Praise for *Twisted Tales from Tornado Alley*!

"These tales are top class horror with a smile, which is just as scary as a scowl or a snarl."

—Maynard Sims, author of the DCI Jack Callum series

"West draws upon our worst fears, turns prejudices back on to us, and puts us in situations against all odds as we recoil in horror but rejoice in delight at the intelligence of the writing and aha moments."

—MJ LaBeff, author of the *Last Cold Case* thriller series

"A Midwest fright-fest that will blow you away."

—Russell James, author of *Q Island* and *Dark Inspiration*

"A collection of horrific gems from a unique talent, *Twisted Tales from Tornado Alley* is one to curl up with on a dark night. Just make sure all the lights are on. Oh, and that you know where your cat is."

—Catherine Cavendish, author of *The Devil Inside Her* and *Waking the Ancients*

Twisted TALES FROM TORNADO ALLEY

A Collection of Short Fiction

Twisted TALES FROM TORNADO ALLEY

A Collection of Short Fiction

STUART R. WEST

A
Grinning Skull Press
Publication

Twisted Tales from Tornado Alley
Copyright © 2018 Grinning Skull Press

This book contains works of fiction. All characters depicted in this book are fictitious, and any resemblance to real persons—living or dead—is purely coincidental.

The Skull logo with stylized lettering was created for Grinning Skull Press by Dan Moran, http://dan-moran-art.com/.
Cover design: ©2018 JK Graphics, http://jeffreykosh.wix.com/Jeffreykosh graphics.

ISBN: 1-947227-15-7 (paperback)
ISBN-13: 978-1-947227-15-6 (paperback)
ISBN: 978-1-947227-16-3 (e-book)

DEDICATION

This collection is dedicated to my fellow Midwest travelers, particularly in these most turbulent, troubled times. Hang in there. And, as always, my continued love and gratitude to Cydney and Sarah.

Table of Contents

GREETINGS

Whoa, Nellie! Didn't see you there, all lurking in the shadows and what-not. Gave me quite a stir. Now, I'm not the type who frights easy, no sir. Not here in Tornado Alley. Kinda get used to that sorta thing after a while.

Come on out where I can see ya. No need to be a stranger. We're all in this together. Anyone who ends ups here, I figure, is meant to be here. Sorry to say, pal, you ain't special. You belong here just like the rest of us. But we're a neighborly sort.

That all you got, stranger? By way of a hand shake? Kinda loosey-goosey, but, hey, I don't stick labels on people.

What's that? Where are we? I dun already *tol'* you once. We're in Tornado Alley.

Well, hell's bells, we're gettin' off on the wrong foot here, friend. Sorry I snapped at you. Let's start over. Tell you the truth, God as my witness, I'm not quite sure *where* Tornado Alley is. I suspect we're in the Midwest somewhere, Kansas or Oklahoma maybe. You see, Tornado Alley's made up of several cities and counties, just a tad off the beaten track, if you know what I mean, and I surely bet you do. I reckon it's more of a state of mind than a locale.

And it ain't no secret strange things happen in Tornado Alley. Ask anyone.

Generally speaking, Tornado Alley ain't that bad. Well, *most* of the time. Dusk lingers here longer than most places, and shadows don't exactly slip away into the night. They sorta move and dance and take up residence and—

Aw, hell, stranger, I didn't mean to scare ya. Just tryin' to help, that's all.

Let's see, where was I? In Tornado Alley, you'll notice a constant, crisp breeze that's both pleasant and unsettling. The smell of burning leaves just kinda hangs in the air as if warning of somethin' bad comin'. Autumn colors of orange and yellow and angry red pert near stay year round 'til they finally wither away into winter. 'Cause you and I both know everything dies, right?

On nicer days, you can near see across the flatlands to the end of the world. Which I kinda reckon it is. End of the world, I mean. Back in the day, I tried to leave Tornado Alley a couple times. Never knew the Midwest could be so damn big. And frankly, it's not.

But, hey, I ain't here to spook you! Don't leave! Not that you could leave, mind you, just sayin'.

Let's see…

Oh! Tornado Alley can be downright nice at times. Parts of it are quaint and charming, big on antiques. If you go in for that sort of thing, that is. And it's not a bad place to raise a family. Well, some parts maybe not so much…

Hell, there I go again, gettin' off on a tangent. If you like small towns, you'll love it here. It's a safe place. For the most part. Most days, children race through the streets, screaming their lil heads off, not a damn care in the world. Of course, I never have figgered out why the lil hellions ain't in school. *Ever*. Then there was that one incident over in Beckham County last year. But the less said about that, the better.

Sometimes you might hear things there ain't no accountin' for. That's true for all towns, I suppose, but it appears to me Tornado Alley's got its own sense of peculiar. From midnight until the wee hours, you might hear that damn pesky coyote, howling to beat the band. Count on it like clockwork. At least that's what the local law calls it: a coyote. Me? I got my doubts, heard all the stories. Don't get me wrong! I'm no over-the-fence gossip. Just rumors, that's all they are, just rumors.

Neighbor, you may as well anchor yourself. You'll be here a while. Set up some roots. Just don't get uprooted, if you know what I mean, and I believe you do.

Did I mention gettin' home before nightfall? No? Shoot, there I go again, forgettin' the important stuff. No, no, no. No reason. You know what they say, better safe than sorry, that's all. Just make sure you're indoors before dusk tucks itself in. Might wanna lock your doors, natch. But I don't need to tell you that, you being a big city slicker and all. Goes without sayin', but don't open your door for anyone. At night, I mean. Even if it's your sweet grandma payin' you a visit with a batch of her cookies. 'Specially if she died some time back.

No, wait, wait! You're fine, friend! Of *course*, you're fine. For now.

Okay, okay, just between you and me…

Well, I probably shouldn't tell you this. But you seem like a trustworthy enough fella. You can keep a secret, right? *Right?* Not that I ever take part in the town gossip, no siree bob, not one iota! But I reckon I oughta tell you a couple things.

There've been a lot of strange incidents in Tornado Alley. Yeah, sure, we get our fair share of tornados, but that's not the kinda "strange" I'm talking about. C'mere. A little closer. Don't worry, I won't bite.

There's been talk about a witch who came back from the

dead. That's right, a witch. Some folks claim to have seen Bigfoot. Don't laugh! I had the same reaction. At first. Then there're the strange creatures—some call 'em monsters—growing in a local farmhouse's cellar.

You might want to steer clear of a certain dentist, forget his name right now. It'll come to me soon enough. Funny guy and not "funny" in a comical way, either. Anyway, word on the street is he's in bed with something…*unnatural.*

I've heard of a late-night school for monsters and creatures of all sorts. We're talking vampires, werewolves, zombies, you name it. But I ain't never seen the school, mind you, just repeating what I've done been told. Then again, the school's supposed to be open only at night, and you won't catch me out after dark. No sir, not me!

No doubt you've seen the webs drapin' from our trees. Got a real problem with bagworms and webworms this year. Of course, it ain't as bad as what happened to that visiting young couple, mind you, but I ain't gonna get into gossip. Just not the way the good Lord made me.

I gotta say it's hard to dismiss what happened to ol' Tillie Johanssen, though; proof's in the pudding. Most folks say she had it coming. Not me. Ain't my place to judge. Except for maybe when it comes to Harv Jenkins. Always said he was a queer duck.

Couple folks might tell you 'bout a secret underground city and its inhabitants. Me? I reckon those folks are done tetched in the head. But here in Tornado Alley, it's hard to say.

Fine. You go right ahead and laugh, Mr. Big City. Seen it all. Done it all. You'll find out soon enough. Then we'll see who's laughing.

Best get goin' now. Gettin' dark. Feel it weighin' on me like the tide dun pulled me under. Dusk lasts long here, but it ain't gonna last forever, you know…

BAGWORMS

Alongside the road, cobwebs plugged the crotches of trees and formed bridges between branches. As Corey zipped past them, foot heavy on the gas, Liza couldn't help but be ensnared by their grotesquely hypnotic pull. Some of the webs draped to the ground, some pulled taut like delicate tents. They tainted the early fall beauty of the elm, hickory, fruit, and maple trees. Every tree Liza could identify. As a child, she loved trees, studied them quite a bit. Things changed when she developed an aversion to spiders.

There hadn't been a traumatic, life-altering occurrence; no shrink and sofa ready tale of woe. If pressed about it, Liza couldn't remember when her phobia started. But it did; oh hell yeah, it did. It came on like Christmas. Now she couldn't tolerate the outdoors, couldn't stand sharing space with her nemeses.

Again, she glanced at the webs—hard to miss them—and shivered. Her arms folded across her chest as she massaged her newly hatched goosebumps. The convertible's roof being down certainly didn't help matters.

"What's wrong, babe?" asked Corey. "Too cold?"

"No, it's just..." She wouldn't dignify the heinous webs by naming them, giving them weight. The farther along the road they traveled, the webs appeared to be encroaching closer to the road. Coming for her. "You know..."

"Oh, yeah. The dreaded 'S' word." Corey smiled, hot-dogging behind the wheel of his daddy-bought Corvette. He flashed his killer smile, pulled off his sunglasses so she could swim in his eyes. Absolutely arrogant and shameless. Totally hot, though, and he knew it.

So did Liza. She knew she'd never settle for Corey, not in the long-run. Sure, his package was strong, sturdy, and pretty, but the gift inside him was pretty ignorant. Damn, if he didn't look good on her arm, though. With pride, Liza would parade him around the University of Kansas campus like a rooster in the hen-house. Younger girls practically frothed at the mouth as he strutted by. She'd just entered her senior year, so he was a last-chance blow-out to have fun before diving into the corporate world, a trip she intended to take alone. No doubt Corey used her, too, for her popularity cachet. Call it a mutually satisfying, exploitative relationship. As long as they both knew it, no harm done. Sometimes she just didn't *know* if Corey knew it. Corey's lighthouse had long gone dim, but the light that remained shone fully on Liza. Somewhere along the Path of Fun, Corey had strayed into Love Land.

"What, babe? The eight-leggers got yer panties in a bunch?"

"Shut up, Corey," she said. "It's *not* funny." Not many things frightened Liza. A few things came close: the fear of how the world was evolving (and un-evolving); terrorism; a potential inability to land a job befitting her status as president of her sorority; the dreaded day *The Bachelor* would be canceled. All of these things bothered her. But there was only one thing that absolutely, positively terrified her, one thing that caused her to wake up in sheet-soaked night terrors. *Spiders.* Not only did the loathsome creatures top her list, but they also weighed it down with irrational fear. For the most part, she knew spiders were harmless, although she had seen plenty of horrifying photos on the 'net of spider-bite victims. Try telling *those* victims how irrational arachnophobia was!

Most people Liza met didn't understand her phobia at all. Generally, guys wanted to tease her. Considered her a "silly, helpless girl," afraid of eight-legged bogeymen. Jackasses. Not a damn thing funny about the "S" word.

To Liza—and, really, wasn't she the only one who should matter in the situation?—her fear was so real, so palpable, it acquired an ugly, misshapen dark form itself, tormenting her waking and sleeping hours. Her goddamn bogeyman.

Of course, when they'd first started dating, Corey'd reacted in the same doltish, teasing manner. Wiggled his fingers, said, "They're coming to get you, Liza." But he'd learned fast not to taunt or even mention the "S" word around her. A cold, harsh slap in the face worked wonders. Train 'em early, before the guys think they rule the relationship.

And now, against her better judgment, Liza was going to some God-awful cabin in Podunk Kansas—"Le Vautour" or some silly French name—for the weekend. Something she fought against with customary ferocity.

"Corey, I *don't* camp," she had told him.

"Sure you do, babe. Everyone camps."

"No, *not* everyone. I don't. Never have, never will. My idea of roughing it is braving the turbulent waters of a hot tub. Or maybe, God forbid, losing my phone."

"But, babe, we're going to a cabin. One of my folks' fall places. We got electricity. And there's a hot tub. If you're worried about…you know…"

"Don't even say it!"

"Cool, cool, babe, wasn't goin' to. Look, if you want, we

can spend most of the time indoors. Plus—" He made a "tss-tst" sound between his teeth, pressing a finger down on an imaginary spray can. "—that's what bug spray's for."

It took a full week of cajoling, pleading, promises, and puppy dog eyes to convince her. A mistake, big-time. From where Liza sat, it looked like they were driving straight into a giant spider web.

"Oh, you're freaking about all the webs in the trees, right?" Corey looked her way, his gaze leaving the crooked road far too long for her comfort.

The road narrowed. On both sides, the webbed trees crept closer. Liza knew it was her imagination gone wild, the gigantic webs crawling through her head. Couldn't be helped.

Miles ago, they'd left civilization—and pavement, for God's sake, *pavement*—behind. Gravel dinged against the under-carriage. Dust rose, swirled into a cloud, and chased them like a late-to-the-haunting ghost. Liza trembled, gripped her shoulders. She sunk down into her seat and tucked into a compact version of herself.

"What the hell do you *think* I'm upset about?" she spat.

"Sorry, babe, want me to put the top up?"

"Not if it means stopping." Liza risked another look. The webs seemed to be multiplying, becoming more common-place than the surrounding foliage. They waved lazily in the breeze, laying traps to entangle her. The image of eight tiny legs crawling over her body burned into her mind. Hideous pincers—or whatever the hell they had—snapped at her body. Liza clamped a hand over her mouth to fight back sickness.

"Nope. I'll put the top up as we go." Grinning like a loon, Corey pressed a button. Mechanical parts hummed. The roof rose. Afraid to leave the comfort of her dugout, Liza waited for her boyfriend to snap the roof into place. As he reached over and latched it, the car swerved, then he corrected course.

"There. Better?"

"A little." She rolled up her window, turned on the air conditioner.

"Anyway, you got nothin' to worry about, babe. Those webs ain't caused by…um, well, you know. You think I'd take you into their territory?"

Yes. "I dunno. You're *sure* they're not…"

He nodded, proud and dumb. "Folks here got a real problem with fall webworms this year. Some call 'em bagworms."

"Webworms? Never heard of 'em."

"Shocker. You're not exactly the most nature-loving babe in the woods, Liza. Basically, webworms are just caterpillars. Some form these weird-ass, hard cocoons around themselves. They spit out silk webs all over the trees. It's their leaf-to-leaf highway, how they travel. They're harmless. Except to leaves, I guess."

"But…there're so many of them." Again, Liza glanced at the roadside drapery. Numerous webs flowed, gluing trees together, and yet they looked a tad less evil now. After all, Liza loved silk dresses, the softness of the material in Corey's ties. And caterpillars were kinda cute, in a sort of don't-think-about-it-too-much manner. At least cartoon ones. Now, instead of appearing like a dark mass of sickening, sticky traps, the webs waved a friendly, country greeting to her. "I guess webworms aren't so bad."

She slid across the seat and snuggled up to her big, beautiful, dopey man, hoping for many weekend hours spent in his loving, protective arms.

The cabin wasn't what Liza expected. *Understatement.* "Cabin," after all, generally denoted a shack built out of logs, a place where Abe Lincoln wasted his childhood, a place not suited for human living, but rather reserved for rugged mountain men who couldn't afford better. There were logs alright, lovely red cedar by the looks of it. But they only formed part of the framework. Intricate columns of lavishly carved stonework comprised most of the ground floor foundation, as impenetrable as a fortress. The second and third floors appeared open and airy, delightfully manufactured by human hands and deep pockets. A warm, orange light glowed in the windows. As far as privacy, Liza could see directly into the bedroom. A problem in the city, of course, but out here where no one lived? Voyeuristically thrilling.

"Dayum, Corey." Liza exited the car. Slowly, she walked toward the cabin, appraising its out-of-place beauty. "When you said we'd be staying in your family's getaway cabin, I thought… Guess I thought it'd be different."

Corey slung an arm around Liza's shoulders. "Told ya you'd like it, babe." He grinned, basking in her adulation. He pushed up his sunglasses with a finger and kept nodding in that dumb way he had. Like a cow chewing its cud, he tortured his chewing gum, round and round.

Before arriving, Liza had already made up her mind she was going to absolutely hate the weekend. During the last leg of the trip, the road had narrowed into a nearly impassable strip of bumps, mud, and runaway tree roots. Not a soul or house for miles and miles. Just those damn webs, strangling the forest. Flowing in the wind like a ship's sails. Silk webs, though. *Silk.*

Things had changed. Not only did she absolutely adore the cabin, but her plan to dump Corey post-graduation now felt a bit hasty. She knew a history of oil pumped through the veins of Corey's family, but the cabin exceeded her highest expectations. And the cabin only represented one of many of his family dwellings. She ran a flirtatious finger up and down Corey's arm.

"You're wrong," she cooed in her best little girl voice. "Liza doesn't like the cabin."

"Wait. What? Babe, you—"

"Liza *loves* it."

Macho confidence possessed him. Moonlight captured his perfect, expensive grin. "That's what I'm talkin' about, babe! C'mon!" He grabbed her hand, pulled her behind him at a trot. "Let's get to it."

And, of course, by "getting to it," he meant sex. Lots and lots of sex.

As they hurried down a short stack of stairs, he fumbled with a ring of keys. A chill brushed Liza's shoulders, kissed the nape of her neck. She folded her bare arms, rubbed her shoulders. A whisking sound—a chorus of whispers—rose from the surrounding woods. Almost as if the trees were communicating with one another, discussing the human interlopers. And the webs—the damn, long, colossal webs—fluttered in the breeze. Waving at her. Welcoming Liza.

Yes, Liza adored the cabin, loved Corey's depthless expense account, and could sometimes tolerate his insatiable passion for sex and clumsy groping. She just wished they were vacationing in a nice, normal neighborhood—something ocean-side or, at the very least, a bland suburbia.

Sprawled out on her belly, Liza groaned. "Dammit! No phone reception or WiFi! What'm I gonna do?" She tossed the phone onto the carpeted floor, but not too hard. The state-of-the-art, top-of-the-line model phone had set her daddy back a lot of green.

Corey sat up in bed, smacked Liza's bare behind, but not too hard; Liza prided herself on her fine, firm ass and wouldn't tolerate any harm done to it. "C'mon, babe, it's not all bad. We got the great outdoors at our fingertips."

"Blech. You can have it." She sunk her face into the mattress. "I miss social media!"

Corey rolled out of bed and into his swim trunks. "C'mon, get your swimsuit on. Time's wastin'."

She looked at him, slack-jawed. "What're you talkin' about? It's night. Liza doesn't go outside at night."

He flung her swimsuit toward her. It landed on her back. "Babe, Corey ain't gonna let anything happen to you."

"Whatever. Already told you I'm not goin'. This place got a TV?"

"Got somethin' better than that."

"I'm missing my *Housewives*, Corey."

He sat on the bed next to her. "You gotta check out my dad's boat."

She rolled over, sat up. Water: good; nature: bad. "A nice boat? So help me, God, if I end up having to paddle or—"

He laughed. "No, babe, Dad does everything big. Come on."

She considered it. He had her at "big." A tale for her jealous sorority girls. Besides, a boat ride beat another round of his slobbering over her. "Are there actual stairs down to the dock? I'm *not* walking through the woods."

"Sure. You haven't lived 'til you been on the water at midnight. I can fire the boat up to 60 knots."

"Okay. I don't know what that means, but I'm up for it. If

I don't like it, though, we quit when I say so."

"Whatever you say, babe."

Damn straight. She wiggled into her suit, added a few extra bumps for show. A final ludicrous touch, he donned his sunglasses.

"Let's get one thing straight," she said. "You're *not* wearing your sunglasses. I mean seriously, at night? What is this, 2014?"

Corey stiffened. "Oh, right. Force of habit." Carefully, he took off the designer glasses and set them on the bedside table. "Put on your sandals, babe. And bring your jacket. Gets a little chilly on the water."

Outside, on the doorstep, chills rippled across her legs and arms. The moon shone pregnant and bone-white, ample light to guide their path. Yet the eerie glow painted the webs—highways of interconnected webs—gray and decaying, like the hair on an old man's scalp.

"I don't know, Corey. Maybe—"

"Oh, hang on a sec, babe."

Corey disappeared into the cabin. Tree limbs saluted with skeletal fingers in the wind. Leaves snapped free and see-sawed silently to the ground. Something—definitely not human, no animal she'd heard before—warbled a somber tune. An unidentifiable bird chirped like a battery-drained fire alarm. An owl hooted. Tiny footsteps flitted across fallen leaves, nimble and fast.

"Corey?" She stepped back inside the cabin. Louder. "Corey?"

"Yeah, babe?" He dashed around the corner, a gun in his hand.

"Jesus!" She fell back, panting, a hand to her chest. "Don't *do* that! And why do you have a gun?"

"Hm? Oh, this?" He looked at it, turned it this way and that, and smiled. "We're in the woods, babe. You know. Just in case."

"Just in case *what*? If you think we need a gun, then I'm—"

"Whoa, slow down, babe. I'm kidding. We're as safe as bumper cars. You ever shot a gun before?"

"No."

"It kicks ass! Wait 'til we're out on the water. Shoot some trees, other shit, whatever. Totally rocks."

"Let me see it." She held out an imperious palm, waited. The gun was heavier than she imagined, but it felt solid, sleek. A comfortable fit. More than that, she held true power, almost an extension of her own inner strength. "And you had this the whole time?"

"What? Of course not. It's Dad's. Everyone in Kansas has a gun."

"And you'll teach me how to use it?"

"Hell, yeah, babe." Their hands met on the gun. She stroked the barrel, licked her lips. That horny ember in Corey's eyes burned hot, close to raging out of control. Time to dampen the fire.

"Let me carry it." Liza couldn't pinpoint a particular reason, but she felt safer with the gun.

"Sure, babe. Hang on." He snatched it from her, clicked something on the side, then gave it back butt first. "Just makin' sure the safety's on."

One last stop and Corey grabbed a flashlight and a bottle of wine. "You never know. Dad usually keeps the boat well-stocked, but better safe than sorry."

"Oh, *hell*, yes. Take me to the boat, Captain." Liza tucked the gun into her leather jacket's pocket. The lump tugged at the right side, reassuring next to her hip.

With her hand gripping the underside of Corey's arm, they strolled down a smoothly paved sidewalk. It curved around the cabin and into a cleared section of woods. Surviving tree stumps pimpled the ground. The sidewalk gave way into a graveled path. Liza's sandals scraped across the gravel, providing a welcome respite from the raucous sound of wildlife. Corey shot the flashlight's beam around, spotlighting things they'd just missed, creatures diving for cover. Soon, the path entered the woods. Liza squinted, strained to see into the darkness. The path appeared to drop off, nothing but blackness beyond. Twin curtains of webs flapped on both sides of the path as if lazily shepherding them into a dream world.

Liza hesitated. "Wait. I thought you said no hiking, exploring, or any of that crap."

"Right. Just goin' down to the dock." He pulled her toward where the path dropped. The flashlight's cone illuminated descending steps of crumbling rock eroded by time and nature. Unruly weeds poked through the cracked stone. Some steps had broken in half, dug into the earth and pitched up their edges like iceberg tips. "We gotta be careful. Dad keeps sayin' he's gonna fix the steps, but he never gets anything done."

"Give me the flashlight." Liza stuck out her hand. Always in control of the situation, she knew she'd do a better job of bringing the light than Corey. She held the flashlight out over the stairwell as far as the beam could travel. A dock and boathouse sat at the bottom of the dark path, lit by the moon.

Perhaps nothing but wishful imagination, Liza thought she heard the oddly soothing *clump-clump* of the boat bumping against the dock inside the boathouse. Over the din of the forest inhabitants, the gentle sloshing of water calmed her. Moonlight reflected off the lake's surface, shiny as diamonds. Blessed redemption after the path through wooded Hell. "Fine. Let's go."

Carefully, Liza planted her feet on the first wide step and shuffled forward. The drop down to the next step was deep, nearly a foot. With Corey as her anchor, holding onto his arm for balance, she hopped down. Slowly, they descended. The rocky path tapered, the trees crowding in. The air thickened, still and humid. Something cracked. A screech, not unlike a monkey in the zoo, sounded overhead in the trees. Limbs stretched over them, formed a dark tunnel of acquainting branches. Leaves covered the ground, rendering it impossible to clearly see the steps. A slow process, Liza slid her feet forward, exploring the environment as tenderly as a new sex partner. Towering trees blocked the moonlight. The flashlight helped little, only capable of cutting through the darkness a few feet at a time.

Something dropped onto Liza's hair. She stopped, nearly tumbled. Her hand flew up, grasped Corey's back.

"What's wrong, babe?" Corey's voice sounded weak, drained of bravado.

"I dunno. I think…" She reached up, felt something light-weight as cotton candy, yet tough as polyester thread in her hair. Immediately, she knew what had fallen on her. But she had to see it. Just had to know. She tugged at the strong fila-ments. They snapped and came loose. She turned the flashlight onto the contents in her hand. *Webs.*

"Goddammit!" Liza flapped her hand, but the webs clung. Near panic, she scraped her hand against her jeans, vowing to wash them thoroughly when they got back to the cabin. Still, the webs hung on. "Get 'em off me, get 'em off!"

"Hold on, babe." Corey grabbed her flailing arm. Care-fully, he pulled at the webbing.

"What about my *hair*? Is there any in my *hair*?" She bowed, offering her head as she bounced. "Get it out!"

"Give me the flashlight." He took it. Liza clamped her eyes shut and felt a ray of heat warm her scalp. "Nope. Not that I can see." To prove it, Corey patted down her head. "Clean as the day you were born, babe."

"Which isn't very clean, duh! Babies are born with all kindsa shit on them!" She'd hit her wall of tolerance. Somewhere inside, she knew she shouldn't take her frustration out on Corey, but he was the closest, easiest target. After all, he'd led her into this. "We're going back."

"But, babe, we don't have that much—"

"I said we're going back! Give me the flashlight." She snatched it, took a giant step up, considered racing the rest of the way. But she didn't want to do it alone. "Coming?"

She splashed the light onto Corey. Above him, threads dangled. Threads that moved, twisted, pulled, and played. Something caused the movement, something alive.

She threw back her shoulders, gulped down a deep breath, ready to release a killer scream.

A low sound rose from the bottom of the path. Humming, buzzing. Purring, like the inner motor of a satisfied cat. But much deeper, more menacing than any common cat. Liza struck the light down the path. A large figure flitted into the beam, then darted away. She shot the light up, down, left, and right. Nothing. Just the ghost memory of what she'd seen. Or thought she'd seen. Something big. Dull grey body. Odd ink-blot-black patterns.

The humming noise grew. No longer a hum, now an inhuman growl. Leaves swept up at Liza's feet and swirled into a mini-cyclone. A fiery draft followed.

"*Run!*" Liza didn't wait for Corey, absolutely couldn't do it. Survival instinct drove her. She jumped up another step. Her flashlight's circle of light bounced over the ground, the trees.

"Liza, wait! They're—*Umph!*"

She heard a hollow *thump*, Corey's startled cry. Heard the leaves crunch and crack as he tumbled down. But more than anything, she heard the buzzing growl. Increasing in volume and strength, fierce with anger.

Behind her, unnatural heat rolled over her back. An onslaught of wind shoved her forward. She steadied, set, ran. Vaulted up the steps, one after the other.

The roar sounded everywhere…above, beneath, and directly at her back. But it wasn't a vocal cry. The sudden gust of wind, the vibrating sound of flapping wings. A dragonfly's wings amplified at an impossible volume. Goddamn scary, nasty, huge, improbable wings!

"Lizaaaa!" Her lover's voice sounded garbled, far away. He screamed again. Bats took flight from the tops of trees.

The thing behind her drew close, closer. Tears bled from her eyes: tears of fear, tears for Corey. But she couldn't go back, couldn't even look back.

Bzzzz…fzzzz…whump…

Please, Jesus God, get me out of this! I'll do anything! Anything!

The top of the path lay in sight. If she could make it, she could run like hell on level ground. Get out the gun, blow away the creature. Come back, save Corey…

She leaped up another step. Her foot came down, slipped on a loose rock. In reality, just a little one; in her mind, as big as a mountain. Her ankle twisted. She ran on, outracing the pain. Close, so close to the open meadow.

The thing at her back buzzed, dive-bombing her now. She felt its oppressive weight, sensed it hovering over her. Treading air. Playing with her?

She unleashed a battle cry. Launched to the top step. In mid-leap, too late, she saw what awaited her. The giant web strewn between the trees trapped her. Wire tugged at her exposed legs. Reverberations shook her gut, her bones. Completely off the ground, dangling like a helpless marionette. Her throat dried out, her voice lost.

The warmth at her back grew in intensity. The thrumming of the wings rumbled through her chest. Her hair whooshed about her shoulders, then adhered to the web.

The creature landed on her back. Warm, wet, heavy. Worst of all? *Gentle.* Legs like sticky rubber hoses massaged her rear, caressed her arms, moved up her body. Antenna, hairy and hideous, scratched her cheeks, then coiled around her neck.

Sweet darkness swept her away.

Cold. So cold.

Liza rocked gently. Light penetrated her eyelids.

The thick molasses of unconsciousness began to melt away. Mercifully, she'd slept nightmare-free, memory-free. Then, the filters in her brain—the ones used for sanity control—unleashed small peeks of what had happened last night. Just small glimpses, not too many. *Not all at once,* her control tower ordered.

I'm alive.

As soon as she opened her eyes, saw the sun rising over the horizon, she wished for death.

"Oh. My—" At first, she didn't recognize her smoker's voice, craggy as a three-pack-a-day habit. Her throat hurt, raw. Memories slammed into her, full on, no mercy. A monster had attacked her last night, a creature she never saw. But it had left its imprint on her, physically and mentally. Her back burned, itched. Pain throbbed throughout her arms and legs. Thick filaments of webbing covered her from neck to ankles and wrapped around her several times like a mummy's dressing.

Strung up between two large oaks, an industrial-sized web held her captive.

She tried to free her arms, but the webbing glued them to her sides. Every time a breeze drifted in from the lake, the web swayed back and forth, threatening to expel Liza's last meal.

"Oh, my God," She whimpered, her voice weak.

Get it together. It's not over yet. Keep cool. Just get outta this... Giant fucking spider web.

Her gorge rose again. This time she leaned forward, let it fly. Her vomit splattered down onto the leaves, lost in the fallen orange and red colors. She bucked forward again for one last dry heave. The web tipped with her, swinging her nearly horizontal with the ground. Afraid of being trapped feet up, she leaned back. Forced gravity to right her.

Remember. Not a spider web. A bagworm's web. It has to be.

Then she remembered Corey. His cries for help. She shut her eyes hard, hard enough to dam the swelling tears. She couldn't get emotional. Soldiers don't cry in the face of battle.

Stay strong. Don't give into this. You can do it!

She surveyed the area. No sign of the monster, creature, whatever the hell it was. Trees surrounded her within spitting distance, deep into the woods. Helplessly enmeshed within a giant web.

No! Never helpless!

A sudden thought struck her, a disturbing one.

How'd the beast move me? Don't think about it, don't think about it, don't—

She listened. Last night, the woods had been alive with the jarring sounds of wildlife. Today, it was quiet. An eerie, empty wasteland.

Maybe I'm still asleep.

Bullshit.

She never hurt in her dreams, not like this.

Prayers couldn't hurt.

Hi, God, remember me? I know it's been a while—

She gave up. Her heart couldn't sell it.

Then she remembered. *The gun.* She couldn't tell if she still had it in her jacket pocket. Something dug into her hip bone, but it could be a wound or something better not considered. She forced her arms outward, strained. A bit of give, but not enough. Like a rubber band, the filaments snapped firmly back into place. She tried again. The strands loosened a little more. If she couldn't break them, maybe she could stretch them out.

Liza clenched. Sucked in fortifying air through gritted teeth. And pushed out. Webbing cut into her balled-up fists like fiberglass. Blood warmed her right hand, fueled her will to live.

Harder, dammit, harder!

She heard a tiny *ting*, nothing louder than a snapped guitar string. Then another. Now she could move her right hand a few inches, back and forth. Tingles zapped her hand, first in a pleasant blood-rushing manner, then in a painful one. But she could move, dammit.

She worked her hand back and forth, each time expanding the gap. Next, she flexed her elbow and met solid resistance. If she could draw her hand up within the cocoon, she could reach the pocketed gun. Not yet, though, the damn web held tighter than a straight-jacket. She continued ramming her hand against her prison, baby steps.

But, really, what could she do with a gun anyway? She couldn't very well shoot her way out, not without possibly injuring herself.

Think, Liza, think!

Last night when she'd dropped the gun into her pocket, she'd heard a *clack*. At the time, she'd recalled it was the lighter she carried on party nights. Possibly burn her way out? Dangerous, but hell, she'd rather burn to death than supply a monster its dinner.

She shivered. Her prison wobbled.

Thump.

"Shit!" Liza's heart beat hard, jackhammering at her chest.

Thump.

The sound again. Below her. She looked down, fearful.

At the base of one of her guardian trees, a large muddy sack clung to the trunk. Tapered at the top and bottom, it appeared comprised of sticks, leaves, other foliage. Branches stuck out in disarray like a mutated porcupine. Possibly five feet tall and as wide as the large oak tree's trunk.

Thump.

The bag moved. Just a bit. But, sure as hell, the bottom had pulled loose, then snapped back to the trunk.

What the hell, what the hell, what the hell —

With her eyes locked onto the sack, Liza dredged up more strength, moved her hand faster.

Back and forth, again, pain, wash, repeat…

Panic gave her a second wind. She recalled what Corey had said about the gross bagworms: *Some form these weird-ass hard cocoons around themselves.* The sack had to be a giant bagworm's cocoon, no other explanation. Maybe the other creature left Liza for its offspring's food.

The sack's back-end snapped out again, settled. The top of the sack wiggled in a small, hypnotic circle, expanding with each twist. A dark bulb crowned. It pushed through the enlarged opening. A thick, green substance gushed out around it, slopped to the ground. The sack's top continued to squirm as the creature within pushed through to the world. Two red hooves, nearly goat-like, squeezed up beside the black mass at the center. Then they were free, extending into black furry legs. They stretched, shook, almost hesitant, and tasted the air. Searching for Liza.

I'm gonna die, my God, don't let—

Liza's fist rammed against her thrust-out hip. More tension released. Able to move her fist about four inches now, she made it five. And kept going.

Two small, wilted antennas rose from the creature's dark head. They waggled, almost as if sensing Liza.

Push, girl! Goddammit, push!

Six inches. Seven…

The antennas snapped to a full-on erect position. The center bulb rose. Another splash of green ooze bubbled out. A black piece of burlap flapped from the crowning head.

No. Not burlap. Hair. Matted hair. Corey's hair!

Liza's scream woke up what few woodland creatures still inhabited the area. Birds cawed. Something broke through the brush next to her. Then deafening, suffocating silence.

The head—what remained of Corey's once-beautiful head—turned. Two black orbs—golf ball-sized—bulged from the side of its fuzzy grey skull, a perverse bastardization of Corey's typical sunglasses. Something flipped over the sack's lip, drooped down like an anteater's snout. Two sharp points—*What in God's name are they?*—extended from the thinly covered skull, next to the constantly probing antennae.

It stopped. Looked at Liza. Opened its snout in a silent scream. An all too human tongue and teeth remained inside its mouth.

Liza's stomach pitched another fit. She had nothing left to offer. The web tipped her forward, swung her back around. Eventually, the web rocked to a halt. Liza's heart kept banging.

The creature—*Corey! Oh my God, Corey, I'm so damn sorry, so sorry*—kept wriggling out of its cage. Its shoulders—sunken, vaguely human, covered with bristly fur—pushed through.

It opened its mouth again, shook its head in rage. Or possibly heartbreaking sorrow.

"Corey, I'm so sorry," she cried.

The creature's sack moved up the trunk. First, six inches, then a foot. Its hoofed legs gained purchase, the sack naturally adhering to the tree, and pulled. Inching along with alarming speed.

Liza created another inch of leeway with her fist. The entire web slackened around her body. Still not enough. She pulled her hand up, tight against her skin. Her body itched; first, on an unreachable kneecap, then the sensation spread like a virus. She imagined creatures of eight legs skittering across her, injecting her with their vile venom. Her shoulder wrenched, possibly dislocated. Worry about it later. Her hand drew up to the pocket. Felt the reassuring lump of the gun. Now she had to get the damn thing unzipped.

The monster stopped moving. Its head bounced up and down, reminiscent of Corey's stupid—but God, she wished she had it back!—nod. Then the creature did something unexpected. It pressed its head, its hooves against the tree trunk and pushed. The creature's upper torso bobbled, wavered in the air before it snapped back against the tree. Another push. This time the monstrosity ripped free from the tree. A viscous substance pulled tree bark along with it.

"Jesus!" Contorting her fingers, Liza managed to snag the zipper pull and yanked. The pocket opened. Her fingers dug inside.

The creature fell onto the web. The netting sagged under its weight. Slowly, Liza lowered to the ground. Her toes grazed leaves. Suddenly more nimble, the monster propelled its cocoon across the webbing. The web dropped farther. Liza's feet slapped the ground. The creature slithered toward her, a foot away. Liza hurled her weight to the right. The webbing snapped. On the way down, the foul mesh draped her face, entered her mouth. The ground raced up. She turned her head and shut her eyes for impact.

Bmph.

Dots of light dazzled her vision. Her shoulder screamed in agony. Yet she rolled and kept rolling. Her wrapping tore, split down the seam. She jutted her elbows out, freed them, but her arms remained confined. She sat up, dazed.

Above her, the monster kept coming, sliding down the webbed ladder. *Fast.* Its snout gaped wide. Saliva dripped from it, spattered Liza's head. Although the creature remained silent, Liza felt Corey's rage, his hurt, his horror. Felt like she owned it.

Beneath her webbed shroud, she managed to face the gun barrel out. Held it tight against the filaments. Pulled the trigger.

Nothing.

Shit! Safety's on!

She had to free her hands.

The creature lowered. A scent like rotten produce, full of decay and death, rolled off its breath. Liza rocked her shoulders. A long rip. One arm slumped out. She lifted her arm, gun in hand, and brought it to her mouth. Her teeth bit at the metal until they latched onto the tiny safety switch. Teeth firmly attached, she twisted her hand.

Corey lowered. His snout opened wider. The antenna found her face, explored it, stroked her features. Her terrified reflection caught in its hideous eyes. Rough legs pressed onto her breasts. Its pink tongue jiggled from within its foul mouth as if pleading for one last kiss.

She had a different last kiss in mind for Corey.

"Sorry, Corey," she managed. "Really."

The gun whipped up. She pressed it between the monstrosity's eyes. Pulled the trigger.

A thunderous roar slammed her back. The gun flew from her hand. A rainfall of color exploded from Corey's head. Blood, bone, fur, flesh spattered Liza's face, soaked her hair.

One of her ears rang. Liza turned, favoring her good ear, and listened for signs of life. She sat up. Waited for her stomach to quit revolting. Through tears and muttered apologies, she managed to unwrap herself. Yet she couldn't bring herself to look at Corey's corpse. Just couldn't do it.

She stood. The earth moved and not in a good way. While not dislocated, her shoulder hurt every time she moved it. Once her right foot came down, her twisted ankle reintroduced itself. Frankly, she didn't care. She'd survived.

She stumbled her way to the path leading down to the boat dock. Lines of blood marked her legs. Branches tore holes in her jacket. Sweat soaked her thoroughly, matted her hair. Burs clung to her. Small needles splintered into her legs. She looked up the trail, didn't have the energy to climb. But she needed to get out of the woods. Reach civilization.

She headed down, the easier direction. The lake remained quiet—no other voices, boats, sounds of humanity.

She'd make herself at home on the boat, even though Corey—*Corey!*—still had the keys. But surely someone would happen by. Surely, hell yeah, they would. Maybe there was a radio she could use. Or maybe she'd get very, very drunk.

She staggered onto the dock. It swayed beneath her feet, an uncomfortable reminder of her time trapped in the web. Her feet clonked hollowly across the pilings. She followed an adjoining walkway that led to the boathouse's door.

Please, God, let it be open.

It wasn't. God disliked her, fickle to a tee. No problem. She struggled out of her jacket, easy on her wounded shoulder, shrugged it to the dock. She picked it up, built a good buffer of material around her elbow and whacked it into the lowest glass panel. Maybe it would set off an alarm.

Silence.

She reached in, found the inner lock, and released it.

Even though the sun blazed brilliantly outside, darkness ruled inside the boathouse. Next to her, the boat sloshed in the water. On the far side of the boat, a thin sliver of light peeped through a hole in the wall. It rippled over the dark water. Her fingertips grazed the wall as she searched for an electric garage opener. Nothing.

Weakened to the state of passing out, she grabbed her lighter. She lit a scrawny trail to the boat. Maybe she could grab an hour of shut-eye, reinvigorate. Find the radio. Or the other way around. She couldn't think straight.

With an outstretched foot, she tried to toe the boat closer to the dock and failed. Stubbornly, the boat fought her needs. Just like the entire weekend. She snagged a foot onto the closest boat seat, the other uncomfortably on the dock.

Something flew by her.

Big deal. A bat. I've dealt with worse.

But when something dropped onto her—something all too familiar—it became a much bigger deal. Webbing spun around her, hissing like a can of hairspray. She stabbed the lighter's flame at the threads, moved it around to no effect.

From above, a loud humming sound filled the boathouse. More creatures joined. She held up the lighter. A flock of monstrous moth creatures descended, the lighter's flame glinting in their black, hungry eyes. The creatures parted. Between them, a barrel-sized, eight-legged, God-forsaken beast from Hell lowered on a rope-thick web. And dropped onto Liza.

God, she hated nature.

MAFIOSO HOLIDAY

"Shut up, shut up, already." Carmelo stood, waved his hands with royal flair. Hefted up his sweatpants. Sometimes it was the little touches that commanded respect. "I know it was hard for some of you to come out today, so thanks to all you guys."

"Anything for you, Don." The men around the table nodded. Even though the suck-up ritual bored Don Carmelo in its predictability, he'd have it no other way. Hell, he'd made most of the gathered men into who they were today. Call it egotism, call it whatever you wanted, just as long as it was complimentary and the truth.

"Alright, it's Thanksgiving. We got lots to give thanks for." Carmelo tilted his wine glass toward his nephew, Sammy, then considered dumping the contents on him. Always with the same after-sex satisfaction smile. Clearly, the boy had inherited his mother's genes, not Carmelo's smarts.

A glorious meal sat on the table before the men. Roasted turkey steamed like a sauna. The complete works, the fixings, the stuffing, all in sweet oranges, candied reds, and crisp browns. Carm kept his eye on the heaping bowl of raw oysters, first on his list. Boss's rights. And from the mean, hungry look in his subordinates' eyes, he'd have a fight on his hands.

"Um, Don?" Like a schoolboy frightened of his own shadow, Troy raised a hand. "We gonna eat soon? Food's been here a while now. It's gonna get—"

"Shaddup, Troy!" Carm never liked Troy. Sure, he was a decent enough soldier, got the job done and everything, but what the hell kinda Italian name was Troy? "We'll eat when I say we do!"

"No offense, Don, it's just…" Troy's voice trailed off like a runaway kite. Smart choice.

Truth of the matter, Carm was fairly famished as well. But it wasn't a party 'til Mikey showed up. Couldn't eat without Mikey.

Where the hell is that dumb lug, anyway?

The group maintained a respectful silence as Carm strolled toward the window. He whipped up the Venetian blinds. *Ah!* Mikey's Oldsmobile—the one that still had a Nixon/Agnew bumper sticker on the back—rumbled into the parking lot. The car visibly lifted as Mikey hefted his girth out of the driver's seat and continued to bob in affirmation—or more likely, relief. Mikey stood outside his car. He pulled his knee-length leather jacket tight around his neck. And stared at Carm.

What the hell's he waitin' for?

Never the most animated of souls, Mikey didn't move. Just stood there, looking Carm's way, waiting for a parade or something. The wind whipped paper cups across the parking lot. Leaves swirled about Mikey's legs. Yet, Mikey's hair stayed immaculately in place. Must've used a lotta hair product this morning.

Carm turned back to the hungry men. "Okay, okay, we'll eat soon as Mikey gets his ass in here."

More fidgety than usual, the men looked at one another,

shifted in their folding chairs, coughed into hands. Howie sneezed, didn't even cover it. Sliver Jimmy lit a smoke. His hand shook as he pulled it from his mouth, puffed a cloud into the air. For a change, his frog-lidded eyes appeared wide open.

"Ah, Don, that's a good one," said Jimmy. "Had us really goin' for a minute." He attempted a smile, not a good look on him.

"Whaddaya talkin' about?" Carm asked.

"Well…" Jimmy's gaze flitted about the table as if seeking corroboration. The men looked down into their laps. Carm had trained them well. "Mikey got himself shot last month." Jimmy sat up, speed smoking, more nervous than when he bet on long shots at the track. "Remember? You remember, right?"

Shit.

It all came rushing back to Carm. The late-night phone call about Mikey getting shot in his own driveway, three slugs in the back (real pussy stuff). The damned pesky Cammara family who denied it (typical pussy stuff), even though Carm knew they'd done it. The call to Mikey's wife, even though she'd been the one who heard the shots and found her husband's body. The fabulous feast at Mikey's wake. Revenge, natch. *All* of it.

But why had Carm forgotten? Drama of the century and Carm had filed it away into the ozone of his brain. In his sixties, senility couldn't have been kicking him to the curb yet. Right? *Right?*

But he'd just seen Mikey. Big as life and twice as dumb.

He looked out the window again. Mikey was gone. His Olds was gone. Carm feared his mind was going next.

Ah, the hell with that kinda thinking.

He just needed to eat. Christ, Mikey'd been with Carm over the past twenty Thanksgivings, no wonder he expected him to show up, hat in hand, and napkin tucked into his collar.

Best not to show weakness, though. Never.

Carm winked, shot out a hollow laugh. "Gotcha, boys!" He sprayed finger bullets through the room.

Strange looks ricocheted back at him. Polite laughter circled the table, worse than a goddamn tea party.

Quickly, Carm sat down at the head of the table. "Alright. Who's gonna do the prayer?"

Grmmmbbb, gurm, spack, tack, tack, tack—

"Damn it, Sal!" Carmelo slammed his wine glass down onto the table. The stem broke. Red wine stained the tablecloth. "Sal! I thought you were closing down the bowling lanes today!"

Sal's sun-burned head popped in, a towel draped over his shoulder, part of his never-changing wardrobe. "Sorry, Carm. I'll kick 'em out now," said Sal. "Thought word got out we were shut down today, but—"

Carmelo rushed toward the door, shoved his cousin out, kicked the door closed. *Badda-boom!* Why he's the boss.

"Alright, alright, back to business. Simmah down." Carm patted the air, tugged his sweats up again with the other hand. All these years, his wife still didn't know how to fit him. He reclaimed his throne, sighed. "Prayer. We need a prayer. Sliver Jimmy?"

Jimmy groused back and forth, a groundhog checking for his shadow. "Ah…okay, I'll give it a shot." He crossed himself, the others followed. "Dear Mary, Mother of God, please, ah…give us thanks for…our money. Help us not to get busted for the protection we offer, 'cause it's a good thing…the gambling—"

"Whoa, whoa, stop!" Like a referee, Carm threw his napkin to the floor. "You can't use the blessed Mary's name in vain like that, idiot! Have some respect! Don't be talkin' 'bout our work in the same breath as Mother Mary."

Jimmy proffered beggar's palms. "What'd I do? What?"

"Shut up, that's what. Howie? How 'bout you give it a shot? Can't get any worse."

Howie trumpeted his nostrils—worse than a sick elephant—blew into a well-used handkerchief, then crossed himself. "Thank you, God, for all the sick, the needy—"

"Why're you thankin' God for the sick, dumbass?" offered Gordon. "Should be askin' God to cure 'em."

"Shut up, Gordo. Let Howie finish." Sweat streamed down Carm's forehead. His kids were easier to manage than his work zoo.

"Thanks, Carm, and…um, God. Anyways…" Howie started over, zipped through a condensed sign of the cross. "…fix the needy, the sick, the stupid—" Snickering from around the table tossed Howie off his game. He licked his lips, clamped his eyes down hard as if summoning his inner angel. Howie was no genius, the proof was in the prayer. Carm could practically count Howie's brain cells struggling to form a true thought. Dense stress lines folded his forehead. "And, dear God, thanks for not letting us get whacked like Mikey did. It really sucked and—"

"Whoa!" Carm brought down a gavel-like fist. "Just shut that right now! You hear me?"

"But, why, Boss?" Howie's eyes moved left, right, up. "Feds listenin' in?"

"No, numb nuts! But God is! Have a little…a little…" Something darkened the window at the far side of the room. A figure. Black curly locks. Uni-brow that'd make a caveman jealous. A nose proudly broken three times. Indisputably *Mikey*.

Again, Mikey didn't move. Didn't break out his fun-loving, dumb grin. Solemn as church.

"Anything wrong, Don?" asked one of his men.

Carm rubbed his eyes, hoped to rub out the image of Mikey. He opened them. The window still framed Mikey, a macabre portrait. Although Mikey would never be mistaken for George Hamilton, his face appeared whiter than usual, his jowls gaunt like he'd had a facelift. Clearly, what Carm had on his hands was something he felt ill-equipped to handle: a haunting. Every fool knew money and bullets were worthless against ghosts.

Bullshit! I don't believe in any of those wives' tales!

Carm bunched the tablecloth in his hands, squeezed the foolish thoughts from his mind. Closed his eyes again. Blinked them open to see nothing but the blessed, ugly, gray fall day outside the window.

Hunched over the table, the boys stared at him. None of them uttered a sound. Half of 'em, Carm suspected, were probably hoping for a heart attack.

"Nothin' the matter with me, boys! Just my eyes bothering me, that's all." He cleared his throat, cleared his mind. Mind over matter, the best way to win, combined with power, money, and violence, of course. "Alright, after those crappy prayers, anyone here...*anyone*...even know what Thanksgiving's all about?"

Eyes wandered. Voices hushed. The way Carm liked it. *Respect*.

But there's always a fly in the ointment.

Milo frowned, one of his two expressions. "Carm, not that I'm complainin' or nothin', but ain't Thanksgivin' s'posed to be about eatin'? Not that I'm complainin', ya see."

"You like cement, Milo?"

Milo displayed his second expression: deer in the headlights. He shook his head but said nothing.

"Then shut your hole. Today's about celebrating. Sal cooked us this turkey day dinner—"

"Probably cold by now," mumbled Milo.

Carm couldn't believe the bitching. Without him, his men—

his brothers—would be nothing, have nothing. His patience raw, burnt at both ends, he remembered what his wife told him, something she brought back from her expensive therapy sessions: *think mindfully*. He didn't understand what it meant, made no sense to him. He thought thinking with your mind was the *only* way to think. Still, on this holiday, he'd give it a shot. He took a deep breath and sent bad thoughts away on a cloud. Along with visions of Mikey, nothing more than his imagination.

Once Carm passed Defcon-2, he calmly addressed his soldiers. "You jackasses rather eat tofurky?"

"What the hell's tofurky?"

"I dunno. But it tastes like ass. It's what my wife's makin' for dinner. You guys rather go to my house and eat that?"

More jowls shook than at a dog pound.

"S'what I thought. Be goddamn grateful. Anybody else wanna give a prayer a stab? Try and nail Thanksgiving? Do it up right?"

No one volunteered.

"Fine, whatever." Carm took his time, made a huge production of it. Bright Broadway lights and "*a-oogah*" horns were the only way to get into these numbskull's noggins. "I'll take a bullet for the team. I always do." He crossed himself, looked up, felt a kinship with Jesus for his suffering.

"Dear Mary, Mother of God, I mean, you know, Jesus. We're all gathered here today to give thanks. Thanks for everything you've granted us. Given us. *Will* give us in the future. Knock on wood."

Table taps danced all around. A few "Amens." One idiot offered a "*Salud*," any opportunity for a drink.

"We're blessed with good health—" Jimmy hacked out a disruptive cough, symptomatic of his three-pack-a-day habit. "—*mostly*. And we're blessed with beautiful families—" Carm peeped open an eye, made sure his nephew wasn't a horrifying illusion like Mikey. No such luck. "—for the *most* part. But, you know—"

Brrrm brrrm brrrm spack tak tak!

The noise disturbed—insulted—Carm's bowels. With his hand fondling the gun in his jacket, he strongly considered opening fire on the errant bowlers. But, no. Deep breaths. Not on Thanksgiving. Lead by example.

Carm rushed toward the door, flung it open. "Sal! Sal, dammit! Get yer ass in here before I rip you a—"

But Sal was nowhere in sight. In fact, no one was. Other than one small light above a table, darkness filled the bowling alley. An indistinct figure sat huddled behind the scoring table, uncomfortably packed into the small seat. The scoreboard above the lane lit up. Scrawled under bowler number one's position: *Mikey.*

Mikey struggled to get out of the tight-fitting plastic furniture. Finally, he stood and turned toward Carm. His mouth opened wide, too wide, grotesquely wide. And within that dark hollow of a mouth, Carm saw many things. Frightening things. Things he knew weren't real, couldn't be real, no way in hell could be real.

Carm slammed the door, put his back against it. Panting and sweating like he'd come in out of the squall of the season.

"Boss? You tell them bowlers to shut their holes?" Uncertainty filled Jimmy's voice.

Christ. Get a grip on yourself, Carm! There's no such thing as spooks, fer God's sake.

Slowly, Carm opened the door again. The beautiful sound of bowling balls tumbled down lanes. Elation swelled in his chest at the sight of the well-lit and populated alley. From behind the shoe counter, Sal gave Carm a goofy, child-like wave. Carm could've trotted over there and kissed his lovely, liver-spotted dome. Anything but Mikey. Anything but insanity.

Carm manned up. He cinched his sweats even tighter and sat back down. "Alright. Jesus…I mean, sorry." For extra protection, Carm crossed himself again. He knew enough about the protection game to not hedge his bets. Especially not now. No more illusions for him, thank you very much. He closed his eyes, folded his hands, and continued his prayer. "Sure, God, we make a lotta bank by providin' protection. Sometimes it hurts some people. But, you know, they're bad people. And we're doin' good work. Protectin' the good people of our land. Just like the Pilgrims."

"Well, howdy, pahd-nuh, I reckon—"

Carm castrated Howie with a slashing glare. Good Christ, now wasn't the time for Howie's pathetic John Wayne imitation!

"Forgive them, God, they don't know how stupid they are. Anyway, the Pilgrims I was talkin' about. Our great ancestor, Christopher Columbus—"

Whispers derailed Carm's train of thought.

"You idiots got somethin' you wanna say?"

"Is Christopher Columbus Uncle Benny's cousin?" asked Milo.

"No, dumbass," said Howie, "Columbus is that TV detective with the glass eye. You know…" He pulled his collar up and hunched over. "Just one more thing—"

"Shut up, already!" shouted Carm. "Columbus was our Italian ancestor who discovered America!" Carm pounded the table until his fist lost feeling. "Buncha idiots! You gonna let me continue or what?"

Silence supplied his answer. "As I was sayin', God, the great Columbus showed us the way. Swoopin' in, takin' what's rightfully ours. The strong shall inherit the earth as the Good Book says. Wipin' out the weak and makin' bank. So, in the name of the Father, the Holy Spirit, the three wise guys, Mary, of course, and all that other stuff. Amen."

Blank stares met Carm. "I said, 'Amen!'" This time affirmations of "Amens" rose, the proper response. "Now let's eat."

"Um…Uncle Carm?"

Leave it to Carm's idiot nephew to ruin an appetite. "What now, Sammy?"

"I, um, don't really think that's what Thanksgiving's about." Sammy ducked his head into his polo shirt, a yuppie turtle. First time the boy had ever spoken out. After the holiday, Carm would see to it he'd never do it again.

"Oh, yeah, schoolboy? You think you know better?"

Sammy's cheeks blushed. He nodded.

"Well, please. Enlighten us all." Carm waved a hand. Everyone laughed. Unlike his nephew, his family—his *real* family— knew how to show respect.

"Okay. Everyone, let's join hands."

The men looked at one another, more embarrassed than a priest at a nudist colony.

Humoring his nephew, Carm said, "Fine, just do it."

Tiny Dancer coughed, dabbed his mouth with a napkin, and said, "Come on, Carm. This is—"

"Shut up, Tiny, and do as you're told!"

Hands were grasped, awkward glances shared. Things they'd never speak about again.

Sammy closed his eyes. "Dear God, thank you for gracing us with people we love. People we break bread with. Like the Pilgrims and the Native Americans did on the original Thanksgiving…learning, sharing and giving. Uniting us into a family, one that goes beyond the bonds of blood. We're thankful for those bonds of love. Nothing's more important than love. Amen."

An uncustomary hush dropped over the room. Even Tiny

Dancer's oxygen machine level mouth-breathing quieted. Sammy smiled, nearly beatific, practically farting haloes.

A strange surge of emotion overwhelmed Carm. Unbelievably, his nephew's prayer moved him. But he wouldn't show it, not professional.

Leaning over, Carm slapped the back of Sammy's head. "Show some damn respect next time, Sammy. You're only here 'cause of your sister. Now let's eat."

Carm shot up, reached over, and grabbed the bowl of raw oysters out of Milo's hands. He dumped half of the bowl onto his plate. And devoured them.

The gorging and drinking went on for hours. Drunk as a skunk, Carm leaned back. He unbuttoned the shirt over his belly, ran his fingers over the impressive mound he'd accumulated since noon. Job well done.

Now, of course, came the holiday aftermath. Carm's stomach roiled, creating sounds that gave the bowlers a run for their money. Topsy-turvy and altogether queasy, Carm couldn't get comfortable no matter how he adjusted himself. Much worse than past Thanksgivings.

Around the table, the men swayed, dizzy, stuffed, ill at ease. Sliver Jimmy had passed out, head on the table. Uncouth as ever, Milo stood, waddled to a corner, hefted a tree-trunk leg and passed gas. Moans leap-frogged across the table, ghosts at play.

And that's when the door opened, and the real ghost strolled in.

Sammy screamed, his true nature showing. Glasses dropped, and so did jaws. Eyes popped. Howie took up a mantra of "No, no, no, no..." Unbelievably, Jimmy slept through it. Lucky guy.

Carm just shook his head, pretty much expecting it.

Like he owned the place, Mikey stood before them and

grinned. "Hi, boys. Miss me?"

"Jesus, this can't be real," said Tiny.

"What's reality?" Mikey shrugged, no sweat off his shoulders. But he did shrug off the jacket. Turned around. Three dots of red spread on his back into butterflies of blood. Calmly, he sat down next to Carm. "Hi, Boss."

"Hey, Mikey. Long time." An odd calm had settled over Carm, his wife's beloved mindful thinking at play. Or something worse.

Howie pitched forward, vomited a disturbing red torrent into his plate. Like an avalanche, more men joined him.

At that moment—that very thin slice of a second that Carm imagined everyone experienced right before death seized them—clarity freed his mind. More than *déjà vu*, he'd lived—and died—through this before.

Gongs went off.

Donnng…donnng…donnng…

From nowhere, from everywhere, and from deep within Carm's tortured gut. Twelve of them.

Although he knew the time, knew it quite well, Carm checked his pocket watch anyway. Same way he'd done for years. Twelve o'clock. Midnight, of course.

"Someone tell me what the hell's going on," screamed Sammy before he bucked forward in a vomiting fit.

"Kid, I explain it to you every year, the exact same way," said Mikey. "But, guess it's my lot in life—hell, I dunno, maybe death—to do it. So here goes."

Most of Carm's soldiers were beyond listening now, too sick to do anything but curl up in grotesque balls on the floor, their meals revisited upon their clothing.

But, as soothing as Carm's late, dear mamma, Mikey's deep tones lured Carm in, hooked him on story-time.

"All of you," Mikey jabbed a meaty thumb around the

room, "died long ago. 'Cause of what happened here."

"What? That goddamn Cammara family finally get us?" asked Howie. "And on Thanksgiving? *Pussy* move!"

Mikey smiled that hideous, toothless black hole of a smile again, and frankly, Carm wished he'd cut it out. "No, but the news called it the 'Thanksgiving Night Massacre.' Everybody got sick from the food. Some got sepsis from the oysters, others got *E. coli*, some of youse guys was already pretty sick, so those illnesses sped up. All of you was dead within a week, some in hours."

Before Carm spoke, he knew what he was going to say, knew he'd said it many times before, but he also realized he couldn't fight destination. Predestination. *Whatever*. "Goddamn Sal! *He* did this to us? Where is he? I'll kill him good! *Real* good! I'll—"

"Sal's still alive. In some rest home somewheres," said Mikey. "He didn't eat any of the food. Brought some of his wife's lasagna to work with him. And it wasn't really his fault. He cooked the food that one of your suppliers gave him. Tainted to hell and back."

"Jesus!" shouted Carm. "I shoulda had my wife's tofurky!"

Mikey sneered. But at least his mouth closed. "I dunno, Boss. Maybe you got the better end of the deal there. Anyway…" He scrubbed the air clean with his hands. "…you're all gonna be dead soon. Sliver Jimmy over there?" His thumb hitched toward the still-sleeping Jimmy. "He's the lucky one. Already dead."

"Lucky? How in the hell is he lucky? No one's lucky if we're all gonna take the six-feet-under snooze," said Carm.

"Um, it kinda gets worse, Boss. You see, this is your restin' place."

"I don't get what—"

"I don't know if this is hell or someplace…worse. But every

day you're all brought back here to die all over again. I'm stuck here, too, as, I dunno, some kinda guide, I guess."

Carm let it sink in. Then he sunk a hand into his pocket, retrieved his gun. And blasted Mikey.

When the smoke cleared, silence reigned. Except for Mikey's laughter.

"Boss, you can't kill me if I'm already dead."

"Goddammit, this can't be happening!" The second Carm jumped to his feet, he doubled-over and released a tide of poisoned oysters. He dragged a sleeve across his mouth, didn't feel a thing. In fact, most of the men were fading in front of him, some translucent, others missing various body parts completely.

"Gotta be going, Boss. See ya tomorrow." Mikey vanished quickly with a delicate *pop*, followed by three loud gunshots, an end of joke drum lick.

The others had slipped away into oblivion, too. But Carm was still alive. He could beat this…this thing. He knew he could. He'd beaten all his opponents, all the other families. Sure as hell he could beat eternity in a bowling alley.

He slipped the gun barrel into his mouth, closed his eyes and…

…"Shut up, shut up, already." Carmelo stood, waved his hands with royal flair. Hefted up his sweatpants. Sometimes it was the little touches that commanded respect. "I know it was hard for some of you to come out today, so…"

BE A MAN

Really, I suppose it's just a matter of setting your mind to something and following through. That's what Mae's always harking about, anyway. At least she did before she became bedridden. You know, before I started poisoning her.

In the kitchen, I applied the finishing touches to her omelet. Three eggs beat the way Mae likes them. Ham, peppers, onions diced into tiny squares. *God forbid I should let large pieces slip in there.* A handful of mushrooms. A pinch of arsenic. Some might think that last ingredient a little extreme, not suited for those with a refined palate.

In my defense, Mae's anything but refined. Blowsy like a hurricane, Mae whips into a confrontation, spews out what's on her mind, cuts me down like a diseased tree, then passes on to another port. An unfettered force of nature. Except, of course, storms tend not to aim for the same target time and time again, are much more indiscriminate in who they bully.

One might wonder why I ever married Mae. To tell you the truth, I ask myself that question every morning when I bring Mae her breakfast. You see, she wasn't always "Hurricane Mae." No, when I met her, Mae had a lilt to her laugh, a graceful tip of the chin, stars in her eyes, and a universe of warmth in her heart. Young, dumb, and in love, we had life by the tail. We planned to use that tail as a whip to tame the world.

But things changed pretty soon after we were wed. Actually, I should say Mae changed. I remained the same—same goals, same personality, fairly same waistline. Mae, of course, would say "same ol', same ol'," a ghastly, broken record.

I positioned the omelet on a tray, getting it just right, centering it nicely between a glass of orange juice and the silverware. A rose supplied the embellishing touch. Presentation is important. Not that Mae appreciates any of my culinary artistry. As soon as we'd bolted from the church ten years ago, she'd quit appreciating anything I did. Which I never quite understood, not really. After all, I accomplished everything I set out to do. I became a pharmacist at a leading retail drug store. The money's good, the hours are stable, no complaints on my end.

"Be a *man*, for God's sake," Mae liked to say. "You gonna waste the rest of your life in that crappy little drug store? We're barely making ends meet as it is. Set some *goals* for yourself!"

You know, it's really hard to set goals, let alone achieve them, when your wife continually stifles your attempts. Pardon the sports metaphor, but Mae's a world-class goalie, blocking every one of my well-aimed kicks. What she calls "making ends meet," I consider living the American Dream. We own a house, a place to lay out the welcome mat. Sure, there's the expected mortgage that seems to multiply like bunnies. And there are the credit card bills skyrocketing out of control, mostly due to Mae's penchant for shoes and strange, expensive, ugly-as-sin figurines. But, hey, we're living the dream, the one marketers and advertisers insist is the only dream to have. Absolute perfection. Except for the wife I can't stand.

The bottom step groaned as I began the ascent to Mae's bedroom.

We'd only spent one year together in the same bed before Mae had fled to the larger bedroom. Our future children's bedroom. The children we'd talked about having before we were married. Funny how the topic never came up again, post wedding ceremony. Of course, procreation seems unlikely now given that sex is nothing more than a barely remembered, occasional incident. Sort of like the vanishing edges of a nightmare.

The omelet looked good, smelled even better. It's what you can't see that'll get you, so the ubiquitous "They" say. Like an undetected tumor rotting away your insides while everything on the surface seems status quo, hunky dory, all systems go. But these days, Mae's systems aren't exactly thriving. They've been shutting down for some time. My decision—yes, one of my goals—had been to take Mae down slowly. Poison her at my leisure. Enjoy it while I can because as the damned Negative Nellie They say, *Every good thing must come to an end*. Feh. What do They know, anyway?

God only knows Mae unraveled our marriage bit by bit. Ten long, agonizing years of bit by bit. Maybe I'm being slightly petty, handing out pay-back. So sue me.

As a pharmacist, I have the knowledge, the tools of the trade, to achieve my long-term goal of Mae's drawn-out murder. Okay, okay, so I'm not *really* a pharmacist. I'm a pharm tech, the next closest thing. A matter of semantics, nothing more. Tomato, tomahto.

But Mae never saw it that way. "You said you were gonna be a pharmacist!" she'd rant. "Not some...*clerk*!"

A *clerk. Right*. This lowly "clerk" has the knowledge and skill to poison his windbag of a wife. Doubt that registers high on a clerk's job description. Besides, I'll eventually get back to pharmacy school. Some day. But now, as Mae so loves to remind me, we have ends to meet.

Half-way up the stairs, my toe caught on the carpet runner. The glass on the tray wobbled. I counterbalanced too far, and gravity beat me. The glass bounced down the stairs, spattering the juice everywhere.

Sometimes I daydream about ending Mae's life quicker, fantasize about watching the blood drain from her body. A quick-term goal, I guess one could say.

But, no, the plan had been put into effect, a damn good one, too. By killing her slowly—naturally, if you will—the shroud of suspicion would fall far from me. I'd already laid the groundwork, tricky devil that I am. Once Mae started feeling fatigued from the poison, losing weight along with her appetite, I took her to our doctor, a notoriously inept quack my family used to swear by. More often than not, the doctor diagnosed everything wrong. Shoved everyone out of his office with the advice, "Take decongestants, drink lots of liquids, call me in two weeks if you're not better." He chalked up Mae's symptoms to a nasty virus, one that'd been making the rounds. And while in Dr. Incompetent's lair, I strapped on my worried husband mask and reiterated, several times, Mae's family history of heart disease. Some of the best goals take a long time to put into action, you understand.

I left the orange juice glass on the stairs. Mae hadn't been drinking it lately anyway. Of course, she'd still scream about her missing juice.

"You *never* get anything right!" Another one of her favorite mantras. "You *never* do what you *say* you're going to do! For once in your life, be a *man*! A man like Kevin!"

Kevin. Did I mention Kevin? No? He's one of those hot-shot, cover-model lawyers in Mae's office. His hair's so perfect

I suspect it's sculpted. In fact, God took His sweet time when He sculpted Kevin's entire appearance while I got a rush job. And Kevin's clothes! A single suit costs more than a year's worth of my salary. He even smells rich with cologne so pungent it's obviously aged and shipped from some exotic locale. Come to think of it, you might find it strange how I'm extremely familiar with Kevin's scent. He's certainly dropped by the house often enough, his heinous odor lingering like skunk spray.

Kevin. I don't like the man, plain and simple. The man my wife's been having an affair with. I knew it then, and I know it now as gospel.

You see, Kevin played a starring role in the downfall of our tragic marriage. As soon as the ring slipped on Mae's finger, Kevin slipped into her life. Once they hit the sheets, I may as well have hit the streets.

But contrary to Mae's caterwauling, I'm not a quitter. Once I commit, I stay with it, a determined dog barking at shadows in the night. It's called *goals.* What the *hell* does Mae know about goals?

I snatched the rose from its vase and threw it against the wall. No big drama, no big fuss, the flower just limply slid to the steps. Very unsatisfying, like most of my life.

But watching Mae slowly deteriorate had proven extremely satisfying. That's what I keep telling myself, anyway, my daily affirmation. The only reason I get out of bed anymore. But, in all honesty, the process has dragged on too long. When I first realized my inevitable course—one that couldn't be steered in any other direction—I'd considered many different drugs, other methods. Hell, as a pharmacist, I even had a mortar and pestle, perfect for grinding glass into tiny, undetectable shards. But, as They say, *If it ain't broke, don't fix it.* And there's those fucking "They" people again, always running my life, always there with a smart-ass comment on everything like they know it all!

Anyhow, anyhoo, I settled on arsenic. As there'd been reports of arsenic findings in several local county water wells, all my bases were covered. Problem is, I hate waiting. Seems like that's all I do: *wait*.

I've spent the better portion of ten years waiting for Mae to come around.

"Take Kevin, for instance," the bitch would say. "He *always* wanted to be a lawyer. So he set his sights high, breezed through Harvard, graduated top of his class at one of the best law schools in the country. A *real* man, taking what he wants. *Nothing* like you!"

Kevin, Kevin, Kevin. Time and time again, Mae praises the ground Kevin strolls on and belittles me in comparison.

Maybe I should expand my goals. Kevin's demise seems like a perfectly wonderful new goal, one I'll enjoy immensely. They say *you only live once*!

But here's the deal. I lied. Just a bit, though. Nothing *too* out there. I don't *really* know if Mae and Kevin ever had an affair. Could be I don't know the back of my hand very well either. Just sayin'. But it makes sense. Nothing else fits. Even if I'm wrong—which I doubt—Kevin's so pompous, so perfect, so arrogant, I'd be doing the world a favor. Call it a mercy killing. Yeah, Kevin's gotta go.

Once I reached the top of the stairs, I heard Mae moan. Well, more like a shriek, her favorite form of communication.

My heart tripped; not out of fear, but, rather, joy. I'd be hard-pressed to put into words as to why I felt so vibrant, so exuberant. But my pushy subconscious found the right words. With a mental nudge, my subconscious said, "It's time, already. Be a man!" Funny thing is, my subconscious carries Mae's grating voice.

A voice that can't be denied.

With nothing on the tray now but silverware and an omelet, I opened Mae's door. Didn't even knock, either. Full-on, take charge, he-man mode.

Mae's brow pulled down in typical disappointment. "There you are. I thought you might've overslept. I was worried about you." Illness tempered her typical banshee shriek into a contemptuous whine.

"Sorry breakfast is late. Good things come to those who wait." Truer words They have never spoken.

She scooted up in bed, a mammoth undertaking. Her skin hung in loose folds, her face skeletal. Her eyes were large and round and glassy, just like her abominable figurines. Yet she kept her scornful gaze rigid, searing me with disapproving eyes.

See, as much as I hate to admit it, Mae spoke the truth about one thing: *goals*. Months ago, I set my goal and had been working hard toward achieving the end. Now I'm finally ready to cross the finish line. In sports parlance, call it "sudden death."

I set the tray on the floor.

Always untrustworthy, she attempted a false face of concern. "Are you okay? You look…upset. Please…" She patted the bed with a weak hand. "…sit with me. You've been so withdrawn lately, honey. We never talk anymore. I don't want you to worry about me. Are you feeling—"

The pillow stopped her nagging, her insistent bitching. Her arms flapped ineffectually, as ludicrous as a chicken with its head cut off. I held the pillow tight, laid into it with my body weight. Weighed it down with ten-years-worth of emotional torment. Waited while she struggled, hardly a fight at all. Her crap-flinging, nail-pounding, emasculating voice ended with a blessed groan.

I completed my goal. The way Kevin would do it, no doubt. Just like a man.

HUSK

First thing upon waking, Harv noticed his wing-ding killer of a hangover, impossible to ignore. His apartment bedroom spun like a dervish, and his head slogged along for the ride. Parched, his mouth hosted a desert. His brain had taken up the conga drums, *bang-bang-bang*ing away in an irritatingly spirited symphony. Oddly enough, Harv didn't even recall drinking last night.

The next thing Harv noticed was his morning wood tent pitching just a bit taller than usual. Strange, but hey, nothing to complain about. Besides, he couldn't track a coherent thought at all, not in his state.

But the third thing Harv noticed really yanked reality's rug out from beneath him. After quite a struggle, he managed to sit up and gawk at the stranger in the chair next to his bed. Well, he supposed, it's not *really* a stranger if it's yourself. Even if Harv knew, absolutely so, that his spitting image *definitely* appeared fatter. It didn't matter, though, because no matter how many quacks, kooks, cult members, religious nuts, or science fiction writers state to the contrary, doppelgängers simply don't exist. Not in Harv's world.

Harv chalked up his illusion to nothing more than that old devil, alcohol, gifting him with temporary dementia. He closed his eyes, leaned back into his pillow, and hit the headboard instead.

After a couple minutes, Harv opened one eye, kept the other locked down tight so he could focus on a single image.

Nope. Still there. Sitting deep in thought, an elbow on the knee and a hand curled up beneath his chin like Rodin's sculpture, *The Thinker*. Naked as a jaybird.

The hell?

"Hello?" Not the most intelligent or applicable introduction to oneself, but Harv figured there probably hadn't been a lot of experience in such a situation to draw from. "Um… Hey?"

Harv reached out, then reeled his hand back in. Sure, he didn't particularly want to touch himself, but he also didn't recognize his own hand. The fingers seemed a bit longer, stronger. And the coloring appeared all wrong.

What, did I go drunk tanning last night?

He turned the foreign artifact of his hand over and back again. Nice olive complexion, a little bit lighter on the underside. He licked a thumb—even though he couldn't dredge up much saliva—and rubbed his hand. Near panic, he scraped it roughly against the wall until the dark complexion turned red.

Nope. Permanent. Weird. I'm never drinking again.

Harv had vowed to give up drinking before, of course. He always meant it, too, until his next outing. Generally, Harv remembered most of his drinking adventures. But he couldn't recall tying one on last night. As a matter of fact, he couldn't remember a damn thing about last night.

What did I do?

Had to be Bill down at the office. Just had to be. Always a practical joker, Bill never knew when to stop.

Haha, very funny, good one, Bill.

But the fake tan had better not be permanent.

Then again, why in hell's my double sitting next to me?

Harv nearly raced to the bathroom, but curiosity held him within its gravitational thrall. His double hadn't moved, kept his eyes shut. His—its?—face was drawn up in a multi-wrinkled grimace that reminded Harv he'd recently ignored his fortieth birthday, one he hadn't told anyone about. But there Harv sat, pretty as a picture in his birthday suit, all forty years of him.

Of course, Harv wondered if sleep still tethered him down into a silly dream. That explanation would wrap up everything nice and tidy, put a bow on it, no need for the men in white coats. But Harv knew he was awake, didn't have to pinch himself to make sure. The awful hangover pretty much ensured that.

He steadied his hands and wiped yawn-induced tears from his eyes, the better to take a longer gander at his double.

Middle-aged paunch? *Check.* Receding hairline? *Check.* Varicose veins in the legs? *Check, checkity, check!* Strange hair growing out of even stranger places? *Check, goddammit, check!*

Bill sure had gone to a lot of effort for this, his ace of all pranks. Obviously, Bill'd cast a statue from Harv's passed out body. Dyes or something explained the coloring of Harv's hands, a mere side effect. Nothing else made sense. Unless, of course, Harv's mind had taken a hike, and it was certainly best not to follow it down that dark alley. No sir, Bill had pulled out all the stops and made an incredibly life-like statue of Harv, warts and all. Bill's sculptor had performed amazing work, although none too flattering—something Harv would take up with Bill later.

Yet… Harv had to touch it, see what the statue felt like. Just like a little kid drawn to forbidden, priceless, fragile things.

But mostly to reassure himself it wasn't skin because it certainly *looked* like skin. That'd be creepy. Maybe even illegal.

A half-hearted alley-oop and Harv planted his legs over the side of the bed onto the floor. It still didn't stop the room from spinning, but one thing at a time and all. He admired his newly lean and muscular legs. Not a vein in sight, either. Of course the negative outweighed the positive: the dark color of his legs, a shade deeper than his hands. *Not* his favorite color.

"Come on, Bill," he muttered. "What*ever*."

Harv rubbed his eyes again, which didn't help at all. Just made his vision blur more. That's when he noticed it. From his bedroom window, a sliver of sunlight sliced through his double. Harv leaned closer toward the statue. The figure appeared translucent.

This time Harv couldn't be stopped. As if standing outside himself—and why not, since he didn't recognize his current body?—Harv watched his hand take on a life of its own. Slowly, it reached toward the body, hesitated a couple inches out, then landed.

Harv shrieked, not a very manly sound, and frankly, he didn't care. Beneath his touch, the body flaked, silently caved in on itself. A cloud of white dust swam in the window's light, swirling like a horde of mites. A strange odor, not unlike talcum powder and sweat, filled the room. The shell of his former body lay on the floor in brittle potato chips and sugar-coated dust.

Harv's stomach flip-flopped. He hurtled into the bathroom, no time to open the toilet seat. A gut cramp doubled him over, face into the sink. His stomach released its contents in a torrential blast.

What the hell is going on?

When his stomach had no more to give, his body thought

otherwise. Several gut-clenching dry heaves shook him down to his knees. Tears rolled down his cheeks. When he knew he was done—absolutely, finally (*please-let-me-be-done*) finished—he straightened. Through blurry eyes, he looked into the mirror.

And met the new, although not necessarily improved model of Harvey Perkins.

Sure, some things were better. His extra five pounds of baggage—okay, 25 pounds, but he meant to take it off any day now!—had vanished, now replaced with a lean, mean six-pack of ribs and muscles, a first in his life. His mousey blond hair that had been crawling away from his scalp had miraculously transformed into waves of black curls. Weak pale grey eyes had changed into solid brown marbles. He popped open his jockey shorts, took a quick inventory. Yep, packing a little more punch there, too.

Ordinarily, he'd be thrilled. Now he carried the physique he'd secretly admired from others, the guys who paraded around naked in his gym's locker room—*and, jeez, who does that anyway?* His new physique and full head of hair would probably even garner come-hither looks from Phyllis, his company receptionist. Not an ounce of fat on his body.

But there remained one huge problem.

Harv Perkins had been somehow transferred into the body of a Middle Eastern man.

Not that Harv had any prejudiced bones, no way! Constantly, he reminded friends and coworkers of this very important fact. He considered himself a fair man, hardly noticed skin color at all. Quite the open-minded liberal, all in all.

But…but…a Middle Eastern man?

Not that there's anything wrong with that, of course. It's just that being a Middle Eastern man in the States right now probably wouldn't be a cake-walk.

Even though he didn't feel it, Harv laughed. A fairly safe

and sane response. The other option? Curl up into a ball and cry. What else do you do when you wake up as a new—*foreign*—man?

Earlier, Harv'd tried to convince himself he'd been the victim of one of Bill's gags. But his tenuous grip on that last string of sanity had pretty much loosened. Even Bill wouldn't go to such elaborate lengths.

"My God! What's *happening* to me? This *can't* be happening!"

His altered image stared back at him in the mirror. Heavy, furrowed dark brows displayed menace. The brown eyes harbored a deadly secret, a trap waiting to spring. With a roar, Harv smashed his fist into the mirror. He did it until his image shattered.

"God*dammit*! I'm not a…a…a *towel head*!"

There. He'd said it. Surprised himself a bit, maybe felt a tad ashamed, but thought it might be cathartic. It didn't do much at all, honestly, but he repeated it quietly, a hymn of loathing.

Insane things like this just don't happen in a sane world. Yesterday, Harv was a happy, white—maybe a little privileged —pharmaceutical rep for a decent-sized Kansas City company. Okay, maybe "happy" might be fudging the truth a bit, but he certainly felt content. Well, he was lonely, no doubt about that, but he'd been doing alright. Kinda idling through life, truthfully, but now he'd love to edge back into the slow lane. The nice, easy, white slow lane of his life.

And where in hell had that slow lane taken him last night? How did this happen? Why couldn't he remember anything? Last thing he recalled was having a drink with Bill at Davey's Landing, then…

Bill! He needed to talk to Bill. Maybe he'd have a clue. And maybe that's what Harv needed: a bit of the old, comfortable, boring stability of his job. Still, it didn't make him jump for joy about the prospects of going to work in his changed form. The guys would razz him mercilessly, bunch of jerks.

Maybe he was looking at things all wrong. What if it's just temporary, God pulling the practical joke strings instead of Bill? Or maybe it was epidemic, people changing color all over the world. But a sinking rock in his gut told him the truth: he'd boarded a one-man boat to Minority Land.

Clothes, I need clothes. No moss on me.

All of his suits were too large now. He still had his sweat-pants from when he joined the gym—one he'd quit going to after two visits—several years and 25 extra pounds ago. They'd probably fit him. Toss on a t-shirt and done. As a general rule, Harv always prided himself on dressing sharply for work; he took great umbrage to the idea of "casual Fridays," but desperate times called for desperate clothing.

Now if he could only find his keys, and he had a pretty good idea where they were. It hadn't been the first time he'd left them in his car after closing up the bar with Bill. He took one last look at his broken mirror image, shook his head in dismay, and left.

The morning air struck him like a slap in the face, too cool and biting for a late Kansas City spring day. A cursory glance up and down the street showed him the world hadn't changed. Business as usual. Yuppies climbed into their sports cars, brief-cases in hands. Trash cans sat on their sides in yards, the union-protected trash collectors returning them any which way they felt like. Birds sang and chirped damn happy songs, mocking him with their carefree, stupid, and short attention spans.

Harv's Celica sat in the drive, one tire in the grass. He really had to watch how much he drank when he drove, meant to change that, but just never had the time. Last night's outing, though, must've been a hella bender, black-out and all.

As he approached his car, that rock in his gut settled lower.

All doors locked, the keys in the ignition.

"God *damn* it!" He raised his hands above him, pleading with the Big Guy in the Sky. "Can't you give me a *break*?"

He kicked the car's fender, did it again for good measure. *Ank! Ank! Ank! Ank!…*

"Fan-freakin'-tastic!" The horn blared, the headlights flashed off and on. Stymied and still unable to think straight, he ran his hands through his hair and released a small "yeep." Temporarily, he'd forgotten about his bountiful gain of hair. Kinda felt a little greasy, though. Could do with a good wash…

Keep your mind on the big picture, Harv!

Something cracked like a gunshot. Next door, Mrs. Sugarman stood in her open doorway, dressed in a robe. A shower cap wrangled her bird's nest of hair. She held her phone out as if ready to detonate a bomb with it.

"You! *What* do you think you're *doing*?"

Usually, Harv dreaded his encounters with the old busybody, carefully avoided her like the plague. But today, he welcomed her appearance. Kind of.

"Oh, hey, Missus Sugarman, I locked—"

"I don't know you! I'm callin' 9-1-1!"

Harv waved his new hands in surrender, nearly got lost in the peculiar dark tone they'd acquired. "No, no, it's me, Missus Sugarman! Harv! Harvey Perkins, your neighbor. I know it—"

"What in the world kinda crap you tryin' to feed me? I know my neighbor. You sure ain't him! You're tryin' to steal his car! Caught ya red-handed!"

Harv nearly corrected her and said "brown-handed." His inner censor stopped him. "Hold on, hold on. It *is* me, Missus Sugarman! I don't know *what* happened, but I woke up like this! Crazy, right?" He flashed her a smile. Too late, he wondered how it looked on her end as he remembered how menacing he'd appeared in the mirror. "I can prove it! Every Christmas you give me a fruitcake and I, um…don't give you anything. But the fruitcake is good." It never was, really. Might make a good doorstop, but it had proven inedible. "I locked my keys in my car—"

"That don't prove nothin'! You think I was born yesterday?" *Absolutely not.* "Feedin' me that cock-and-bull story! You're stealin' the car, you *damn* foreigner! That does it, I'm callin' the police!" She squinted at her phone and pecked at the pad. "They'll be here any second now!"

Dammit. The police wouldn't believe his story. How could he expect them to when he had a hard time wrapping his head around it? Until he had answers, it'd be best to fly under the radar. Mrs. Sugarman proved that.

"Fine. Fine. I'm going! You can put your phone away, Missus Sugarman!" Slowly, he walked backward down the driveway, hands up in the air as if held at gunpoint.

"Yeah, you'd better run! Damn camel jockey! Go back to Iran, you and all your type!"

Like a shiv to the back, the words cut deep. His mounting fears cut even deeper.

The bus rolled, the occupants shook, and all eyes eventually crapped out on Harv. Some people glanced at him surreptitiously, never a single look, not the socially acceptable and nearly required look one expects from people while sharing a communal experience. No, Harv's fellow travelers looked at him with suspicion, quickly averted their gaze, then glanced at him again. Whenever he tried to meet their eyes, they'd turn away so fast he thought they might develop some seriously high chiropractor bills. Those were the polite bus travelers. The others were the ones who really bothered Harv. Hard stares, grimaces, unforgiving frowns. One older man kept working at something tucked into his lower lip as if ready to hawk a loogie at Harv.

When another man of Middle Eastern descent boarded the bus headed downtown, Harv nearly cheered. Yet Harv had to stop himself from staring at the newcomer. Clearly, Harv's curiosity could be mistaken for the obvious prejudice he'd just experienced. Truth be told, though, the bulging backpack weighing down the young man gave Harv pause. In this day and age, it never hurt to be on guard, observant, and always vigilant.

The guy slipped into the seat in front of Harv. Immediately, he took off his backpack. Except for a narrow opening, he kept the pack zipped up tight. Then his hand vanished inside it. Moving to the edge of the bench, Harv checked for any suspicious activity.

Now who's being racist? Gah! Talk about the pot calling the kettle…well, brown, I guess.

Harv settled back, mentally slapping himself. *Stupid, so stupid.*

Still…the guy kept glancing around, nervous. Clearly up to no good. Finally, he pulled out a textbook, engineering or something. Harv let out a thorough, cleansing sigh. Not nearly as hushed as he'd meant it to be. The student turned around, gave Harv a quick up-and-down appraisal. Apparently, Harv met his standards. The young man nodded at Harv. His lips turned up, just a tad. Not an open, friendly smile. Rather a tired, world weary smile: *I've been there, brother.*

Tired of the endless mind games and cold fish faces, Harv

sought solace by staring out the window. Sunlight caught and captured a reflection of his new face in the glass. As the bus entered a tunnel, his refection disappeared; a perfect metaphor for the mess Harv's life had turned into.

As Harv exited the bus, he offered a smile and "thank you" to the bus driver. The driver said nothing, didn't acknowledge him, just whooshed the door closed with a rude *clumph.*

The elevator ride up to Harv's company held no shocks or surprises. Harv stood his ground, tried to put his newly broad shoulders back and single chin up. But as more people entered, his pride sort of deflated and whiffed away. He stayed firm in his polite everyman stance, hands folded reverently in front of him, but the elevator may as well have been segregated. Overloaded with white people on one side, Harv stood on the other by himself. Part of him—the old part he knew—felt like joining them. He wanted to shout, "I'm a white man, dammit!" Instead, he folded into himself, kept to himself. The new world order hadn't invited him to either side.

A sharp *ding* signaled the end of the hellish trip. The doors whisked open. He welcomed the comfortable sign of his company, *Roker's Pharmaceuticals,* hanging on the wall. Damned near ran over and embraced it. Behind the receptionist's desk sat Phyllis, wearing a rather unwelcoming frown.

"Can I help you, sir?" She afforded Harv the briefest of looks before busying herself by moving the stapler back and forth.

Phyllis knew Harv well. Encouraged by alcohol, he'd hit on her at more company outings than even their boss. With an annoying eye roll, sometimes derisive laughter, she'd always rejected Harv's good intentions. Which just burned Harv at both ends.

Phyllis wasn't *all* that, as the kids say (and Harv prided

himself on keeping up with the "hep" trends). Barely attractive in a kinda squinty-eyed, last-call manner, Phyllis paraded around the office like a royal queen. Harv always wondered what had happened in Phyllis's past to buoy such delusional and unwarranted confidence. Still, after a long dry spell in the romance department, Harv had decided to lower his standards. Considered Phyllis a slam-dunk. Especially since Bill bragged first dibs on having a short-lived fling with her. But she'd always flat out let Harv (and everyone within hearing distance) know exactly what she thought of him.

"I wouldn't go out with you if you were the last man on earth!" she'd said once at a bar (and much too loudly). She followed up with that horsey guffaw of hers, more grating than squeaking Styrofoam pieces.

To show he was a good sport, Harv had laughed it off (tried to anyway) and bought her a "no sweat" drink. Then another. And another. And she still wouldn't sleep with him.

Now, as he watched her fussy, bird-like movements, he wondered what in the world had ever possessed him. Then, in that round-about way, he wondered if Phyllis might change her mind if she knew what he now packed in his sweats. He smiled a revenge smile. He'd play hard to get; too bad, her loss.

"Good morning," Harv said. "Is Bill Thackett in?" After his next-door neighbor mess, he'd decided to not play his "Old Harveyness" card too much.

"Mm-hmm. Do you have an appointment?" Phyllis pinched her lips together. Wrinkles Harv never noticed before encroached upon her mouth and rode her brow.

What was I ever thinking?

"Actually, I don't. But I'm sure Bill will want to see me. Can you just—"

"I'm sorry, but you need to have an appointment to see

one of our sales reps. If you'd like to call back to schedule—"

"Oh, for God's sake, Phyllis! I know damn well that's not one of our rules! Everyone knows sales reps will see practically anybody! Just pick up your—"

"I don't know how you know my name, sir, but..." She slapped her name plaque face down. "...I certainly don't like your attitude or the way you're talking to me."

"Ohhh, I get it. It's because of how I look, right? My skin color! Is that—"

"Sir, you need to calm down and lower your voice or I'll call security."

"What? Security? Fer cryin' out loud, I haven't *done* anything!"

"Either leave or I'll call security." In a flash, she held the phone to her ear, her unappealing, ropey fingers hovering over the keypad.

Exasperated, Harv tossed his arms up in a remarkable display of hissy fitdom. "Fine. I'll leave, dammit."

Harv feigned a path toward the elevator, then bounced back, much faster than his chubby legs used to carry him. He bypassed Phyllis, cupped his hands over his mouth, and called out down the hallway. "Bill! Bill Thackett! I need to talk to you! It's important! Bill!"

"Sir! You need to leave! *Now!*"

The elevator doors slid open. Several men rushed into the waiting area, Roker's security team hard at work. "Security! There a problem here?"

Harv whirled. His heart thumped. Manic thoughts crowded his mind. "Yeah, there's a problem!" He pointed at Phyllis, now backed up against a file cabinet. "That racist woman, for starters! You shoulda seen how she treated me! It's—"

"Sir! Calm down!" One of the blue suits held up a pacifying hand, the other had his stun gun out. Hardly reassuring.

"Take a deep breath and settle down! *What* are you doing here?"

"I'm an American citizen! I've got just as much right to be here as you do!" Never in his wildest dreams did Harv believe a day at the office would turn into a tolerance and rights rally. Certainly, he never envisioned himself leading one. Plain as day, he hadn't *thought*. Period. "Just because I have dark skin doesn't mean—"

"Sir! Do you have any weapons on you?"

Phyllis screamed. "He's got something in his pocket!"

"What? No, I don't! Just my wallet and—"

"Whoa! Slowly put both hands in the air! I'm not playing here!"

The way the guard toyed with the stun gun, tossing it between his hands like a knife, Harv thought the blue suit definitely wanted to play. The guard's eyes brightened, his smile widened. Harv suspected he'd enjoy his chance at playtime quite a bit.

Not ready to embrace electric volts, Harv took a deep breath, let it out. "Okay, look, I'm sorry. Can we start over? Please? I'm a nice guy. Really! Just ask my friends! I—"

"Nice don't matter since nine-eleven," spat out the other guard.

"Oh, good God! I'm not a terrorist! I just want to talk to Bill Thackett! Can you—"

"What the hell's goin' on here?" Like a genie—an overweight and out-of-breath one—Bill popped around the corner. He stared at all the showdown's major players, clearly trying to put the pieces together. "Phyllis? What's going on?"

In a shaky voice, she said, "That…that *man*!" She hit "man" like she'd stubbed her toe. Her finger wagged at Harv. "He… came in here, making threats and—"

"*That* didn't happen."

"Quiet, sir!" said the trigger-happy guard.

"I need to talk to you, Bill. It's important! Please!"

Bill squinted, jerked his head back to peer through his bifocals, and looked Harv up and down the way Harv was growing accustomed to. "Um, do I know you?"

"Yeah…no…sort of. Just give me five minutes. It's all I'm asking."

"What's this about, Mister…uh…"

"Smith." First name other than Doe that popped into Harv's head. "Ah…John Smith. I've got something important to tell you."

"Did you make an appointment with Phyllis?"

Harv's eyes rolled a complete, sarcastic orbit. "Bill, that's not how we operate and you know it! Oh, for God's sake…" Time to play hardball, the only way to get Bill's attention. He raised his hands, slowly approached Bill as if walking into a hostage crisis.

"Sir, hold it right there!" The guard dropped into a crouch, legs apart, stun gun locked in his arms. Looked pretty cool, thought Harv, just like on TV. But he doubted the stun gun's range would reach him this far.

Harv grabbed Bill's arm. Bill flinched. Bill never flinched. In fact, he got overly touchy to the point of irritation whenever he had his drink on. Harv leaned down, whispered, "Bill, I know you had an affair with Phyllis." Best way to get his undivided attention.

Bill stammered, stuttered, fluttered his eyes as if fighting a sandstorm. Harv nodded, mouth set in a serious straight line, letting him know he meant business.

"Sir, you need to come with us now," said guard number one.

White as chalk, even whiter than his usual WASPy self, Bill waved a hand. "It's okay, Bob, I've got this."

"You sure, Mister Thackett?"

Looking quite unsure, Bill said, "I'm sure."

"Alright then. You need us, just holler." Trigger-happy pocketed his stun gun, hitched up his pants. The two of them swaggered toward Phyllis, thumbs hooked into their belts, no doubt seeking accolades and a phone number.

Bill hurried down the hallway, more urgently than he'd ever moved, and Harv followed. In his cramped office, he said nothing, pointed at the seat usually occupied by rubes or other salesmen. After a conspiratorial glance down the hallway, he closed the door. With a deep sigh, he collapsed into his worn chair. "So…you're blackmailing me? Barking up the wrong tree. I don't have any money."

"What? Of course not! I don't care about your sleazy past!"

"Back up a minute. First of all, how do you know about, ah, Phyllis and me? I'm not sayin' it's true, but if it was, how'd you find out?"

"You're gonna play that card with me, Bill?"

"You act like I know you. I'm pretty sure I've never met you before. At least, I don't think we've met. Who are you? If you don't want money, are you trying to ruin my marriage?"

"I wouldn't tell Muriel, for Chrissakes! Just listen—"

"Wait, what? How do you know Muriel?"

Harv sighed. Salesmen always made the toughest sells. "Before you say anything, before you call me crazy, just hear me out. Okay?" Bill sat motionless, quiet. Color—and possibly a few years—leaked away from his face. "I swear I'm not after money, and I'm not gonna tell Muriel about your stupid affair."

"Hey, it wasn't stupid. It—"

"Quiet, Bill! Just listen, okay?"

Bill nodded.

"It's me."

Bill shook his head, lines of confusion riding his forehead.

"Harv. Harvey Perkins. This morning, I woke up like this. My old body—just a shell—was next to me, and when I touched it, it crumpled. Poof!"

Bill said nothing as promised, his face blank as well. He opened his drawer, pulled out his whiskey bottle. Set down a single shot glass and filled it full. First time he'd never offered Harv—the old Harv—a drink. Finally, "You're right. You're crazy." Downed his shot in one tilt.

"I'm not crazy, Bill! *That's* the crazy thing! *This* is the crazy thing!" Harv flourished his hands over his chest. "I'm not crazy, but what happened to me definitely is! Say something!"

"First you don't want me to talk, now you do." Bill shrugged, filled the shot glass again. "Whoever you are, what you just told me is ridiculous. People don't wake up changed into a…a, um…" Bill, never the most tolerant of people, held back whatever colorful racist slur he wanted to unleash. Harv had heard them all. Liberal to a fault, Harv never joined Bill in his racist tirades. At least, he didn't think he did. Maybe an accidental slip of the tongue once in a while. Everyone's human. Or if Harv had been drinking, he didn't mind repeating a racial joke. All in good fun. Blame the alcohol. Made quite a few sales that way, too. On the other hand, Harv never chastised Bill for his blatant racism. Thought it was kind of amusing in a "bad boy," vicarious sort of way.

"Well, clearly you're delusional," Bill continued, "or just flat out nuts. Maybe I better get security back—"

"Don't do that, for God's sake! I'm telling you the truth! How do you think I know about Phyllis? Or your wife's name?"

"Only two people know about Phyllis." He stuck out two fingers, counted them down. His middle finger remained up. Then poured another two fingers. "Phyllis and Harv." He brokered a smile. A tide of calm washed over him. Alcohol-fueled redness flushed his cheeks. "Wait…duh. Harv set you up to this! You actually had me goin' there for a moment. Where's Harv?" Playfully, he peeked under his desk. "Tell him the joke's over. Good one, though."

"You're not hearing me! It's me, Goddammit! Harv!" An idea struck him, should have thought of it earlier. "You remember that one night—six years ago? The night we *really* tied one on?" He stood, started undoing his sweatpants.

"Um…I mean it, joke's over. I don't fly that way, no sir!" Offensive again—the only way Bill knew how to fly—he dropped his hand at the wrist in an unflattering gay stereotype.

"We got tattoos on our asses, Bill! 'Member that? You got Muriel's name on yours, and I got the last girl I dated, Cheryl, on mine! You wanna see it?" Harv hoped his gamble would pay off. True, they'd gotten the tattoos. False, he'd never dated Cheryl, though sorely wanted to (although Bill never needed to know that inconsequential tidbit). He prayed his tattoo had transferred to his new skin, hadn't thought to check earlier.

Bill threw his hands up and threw in the towel. "No! Don't take your pants off! Christ!" He stared at the bottle. This time he forewent the glass and took a long slug from the bottle. He released his lips from the bottle with a hollow-sounding *clump*. "Only Harv knows about those tats. We swore one another to secrecy. Not even Muriel's seen my ass for about fifteen years now."

"You believe me now?"

Again, Bill shrugged. "I don't know what to believe. Say I do believe you—and again I'm not saying I do, we're just pretending for now—but…how in the hell did this happen? Are you gonna change back? You goin' to synagogues now or what? What—"

"Bill! I need your help!"

Bill sat back with a sigh, loosened his tie. Resigned to temporary insanity.

"What did we *do* last night, Bill? I mean…I kinda remember going to Davey's Landing for drinks, nothing new there. But then…nothing. Zilch. Last thing I remember, I was warming a bar seat next to you, then I wake up with my old body looking at me. Well, it wasn't really looking at me."

"Jesus. You—*Harv*, whatever, whoever—were well into your fifth scotch when Muriel called me," said Bill. "She couldn't figure out the damn DVR, so I had to skedaddle. You don't remember that?"

"Vaguely." *No, not at all.* "So you left?"

"Yep. Damn Muriel never met a piece of electronics she understood. Although I suspect she's got a vibrator that—"

"Stay focused, Bill. Anything else you remember about last night? What'd we talk about?"

He grinned, his eyes lost. He rocked in his chair as if recalling a nostalgic childhood memory. "Well, that's the kicker. You, or whoever, were in a real funk. Talkin' about how life was disappointing, all that kind of crap. Goin' on about your looks, your overhangin' belly. Age. Loneliness. Frankly, I was kinda glad to get out of there before you started cryin' like a sloppy drunk."

"So you left me there?"

"No. I left Harv there. You, I've never met before. Look, tomorrow at this time, I fully expect to have Harv—the *real* Harv—sitting in that chair you're taking up space in. End of the joke. Either that or I've gone crazy. Or you're a lunatic, whatever! But if you wanna play this thing out…and I'm not sayin' I believe you 'cause that would make me crazy…I'd go down and talk to Shakey at the Landing. He was tendin' bar. He'd probably be more help. But right now? I'm gonna get quietly drunk and laugh this off."

"Yeah, wish I could."

"Now, get outta my office. And if I ever see or hear from you again, I'll call the NSA or somethin' and report you as a terrorist."

Harv didn't quite know how to respond. In a way, he supposed he owed Bill his thanks. But Bill had threatened him. Always an ornery drunk, Harv suspected Bill was getting in his cups already. Time to go.

"Fine, then. Thanks, Bill." He extended his hand.

Bill looked at it, sniffed. "Don't let the door hit you on the way out."

Harv slammed the door, stomped through the offices. He pressed the elevator button, then turned around. In a nice, loud voice, he yelled, "Hey, Phyllis, you still sleeping with Bill?"

Before Phyllis could call security again, he jumped into the elevator, giggling like a madman (to which he felt a certain kindred fellowship). All the white passengers stared at him.

A fine American establishment (since 1959!), Davey's Landing posed a bit of a problem. Harv and Bill had spent many nights propping up the bar, usually under the vigilant, googly eyes of "Shakey." The proprietor hated his nickname, of course, but due to his hands making like a paint shaker, the moniker stuck. Fiery to the point of a two alarmer, Shakey was also the whitest guy Harv had ever met, and that was saying quite a lot. Harv hadn't really looked at Shakey in that light before. Hell, he'd had no reason to. But Shakey—proud to be an American, dammit! Try telling him all "Americans" have foreign blood streaming through their red, white, and blue veins, and he'd threaten you with his baseball bat—could drop a racial slur like a rapper with his microphone. Once Shakey got going, he couldn't be stopped, a runaway train of racial epithets. Come to think of it, Harv couldn't remember ever seeing a person of ethnicity or color in the bar. Unless you counted Jewish people, and they didn't really count as minorities. Not that Harv ever harbored a racist thought toward the Jews, mind you.

Regardless, Harv didn't look forward to his impending chat with Shakey.

At three o'clock, Davey's was generally empty, a good thing. Harv squared his shoulders (giving him a masculine boost he hadn't felt, well, ever) and entered the dive. He half-expected to see the bar in a new light, maybe in a more enlightened manner, but it appeared as homely and oddly homey as ever. Dark to the point of twilight, faded beer signs decorated the walls. Country music (*always* Garth Brooks, if Shakey had his say, and he usually did) blared out from the ancient jukebox. As he strode to the bar, Harv's sneakers stuck to the beer-covered floor, then released with a ripping sound.

Shakey was busy wiping down the bar with a hand towel—although it never seemed to make a difference—and hadn't seen Harv enter. For a full nerve-wracking minute, Harv stood in front of the bar, hoping to catch at least one of Shakey's wayward eyes. Frustrated, Harv cleared his throat. Shakey's scattershot gaze traveled east and west, then dropped to a distrusting half-mast.

"What do *you* want?" Since Shakey's eyes rarely focused on a central point, he could've been speaking to anyone, but Harv knew his ire was aimed at him.

"Hey, Shakey. Can I ask you something about last night?"

Shakey spat on the floor, wiped his mouth with his arm.

"Free country, I reckon. Not that *you'd* know much about that."

"Um, I'm a private detective. I'm looking for info about a man who was here last night. Harv Perkins." Harv figured the cover of a P.I. might warm the long-dead cockles of Shakey's macho heart.

"Harv? I know Harv. What's this all about? What's it to ya?"

"Just routine questions. He's not in trouble or anything like that. I just—"

"Show me your credentials."

"Ah…"

"Your credentials. If you're some hotshot detective, I wanna see some credentials."

Harv patted down his pockets, a shameless ploy to buy time. "Guess I left my wallet in the car."

"Yeah, right… Just as I thought. What's your angle, raghead? Gonna shoot up my bar? And Harv! What'd you do to Harv? You kill him?"

"Course not! I *am* Harvey!" *Whoops.* All in now, Harv yanked out his wallet. He flipped it open, displayed his driver's license. "See? That's me! Harvey Perkins! Bill and I've been comin' here for years! I sit—"

"Son of a bitch! How come you got Harv's wallet? You roll him?" Shakey's face burned red. He wheeled around, dropped behind the bar, then popped up, baseball bat on his shoulder. He smacked the bar.

Crack!

An empty mug danced close to the bar's edge.

"You fuckin' camel jockeys! You're ruinin' our country!"

Thwack!

"It's high time we took it back! Make America great again!"

Brack!

Despite the threatening baseball bat, Harv couldn't hold

his tongue. "You think you're a true-blue American, right, Shakey? Well, news flash! None of us are! We're *all* immigrants. Sorta! And not all Middle Eastern Americans are terrorists, dumb-ass!"

"You just signed your death warrant, Ali Baba!" Shakey raced down the length of the bar, cursing and swinging his bat. His white shirttail loosened and flapped behind him like a kite tail. "Gonna kick your ass, ya Goddamn camel jockey!"

On his new legs of iron, Harv bolted. He burst through the door and left Shakey far behind, screeching in the parking lot. At a safe enough distance, Harv saluted Shakey with his middle finger. Standing up for Mid-Easterners. Or the *good* ones, at least.

A cloud of troubling confusion settled over Harv. Bad enough he'd lost his body. He hoped to Hell he could maintain his American identity.

It took forever to flag down a cab. Earlier, a couple of white drivers had slowed, checked out Harv, then floored the gas as if Harv was sporting a suicide bomb jacket.

The cabbie who finally stopped appeared to be of Middle Eastern descent. Frankly, Harv couldn't be certain, so he played his cards close to the sleeve.

Harv strained to see the I.D. card hanging from the rearview mirror. Nothing in the least exotic about the name Fred, yet the man couldn't look any less "Fred-ly." "So, where you from, Fred?"

Fred shrugged, scratched his beard. "Here. Kansas City. I

grew up on a farm 'bout an hour-and-a-half away. You know…
Kansas." Again, he shrugged, as if evoking the name "Kansas"
said it all, a topic he seemed disinterested in discussing further.

"Huh." Given the strange circumstances, it was Harv's
best, safest response. A Middle Eastern farm kid. What next?
A Middle Eastern president?

Fred remained quiet. Occasionally, he glanced at Harv in
the rearview mirror. Finally, he said, "That surprise you?"

"I'm sorry?"

"You seem shocked, or I dunno, maybe disappointed I
grew up on a farm. I get that a lot. Just, you know, usually
not from someone who looks like us."

Looks like us?

"No, sorry, it's not that," said Harv. "It's just…it's been a long
day."

"Where're *you* from?"

"Me?"

Fred laughed. "Nobody in the cab but us."

"Kansas City. Pretty much grew up here."

"Huh," said Fred

What was *that* supposed to mean? Harv wondered if Fred
had punked him. Pigeonholed Harv into a stereotype, a hole
he didn't fit. Jesus, his head hurt.

"Now that that's outta the way, where you goin'?" asked
Fred.

Good question. Harv hadn't worked that out yet. He just
knew he had to keep on the move, be proactive. Keep the nightmare at bay. "Dunno yet. Can you just drive for a while?"

"Hey, it's your money." Yet another shrug, the Zen of
Fred.

Think, dammit, think! Where did I go after the bar last night?

He rode quietly for a while before an idea hit Harv. Something so glaringly obvious, he felt like a fool for not having considered it earlier. Of course, when your whole world has changed, cell phones no longer seemed so damned urgent.

He plucked his phone out of his pocket. No missed calls. No messages. No drunk texting. Maybe his recent browsing history held a clue…

Big Boob Bonanza? No, not pertinent. Quite a few hits last night, though.

Kansas City Cuddle Corner? Oh, *hell* no! He'd never cough up an online dating fee. Not Harv Perkins, a man who didn't need to pay for a date. (Apparently considered it last night, though.)

Funny Frog Fotos? Good God, how pathetic was he?

One Wish.

One Wish? The *hell* is that? Dread formed in Harv's gut, wormed its way into his head. In his drunken stupor last night, had he made a ridiculously large donation to a Make a Wish Foundation, or something worse? Of course, he had no issue with such a worthy charity, always meant to do his part and donate, but Harv led a busy life and just hadn't gotten around to it yet.

Harv looked upward, winked, then closed his eyes.

You know I'm good for it, God, just fix my life, okay? I'll donate whatever as long as you make me white again. But can I keep this body, just in a whiter shade?

To see if God had listened—although, honestly, he knew it was a long shot at best—Harv opened one eye, then the other. He looked down at his hands, rolled them over. Still despairingly olive-colored. For whatever reason, Harv suspected God didn't like him very much.

But *One Wish?* Something about the name chilled Harv. A familiarity, perhaps, and not necessarily a good one either. Like a nearly forgotten dream, any association Harv could muster with *One Wish* flit away like smoke.

As he waited for the *One Wish* homepage to load, he set his phone on the bench seat. He gripped the edges of the seat, squeezed, inhaled deeply. Seeking some of the calm cool Fred had to spare in buckets.

He picked up his phone. On the screen, animated red curtains pulled back at a tortoise's pace. Trepidation filled Harv as (*Something about those red curtains…*) he waited to see what lay behind the curtains, the identity of the wizard pulling the strings of his so-called life. On an endless loop, the American Flag waved, snapped in the wind, then preternaturally reset back to normal. A country song (*I've heard that song before…*) detailed American values and the need to stand together in troubled times. *One Wish* popped up in minuscule sized type, then zoomed out to the viewer like a head-on collision. Below *One Wish*, a scrawl unrolled…

One Wish. That's all you want, it's all you need. Have you ever thought about your life, truly thought about it? Is there something in your life you'd like to change? At One Wish, Incorporated, our mission statement is to grant you that wish. For a price, but don't worry about that now. We'll dicker over the actual fee later. Call it commerce, one of America's best foundations!

Not a hoax, not a rip-off, One Wish stands by its claims.

Call manager Louise Saffer for a free consultation.

What have you got to lose?

After the last line, the scrawl sped up. The address and phone number zipped by and repeated several times. A poof of smoke obliterated the scrawl. When the smoke cleared, a leering, smiley face emoticon appeared. *Cute.*

As if destroying the evidence, animated fire jagged across the screen and burned the contents inward. Resultant gray smoke curled into a question mark before it too vanished. The screen went blank. *Strange.*

Even stranger, Harv's phone grew hot.

"Ow, dammit!"

Harv dropped the phone and frantically shook his hand.

"You okay?" asked Fred.

"Yeah, just...got a cramp. Or something."

"Hate it when that happens."

With a dart of his fingertips, Harv tested the phone. Cool to the touch now. Once he fixed his life, the phone company would hear from him, count on it.

He checked his recent calls listing, something he should've done first. Sure enough, he'd dialed *One Wish* last night at about 11:30.

"Fred, take me to 1312 Holmes on the Missouri side."

"Hey, you sure? Kinda bad down there. 'Specially at night."

"I'm sure." Or at least as sure as Harv could be of any-thing.

Fred hadn't exaggerated the neighborhood's character. Even a stray cat appeared anxious as it poked its head up behind an overflowing trash can. It stared at Harv as the cab slowly rolled onto the street. The cat opened its maw and uttered a questioning "*Mrawr?*" Harv interpreted it as "*Really?*" The same disbelieving question Harv had been asking himself all day. As soon as Harv stepped out of the safety of the cab, Fred left street rubber behind as he high-tailed it away.

A low-riding car, the bumper practically dragging the ground, turned onto the street. Rap music thundered from the trunk. Four young black men sneered at Harv as they cruised by. Any second now, Harv expected the guns to come out, because, well, everyone knows that that's what *they* get up to late at night.

He chastised himself for stereotyping, knew it was wrong (*hey, I'm no bigot!*), yet he didn't take a breath until the car vanished around the corner. The music faded into the night.

As Harv stepped over a passed-out drunk, he wondered what circumstances had led to the man's unfortunate state. The drunk was black and was probably never afforded the opportunities white men have handed to them. Doing his part, Harv tossed a quarter onto the unconscious man's belly. Maybe even buying himself some goodwill points. It certainly couldn't hurt. *Tough times, my friend.*

With every streetlamp out, Harv couldn't read the addresses until he walked closer to the stoops. None of the buildings looked familiar, a feeling he could equally apply to his new life. He looked left, right, padded up and down the sidewalk, mathematically figured out where the address for *One Wish* should be. The address simply—*impossibly*—didn't exist. Frustrated, Harv kicked one of the brick building's walls and immediately regretted it. Pain shot up his leg. He grabbed his foot, bounced out a jig in a dizzying circle.

Ratty buildings and apartments, boarded-up and abandoned by all but the hardiest of tweakers, hovered over him, mocking him in his impotent humanity. Hardly the venue for a life-changing ballyhooing company.

Then he heard it. Like a buzz from a bumblebee, a distant neon sign hummed with life. At the foot of the closest building, a flash of red light flared up from a stairwell. A stairwell he hadn't seen before. And he knew damn straight, knew it like the back of his hand (although quite honestly, he didn't know that very well these days either), that he'd walked by that stairwell at least twice. More of God's cosmic jokes.

Ha, ha, God. You've had your fun, now cut it out!

Harv approached the beckoning light. He leaned over a railing, peeked down the dark stairwell. The steps led to a door. Above the door, in a cursive font, *One Wish* flashed intermittently in strikes of red lightning.

The sign blinked off. The ghost image fluttered in Harv's mind, then swam into an impression of déjà vu. He'd been here last night, no doubt now whatsoever. Endgame. Time to play.

The steps were steep and short, hardly manageable for a man of the original Harv's size and coordination. How he'd managed them while blitzed out of his mind seemed impossible. On the second to last step, his toe caught, thrusting him forward. His hands flattened against the cold metal door. Above him, the word *Wish* fizzled, briefly lit up, then died. Tentatively, he knocked on the door. Felt it wasn't a very manly knock, so he let loose and gave it a good pounding. The door opened, just an inch. No creak like in the movies, not a peep. Even scarier than the movies.

He pushed the door open all the way. One foot inside, he hesitated. A voice told him maybe he was better off not knowing the truth, perhaps a memory he'd suppressed. But a cure for his minority-itis might lie beyond the door. He forced his other foot inside. Sweat ran from his hairline, trickled down his cheeks. Not overweight sweat, either, the kind he'd give anything to have back again.

His feet moved silently over the red carpet as he followed the hallway. Three red bulbs hung from the ceiling, naked, no shades. Everything red, red, darker shades of red. Although an interior decorator's worst nightmare, the color scheme struck Harv as definitely memorable. Too memorable. He remembered walking—well, stumbling—down this very hallway last night.

The hall ended in another red curtain, billowing out as if

wind-tossed. He pulled the curtain aside. Like fingernails on a chalkboard, the curtain's rings scraped across a rusted rod.

Screeeeee…

Another hallway, this one dark. A finger of moonlight poked through a sole window. The beam fell across several doors.

"Hello?"

Quiet. As they say in the movies: "too quiet." A cliché he'd never quite understood until now. He pulled out his phone, turned on the meager light.

The first door was the old-fashioned kind, the type he hadn't seen since grade school. A panel of smoky, frosted glass sat precariously within the rotting wood frame. On the dusty glass, the words *Customer Service and Complaints* had been crudely painted. Again in red. Below it and extending to the doorknob, paint spattered the woodwork. At least Harv hoped it was paint.

The next door, this one in slightly better shape, read *Wish Fulfillment.* Harv tried the doorknob. Locked and iron hot. He heard movement from within and placed his ear against the warm glass. From far away (and just how big could the office be anyway?), he heard a low thrumming. Clanks of steel, like a blacksmith hard at work. And a hushed, simpering cry? A muffled scream?

Harv straightened, his heart matching the pounding of the steel. He moved to the third and last door. *Louise Saffer, Manager.* Paydirt.

Harv wiggled the knob. To his surprise, it opened with a mouse-trap *snap.* Another door opened in his mind, replaying a nearly identical trajectory of events from late last night. Before he remembered too much—and he was truly beginning to fear his memory—he slammed his mind's door shut. And stepped through Louis Saffer's office door.

Darkness cloaked the office. Harv found it hard to breathe, the air stifling and heavy. Fluorescent lights snapped on above him, one after the other: *clack, clack, clack.* A gorgeous blonde woman—a film noir vision—sat with perfect posture behind a desk. She looked up from a pile of paperwork, peered over the top of her cat-eyed glasses, and said, "Hi, Harv. Took you long enough."

The fog broke. Memories—snippets and nightmarish glimpses—flooded through him with the force of a tsunami. His knees weakened. A hot fever rushed up from his toes to his scalp, leaving him shivering.

"You better sit down, Harv, before you fall down." Ms. Louise Saffer, manager of *One Wish*, gestured with a long-nailed finger toward the chair on the other side of the desk.

"Oh my God… What…" Harv did as he was told, the way he'd always conducted his life. His hands, moist with sweat, nearly slid off the chair's arms. "Good God… Last night didn't happen… It…"

Saffer smiled, teeth as brilliant as snow on a sunny day. "Heh. Good one, Harv. You and I both know God didn't have anything to do with what happened last night."

"I don't remember… Just bits and pieces…"

"Yes, well, most of my clientele react the same way at first. The client's way of protecting their sanity, I suspect."

"I came here last night." Harv didn't frame it as a question. He didn't need to.

"You did."

"And…how much did my wish cost me?"

"What do you think, Harv?" Saffer rolled back in her chair, exposing her very shapely legs. For once, Harv's gaze didn't linger as it so often did with Phyllis at the office. "You signed the contract. I gave you a copy of the contract. Surely you *read* the contract." She frowned, lips pouting. "Oh, wait. It must be in your car. Your locked car."

"How…how'd you know about my—"

"Oh, get real." Her hand slashed the air. A trail of translucent red followed it. "You know who I am, right?"

"You're…you're Louise—"

"Duh. Hell's bells, Harv! Even a grade school kid could figure out my name. Think about it!"

Louise Saffer. Harv knew something about it sounded artificial, kinda like a stripper's stage name. But that wasn't quite it… *Lou Saffer. Lousaffer.*

Lucifer.

Harv's muscles went limp. He worried about bowel control, the potential embarrassment he'd face. Mostly, he worried about his soul.

Dear God in Heaven, no…

His right arm tingled. Paralysis seized him. Heart attack onset. Only his lips clung to life, and even then, his tongue felt like a bloated slug. "You're…Lucifer."

"Ta daaa!" She shook out jazz hands. "Took you long enough. I mean, honestly, the clues were all there. How in the world could anyone else make *One Wish*'s claims? Honestly…some of you mortals are so damned stupid. And, really, the red motif? The website? It's not like I've been hiding the truth or anything."

A cavalier attitude from the Devil didn't exactly brighten Harv's day. Frankly, once the initial shock passed, it irritated him. "You tricked me! You took advantage of my drunken state and made—"

Violin music piped in over unseen speakers. "Oh, spare me. You were drunk. Hardly my fault. Free will and all that malarkey. And everything's specifically explained in the contract. Which you signed, by the way. It's a legally binding and valid contract. Your soul is mine, Harv. Although, to tell you the truth, after watching you in action today, your soul's not all that. Not even really very interesting. But that's neither here…" She pointed up. "…nor there." Her finger went down. From nowhere, she produced a scroll. Whipped it open. The bottom rolled off her desk, onto the floor, and over Harv's foot. His signature, or at least a drunk approximation of it, had been scrawled across the bottom.

"But…but…why in the *hell* am I *Middle Eastern*?" The million dollar question. Sure, he'd sold his soul and all that crap, but priorities.

"It's what you wished for." She kicked a leg high with the panache of a Vegas showgirl.

"I never wished to be a…a *goddam*—"

"Ah, ah, ah, Harv. Don't go racist on me. I swear I'll never understand you mortals. You can't even get along with your own kind. Try living through the fall of Heaven. Then you'll understand—"

"I'm *not* a racist!"

"You sure about that? Look in a mirror lately?"

"Of course I have, goddammit! I want my own body back! My old life! My old, comfortable—"

"Boring, WASP, privileged, racist life. Remember what you wished for, Harv?"

"No." He closed his eyes, massaged his pounding temples. Then he remembered. "Yes. I said…I wanted to be…attractive."

She bowed her head, rolled her arms, thrust them toward Harv. "And that's what I gave you. You're hot now. *Hawt*." As if to demonstrate her point, she licked a finger, hiked up her rear end, and touched it. A hiss and wisp of smoke rose.

"Not by *my* standards."

"Exactly." She smiled, a blandly arrogant salesman smile, a smile Harv had mastered.

"I don't understand *any* of this!"

"Read the contract. It's all there."

Harv wanted to grandstand, righteously rip the contract to shreds. Things never played out quite like they did in Harv's head, though. He settled for folding his arms. "I don't care what's in the contract! I'm an unsatisfied customer! I want—"

"Want, want, want. Ick. Typical greedy mortal. I swear I'll never know what Dad sees in you humans. If you actually *read* the contract—and honestly, drunk or sober, you're a salesman and should've known better—you'll see there's a no return policy."

"But you tricked me."

"Of course I did! That's my job! Lucifer! Satan, ol' Scratch, the Devil, call me what you want, but at least I'm consistent in my actions. Unlike dear ol' Daddy." She sneered, ugly and inhuman, her devil showing through.

"This sucks! All of it! Goddamnit! I don't care if you *look* like a hot woman, I'm going to—"

"Oh, really? You don't care what I look like? Then, by all means, let me shed this grotesque mask."

Harv knew he shouldn't have done it, considered himself a mature man above name-calling. Wished he could take it all back. Because whatever Lucifer had in store for Harv, he knew it wouldn't be pretty.

Saffer's locks of hair burst into tiny flames and sizzled like firecracker fuses. The flames crawled toward her flesh, melted, then peeled the skin away into falling black chards. Through a hideous mess of muscle and bone and eyeballs, she grinned. Her teeth fell out, pitter-patting onto the desktop. Next, one eyeball popped, then the other. Green, gelatinous liquid gushed out from the sockets, violently pumping like blood. The remnants of her mouth opened wide, wider, impossibly wide—*Oh God, make it stop!*—until the jawbone dropped.

Tentacles unfurled from within her hollow skull. They stretched and danced like the mythical Medusa's head of snakes. A small face birthed at the end of a long tentacle, a human face. Tiny eyes opened, milky and wet. It unleashed a horrific shriek. Faces grew on the other tentacles, all human—or were at one time—and all screeching in agony. One licked Harv's cheek, sharp as a cheese grater. The devil's skull shot up, thwacked into the ceiling. A larger, segmented tentacle jabbed out of the devil's dress. It thrust up, then toppled in front of Harv like a fallen tree. A penile head grew from the tentacle, hard and angry. And olive in color. A foul, hot liquid spat onto Harv's face.

Harv screamed. Frantically wiped his face. Thrashed his hands about, tried to jump out of the chair. But the chair fell back, taking Harv along for the ride. He shut his eyes hard, so hard he thought his eyeballs might implode. Truly, he *wished* they would implode.

And then he remembered. All of it.

Dear God, all of it…

He remembered drunkenly stumbling into *One Wish*. How Louise Saffer had welcomed him—quite friendlier last night, a salesperson, after all—and how she'd painstakingly explained everything to him. But he hadn't listened. Too pumped to get to the end result.

Once he'd entered the Wish Fulfillment department, his internal pump ran out of air. Horned monstrosities grabbed him. Forked tongues lashed at him. They strapped him down onto a bloodied iron table and went to work, delivering excruciating pain. He screamed, cried like a little baby, wet his pants, and didn't give a good goddamn about dying in dirty underwear, either. He howled, bawled, begged to be put to death. Anything to stop the agony. They bashed every bone, chiseled every orifice. They broke him with spiked mallets, hot irons, electric drills, thorned vibrators, any torture instrument imaginable and then some. Using a funnel, they forced scalding liquid down his throat, into his stomach, up into his ass. They knocked out his teeth, ripped out his gums, tore out his bones until only tenuous flesh stitched him together. As an afterthought, they slowly, lovingly, tore his flesh away, too. At one point, he passed out, but they wouldn't stand for that. Using electricity, they jolted his nerves awake, forced him to watch the destruction of his body. And fully experience every unspeakable violation. His brain, eyes, and groin were the last to go. Well, those and his pain receptors, of course.

The last thing he remembered was the laughter. In the center of a hellish operating arena, the stands overflowed with inconceivable creatures. Fish monsters constantly dribbled murky liquid. Three-eyed fur balls with giant teeth and tiny feet bounced around the coliseum. A beast with a snout full of dangling tusks and glowing red eyes clapped its three-fingered claws in polite approval. A monster turned its large lamprey mouth onto its companion's shoulder, sucked, then spewed blood out in spit-takes of hilarity. Horned demons, faceless creatures, flying genitalia, things Harv never imagined and could never unsee. All laughing at his expense. The way life had pretty much treated him…

Then he woke up the next morning, blissfully unaware of the previous night's devastation of his body and his soul.

Now he was *truly* pissed off. He snapped open his eyes. Tentacles wagged above him. He beat at them with his fists. The results were rather ineffective, but he took charge of his life. Downright owned it (as the kids say). The all-new-and-improved Harv Perkins.

The room warmed. Not the Devilish heat he'd felt, either. Rather, something akin to nostalgia enveloped him. Like when his mother used to cradle him after he'd been bullied at school, reassuring him that everything would be fine. Realistically, he always knew the bullies would be there the next school day. Didn't matter. For when he sat nestled in his mother's arms, coddled by her reassuring words of nothingness, the world was a nice and safe and warm place. How he felt now.

The Devil reined in his tentacles. In an incredibly quick display of showmanship and compact packing, Lucifer folded back into her more pleasant form. Then, she said, "Oh, crap."

The Calvary rolled in on a white cloud. Not really, but Harv liked to envision things that way. Instead, She strode in wearing a polyester pants suit.

"Hello, Dad," said Saffer.

"Son…you're up to no good again."

Harv studied Her. Middle aged, a bit frumpy, hairstyle and large red glasses straight out of the Sally Jesse Rafael era. Probably quite the savvy businesswoman, Harv imagined. But Her Middle Eastern ethnicity and accent really threw Harv for a loop.

"Oh…my…God!" Harv clambered to his feet, legs shaking and barely working.

"What?" Very put out, She sneered, the way a tired parent responds to their sugar-addled kids.

"You're… You're Middle Eastern? And a woman?" Despite the present company, Harv laughed. Sometimes it's the only thing that makes sense.

"I'm everything, Harv. Just thought this shell was appropriate given the circumstances." She still seemed kinda pissed. Harv hoped Her irritation was aimed more toward Lucifer than him.

"What're you *doing* here, Dad?" asked the Devil. Like a surly teen, she slumped down in her chair, kicked her high-heels up onto the desk.

"I've been watching your current little experiment with some interest. As you know, things that interest me are rare."

"Yeah, I know, Dad! *Gah*!" Saffer picked up a piece of stationery and started ripping long strands away. Casually, she pitched the wadded up pieces onto the desk. "But…why are you here *this* time?"

"Well, Harv amuses me. And I see potential in his special situation."

"Um, thanks?" Insecure, Harv tried to man up, roll into his broad shoulders. It's not every day he got a compliment from God.

"Luce, I propose a bet. I know how much you love to gamble, sinful as it is and all that."

"Oh?" Her/His eyes lit up like winning slot machines. "Now *I'm* interested."

"So, Harv signed his soul to you in exchange for becoming handsome."

"Yes, he did."

"Well," stammered Harv, "it wasn't *quite* like that. You see—"

"Silence!" shouted God. "Luce, here's the bet, if you're interested. Harv's lived on both sides of the race table. He—"

"Not a racist," Harv whispered.

God ignored him. Thankfully. "That puts Harv in a very unique and special position. With the knowledge of his old, racist life…" Harv started to interject again, thought better of it. "…and his current physical state, he stands the chance to truly make a difference."

Saffer sneered. "And what would that difference be?"

"Maybe he could accomplish something about racism. Spread the word. *Be* the word."

Silence. A quiet, nerve-wracking, potentially soul-saving silence. The Devil laughed, loud and staccato-like drum beats. Harv nearly jumped out of his new skin.

"You really think this weak, simpering, racist fool is capable of something like that?" asked the Devil. "He can hardly tie his own shoes without someone motivating him."

"I can tie my shoes just fine."

"Don't *make* me come over there, Harv," shouted God. "Anyway, I'm willing to give him a chance. Something you never do, Luce." God walked over to Harv. Her pant-suited legs whisked together like zippers. "You think you're up to the challenge, Harv?"

"Oh *hell*, yes!"

"Ahem." God cleared Her throat. The floor shook, and items on the wall rumbled like a Celestial bowling alley. "If Harv lives up to his potential—makes a difference—then I get his soul. Do we have a bet, Luce?"

"I won't let you down, God," said Harv, manically shaking God's hand. "I swear I'll—"

"Whatever, Dad," said Saffer. "You're on. Easiest bet I've ever made."

"We'll see about that."

Both God and the Devil eyed Harv, the way people had judged him all day. The Devil laughed. God sighed, shook Her head. Then waved Her hand.

During the split second it took Harv to blink, everything changed. Harv hadn't changed, of course. Still dark, still Middle Eastern. But he no longer stood in the offices of *One Wish*. He was back on Holmes Street. The *One Wish* offices had vanished, out of business.

Harv felt like dropping to the filthy pavement and kissing it, but the fear of discarded needles put a damper on that victory parade. Instead, he tapped his chest with two fingers, then held them up to the Big Gal in the Sky. The way he'd seen all the homeboys do on TV.

Like a sign from above, a group of homeboys had gathered

across the street. All black (not "colored," no sir, never again!), probably sporting guns in their hoodies or tucked into their low-hanging pants. Obviously selling drugs.

Harv had never had a black friend before, not really. Unless he counted Bernie, the night janitor, and that was just more like saying "hello" in passing. Doing his due diligence for tolerance.

Of course, there was his black acquaintance (not really a friend), Tyrone, in the sixth grade. A new student that year, Tyrone stunned, scared, or repelled Harv's classmates with his invading presence. After all, they'd never had a black student in school. Never even met a black person. But Harv made it his duty to befriend Tyrone. Show everyone he wasn't racist. And he was curious about the black experience, after all, wanted to experience it for himself.

So, really, Harv thought, *I've been at this battle for some time.*

He considered the homeboys across the street again. If he was serious about his new mission in life—the fight to stop racism (and save his soul in the process)—maybe he'd join the homeboys, make friends with them. Wheedle his way in nice and easy, ask them if they had any drugs he could buy (not that he'd follow through, of course; just his way of gaining their trust so he could discuss the bigger issues at hand).

Then again, what good would it do if one of the homeboys shot Harv?

He'd start his new mission of racial harmony tomorrow.

LAST RITES IN BECKHAM COUNTY

That summer afternoon had been a blistering one, hotter than a three-alarm fire. Hardly a proper send-off for Mrs. Sowers, town witch and killer of cats. At least so the stories went around these parts. And around Beckham County, stories grew taller than well-tended stalks of corn and gossip fattened the tales until they were good and plump and ripe enough to scare.

Daddy made sure I didn't buy into such nonsense. Tried to, at least. Course Daddy didn't much understand me, either, being a girl and all with no momma to shine my problems on to. It was hard enough growing up in a funeral home without all the campfire tales burning a path into my nightmares.

But the day Harry ("Harry's Hearses: Going out in Style!") rolled Mrs. Sowers in through the back door of our funeral parlor proved to be especially peculiar. A cluster of cats had gathered at the back door. They mewed and purred the way cats do, kinda reminding me of a low-grade generator. Their bodies rubbed up against one another, their tails swattin' the dive-bombing flies. By way of how-do-you-do, ol' Mrs. Sowers said nothing, of course; everyone knows the dead can't speak. But the wheels on her gurney squeaked to high Heaven (although, I hardly think that was going to be Mrs. Sowers's final resting place), sort of the old woman's final rant against cats.

If I didn't know any better, it appeared the cats were rejoicing. A clowder of well-wishers. Because in Beckham County, Mrs. Sowers was a cat's natural enemy, far worse than the dogs.

From my upstairs bedroom window, I watched; it was better than going to the movies. Daddy's red scalp gleamed—waxy looking, just like the corpses he worked on—through the long spider legs of hair he combed over, fooling absolutely no one except maybe himself. He conferred with Harry, grown-up talk with down-turned faces. Harry helped wheel Mrs. Sowers down through the cellar steps into Daddy's work area, an area he only let me visit when invited. Not that it was a nifty place to hang out, mind you (although I've had more than several acquaintances, all of them cute boys—my friends didn't tend to last long—beg me to take them down there). Daddy always told me, "Becca, my workplace isn't a place for young girls." But sometimes I got the feeling Daddy kept secrets from me. As a man of mountain-tall pride, Daddy always claimed he was an open book, as honest as ol' Abe, but something in his eyes, how his shoulders rounded, maybe the way he always looked askance when talkin' 'bout his work, told me that below our house lay an unexplored world of dark mystery. Sometimes it excited me; at other times, it frightened me.

Still, Mrs. Sowers held a special fascination for me. In life, she was a curious person; death only cast more mystery upon her. The legacy she'd left behind had been built on stories most people only reckoned to be true. But true or not, the tales were enough to keep me out of her pasture, off of her front porch at Halloween, and dodging her at the general store.

Suzette (a rightly beast of a different kind whose expensive braces hid the fangs I just knew she had) swears to the fact that one night, while bicycling by Mrs. Sowers's house, she saw the body of Tommy Talipin swinging from the ol' elm tree in the front yard. Most folks say Tommy—a handsome teen of movie star fashion, but troubled by wanderlust—just took off, tired of the country way. I might've believed it, too, if Tommy's folks hadn't done got Sherriff Landry involved, sniffing out the woods and other unsavory parts of Beckham.

I can't imagine a soul just up and leavin' one night without letting his folks know his whereabouts. I'd never do that to Daddy. It was hard enough when my mother left, talk of the town and all. But I'm gettin' off-track like a sidewinder.

Other stories about Mrs. Sowers meandered on at great lengths about her practice of witchcraft, the details muddier than a country road after a downpour. Take, for instance, the tale about ol' Sy Norton. Everyone knew Sy liked to tip at the bottle, no secret there, but rumor had it he made the mistake of sayin' some mighty disparaging words about Mrs. Sowers down at his favorite drinking hole (only one in town, I mean, Beckham not lookin' too kindly on alcohol). Once word got back to Mrs. Sowers (and 'round here, word travels faster than electricity) about Sy's verbal trespasses, ol' Sy found his foot takin' a turn for the worse. It just started rottin' away, the end shriveled up like a sun-baked walnut. Course, Daddy, as a stern man of science, explained Sy's ailment with an educated diagnosis. It sounded good—comforting—to me, science being much more reasonable than witchcraft.

Truth be told, though, growing up in Beckham County, it was hard to know what to believe.

Then there were the stories about the cats and Mrs. Sowers. I tend to believe those tales as they remain constant (a term Daddy says is important in science) and rarely change. Now, a missing cat in the country isn't an unusual occurrence, mind you. Like Tommy, cats are prone to wander, following lust of a different sort. And in Beckham County, cats are mighty plentiful. You can't swing a, well, *a cat* without hitting another. But the story has it, every time Mrs. Sowers fancied dropping a spell on somebody, she'd sacrifice a cat to her god, who I assure you was a far cry from my God.

Guess what I'm sayin' is even Job himself would surely have his patience tested by having Beckham County's biggest mystery lying flat on her back in his basement.

So, that night, after Daddy had tucked himself in with a nightcap, quiet as a whisper, I stole out of my room. I snuck down the two flights of stairs, avoiding every telltale squeak and groan of the treads I'd committed to memory. The moon, full and glorious and sort of tetched by the wild side, shone through the windows, lighting my barefooted path through the kitchen. I tiptoed down the basement steps and entered Daddy's workshop.

The cold air struck me first. Fingertips of ice softly caressed my cheeks. Daddy never said it, but I imagined he kept it cool to preserve the mortal remains of his customers for as long as possible. The notion sometimes gave me chills of a different nature, but after a while, I suppose I got used to livin' over a funeral home. *Most* of the time.

I flipped on the light switch, hoping to chase away chills, real or imagined.

Clak, chak, chak…

Like dominoes of lightning, the overhead fluorescents clacked on, one after the other, painting the room with a dull yellow glow.

For what I imagined to be one of the messiest jobs in Beckham County, Daddy always kept his workspace cleaner than freshly laundered linen. His tools were lined up on his cart in an orderly fashion, biggest to smallest: all manners of scalpels, something he called a trocar, various ointments and disinfectants (both for him and his customers). Several tubes snaked from the great chugging (now, blessedly hushed), gray beast of an embalming machine. The sink, longer by a foot than the tallest fella' Daddy had ever buried, remained sparkling, good as new in its TV commercial sheen. On the few occasions Daddy had allowed me down there, I'd never seen a drop of blood.

But the body beneath the blue blanket drew me, surely as a magnet attracting paperclips. Mrs. Sowers's scouring pad of black and gray hair stuck out at the top, wiry and mean as the woman herself. Her toes poked out the bottom. Tiny blue veins wrapped around her feet, as if tying down the orneriness. Corns erupted into swollen, orange carrot tips.

I didn't know what I expected to see, but I was pretty dang sure what I *didn't* want to see. Sometimes things just don't work out the way you'd hope.

Slowly, I inched the blanket down, exposing Mrs. Sowers's forehead, shiny and lifeless as plastic fruit. Another slight tug and I gasped. Her eyes were open: unblinking, milky, and nobody home. And that struck me as a might bit peculiar. Daddy always closed his customer's eyes first thing. He said he did it out of respect for the deceased. But after seeing Mrs. Sowers's eyes, I suspect he did it to keep the dead from watching him as he worked.

I wanted to stop, I really did, but I'd come this far, and if nothing else, I wanted to prove to the pestering voice in my head that I could do it, not a chicken at all.

The blanket rode the ridge of Mrs. Sowers's nose, a crooked, blue snow jump. I pinched the blanket and gently pulled it farther down until her nose popped out. Tiny hairs rimmed her nostrils. And I swear what I saw next was only a trick of the flickering overhead light. I really, truly wanted to believe that.

One long hair withdrew up into Mrs. Sowers's nostril, then blew out again.

I tried to convince myself it didn't happen, wasn't possible, not here, not anywhere. My brain told me to run, go crawl back into bed, but my feet didn't listen; instead, they sidled up next to the ornery devil on my shoulder, sayin', "In for a dime, in for a dollar."

As I pulled the blanket down below her chin, my hand shook worse than ol' Sy's three-day tremors. I withdrew my hand fast as a jackrabbit, afraid of things I couldn't understand.

Mrs. Sowers's mouth opened. Not an involuntary movement caused by gas either, the way Daddy explained sometimes happened. She made a sound, something not human, more akin to a hissing radiator.

Shhhhhhhsssssssss…

Spit gathered at the corners of her mouth like condensation. It ran down her cheeks in teary streaks.

I clamped my hand over my mouth, captured a scream. I turned tail, willing my legs to cooperate.

Behind me, the gurney rattled. Cloth rustled. I didn't want to look, but I had to. Just had to.

She sat up. Her head twisted at a sharp, unnatural angle. Chin cocked. Glaring at me. The milk had siphoned out of her eyes, now fully clear. And full of gray, cold hatred.

"I…didn't do this," was all I could say, all my addled brain could muster. A weak apology so I could stay out of Hell, for surely that's where she intended to send me.

Varicose-veined legs swung over the side of the gurney. Her gnarled toes dangled above the linoleum. Although Daddy never really held much to the Bible and all its teachings, I nearly dropped to my knees right then and there to plead my case to God Himself. I wanted to scream loud enough to wake all of Heaven. But my throat went dry. My tongue felt like it'd clogged up my windpipe. My big girl voice had stepped back in time, now only weak whimpers and ill-formed words. Dang near wet myself, too, and ain't too proud to admit it, either.

Something scampered across the room. Soft pitter-pats of timid rain. A golden cat padded toward Mrs. Sowers, its white paws prancing with a casual stride. It picked up its pace, more determined than Mr. Jones and his prized pig at the fair.

Mrs. Sowers framed an ugly oval with her mouth and hissed between gaudy red lips, part feline herself. The cat took no heed. Jumped right into her lap. Its claws dug into the blanket. Mrs. Sowers gasped, then lay back down where she belonged. The cat strolled up to her face, lowered its head, and performed a strange mouth-to-mouth resuscitation ritual. Only it had the opposite effect. Mrs. Sowers's eyes closed. Her chest rose once more, then fell, and stayed that way.

The cat looked at me. Licked its chops like it'd just eaten the plumpest mouse in the county.

As soon as the cat hopped down, I ran like the devil himself was pitchforkin' my behind. Straight up to my room. Buried my head beneath the quilt. I don't recall (as you may well imagine, there were quite a few other things to recall) sleeping, either.

I never told Daddy what happened that night down in the basement. Not only did I want to avoid punishment, but I reckon I wasn't rightly sure what *did* happen. Couldn't explain it if I tried.

It's hard enough being young—deliberating between science and religion, navigating the rough and turbulent waters of school, discovering your sexuality and body—without having some unknown element introduced. Something no one could explain, something better left to the world of nightmares.

They say that life in the country is different. I reckon so is death.

MIDNIGHT SESSION

As soon as Harry saw the state of the building, he considered the hefty tuition he'd paid wasted money, green currency just floating away on a draft of chicanery. *Sucker*. Ironic, Harry thought, as the name really suited him in more ways than one. He turned away from the industrial warehouse and yelped, startled at the sudden appearance of a brunette behind him. A *gotcha* grin tugged her cheekbones high.

"Hey." She clutched her trench coat tightly around her throat, the part of her body that intrigued Harry the most. And that was saying something. "I'm Katrina." Even though her name spoke of exotic faraway lands, her accent didn't travel farther than Chicago.

"Sorry. You scared me. I'm Harry." He stuck his hand out. Hers felt very cold, arctic blast cold. Delusional maybe, but he tried to hold onto the notion that his skin was still warm.

"What can I say?" she said. "Around here, we move pretty quietly. You must be new."

"Yeah. Guilty. I'm…pretty new."

"Well, c'mon, Harry. You're in the right place. Don't worry about the venue. It's a pretty good class."

When Harry first saw the flyer for "Vamps 101," he imagined it was a stripper school of some sort, teaching about the fine art of pole dancing and other ins and outs. But after calling the number, the supportive operator assured Harry he'd found the right class. After all, he needed all the help he could get. This vampire business was beginning to play havoc on his social life.

Katrina rang a bell next to the "Thomason Label" sign and waited. Harry expelled a breath in the cold winter night. Of course, he didn't expect to see his breath, not really, but he looked anyway. Old habits die hard and all. Still, he couldn't quite figure out why he could smell things, keener than ever. One more reason he needed the class.

A night watchman peeked through the window next to the door. "Good evening, Miz Katrina. I was worried you wouldn't make it."

"Just running late. You know I'd never miss a class."

"Teacher's pet!" The watchman laughed. His pornstache hopped along with his joke.

Katrina led Harry through a maze of front offices and hamster-challenging cubicles until they reached a large meeting room. Inside, people had gathered around a back table, sucking out of hospital blood bags. A few of the more etiquette-inclined dabbed their mouths with wet wipes. Chairs stood in rows, even and precise as gray tombstones in a military cemetery.

"Class, let's begin." A mild-mannered clerk of a man commandeered a podium. Straw-colored hair, wispier and thinner than a fleeting cloud, sporadically dotted his head. "Welcome back. I see we have a few new students joining us tonight." Behind bottle-thick glasses, he eyed Harry. "I'm Seth. The gentleman to my right is my T.A., Kevin."

Harry withheld a gasp before remembering he no longer had the wherewithal to draw in air. He'd never seen an old-school vampire before—true Transylvanian style, gaunt, bald, the pointed ears of an elf, and eyes so pale the pupils barely existed. By way of greeting, Kevin hissed through a mouthful of needled teeth. Ever the accountant, Harry tabulated how exorbitant Kevin's dental bills must be.

"The purpose of our class," continued Seth, "is to help fellow vampires indoctrinate themselves properly into human society. How to live amongst them as equals. We have an open forum, so please, if any of you have questions, concerns, challenges, please do speak up."

Katrina dropped a well-manicured hand on Harry's knee. He jumped, and he hoped she hadn't noticed.

"Now, as you well know," said Seth, "we've been fighting for a long time to put the old stereotypes behind us." He unleashed a poor Bela Lugosi accent, complete with clawed hands. "I vant to suck your blood."

Polite chuckles rippled throughout the classroom, a wave Harry awkwardly joined.

"Our goal is to reassure the humans we mean them no harm. Rather than sup on humans, we've found other ways to satiate our thirst. For instance, there's animal blood, hospital donations—"

A little girl, possibly no older than thirteen (at least when she turned), shouted, "But, Seth, animal blood is *so* gross!"

Seth's lips tightened into a bone-white scar. "Lucinda, when you were human, you ate beef, correct?"

"Well, yeah, I guess."

"And did you like it?"

"Sometimes." She crossed her arms, grumpy at the world and refusing to be pigeon-holed.

"Well, there you have it." Seth spread his hands in a giving manner. "Now, if you're having problems procuring—"

"What about dogs?" asked a burly lumberjack of a vampire.

"Is it okay to eat dogs?"

Harry could see Seth's patience bubbling like a boiled-over teakettle. Briefly, Seth closed his eyes. Then like a rubber band, he snapped back. "Borney, you know better than that. Anything that's considered a pet is off limits. Once we officially come out, humans won't smile kindly on dog snacking. Does that answer your question?"

Borney slid down into his chair, kicked his denim-clad legs out. "I guess." Harry imagined he had his mind set on a rather plump dachshund, only to have that meal whisked off the table.

Someone sniffed three times, then repeated the loud effort. On the other side of the room, a Goth girl trailed her nose along the length of the man's arm next to her. A disgusted frown cut through her make-up.

The man, even paler than Kevin, blurted out, "Leave me alone." He gargled the words, sounding like a man trapped underwater. Pretty much looked that way, too. His skin—alternately bloated and flaking—would provide a more adventurous dermatologist a nice case study.

With a sneer, the girl jacked a thumb toward the sickly-looking man, and asked, "What's *he* doing here, Seth?"

Next to Seth, Kevin hissed, possibly an enforcer more than a T.A.

"Devon, I'm well aware of Charlie's unfortunate living dead predicament. He—"

A businessman spat out, "Zombie!"

"Bloodsucker!" gave back Charlie.

Nervously, Harry sank into his chair. He wondered if the seed of a riot had just bloomed.

Seth banged the podium with a tightly coiled—but ultimately weak—fist. "Ladies and gentlemen, enough! Please! No ugly names! One of the reasons we're here is to get past vile name-calling—"

"We prefer to be called living-challenged," offered Charlie. Even though nearly indecipherable, Harry detected pride in the man's voice. A man who'd fought an uphill battle most of his undead life. Then his ear slipped off and splatted onto his shoulder, and some of his pride slipped away, too. Thoroughly humiliated, he quickly scooped up his ear and pocketed it.

"My apologies, Charlie. Class, from now on, we'll refer to Charlie's predicament as 'living-challenged.' No more name calling. Is that understood?"

Kevin leaned forward. His mouth gaped wide, large enough to inhale a pig. The class quieted.

"As I was saying…" Seth shot the fighting duo a "that's-the-end-of-that" look. "…Charlie had my pre-approval to join the class. He, like us, is persecuted. We aim to end that. Through education, understanding. Getting along as a community. Peaceful protesting, so to speak. Let's move on…" After visually inventorying his students, Seth's bug-eyed gaze fell on Harry. "Harry's new. Everyone meet Harry."

"Hi, Harry!" the students said in a well-practiced choir of voices.

Always shy, Harry loathed the attention, dreaded what would come next.

"Harry, please tell us a little bit about yourself."

Harry hesitated. Katrina's hand squeezed his knee and goosed him into action. "Um…I've only been turned for a couple weeks now. It's hard…tough. I met a girl at a bar…"

Nods from the men, affirmative sour grunts. Women smiled knowingly. Harry didn't want to be a cliché, but apparently, he fit the shoe.

"…anyway, it's been tough adjusting. I'm really not into eating people. Just not my thing. So, any kind of help…" His voice ran away on a traitorous journey. He swallowed dryly, felt a golf ball slowly work down his throat.

Katrina stood first, then the others followed. Together, they circled Harry. Even Charlie, the living-challenged person, offered him a hug (one Harry hoped wouldn't be repeated; casually, he brushed Charlie's flakes of flesh away). All in all, though, a true vampiric showing of brotherhood.

After class, Harry's spirits (*did he still possess one?*) lifted. Empowered, he vamped up and approached Katrina. If nothing else, he wasn't too proud to dig a pity date out of her. He certainly didn't trust himself around human women, their necks so silky and long and juicy and…

Dammit, stay on track!

"Um, Katrina…would you like to maybe, sorta—if you're not too busy and if you are, I totally get it—join me for a cup of coffee?" Immediately, he realized his mistake. A lifetime of human living would take a while to shake.

She smiled. "Not coffee. But I know where there's a field full of cattle, ripe for the taking."

As far as first dates went, it hardly sounded romantic. But Harry did feel a little parched.

HALLOWEENIE ROAST

Prepared for battle with candy bowl in hand, Tillie answered the door. She said nothing and waited. Surely, the onus belonged on the little bastards.

"Trick or treat!" Greedily, the first child opened his pillowcase. He smiled, expecting a cascade of riches.

He'd come to the wrong house. "The hell you s'posed to be, anyway?" Tillie clutched her bowl tightly, just out of the brat's reach.

"I'm a wizard!" He wore a ridiculous purple hat that rose to a point. Cheap glued-on gold stars adorned it. His foolish mother had wasted time and money by sewing a matching purple costume that wrapped around him.

"Huh. You know that magic crap's not real, right?" offered Tillie. "You look more like a bargain basement tent."

The boy's already meager shoulders sunk. He shuffled, performed a little potty dance, and looked down into his nearly empty pillowcase as if he could conjure a spell to fill it with candy. Much to Tillie's delight, the boy looked like he'd do anything to leave the mean old lady who'd derailed his Halloween fun. In a soft voice, he repeated, "Trick or treat?"

Tillie grabbed one of the hideous orange circus peanuts from the bowl and chunked it into the case. "There you go, Merlin. Your teeth are gonna rot and fall out." She grinned, exposing her few yellowed teeth.

The boy trudged off the porch and dragged his pillowcase through the fallen leaves. His two cohorts—a sickeningly sweet princess and a ludicrous boy wielding a space gun and stuffed into a vest with knee-high boots—also received a blast of Tillie's bitter *bon mots*.

"You're wearin' girly boots, kid," she said to the boy. "And you, princess! That the way your momma dress you? The finest in hooker-wear?"

Tillie closed the door, laughing to beat the day. Most fun she'd had in, well…a damn long time. Not that she enjoyed Halloween, far from it. She absolutely loathed the holiday, considered it infantile, nothing more than a cheap and shameless marketing ploy created by mega-corporations to sell costumes and candy to the masses. And just like a miniaturized unemployment line, the grubby little kiddies stuck their hands out demanding free candy. No wonder America was in such turmoil; the kiddies learned early to ask for hand-outs. Hardly one of America's finer foundations.

Oddly enough—and in spite of Tillie's best efforts—parents never warned their children away from Tillie Johanssen, particularly on Halloween. Perhaps parents considered a visit to Tillie's house a rite of passage, one every child in Welton, Kansas, should experience; akin to a boy's first shave or a girl's first menstrual cycle. Maybe parents had forgotten how Tillie had verbally taunted and insulted them, although that theory hardly held water as she'd ended years of Halloweens prematurely, most of them in kiddy tears. Of course, there's the silly old theory—the one tossed about annually by the regulars at Lucky's Grill & Bar—that this would be the Halloween that ol' Tillie Johanssen would soften. And every year at Lucky's when the betting pot was posted, one newbie would always bet big on Tillie's kind heart, a myth as fanciful as unicorns or government intelligence.

The truth of the matter was that Tillie Johanssen scared most adults in Welton; they just didn't want to rock the boat and say anything disparaging about her—in case the rumors about Tillie's being a witch and all were true.

While Tillie wasn't a witch—supernatural or otherwise—she was considered a bitch of the highest order. Which suited Tillie just fine.

Still cackling—similar to a sick crow: *aw, aw, awwww!*—over her last verbal onslaught, Tillie gripped her gut and attempted to tame her hilarity.

"Land o' Goshen, most goddamn fun I've had since I can remember." *Aw, aw, awww!*

Tillie wore her badge of anger with highfalutin honor. She relished her reputation as a card-carrying member of the embittered little ol' lady club. Hell, she founded the club. She did absolutely everything in her power (which, frankly, amounted to quite a bit in the Podunk town of yellow-bellied Welton, Kansas) to rankle her neighbors. If the hedges weren't shorn short enough, she'd call the cops and scream loudly and proudly how it broke city ordinances. If the hedges were *too* short, she'd demand that Mr. Rebus next door grow them out along with a set of balls. And just like the cliché, she never allowed kids in her yard; no one, for that matter. Even the mailman timed his delivery during her regular afternoon siesta. God help the unsuspecting salesman or Jehovah's Witnesses who should darken her doorstep. As a precaution—no, scratch that. For pure fun, she kept her trusty shotgun in the hallway closet, just waiting for such visitors. One of these days, she just might use the gun, too, damn skippy.

She smiled at the thought. Her jaw jutted out in self-right-eousness. Her face, tough as elephant hide, wrinkled. She scratched at the whiskers on her chin, durable enough to strike a match against.

Only Tillie knew the true reason why she celebrated Hallo-ween (in her own fashion, of course). It gave her the opportunity to belittle as many kiddies as possible. Like a female Pied Piper, she'd lead them to her door, toss them the worst candy she could find in the most pitiful quantity (candy didn't grow on trees, after all), and then unleash upon the little darlings the most hellish tirade of insults and name-calling she could legally get away with.

Not only did it bring her great joy, but she considered it as doing her part: toughening up the little candy-asses for a tougher future. But that was a fib of sorts. Flat-out, she loathed children; they were nothing more than little gummy-handed reminders of her mortality.

"C'mere, Brick!" Tillie knelt down as far as her rheumatism would allow. Sure, it hurt like hell, particularly on swampy days, but tonight she felt like a mean, lean fighting machine. "Here, Brick, kitty, kitty, kitty!"

The zebra-striped tabby skulked out from beneath a coffee table, apparently sensing one of Tillie's rare good days. Tentative at first, it stopped and looked at Tillie, its tail curled up into a question mark. Tillie's fingers waggled. Finally, Brick surrendered into temptation and nuzzled his way into Tillie's arms.

"That's a good kitty. Good kitty."

Tillie didn't just hate the brats. She had a large amount of hate to give, an equal opportunity hater. Unlike the other old ladies in Welton, she didn't restrict her hatred toward the triad of terror: the blacks, Catholics, and gays. Well, truth be told, she *did* hate the minorities, but it wasn't an exclusive hate.

Hell, she even hated her late husband, Frank. Maybe "hate" was too strong a word when she considered the spineless, pathetic, boring, bad-breathed, hairless slug of a man who'd occupied half of her bed; she just didn't ever like him very much.

When Frank passed from a heart attack (the most emotion he'd shown during their marriage), she'd been tempted to parade around the city square with a trombone and a big bass drum strapped to her chest. Instead, she'd contented herself with a quiet celebration of wine (lots of it), a bubble bath, and the luxury of sleeping in peace.

She may have hated everyone, but she didn't hate everything. She treated her lovely garden in the front yard like her own offspring, one that wouldn't talk back. She spent hours, days, and weeks cultivating the garden into the most beautiful collection of perennials in the entire town. Blanket flowers bloomed in sunset reds and oranges; blue spikes of Veronica stretched achingly for the sky; tall magenta Phlox smelled as fragrant as classy perfume; sage, aster, coneflower, you name it, Tillie planted and nurtured it. The beauty in Tillie's life. Her neighbors' obvious jealousy provided the icing on the cake. Just another notch in her belt of pride.

Of course, Tillie also loved Brick. Her friend, the tabby who'd never betray her. The pet who—

"Ow! Goddamn cat!" Tillie thrust the cat down. She kicked, missed, and jagged a foot into the door. The corns on top of her toes throbbed. Pain raced to her arthritic knees. "You've had it now, damn animal!"

She sucked on her hand where Brick's claws had dug deep, tasted the metallic tang of blood. Every time she thought she could trust Brick, he'd turn on her fast as quicksilver. "Come here, you lil bastard!"

Next to the secretary in the living room—the one where Tillie stored her figurine collection—Brick cowered. Clearly sensing her anger, he tried to squeeze beneath the secretary. Porcelain angels wobbled, and little boys with their pajama flaps down clanked hollow heads.

"I'll *roast* your furry ass if you break any of my collection!"

Slowly, Tillie lowered to the floor. She held out warm and open arms, tried to quell her mounting rage. "Here, kitty, here, boy. Momma's not mad at you. C'mere, boy…"

The cat, as stupid as it was devious, slinked out. It's back arched, then fell. The tail flicked back and forth like Tillie's Veronica plants in the wind. He crawled toward her.

She lunged, snatched the beast. Like a woman half her age, she jumped to her feet in one effortless move.

"Gotcha now, you little bastard!" Her hand curled around the cat's head. Callus-toughened fingers closed tightly around its neck. For a brain-fried second, she considered ending the cat's life. Power to take a life rested in her hands. But, as always, she came to her God-given senses. "Teach you to scratch momma, you little shithead…"

With the cat pressed against her chest, she whipped open the front door. She tossed the cat into the dark of night, followed it with a pointless air-kick. Brick yowled, an airborne missile, then landed on his feet. The Rebus' hedges rustled as Brick slipped into them.

"And don't come back 'til you're sorry! Goddamn cat!"

Tillie noticed she'd acquired an audience. Midway down her sidewalk, three costumed trick-or-treaters stood. Strangely motionless for rambunctious brats. Watching her. At least she thought they were watching her. Hard to tell behind their white-sheeted heads, nothing but two dark eyeholes torn into the fabric. They didn't budge, didn't shout, not so much as a "boo." They clutched plastic pails in their grimy hands: a grinning pumpkin, a mummy (or so Tillie thought; didn't look like much to her at all in the darkness), and a skull grimacing in torment.

Tillie stared at them long and hard, refusing to give in to terrorism. "What? You little brats just gonna stand there all night gawking?" She tossed up a hand, half an invite, half a challenge. Finally, the children stirred, their feet shuffling forward in slow and measured unison. A far cry from the miniature demons, ghouls, and witches who usually rushed her doorstep with visions of candy bars dancing in their idiotic little noggins.

Attached at the hips, they mounted Tillie's three steps. One proffered his skull bucket. Up close, Tillie saw the bucket had been converted from a friendly ghost into a grim skull by way of creative carving. Large eyeballs had been drawn onto its face. At the bottom of the bucket, a line of crooked, yellow teeth had been glued on, dull and realistic looking. Hardly a jolly-looking bucket worthy of sugary treasures.

The bucket was empty.

"Trick or treat," said the boy, his voice low and calm, belying his age.

"Well, what the hell you s'posed to be? Klansmen?" Tillie grinned, hoping to light a cross-burning fire beneath their arses. Again, they didn't move, didn't speak.

Finally, skull bucket said, "No, ma'am. We're ghosts." The other two sheets rustled in what Tillie assumed to be corroborative nods.

"Ghosts, huh? You look... You look more like..." For the first time ever, Tillie lost her game. Something about these kids seemed *off*. Dirt soiled the boy's hand, his fingernails split and gray. His knuckles were green and purple, bruised and cut.

But Tillie wouldn't let them get to her, not on her watch. "Hey, you know what your parents been doing on those sheets you got on, right, kiddies? They—"

"Trick or treat." The boy interrupted Tillie. *Unacceptable.*

"Listen, you little brat, don't interrupt your elders when they're speaking!" She shook a finger in his face. "Your parents not teach you any better?"

"Trick or treat."

"Well, I'll be goddamned! You're gonna play your lil charade out to the end, huh?" Under her breath, she cursed, grabbed the bowl on the table. She held the bowl out, waited for them to take the bait. They didn't.

"Trick or treat."

Tired of the game, Tillie grabbed three marshmallow circus peanuts. She dropped two orange ones into the quiet kids' pails, saved the pink one for the monster of the pack. Skull Pail stared down at the lone pink nugget grotesquerie.

"There ya go. Don't eat it all at once," said Tillie.

Tillie heard a slight hiss, possibly a sigh. The three ghosts turned and walked down the steps.

The gall of their rude behavior set Tillie in a tizzy. She envisioned grabbing the shotgun and putting the scare of their lives into their sugar-addled brains. Instead, she decided to kill them with more insults. "Hey! Goddamn lil brats! You're *welcome*! Raised in a damn barn, were you? No, wait... I know where you were raised! Your mommas screwed their customers on those sheets, boys! Didn't even wash 'em either! That's..."

Her tirade landed on deaf ears. Unaffected, the trio strode somberly toward the front picket fence. They left the cone of light provided by her porch lamp and slipped away into the shadows.

Little bastards!

Tillie looked up and down the street. Now that night had fallen, Halloween traffic had trickled to a standstill. One father stood on the sidewalk, hands stuffed into pockets, obviously wishing he was anywhere but where he was. A sugar-overdosed yelp rose, far away and ghostly.

Time to wrap it up for another year. Too bad it had to end on a sour note; Tillie much preferred sweet endings, her way.

Smart-ass, self-entitled punks!

She closed the door, grabbed a circus peanut. She gnawed through half of the artificial tasting nugget, then tossed it back into the bowl. Some things never change; the circus peanuts tasted just as awful as they had back in her childhood, which is why she'd picked that particularly toxic candy.

The doorbell rang. Tillie jumped. Her heart pounded. She grabbed the bowl and wrenched open the door. Her voice caught. Three familiar gift-wrapped gifts from Hell met her.

"Trick or treat." Same dull monotone, same stupid ghost costumes, same belligerent attitudes. Skull Pail held up his container as if Tillie had never seen it before.

"My stars and Heavens, isn't this a surprise?" Tillie feigned a nice little ol' lady act, smiled sweetly, fluttered a hand over her heart as if she might break a hip over the cutesiness of it all. The better to catch them off guard. No one ever got one up on Tillie.

"Trick or treat," he repeated, this time a bit more stridently.

"That ship's passed, you little shits. What, circus peanuts not good enough for ya? They were in my day. Hell, I—"

"Trick or *treat*." Now Skull Pail spoke it like a quiet threat, one loaded with spring-action malice. Clearly, they didn't know who they were dealing with.

"Okay, playtime's over. You're lucky I didn't give you cigarettes like I did last year! But your mothers—all the P.T.A. bitches—put a stop to that now, didn't they? Find someone else to harass, shit-stains." The kid gloves were off. The brats had crossed Tillie's line of good humor.

"We talked about it and—"

"Oh, so the other lil spooks *can* talk. I thought they were mute and dumb instead of just dumb."

"What you gave us wasn't good enough." Spoken coolly like a politician, probably learned it from his yuppie dad. "Trick or *treat*." Tillie couldn't believe a kid—*a kid just up to my apron, for God's sake!*—dared to challenge her. Halloween was her night, not his.

"Look, you little *bitches*! You have any idea who in *hell* I am? I made your momma and daddy piss their pants before you were riding in your daddy's balls! I own this town! I can—"

"Last chance. Treat…or *trick*." Tillie didn't care for what the little brat said, not one iota. He'd made a threat. One she wouldn't stand for.

"That did it! No more Missus Nice Guy! I'm gettin' my gun and sending you straight to Hell!" Quickly, she yanked open the closet door. Nice and shiny, her shotgun stood valiantly in the corner awaiting her loving caresses and deadly discharge. She hoisted it up in one hand, barrel pointed toward the ceiling. Usually heavy in her grip, it felt lighter tonight. In fact, she felt lighter, too, floating on a wave of excitement.

She turned back to the door, ready to scare the bejesus out of her tormentors. "Alright, now let's see who—"

The ghosts had disappeared. Disappointed, she dropped the gun butt to the floor with a clump. Far away, she heard giggling drift toward her like an unseasonably cool breath of wind.

"You were warned," one of them shouted in a sing-songy voice. "We gave you every opportunity!"

Tillie stomped out onto her porch, the boards loose beneath her slippers. "You lil bastards! You threaten me? *Me*? You pull anything on me, and I'll blast you! I'll blow your goddamn heads off if you show up again!" She felt a little foolish, shouting into the dark, screaming at an unseen menace. But the neighborhood could always use a reminder.

Next door, the Rebus' porch lights snapped off. So did the neighbor's lamp on the south side. Which added fuel to Tillie's fire. No one shuts Tillie out.

She screamed, "All of you are chicken-shits! Just cowering in your damn cookie-cutter houses! I'm the only one in this neighborhood with balls enough to fight! To stand up for myself!"

She slammed the front door. It echoed throughout the house like a gunshot. She paced the well-worn Persian rug (one she'd snatched from a very lucky estate sale), the gun held at the ready. She stopped at the closet. On tip-toes, she plucked down the box of bullets and loaded her pocket with them.

Bastards! All of 'em! Young and old!

Honestly, though, had Tillie been hard-pressed—lined up against a firing squad, maybe—she'd admit the truth: the kids made her feel vital, more alive than she had in years. Even her old, annoying sidekick, rheumatism, seemed to have taken the night off. She almost prayed to God to have the little turds come 'round again but thought that might be a bit too much for personal gain. Quickly, she reclaimed her wish before it traveled too far on the highway to Heaven.

If given the opportunity, she wondered if she would pull the trigger, turn the brats into real ghosts. She couldn't come up with an answer, none that felt honest.

Timp, tump, crump…

Footsteps on the porch.

"Tee hee, heh, hehhhh…

Muffled giggles, receding. The little bastards were making a run for it.

Tillie swung open the door, poked the gun's barrel out. "Gotcha where I want you, you little—"

Nobody. No ghosts. Just a flaming paper bag on her porch.

Tillie set the gun aside and grabbed her other most important Halloween defense: the small fire extinguisher. A white whiff of nitrogen snuffed out the fire.

Carefully stepping over the smoking bag, she hollered, "Ha! That all you got? Think I've never seen this gag before? Hell, I practically invented it! You ain't gettin' no satisfaction from me! Come get your dog-shit, idiots! You hear me? I know you're out there!"

From a distance, a voice sang, hollow and eerie and lilting like a lullaby, "Trick or tree-eeeeeet…"

Bastards!

To satisfy her curiosity, Tillie retrieved a couple of dirty rags and knelt before the charred bag. The flaps pulled apart with a wet ripping sound.

What the hell?

Not dog crap, not by a long shot. She knocked away a burning ember and reached inside, cautiously keeping her fingers away from the center. She pulled out a twelve by eight plank of wood, burnt around the edges. Nails—rusty, long, and vicious—formed a circle, dangerous tips up. Hammered in from the bottom.

Jumpin' Jesus!

She bolted up, arthritis knocking at her knees again. Her heart pitter-patted out a manic drum solo. Had she not been around the block a few times, she surely would've stomped down with her foot, the nails impaling her foot through the slipper. What the little bastards intended to happen.

She retreated into the house, closed the door, threw the bolt. Her hand trembled. The chain-lock shook like skeleton bones. She couldn't believe the little monsters tried something like that. Not on her.

Way beyond simple, childish pranks. She wouldn't have it. They wanted war? Tillie would give them war.

"Give 'em hell, Tillie," she muttered through clenched teeth.

She opened the living room shade, crawled onto the sofa,

and peeked out the window. Beyond the porch light's arc, she saw nothing. She considered turning off the lights, lure the little rats out of hiding. Hit 'em with good ol'-fashioned Yankee duplicity. But frankly, the light provided comfort. Not that she was scared, mind you. Nothing scared Tillie.

She cupped her hands around her eyes and pressed them against the window. Nothing, just a flickering jack-o-lantern across the street. And shadows upon more shadows.

The moon silhouetted swaying tree limbs. Leaves dropped, wafted leisurely down. A few leaves docked on the porch, then caught by a breeze and were whisked away across the boards. Still no sign of Casper and his unfriendly ghost pals.

Bak, bok, bak!

The pounding wrenched Tillie's heart.

Brak, bak, bak!

The back door! Little bastards were trickier than she gave them credit for. Propelled by adrenaline, she scurried down the hallway to the back of the house. Her slippers slid across the bare wood floor. She crashed into the wall, knocked down a picture of Jesus, upsetting his eternal suffering. She entered the kitchen, flipped on the light. Hefted the gun up. Set the chain-lock on the door free. With gung-ho gusto, she cocked the trigger and threw open the door.

"Gotcha *now*, you lil—"

Silence. Heavier than a clammy, humid day. She propped the gun up against her shoulder and flipped on the backyard light. Nothing out of the ordinary as far as she could see; no egg yolk on the paneling, no smashed pumpkins, no surprise burning packages. Just a rusty old grill that hadn't felt the fiery kiss of charcoal since Frank's passing, a weather-beaten lawn chair, a small table, and a wooden fence that had more missing teeth than a lousy boxer. The ghosts hadn't done a damn thing except ding-dong-ditch her.

Unless…unless… Goddammit! Subterfuge!

Breathlessly, she locked the kitchen door and raced back down the hallway. The gun grew heavier in her grip. Her left arm tingled in a worrisome manner. No time to worry about it. Right now war came first. She didn't stop running until she slapped hands on the front door. She undid the security chain. On the outskirts of her yard, white heads bobbed up and down like mimes dressed in black. The ghosts. Laughing at her.

She stormed the porch. Her hands went limp. The gun dropped with a clatter.

Her garden. Her once majestic and beautiful garden had been stomped through, gutted and pruned of all life. Every last loving bloom and bud of color and vibrancy, all gone. The corpses of her babies lay strewn through the yard, their stems crisscrossing in sad little knots of death. Flower blooms wilted. Petals draped the ground. What once had filled her with awe now carried the gravitas of a funeral parlor.

Rage turned her stomach sour, filled it with bitter bile. Tears threatened to fall, but she wouldn't allow it. Through sheer force of mind, she willed them away. If the town thought she hated before, they couldn't possibly fathom the unholy Hell she planned to unleash on these three monsters.

"You little cocksuckers," she screamed. "I swear to *God*, I'm gonna gut you like you did my garden! You wanna fight? You're gonna get a fight! I won't rest 'til I shred your pimply asses with gun shot! I know who you are! I know who everyone in this pissant town is!" Of course, she didn't know the ghosts' identities. Couldn't quite peg the kids, not with their sheets on. But it was a fine tactic, one that would scare most ordinary kids. But she wondered if these kids *were* ordinary. "Gonna kill you shit-stains real good! *Goddam*—"

Flump.

Tossed over the picket fence, a bundle landed in her yard.

Visible only as a solid, black shape, darker than the night. She stepped off the porch. Trotted into the yard. Swung her gun left, then right, as she approached the object. Leaves crunched beneath her slippers.

Crip, snik, tak…

She stopped. Listened. Footsteps raced down the sidewalk. Giggles followed like shadows.

She approached the bundle, prepared to blow it sky-high if necessary.

She dropped to her knees. This time, unwilling—unable—to stop the tears from falling onto her dead cat, Brick.

She picked up his limp body, held him to her breast one last time. His head drooped at an unlikely angle. Broken neck.

An eye for an eye, so sayeth the Old Testament. And Tillie damn well intended to pluck out all of the ghosts' cursed eyes.

"You goddamn little bastards! I swear I'm gonna get you! Kill all three of you! I'm…" She screamed until her throat turned on her, raw and ragged.

War preparations needed to be made.

She ran back into the house, locked the front door. Dragged a dining room chair out and lodged it beneath the doorknob. Overkill, maybe, but she wouldn't be caught with her britches down again.

Angry momentum thrust her up the staircase, two steps at a time. In her bedroom, she sat on the bed—gun across her lap just the way Brick used to sit—and shed her slippers. Replaced them with her sensible action flats. They'd provide good pro-tection, solid support, and she could move in them easily. No problem conquering two flights of stairs.

Down in the basement, Tillie batted away hanging cobwebs with the gun's barrel. In the east corner, she found what she needed: a vermin-chewed and urine-sodden cardboard box full of rat traps. Most of them had been used successfully before (some of them triple winners); why throw out the baby with the bathwater?

Next to the box, something caught her eye. Something she'd long forgotten, and for good reason: Frank's never-used steel jaw trap. No surprise, Frank never hunted a day in his life.

With the monstrous trap piled on top of the box, the gun tucked under her arm, Tillie bounded up the stairs.

Tillie flicked off the porch light, grabbed the closest emergency flashlight. In full-on stealth mode, she tip-toed onto the porch. She scattered the traps, carefully opening their jaws and pinning them wide. Hidden in shadows, she placed the big trap on the first step. She straightened, chuckled, and felt her back groan.

That'll teach the little bastards. Hope I lop off one of their feet.

With the flashlight guiding her way through the maze of traps, she reentered her dark house and closed the door. Now for the hard part: waiting. Excitement zipped up and down her spine, Brick all but forgotten.

She dragged her rocking chair to face the front door, practiced getting out of it in a jiffy. She fired up a celebratory cigarette (*A pack a day for sixty years! Feh. What do doctors know?*), inhaled the smoke into her lungs. And listened.

Tick-tock…tick-tock…

The grandfather clock in the hallway—the one that used to drive Frank bonkers, not that it took much—ticked off the long seconds filling Tillie's waiting game. Outside, all Halloween caterwauling had died. An owl hooted, just once. Everything quiet as snow-covered winter in the dead of night.

Tick-tock…tick-tock…

A car slowly passed Tillie's house. Tires hummed. Headlights swept in through her window and then blinked back out. She held the gun carefully in her lap, stroked the barrel. Her eyelids drooped. She snapped them open, shook her head.

Tick-tock…tick-tock…

"That goddamn clock!" She couldn't hear anything over it, just the rhythmic sound of an ax on a chopping block. Cigarette dangling from her lips, she jumped out of her chair and embraced her new burst of energy. She reached the trouble-making clock and prepared to end its life.

Dong! Dong! Dong! Dong!…

"*Dammit!*" Startled, she hopped back as the clock chimed ten times. She took a long drag on her cancer stick and blew a huge cloud at the clock. She whipped open the clock's door and stopped the pendulum.

Silence, deeper than a tomb.

Tump, timp…

Her shoulders cocked up, her head angled to hear better.

Timp…timp…tump…

Cautious, measured footsteps on her porch.

Timp…

Tack! Spack! Takkity-tak-ak!

Like a string of firecrackers, the traps snapped.

"*Aieee!*" The scream sounded fragile, hurt, frightened. The way damn kids are supposed to sound.

"Ha! Gotcha now!" Tillie raced to the door. She flung it open, flipped on the light. Two of the white-sheeted figures had hightailed it to the safety of the sidewalk. The third, favoring one leg, limped quickly behind them. She whipped up her gun, fired.

Ba-blam!

The gun's kick jolted her back. She half-twisted, planted her feet, no time for a tumble. Smoke curled from the barrel and from her cigarette. She squinted into the yard. No corpses, but sure as shootin', she'd scared them off for good this time. Disappointment over the anti-climactic end of the game weighed

Tillie down. Little bastards deserved an arseful of buckshot from what they did to Brick and her garden.

She tromped onto the porch, called out, "Come back here again, and I'll blow y'all into bite-sized pieces!"

Most of the traps lay on their bellies, sprung. The big trap, though, had nailed one of them. She'd drawn first blood. *The Lord provides!* She knelt down, inspected it further. A tip of a tennis shoe—one of those fancy-assed, neon-colored ones—sat beneath the clamped steel teeth. Blood dripped from its ragged edge. Tillie stubbed out her cigarette on it. Using the butt, she pushed the tennis shoe remnant over. Half a toe slipped out, just a nubbin, the blood still fresh.

Jesus on a jump-ski, what kinda kids are these?

Nauseous, yet mentally empowered, she raised the gun over her head. "You don't mess with Tillie Johannsen! Hope you bleed to death, you little bastard!"

She looked around, waited for neighbors to applaud her efforts (not that the spineless, pathetic liberals ever would) or call the cops. She saw no one.

Oblivious to the few still-set rat traps, she tromped across her porch in a victory lap, then thundered into her house. Her hands shook, but not out of fear, never fear. A rush of adrenaline electrified her nerves, woke them from hibernation. No more pesky, tingling arms either. For a brief moment, she felt like an energetic woman in her forties. Pity the battle had to end so suddenly.

Her momma had always said, "Be careful what you wish for."

Without a sound, the lights went out. Just dropped away like sudden death.

Tillie raced to the front window to see if the neighbors had been hit as well. Stupid plastic electric jack-o-lanterns lit up their windows. Definitely not a neighborhood power outage.

She determined the little brats had something to do with it (in a sense, a heart-warming notion). But, surely, they didn't have the know-how to pull off such an adult accomplishment.

Better safe than sorry. With the gun in one hand, the flashlight in her other, she laboriously shuffled toward the basement stairs. Just for shits and grins, she flicked the basement stairwell's light switch back and forth. Nothing but a hollow *click-clack*.

"Fine. Gonna have to do it the hard way, then." Ordinarily, Tillie wasn't prone to talking to herself, never saw much use for it unless she had a notion to be fast-tracked to the nuthouse. Still, she needed to cut through the heavy quiet that lay over the house. And since her own company was about all she could tolerate anyway, she saw absolutely nothing wrong with it.

"Damn skippy." She nodded.

As Tillie descended, the flashlight's beam bounced off the wooden risers. She zipped it over the stone, mold-touched walls, on the lookout for shadows that moved of their own accord.

"Nothing down here but Frank's worthless crap," she said. "A few spiders, couple mice, nothing but fear trying to run upshot of you." At the bottom of the stairwell, she did another full basement scan with the beam.

Boxes piled high. Cobwebs draped like Spanish moss that had aged and gone gray. A few wet spots here and there, damage from the insufferable amount of rain they'd been having. A long-snuffed-out dehumidifier leaned against the western wall. Frank's suits lay dumped unceremoniously in the corner. All of it ordinary, forgotten, and discarded junk that didn't merit first- or second-floor status.

At the fuse box, she swept away a stubborn string of webs and opened the panel door.

"The goddamn hell?" She dropped the flashlight. It spun in a dizzying circle of light. Tillie turned around with it, half expecting to be shanghaied. She snagged the flashlight and checked out the panel again.

Completely destroyed, gashes sliced through the internal hardware. Fuses lay cracked on the cement floor.

Cool air brushed the back of her neck. She whirled, aimed the light at the source. Another breeze rushed in through the broken well window. Little bastards snuck in while she was on her front porch.

"*Tee hee hee!*" Footsteps—light, airy and playful—dashed up the stairs. Two sets. She whipped the flashlight over the stairwell. At the top of the steps, one of the damned ghosts—she recognized his voice as Skull Pail—said, "You should've given us better candy."

"Fine day in hell when I take orders from little bastards like you," Tillie screamed.

Like his namesake, the ghost vanished. The basement door slammed with a damning *crack*. The door's lock snapped into place.

"You little bastards wanna *play*? *I'll* show you how I play!" Tillie charged across the basement, tipping over a stack of boxes in her rush. China toppled and crashed on the floor.

Near the base of the steps, her foot slid in a puddle. Frantically, she threw out her gun-wielding hand, caught the barrel on the railing. Something in her shoulder wrenched, an angry pain, one she'd baby later. War had been brought into her house.

Into her goddamned house.

The violation and personal attack burned her more than the murder of her cat or the loss of her garden. Fun and games were over. Never had she felt so dirty, so sullied.

No mercy.

She flew up the steps. An animal-lusty growl emerged from deep in her chest. She should've known better, but it couldn't be helped: without thinking, she threw her shoulder into the locked door and nearly threw it out. Open-palmed, she slapped the door until her hand numbed. "You think a goddamned *locked* door's gonna keep me outta my own *house*?"

"*Hee hee heh!*"

"You even laugh like little girls!" With the flashlight tucked into her pants, Tillie gripped the gun by its barrel and brought the butt down on the doorknob. No damage, just a blow that vibrated well into her bladder. She tried it again.

In her kitchen, pots and pans clanged to the floor. Jars broke. Drawers were yanked out, emptied, then heaved to the floor. And laughter. Lots and lots of hideous, mice-like tittering. Taunting her.

"The hell with this!" Tillie backed down two steps, braced her feet, stuck the gun's barrel next to the doorknob. She clenched her teeth and pulled the trigger.

Ka-rack!

The stairs shook. Wood projectiles sailed by Tillie's head. Her arms thrust overhead. The gun dropped, slid down the stairs. She grabbed the railing and waited for the world to quit wobbling. Even though fully indoctrinated into the fine art of the cigarette, the resultant gun smoke forced tears from her eyes.

When everything settled, the door stood open. Rather, half of it was open; the other half lay on the floor.

The merry ol' time in her kitchen stopped. She caught the backsides of two of the sheeted monsters racing out of the kitchen, the third nowhere in sight. On unsteady feet, Tillie clambered down the steps and retrieved her gun. She bounded up into the kitchen like a marauding soldier.

She didn't want to look, would've been impossible not to. She shifted the flashlight around the dark kitchen. War-torn aftermath inadequately described the mess. Her favorite China set had been smashed into small porcelain puzzle pieces. Cabinets had been pilfered, cans of cat food and bean soup lobbed about like grenades. Worst of all, a pungent odor rose over the still-lingering smoke, one Tillie immediately recognized: *urine.*

"Ahhh*hhhhhh!*"

At that moment, she absolutely knew she'd kill them. No more pussyfooting around. First, she'd make them lick up their urine, then she'd plug 'em full of lead. And kill them all over again.

Bump, bomp, tromp…

Above her, the light fixture wiggled. The little bastards had taken refuge on the second floor. Where her bedroom was, her personal domain.

She hurried through the kitchen, tap-dancing objects out of her way. The flashlight beam bounced across the walls like the old bouncing ball cartoons of her youth. A crudely written message (possibly scribed with cherry pie filling) sprawled across the cabinets: *Old bag!*

Her toe stubbed on the first-floor stairwell, and she didn't take time to give a damn.

Upstairs, the giggling continued. Something pounded, dull and muted. Images of her most private belongings torn to ribbons flashed through her mind. At the top of the steps, she stopped and listened.

The *trompity-trompity-tromp* sounded akin to an elephant in slippers.

She crept up to the bathroom, swung the light and gun simultaneously. Felt like blasting a bullet right through the shower curtain in case one of the little beasts lurked behind it. The voices down the hall rose, full of indecipherable jibber-jabber. Coming from her bedroom.

"*Tee-hee-hee!*"

Whump-rump-bump…

Three of them, one of her. And one of them wounded. Tillie

liked her odds.

But she hadn't seen the third one yet, the one with the limp. He could be hiding anywhere.

She nudged open the door to the guest bedroom and hopped inside. A quick search with the flashlight displayed the room a-okay, everything unsullied by young, filthy, sticky hands.

A sliver of feeble light slipped out beneath her bedroom door. Like a TV cop, she stood next to the door, back against the wall. From within, the thumping sound grew louder. Flashlight in hand, she managed a thumb and finger over the doorknob. She twisted it slowly, quietly. The door opened. She jumped inside, brought the gun up, the flashlight pressed against the trigger guard.

One of the brats stopped jumping on her bed. He landed in a squat, tossed his arms to the sides to maintain balance. Feathers floated in the air, snowed to the floor. The ghost held a gutted pillow, knife in his other hand. One of her kitchen knives.

He said, "You're not gonna kill us. We're just kids."

"Wanna bet?" Something cracked the back of Tillie's ankle. Her trigger finger twitched, squeezed. The gun cracked. She fell backward and hit the floor along with falling plaster. The gun spun from her grip. Heart racing, she raised the flashlight.

The ghost jumped off the bed and ducked down behind it. The other ghost hovered over her in a beast-like crouch.

Tillie screamed. Her flashlight caught on something in the boy's hand: a hammer. He growled, brought the hammer down. Tillie rolled, scooped up the gun. The hammer exploded on the floor with a loud *spack*. Behind her, she heard a sheet whisk, the knife-wielding ghost. Tillie rolled again, the gun hard beneath her brittle bones. And tried to remember how many bullets she'd fired.

While grappling for more ammo from her pocket, she

dropped the flashlight. The beam spun, then pinpointed the ghost's legs closest to her. She sat up, scooted back on her rump and kept moving until she hit the wall. In the dark, she broke the gun, jammed in two bullets, slammed it together again. And fired.

Ka-blam!

Just like a real ghost, the hammer-carrying demon flew across the room. His back hit the wall opposite Tillie. He collapsed into a red-soaked pile of laundry. Hands flumped out beside him, palms up, pleading one last Hail Mary to God.

Tillie wasted no time feeding the gun more bullets. The flashlight lay in the middle of the room, its beam locked onto the ghost's corpse. She couldn't see the knife-carrying ghost, but she heard him move across the room. *Shh-shsh-shhh,* a dragging sheet's whisper.

"You want some of this, you little bastard! I'll make a real ghost outta you just like your friend!" She waved the gun around in the darkness, trying to hone in on his location by sound. First, he landed next to her, then quickly flitted to the far side of the room. He rushed back again, damn near floating. She blasted a random shot to momentarily light the room, maybe get lucky. There, by her lamp, then he darted away. One chance, lure him in.

"Come on, I'm ready for you! Let's do this!"

Slsshhh…swsh…shhh…

The gun shook, an extension of her muscle-weakened arms. She wished the kid would say something, do something.

Shhhh…slishhh…swish…

Games, cat-and-mouse style. But Tillie refused to be a mouse. The brats didn't stand a chance in her tiger's lair.

"Pissin' in your britches yet? Gonna cry next? Too scared to do anyth—"

A tiny beam of light clicked on and floated in the darkness.

The light penetrated Tillie's eyes, stung like a migraine. She glanced away. No longer than a brief second, but a huge mistake.

Ssss, shssss, slish...

Faster now, coming at her. The light grew from a pinpoint to a blinding nickel of sunshine. She blinked. The light snapped off. She listened. Held her breath. Couldn't hear the kid breathing, moving, *living.*

A sudden whiff of air. A minute ruffling of the sheet. On pure instinct, Tillie leaned right, her head practically to the floor. Body warmth filled the space before her. A swish of the knife raised the hair by her ear. A small hand found her throat and squeezed. It was the other hand Tillie worried about.

The boy fell on her, all 60-pounds-when-wet boy. She couldn't free the gun pinned between their bodies. The boy stuck to her, rode her. Tillie found his knife-wielding hand, gripped it by the wrist. For his size and age, he packed solid strength. She kept in motion, dodged, twisted. She released his knife hand, knocked it aside with her forearm. The knife fell. It bit into her side, just below the ribs. Shock diffused the pain. Stubborn as Tillie, the knife wouldn't release as the boy tugged. He growled. Tillie relaxed, collapsed back against the wall. In that smallest window of opportunity, Tillie wrestled her gun from between them to freedom. Surprised, her opponent flopped on top of her, arms splayed out. Sweet victory in sight, Tillie brought the gun around and up. One-arming it, she poked the barrel into the ghost, hoping she wouldn't catch any friendly fire.

And sent him directly to Hell.

Ka-krak!

Flump.

Tillie waited a good long minute before she allowed herself the mother of all deep breaths. She wanted to wait out the ghost, see if she'd handled the job thoroughly. Doubtful, of course, anything could've survived that up-close blast, ghost or not. Still, they were resourceful shit-stains.

But this time, the ghosts appeared to have fled their mortal coils.

With some doing, she hauled herself up. Her side caught like the world's worst cramp and then some. She touched the knife, her fingers seeking out the extent of the damage. Hard to say, but she thought it nothing more than a superficial wound. A constant diet of medical dramas had taught her well. She shuffled forward. Her foot caught a corner of the sheet where the boy had lived and died. She contemplated taking off his costume, get a good, long look at the monster she'd slain. Then remembered what her other favorite stories—the police procedurals—had taught her about not disturbing evidence. Slowly, she walked to the beacon of light in the middle of the room. Again, her side wrenched when she bent to pick up the flashlight.

After admiring the carnage she'd brought to the party, she hobbled toward the bathroom. Occasionally, she stroked the knife handle sticking out of her. A reminder of how lucky she'd been. The boy hadn't chosen a big knife, just one of her smaller utility knives. But Lordy, it was sharp!

Looking into the bathroom's vanity mirror, she further assessed her injury. She inched her shirt up, bunched it around the knife handle. The wound still bled. Not much, not yet hysterical 9-1-1 ready, but she knew damn well if she yanked the knife out, it might cause more bleeding. She managed to prop a folded towel around the knife, tucked her shirt back in. It'd hold for a little bit. She hoped.

"Ring around the rosieee…"

The song, quiet and sweetly rendered, startled Tillie. From downstairs.

Two down, the toeless one to go.

As quietly as Tillie could, she reloaded her gun, her pocket now out of bullets. Pain worked its way from her side into her brain. Tenderly, she planted each footstep down the hallway, each step further into agony.

But she wouldn't stop. Not as long as her castle was under siege.

Little bastards!

"*A pocketful of posieees…*"

The stairwell had never given her any problems in the past, but now Tillie imagined it would be tantamount to descending a treacherous mountainside. With some effort, she finagled her way onto her bottom, placed the gun in her lap (locked, stocked, and ready to kill!), and painstakingly quiet, she lowered herself down.

"*Ashes, ashes, we all fall down!*"

She forced her weight into her arms, onto her hands, attempting to muffle the sound of her rump touching the stairs. Downstairs, the brat continued singing, nothing but the first verse.

As Tillie neared the end of her arduous slide, she smelled something. A very faint smell; one she recognized, knew, but couldn't hang a name on. Slightly off, slightly bitter. Absolutely not right.

"*Ring around the rosieee…*"

On the last two steps, Tillie climbed to her feet. Each step through the house ratcheted up her pain.

"*A pocket full of posieee…*"

An eerie orange glow crept out from the kitchen doorway. Tillie followed it with no more control than if she'd been hypnotized.

The heinous child's voice grew louder, more playful, apparently lost in the song. Innocent as can be, and all the more deadly for it.

In the hallway, just outside of the kitchen, Tillie set her flashlight on the floor and freed both hands for shotgun duty.

"*Ashes, ashes, we all fall down!*"

Tillie bounded around the corner and cocked the gun. *Chik-chak!*

Calm and cheeky as the bloody Queen of England, the ghost sat at Tillie's kitchen table, a sandwich in one hand. One of his legs kicked idly beneath the table, not long enough to reach the floor. On the table, an electric jack-o-lantern bathed the kitchen in a dull orange glow.

"Hello. Wondered when you'd be down." The ghost's hood was pulled up. Shoulder-length, dirty hair dropped from beneath it.

"You're…you're a *girl!*" Shocked, Tillie nearly lowered her gun.

The girl laughed, just a hollow knock at the door. *Ek, ek, ek.* "So are you," said the girl. "I mean, you're an old lady. You hurt my foot." She lifted the non-kicking foot, a darkened pillowcase swathed around it.

"I really feel terrible about that, you little shit!" Tillie wagged the gun in her direction. "Now I'm gonna blow your—"

"You better not." She dropped the sandwich, a frown on her dirt-smudged face.

"Why's that, you little hell-spawn?" Suddenly, Tillie's olfactory senses clanged out a five-alarmer. She looked at her stove. Her *gas* stove.

The girl stood, grabbed the pumpkin light, and limped to the appliance. She held up the lamp. "The gas has been on the whole time you were upstairs. If you shoot your gun, you're gonna blow up. Boom." With a malicious grin, she spread wiggling fingers.

A bluff, surely. Maybe the gas hadn't been on long enough.

Or maybe… Maybe, *nothing*. Under the glow of the pumpkin, the area above the grill shimmered like a desert mirage. Defeated, Tillie lowered the gun.

"Fine. I'll put the gun away." Tillie lowered it to the floor. Kicked it behind her so the brat wouldn't get any crazy idea about blowing them both to kingdom come. "Why'd you little fucks do it, anyway? Why'd you and your lil bastard buddies attack me?"

She shrugged. Stepped closer. "You gave us circus peanuts. They suck."

"This is about *candy*?"

"Course, silly. It's Halloween." She said it matter-of-factly, took another step forward. With one hand behind her back, she swung the lamp. Under the bouncing, unreliable light, her filthy hair, matted in thick clots, appeared to crawl. Dark circles hollowed her eyes. Sallow and sunken, her cheekbones pulled tight to expose teeth the color of candy corn.

"Because you didn't like the candy, you ruined my garden, killed my cat, invaded and destroyed my beautiful home—"

"It's not so beautiful."

"Shut your hole! And your friends—who're deader than doornails and I'm happier than a pig in shit about it—*stabbed* me. I'm gonna kill you. *Bitch*!"

Tillie lunged, lassoed her hands around the girl's scrawny throat. The sheet ripped away in Tillie's hands. She tottered back, arms flailing, searching for balance.

From behind her back, the girl whipped out an ax, almost too much for her to handle. Tillie crouched the best she could, arms open, fingers beckoning in a come-hither manner. *Ready*.

The girl shrieked, dropped the plastic lamp, and rushed Tillie. With Tillie's longer reach, she gripped the girl's wrist. The girl rolled into it, forced her back into Tillie's belly. They swayed, struggled for control of the ax. With a painful-sounding snap, Tillie twisted the girl's wrist. The ax fell. They stopped, stared at it for the longest second of Tillie's life.

Tillie didn't dare let go of the girl. She stuck her leg out and kicked the ax beneath the kitchen table. A near split took her farther down than she'd planned. The girl wrenched away. Tillie's body screamed surrender. She buckled, fell sideways. The knife in her side jabbed deeper inside. A painful, yet welcome reminder of the weapon at hand.

The girl raced for the ax, dropped to her knees, snatched it up. She jumped to her feet, glowered at Tillie. Ax above her small body, out-of-control rage burning in her eyes, she rocketed toward Tillie.

Tillie clamped her teeth together, screamed, and wrenched the knife from her side. The pain fed her, empowered her. She sat up, thrust the knife out with both hands. The girl ran into the knife, impaled to the hilt in her belly. The ax slipped from her hands, clunked next to Tillie's leg. Shocked, the girl's mouth formed a satisfying "O." She cupped her hands around the knife and toppled onto Tillie.

Tillie scrambled out from beneath the foul child. She struggled to her knees and crawled to the cabinets. Using a cabinet door as a crutch, she made it onto sailor's legs. Her side burned, the towel now more than half red. She hobbled toward the girl, gave her a swift kick to her ribs. Some things are worth the pain.

"Hah! I *won!*"

She nearly fell back onto the kitchen counter. Turned around. Reached into her pocket for her smokes. She fished a cigarette out, stuck it between her lips, a solid manifestation of her victory.

"Teach ya to mess with ol' Tillie, by God!" She grinned at the dead girl, rejoiced over the dead boys upstairs. No one could beat her, many had tried, all of them failed. "Be a cold day in Hell afore anyone gets one up on me!" She plucked out her lighter. "Goddamn little punks!"

Her smile faded once she glanced at the stove. The exact second the lighter's flame jumped to life.

"Oh, *goddam*—"

HISSY FIT

Of course, I've heard all the names, all the mean-spirited put-downs. There's "Bigfoot." I suppose my feet are large, but they're not all *that* big, not really. Then there's "Sasquatch," whatever that means, a nonsense name. And possibly the worst of all, "Skunk Ape." I don't look, nor smell, anything like a skunk. Humans can be cruel, quick to strike out against anything that's different, anything outside of what they're comfortable with.

Yet, I'm the one proclaimed a monster.

Actually, my name is unpronounceable in human language; the closest approximation would be "Mmgawalla," but that's still not quite right. There are lots of clicks, syllables humans wouldn't recognize, notes too high pitched for the human ear. Humans seem to have a short attention span and would probably never fully comprehend my complex language. Unlike me. For many years, I've studied the strange human species, attempting to understand their language and ways.

To put it into perspective, my people were an ancient species, older than man. Not quite as old as the great beasts that once roamed this world, but we certainly were around before those annoying cavemen with their foul manners and violent temperaments. But that's hardly here nor there. Because of the callous whimsy of the fates, I've become the last of my breed.

I'm not certain how it happened exactly. Mother and Father tried their best, I suppose, to form my youthful mind with past history and legacy, but the tales seemed incomplete at best. Before each hibernation, my father would tell me how our race had dwindled due to weather, sickness, and men brandishing weapons. Father had called it "evolution," an unfathomable term that terrified me as a youth. When I grew older, I came to understand evolution. Then I grew to hate it. Such an ugly word, evolution.

Simply put, my race didn't evolve with the rest of the world. Just me.

Once, long ago, after a three-moon sleep, I awoke. *Alone.* Not quite alone, I suppose, but the only living entity in the cave. Mother and Father lay across the leaf-scattered ground, arms entwined in one last embrace. Mother had buried her face in Father's chest. Even though I longed for one final look at her beautiful features, I thought better of it, choosing wisely to remember who she'd been, not the shell she'd become. Seeing Father's face had been awful enough. His eyes had dulled to twin dried berries. His jaw sagged down, frozen in a silent scream, a death scream. Even though I knew Mother and Father were now roaming the skies with the rest of our breed, the horrors I imagined them going through during their last moments of life filled me with fear, then a crushing sadness. Finally, anger consumed me. I sat beside them, moaning, cursing the unjust gods. My emotional devastation lasted an eternity, yet not nearly long enough.

For I was truly alone. Forever.

For many seasons, I stayed in the cave. As many moons passed, Mother and Father decayed, their bodies returned to the ground from whence they'd come. Self-torture though it was, as the last of my kind it was my duty to ensure them peaceful passage into the skies. Finally, when they'd transformed to little more than dust, I explored—not too far—outside of my home.

On my first venture, I found a fallen branch, long and sturdy. As a way to pass the seasons, I cleared the dying leaves and used my claws to fashion a nice sharp point on the end of it. I then carved intricate designs into the staff, pictograms of my ancestors. When I'd finally completed the task, I felt empty again. No prospects, alone, disheartened.

I rolled the sharpened branch between my hands, wondered what would become of me if I thrust it into my chest. Would I lap at the air like a fish, gulping for one last breath of life? Would I hurt? Or would I be thrust into a deep darkness, consoling in its quiet warmth? Perhaps a loving embrace from Mother waited for me on the other side.

Mostly, I feared if I took my own life, I wouldn't be allowed entrance into the heavens, fated to wander the earth forever as a restless spirit.

I left the cave, alive yet despondent with no idea what I'd do, where I'd go. But I had to move, to do something. Fill my empty husk. But as Mother used to say, be cautious of what you seek. It wasn't until I saw my first human that I truly understood her cryptic, yet prophetic meaning.

That day, strange sounds echoed from within the forest—not unpleasant really—rhythmic and resonant. I smelled something sharp and full of destruction (which I later found out the humans named *fire*). Unintelligible gibberish—shrill and deep—rose, punctuated by loud, violent bursts. Keeping my distance—our species had been blessed by the gods with remarkable eyesight—I pulled back a tree branch and watched.

Humans.

Father had warned me about them, told me they were

dangerous, evil. As a youth, I'd imagined them as demons, beasts with eyes of fire and a serpent's mouth of pointed teeth. But they weren't at all what I'd imagined. Somewhat homely, really. Ridiculously hairless, awkwardly proportioned, hardly the bodies of warriors or foragers. After a while, I was able to differentiate the females from the males based on sound, appearance, and how they interacted. I studied them for hours until they went into hibernation.

I don't know what compelled me to do so. The humans had acted primal: urinating and defecating wherever whimsy led them, tossing their refuse without care, disrespecting the gods of nature. They flocked together, shrieked constantly, their tones belligerently challenging the heavens in defiance. Absolutely bestial behavior. Yet I was drawn to them. Perhaps it was my crushing despair and loneliness. Or maybe I saw them as a lower life form, something to be pitied, possibly aided. Regardless, I couldn't stop examining them, drawn in like a cub to its mother.

I returned the next cycle and the next. Disappointment set in as I watched them gather their belongings. Terror seized me as a frightening, gleaming shell transported them away. Once my fear subsided—and in my youthful naivety—I felt a colossal loss.

Only youth could commit such a horrific error.

Soon enough, more humans replaced the earlier ones. None of them ever stayed very long, all of them performing tasks at high speeds, all of them nearly impossible to distinguish from the rest. But as the moons waned, I became bolder, moved in closer. And I learned. I began to understand some of their words. I listened to what they called a "radio," their tribal music. At times, the humans talked about "Bigfoot Country." Later I realized they were talking about me.

And every time the humans left, I cleaned up after them,

burying their abandoned rubbish and stamping out their fires. So uncaring, so insolent.

After a while, I grew restless, impatient. A deep resentment built within me like mounting sky storms, something that couldn't be harnessed. One eve, under a pregnant moon, a particularly awful group of humans ran rampant through the grounds. The males drank from shiny receptacles and threw them into piles. One human hacked at a newborn tree with a weapon for no apparent reason other than a joy for aggression. Several humans set fire to small hand-held twigs, then threw them as they cracked like thunder. When one extremely loud and braying man urinated on my foot, I'd had enough.

To borrow a quaint human idiom, I lost my cool.

I whipped back the tree branch. With arms and claws out, I stalked toward the humans' encampment, hoping to instill understanding. I attempted to approximate their words. In my head, I clearly heard "Show respect and practice honor." Truth be told, though, it probably sounded like a monosyllabic roar, humans hearing only what they want to. Several of the pitiful humans screamed, prompting me to shout louder. An extremely frustrating effort.

They wouldn't listen. They would never *respect* the lands and gods they sullied.

One man lifted a stick, a weapon I'd seen them use to slaughter animals. I grabbed the end, tore it from his grasp, and flung it into the woods. I stomped on their fire, tore down their flimsy dwellings. Bird breasts and thighs sizzled upon a foul, black, smoking contraption. I lifted it over my head, banged it on top of a male. Sparks flew like a great constellation at unease.

My jaw grew taut, tighter, my fury escalating.

Did I forget to mention I have a bit of a temper at times?

A female's screams burrowed deep into my head. She

wouldn't stop. I grasped her around the throat, gripped a weak arm and ripped it from her body. Unbelievably, she still shrieked. Using her own detached arm, I slapped her with it, effectively ending her hellish wail.

One man pointed his weapon stick at me. With a loud noise, it discharged discomfort into my arm. Truthfully, it hurt no more than a bee's sting, but the man's intent to harm was evident. I shoved him. He hit the earth. I grabbed his legs, tore him into two halves, one for the god of Earth, the other for the god of the skies.

Two males attacked me, both armed with ineffective weaponry. One slash of my claw severed the head of the nearest male. The other's head stayed doggedly on its body. Which wouldn't do. Finally, after great labor, it detached. Blood, other liquids, and weak strings of humanity draped from it. As an afterthought, I switched heads on the bodies, my playful side unleashed.

The rest of the humans scattered like field mice. Their horrific transport swallowed them. Dust kicked from the spinning silver beast's back legs. I couldn't let them depart on such an ugly farewell note. It wouldn't have been hospitable of me.

I grabbed the back of their transport. Picked it up. The back legs spun, moving nowhere. But I had already planned their destination. I pushed the wounded beast through a clearing. At the edge of the cliff, I dug my feet into the earth and shoved. Slowly, the monstrosity slipped over the edge, dipping and vanishing a bit at a time. Screams rose from within the receptacle, put to rest by a mighty roar of thunder and fire that rose to the cliff's precipice.

I had a very bad day.

While I felt awful for precipitating the explosion in my hallowed grounds—a fully unexpected, though curious event— I suspected the gods would look kindly upon me for the bountiful sacrifices I'd offered them in its stead.

I stalked back to the human's trash site, everything in disarray. And cleaned things up once again, set the grounds back to normal. Upon completion, I smacked dust, blood, grime from my paws, the way I'd seen humans do after toiling.

Yet...I was alone again. I hoped my temper tantrum wouldn't dissuade other humans from visiting my grounds in the future.

Even if their prejudices continued, unwarranted and unfair.

Another voice, tinny and far away, pulled me out of my reflections. Not a real voice, though: a small human from within the radio.

"...I dun saw it, I did. Wouldn't've believed it myself if I heard it from someone else. But there I was staring into the face of a Bigfoot creature, a female from the looks of her bosom..."

I knelt, prayed to the sky gods there might be someone else out there like me. The human in the radio said the sighting had occurred at a place called Honobia. I didn't know where it was, but I'd find it; yes, I would. For the first time in many moons, I dared to hope, to hope for the future.

VEGETABLES ARE BAD FOR YOU

Eleven years old, Kyle considered himself way too mature to believe in ghosts or any of that silly playground crap. Just the stuff of scary movies, nothing more. But regardless of his age, he couldn't deny the sounds he heard coming from the cellar. Actually, more like he *felt* the noise: high-pitched humming, circling round and round in his head and throbbing in his chest.

The song drew him down the steps.

He couldn't decipher what the voices were singing, not really. Just sort of a sad song, a desire, a longing for companionship.

Something Kyle missed as well.

With his mom at work and Dad hitting the pavement for a job, Kyle had no reason not to investigate. His parents weren't there to tell him to stay out of the cellar. Not that a lecture would stop him, never did. In fact, every adventurous kid worth his salt usually accepted such orders as a challenge. Just part of the deal between kids and parents.

His family hadn't lived in the old house for long. One day, out of the blue, Kyle's dad had come up with a stupid idea about country living. Cleaner air, better values, living off the land, blah, blah, blah. Whatever. Kyle knew the truth. Dad's company had laid him off. The bank had foreclosed on their house. It's amazing what you can learn from eavesdropping.

Kyle had been against the move, opposed it mightily. But his voice never carried any weight in family decisions, the curse of being eleven. So when they packed up, Kyle had no choice but to man up and say goodbye to his friends. The friends he thought he'd have forever. But when you're a kid, things never last forever. And you're always powerless to do anything about it.

And move they did, too, straight into a rotten dump way out in nowhere, backwoods Kansas. Mom had said, "It's a real fixer-upper! It'll be fun!" Dad rallied with, "Sure has potential, this country living." If you learn to speak Parent, though, clearly what they meant was, "Yeah, this house is crap. Sorry, Kyle. It's all we can afford this side of a cardboard box. Suck it up."

The steep and narrow stairs to the cellar slanted. Like dirt-covered piano keys, they banged out sour notes with each footstep. Kyle had been in the cellar before, not his first rodeo. But when he'd gone down with his mother, he'd shamefully cowered behind her the entire time. For good reason.

Shadows danced and swooped, threatened to snatch him up and whisk him away to a dark world. Rusty, weird-looking, teeth-lined tools propped up against a sagging stone wall. Filthy shelves packed with bottles covered another wall. In the bottles, bulky yellow globs swam in murky water. Kyle spent many nights in bed wondering just what was in those bottles.

Kyle jokingly called the cellar a Grim Reaper's one-stop shop. But only when he was upstairs.

As mothers do, Kyle's mom warned him not to go down there alone. At the time, he'd agreed, thankful for his mother's wisdom. Later, he thought differently, pooh-poohed the baby notion to hell and back. Absolutely the day would come when he'd have to rise to the challenge. The attraction pulled at him stronger than a double-dog-dare.

Today was the day. He answered the calling, had to find out the source of the sounds coming from the cellar. Simply, he had no choice. Just like so much of his life.

The light bulb at the bottom of the stairs provided limited light. He pulled the string; the bulb swayed. So did everything else. Shadows darted to even blacker places. Eyes and grins formed in the jars' globby masses. The bulb continued swinging, alive, back and forth. Like a metronome, it counted out the beats of Kyle's hammering heart.

The strange humming intensified. One voice, two voices, a disembodied glee club.

At the foot of the stairs, he grasped the flashlight his mother had placed there. He swiveled the beam, getting reacquainted with the creepy cellar, a far cry from their refinished basement in the Kansas City house. Green splotches of mold—or something else entirely—blemished the stone walls. Spider webs hung from the maze of exposed pipes. Leaves crunched beneath Kyle's feet. With no windows or doors in the cellar, Kyle wondered how leaves had gained entrance. A chill rollercoastered down his spine, but he couldn't turn back now, no way. That's not how a man would act.

A large, sad bookshelf leaned against a back corner, the bottom warped and crumbling from mold and water damage. Kyle knew—absolutely so—the voices issued from behind it. The flashlight beneath his arm, he planted his feet solidly and yanked the bookshelf. He bounced back, watched as it toppled forward almost in slow motion. It clumped across the dirt floor. A dust cloud lifted from its fallen body. So did a rotten scent, so strong Kyle's eyes watered. He turned his head, plugged his nose, and coughed until the fumes passed. Then he aimed the light toward the uncovered corner.

Glistening stalks of varying sizes grew out of the dirt, similar in shape and texture to the asparagus Kyle loathed. Except these were slug-colored, pink, white, and grotesque. Black rings circled small nubs, almost limbs. Kyle rubbed his eyes, swung the flashlight away, then looked again. No illusion, the stalks moved, *actually moved*! They twisted and bent as if uprooting legs from the ground. Ignoring his mother's warning, Kyle dropped to his knees for a closer examination. Some of the strange growths dodged the flashlight's beam, stretching toward the shadows, but the dirt cemented them firmly, allowing them little mobility. Little holes popped open at the top of each stalk, mouths silently gasping for air. *Whispering*. Small hairs (teeth?) flitted out with each puff of breath.

Kyle's gaze followed the flashlight's beam up the tallest stalk. He shrieked and didn't even feel like a baby for doing so. A smaller stalk branched out of the top of the stalk. An eyeball dangled at the end. Yellow and wide-eyed and horrible. The branch stiffened as if tugged up by a hidden string. It darted toward Kyle, snapping its miniature mouth at him.

Kyle fell back in the dirt. He scrambled back on his butt, his sneakers trailing dust.

Suddenly the sounds in his head clarified. Voices from another place, far, far away from Podunk, Kansas. Comforting and warm, mesmerizing.

Hi, Kyle...

We need your help.

Won't you help us?

We're your friends...

"No!" Kyle locked his eyes down. He slapped his temples, hoping to stop the voices, things like this didn't happen. Only in nightmares. But he knew this wasn't a nightmare. Confirmed it with open eyes and a bitter bite of his tongue. The stalks stirred, shifted, and sang in perfect harmony.

Kyle…

Listen…

We need you to do something for us…

You help us, we'll help you…

You don't have to be lonely any longer…

Kyle propped up on his elbows, relaxed. Warmth filled him, sunshine on an August day. He floated in an invisible raft, bouncing and bobbing on tranquil waters. Not a care in the world. The cellar's rank odor vanished, replaced by flowers and cinnamon and freshly cut grass. Everything fine and wonderful and comforting and, above all, safe that he associated with his childhood.

Just like the way Kyle used to fall asleep in his mother's arms, he stretched across the floor, closed his eyes, and drifted off to the dulcet tones of his new friends…

"What'd you do today, Kyle?" His mother gently set her fork on the side of her plate while she spoke, good manners played out to annoying lengths.

Kyle shrugged, continued cutting small chunks from his baked potato. *Always* baked potatoes now, as if it was a main course. "Nothing. Same as usual."

"It was beautiful out today. Tomorrow's supposed to be the same. Why don't you take a bike ride, meet some other kids or—"

"Because there *aren't* any, Mom! There's nothing but old people or…farmers for miles!" To really paint a picture of drama,

Kyle tossed his fork down with a clank.

"That's not true, young man. Why just the other day I saw children playing at the school."

"How *old* do you think I am, Mom? I'm not a baby. I don't *do* recess anymore." Kyle knew he shouldn't take it out on his mom, but at least she was there. Not like his dad. Oh, sure, he sat at the dinner table, physically at least. But more often than not, after a failed day of job hunting, Kyle's dad would slouch home, sink into a quiet shell of himself. Do nothing but drink beer, eat, and sulk. Frankly, Kyle sorta wanted to whip up some life into him. Anything.

Instead, his dad stared at his sparse meal, endlessly sawing at his salad with a steak knife, the only thing they'd used steak knives for in a long time.

"Don't you get snippy with me, Kyle Peter Thomason!" His mom strapped on her parenting pants. Somebody had to, Kyle supposed. "Robert? Are you going to let your son speak that way at the dinner table?"

Nothing. Just the endless *scritch, screech, scritch* of his steak knife grinding against the plate.

"Robert! Did you *hear* me?"

Finally, *contact*! His dad looked up, puzzled, eyebrows lifted behind his glasses. Since moving to the country, he'd changed not only in action, but also in appearance. Dark circles that would make a raccoon jealous ringed his eyes. His cheeks drew in to the point of being skeletal, surprising giving the amount of beer he'd been sucking back.

"I'm sorry?" he said.

"Robert, your son… He's getting snippy with me."

His dad looked at him, but his hands kept carving at the salad on his plate.

Scree, scree…

"Don't be snippy, son." Immediately, he returned his attention to the mess he'd made of his salad, hardly the thorough scolding Kyle had expected—and feared—from him in the past.

"Whatever…" Kyle threw in his napkin, threw in the towel, pushed back from the dinner table. "Can I be excused?"

Obviously frustrated, Kyle's mom looked at him, then his dad. Shook her head, sighed. "No, finish your meal, Kyle."

He wanted to say, *meal, what meal*? But there was no sense in rocking the boat, although honestly, he wished his dad would tip over, splash himself awake or something. Clearly, Kyle wasn't the only one unhappy in their new living situation.

"Fine," Kyle huffed, then forked a chunk of potato. He thrust it into his mouth, chewed it animatedly. Gave his mom a "Happy now?" sassy face.

His mom was determined to hit the reset button, turn them back into the normal family they once were. "Robert, how did the job search go today?"

Kyle gulped, stared down at his plate. He knew his dad's joblessness provided prickly conversation. Always a prideful man, his dad hadn't taken the layoff easily although he'd put up a strong front. In the beginning, at least. But every day he failed to get a new job—and really, he was a medical supplies sales rep, so how hard could a salesman job be to find even in the boonies?—he seemed to crawl deeper into himself every night. Kyle wondered if his mom even saw that, and if not, why?

"It went great," said his dad, although he sounded anything but great. "Got a couple leads."

Scree, scritch, scree…

"That's wonderful, honey!" His mom put on adoring, round anime eyes and clasped her hands together as if warming up to swing the bat. "I told you perseverance would pay off. It was just a matter of time before—"

"I haven't got a job *yet*," his dad spat through clamped

teeth, angry at the world and then some.

Kyle just wanted to get out of there. Maybe sneak back down to the cellar to visit his new friends. The friends who didn't bring the drama because that's all his family gatherings amounted to anymore: world-class drama.

Scree, scritch, screeeee...

As he always did, Kyle woke to the sound of his mom slamming her car door. He listened as the car crunched down the graveled driveway. Although he'd been in bed for a good eight hours, he felt like he hadn't slept at all. Even weirder, his legs ached as if he'd hopped over a triathlon's worth of hurdles. He released a yawn big enough for a bird to fly in and out of his mouth.

His clothes lay in a messy pile next to his bed, definitely not the way he'd left them when he went lights out. Dirt stained the knees on his jeans. A dried leaf stuck to the bottom of his sneaker.

The hell?

He'd never been prone to sleepwalking before, not that he knew of. Then again, he wondered, would anyone know if they'd been sleepwalking if they slept alone?

Honestly, it didn't bother Kyle, not really. He knew where he'd gone, absolutely no doubt. Since stumbling across his strange, new friends in the cellar, he'd thought of nothing else, couldn't wait to visit them again. If only for a few hours, they'd sweep him away from the mundane reality of his new life, of the depressing drama of his parents.

Last night, he must've worked himself into such a fit that his mind won out over his body, even in sleep, and he'd paid a nighttime visit. Which just made him more eager to see them again.

For the first time since their move, Kyle sprang out of bed with youthful anticipation of something to do finally—*finally*—in this God-awful town.

Except, once he bounded downstairs, his plans were derailed by his dad's unexpected appearance. At the kitchen table, his dad studied a cereal box with the intensity of a spy who'd just discovered top secret plans. Unaware of Kyle, he scraped a spoon into a bowl, stabbed the cereal into his mouth. He'd dressed for the occasion, too: wife-beater t-shirt and boxers.

"Um, morning, Dad." Kyle grabbed a bowl from the cabinet and sat down next to his dad.

"Hm? Oh, hey, Kyle. Sleep well?" For a second, he smiled, a nice, warm dad smile from Kyle's childhood. Then the cereal box once again became the most important thing at the table.

"Sure." *Nope, not one bit.* "How're you doin'?"

"Me?"

"Um, yeah."

"Okay."

The kitchen clock ticked. The dry cereal crunched between his dad's teeth. The spoon ground against the side of the bowl.

Reeeeet, screee…

Plain and simple, Kyle was afraid to ask the question, but the longer his dad sat around in the kitchen, the longer Kyle couldn't see his friends. Just thinking about the stalks brought back that old Christmas morning feeling, the feeling Kyle thought he'd packed away long ago with his teddy bear and other childish things.

"Dad, are you gonna look for a job today?"

Chak!

The spoon smacked into the bowl. Cereal flakes flew. He glowered at Kyle, eyes wide, kinda crazy big. Like a turtle, Kyle wanted to retract into his hoodie, wanted to take back the question.

His dad's hand whipped up, open, hovering in the air as if ready to smack Kyle. Something he'd never done before, something Kyle couldn't imagine. A small smile cracked his dad's anger. His hand lowered. Kyle flinched, shut his eyes. But his dad only ruffled his hair, the way he used to do in less-troubled times.

"Of course I'm going to hit the trail, son. Just…getting a late start, that's all." He continued messing Kyle's hair, a little rough around the edges, as if playing with a rowdy dog. Finally, he stopped. Kyle straightened, found himself backing up a bit. His dad set down the cereal box, blinked his eyes rapidly as if batting away confusion. "Hey…you know, Kyle, this has all probably been upsetting to you, am I right?"

Kyle shrugged. "I dunno. Maybe. I guess."

"Well, I don't want this to upset you. Mom's right, you know. It's just a matter of time before I get a job. Then we'll be back to normal. Just like the old days. Everything will be all right. I promise."

But, for some reason, it was a promise Kyle no longer believed in, kinda like Santa Claus.

It took *forever*—and for an eleven-year-old, that meant an eternity—for Kyle's dad to get his act together, put clothes on, and leave. Kyle didn't even wait for the car to leave the driveway before he filled up his mom's watering bucket. From the breezeway, he grabbed his mom's bucket of plant feed, and that's when he heard the beautiful siren song of his friends again. As if they knew Kyle was on his way, serenading him with their gift of music.

He hurried down the stairs, his arms full, a wide, stupid grin on his face. The light flicked on. The music grew louder, at least it did in Kyle's mind.

Apparently, Kyle had been busy last night. He'd managed to wire a rod up from low-hanging ceiling pipes in front of his friends' garden. An old shower curtain—don't ask him where he found it, either!—draped across it, black mold splotching the bottom. The beam of his flashlight played over the thick plastic. Silhouettes of some of his more boisterous friends danced behind it. He yanked the curtain across the rod—*screeeeet*—and kept grinning that dopey grin; he just couldn't help it.

Hard to believe, but his friends appeared to have grown overnight. They were nearly an inch taller, their stalks sturdier, firmer. Their swaying, hypnotic dance seemed more polished, kinda weird if Kyle really thought about it. Yet their voices remained as soothing, as pleasing, as innocent as the day before. As if their voices would *never* change.

Kyle…

We've been waiting for you…

We've missed you…

We need to tell you some things…

"Hey, guys. I missed you, too." Now on his hands and knees, Kyle leaned in close. The fresh smell of summer—the memorable taste of days gone by—swept over him again. Like Elvis, the odor of rot that first filled his nose upon entering the cellar had left the building.

From the look of things, he'd done some gardening last night as well. The dirt had been carefully combed through, swerving around his friends' bodies. Nice, orderly rows raked through their playground. Kyle had no idea how he'd managed it, but he suspected it'd taken a good chunk of work. And tender loving care.

"Oh, hey, I got something for you." Kyle dumped some of the plant food into his hand, sprinkled it about his garden.

The tallest stalk swooped down, studied—*sniffed?*—the food. Its eyeball blinked. Kyle didn't understand how it expressed itself, not without eyebrows, but he swore its eye narrowed. Mad, even. The last thing Kyle wanted. Now that he finally had friends, he didn't want to blow it.

What have you brought us, Kyle?

What do we do with it?

It's not what we want.

Why would you give this to us?

"Oh, wow, guys, sorry you don't like it." He looked at the label on the bottle. "It's, um, plant food. Thought you might be hungry."

The tallest stock wagged, looked at its fellows. Almost like they were communicating between themselves, and this time Kyle was not on their frequency.

We're not plants, Kyle…

Of course, Kyle had assumed that's exactly what they were. But his dad always said, "Whenever you assume something, it makes an ass out of you and me." Kyle'd never really understood what Dad meant by that until now. Welcome to the mysterious world of adults.

"I'm sorry. I just thought—"

Don't think, Kyle.

We'll do that for you…

For now, give us water…

Food later…

"Oh, yeah, right." Kyle grabbed the water bucket and poured

water throughout his crops, careful not to go crazy and drench his friends.

They straightened, rigid as logs. Their mouths gaped open. Moans flitted through Kyle's head, his friends clearly enjoying the refreshment. Teeny-tiny *smecks* plopped from what passed for their mouths. Kyle smiled. Slowly, he extended a hand, index finger out. He held it up to the tallest one, let him get used to his odor. Kyle didn't know if they could smell, but figured it's how you'd approach a dog, so why not his new friends? Although there he went again, assuming things.

Next, he meant to stroke the leader's head, just ever so gently. But the creature opened its maw and enveloped the tip of Kyle's finger. Startled, he tried to wrench free. But the creature held on tight, tighter, tightening like a knotted rope. His finger numbed, went cold. Then the stalk released it. Turned its mouth into what looked like a satisfied grin. And Kyle couldn't swear to it, not absolutely, but he thought he saw a silver tongue lap out and lick around the perimeter of its mouth.

Alarms went off in Kyle's head. He fell back, his legs sprawled out in front of him. He shook his finger, nearly sucked on it to bring back some warmth, but then remembered where it'd been.

Then the soothing music spun up, carrying his momentary panic away like departing storm clouds.

It's alright, Kyle…

We'd never harm you…

Others mean to do that, but never us.

We're your friends.

Let's talk about your parents, Kyle…

Kyle's finger warmed first, lit the way, then his body slowly sizzled all the way up into his mind. And just like those drifting storm clouds, he drifted away, too…

Kyle half-way heard the door slam, incorporated it into the disturbing dream that had him trapped. A shotgun blast. He sat up, momentarily confused by his dark surroundings. Next to him, the flashlight's ray spotlighted a few of his friends, all now standing still.

And quiet… Unusually so.

But the heavy tread of his dad's boots across the floor sounded anything but quiet.

His father must be home early, no other explanation. No way had Kyle spent the entire day sleeping on the cellar floor. But he knew, as sure as he knew it would piss off his dad, he couldn't get caught down in the cellar.

He climbed to his feet. Quietly, he drew the shower curtain back across his friends' hiding spot, carefully guiding the curtain rings to ensure as little noise as possible.

At the bottom of the stairwell, he listened. And hoped his dad would retreat upstairs so he could make his break.

Booted feet tromped across the kitchen floor. To the refrigerator. Kyle held his breath, thought he could hear the hum of the appliance as his dad opened the door, then clomped it shut. *Ftsss.* A beer opened. His dad stomped out of the kitchen. Probably settling into his recliner to watch TV.

Carefully, Kyle crept up the stairs, taking his sweet time, trying to still some of the squeaks and groans of the ancient wooden stairwell. At the door, he opened it slightly. Put his ear to the crack. Heard the TV blasting, a rowdy, screaming western from the sound of it.

He swung the door open and stepped into the kitchen.

An iron grip yanked his arm up in the air. Startled, he wheeled to face his father.

"What the hell are you up to?" His dad's nostrils flared, deflated, did it again. Tiny red lines jagged through his glassy eyes. For once, Kyle had his father's full undivided attention.

"Nothing! I swear!"

"What were you *doing* down there?" He shook Kyle's arm, gave it a painful twist.

"Nothing, Dad! Really! I was just…I was bored, so I thought I'd clean up some stuff down there!"

His dad said nothing. A vein in his forehead popped, scary, close to blistering. His face burned red, the color of a blood orange. And still, he held on. Shook Kyle's arm again. In one swift movement, he spun Kyle, wrenched his arm up behind him.

"Ow! Dad! Stop—"

"Liar! I wanna know what you were *doin'* down there!"

"*Seriously*, I was bored and—"

"You keepin' something from me, boy? Got a little secret you're not sharing with me? I'll make you talk, just a matter of how much pain you're willing to put up with." For the first time in a long time, his dad smiled. Full of barely contained danger, hardly a loving father's smile.

Kyle knew his dad had changed, absolutely no doubt now. He meant Kyle true harm. Kyle struggled, then stomped on his dad's toe. The boot provided full-strength protection from Kyle's sneaker. And only made his dad angrier.

He brought Kyle closer. He rested his chin on top of his son's head. And he whispered, "You little shit. The only reason you're still here is because of your mother. I know what you've been up to. And I'll put a stop to it one way or another."

Kyle's world flipped, everything viewed through a confusing kaleidoscope of conflicting imagery. His mind's screen went fuzzy, white noise filled his head. Pinpricks jabbed at his brain, punctured his vision. He knew he was still in the now, felt his father's bear grip around his body, smelled the alcohol on his foul breath. But his father's voice sounded distant, a man yelling from a well.

Visions—Kyle had no other name for them—flooded his mind. Terrible, violent visions that made no sense. He saw a knife enter a man's stomach, then carve up to his rib cage. An ax came down, chunking into something, the sound of a watermelon being halved. Fire spread across Kyle's mind, ending in flames so large and out of control, he felt the heat.

And over it all, his friends sang, their words crystallizing into a soundtrack for the horror show. A beautiful, tiny, delicate melody belying the underlying threats.

Your father's evil, Kyle…

Don't let him do this to you…

He means to kill you…

Kill him first, Kyle!

Do it now!

"I hate you, Dad!" Kyle screamed. He meant it to. If he'd had a knife, he surely would've plunged it into his dad. Nothing else mattered but survival. "I'll *kill* you!"

Kyle's arms went up. Powered by adrenaline, he broke his father's grip, twisted to face his father. And thought of nothing but ending the man's miserable life.

But his father no longer resembled the madman of seconds ago. He appeared weak, confused. He took off his glasses, held his hand over his eyes, and staggered back until the kitchen counter propped him up.

"Jesus, son…I…I'm so sorry. So damned sorry. I don't know what… I just don't…" His words swam away, close to breaking. No longer dangerous, just kind of sad.

Kyle, too, felt his passion—his awful hatred—fizzle out. And like his dad, he felt confused, wanted to take back the last several seconds. But he couldn't. Some things just can't be taken back, a painful lesson to learn.

He wanted to hug his dad, unleash childhood tears, not embrace adult terrors. His dad held a hand over his mouth, gulped. Couldn't even look at Kyle. Definitely not open to a mending moment.

"What's going on?" The serene voice of his mother made Kyle jump. She set down a sack of groceries. A potato rolled from the top, plopped down onto the counter. Her eyes grew worried, wrinkles swimming around them.

His dad just kept looking down, said nothing. Kyle took one for the team. "Oh, hey Mom." His voice shook. Not nearly as much as his hands. He swept his hands behind him. "Nothing. Just talking. I guess…Dad didn't have any luck again." Not really a lie, possibly the truth, just sort of hiding the absolute truth.

Always the easier parent, his mom bought into it. Not fully, though. She tried on a weak smile, flimsier than a house of cards. "Well, it looks like I just walked into a funeral."

And Kyle worried that might've been closer to the truth than she realized. Whose funeral could've gone either way, though: Kyle's or his dad's.

Kyle just couldn't take it.

As soon as his folks started talking about money, life returned as normal. His dad got mad, yelled a lot, blew Mom off in his quieter moments, whereas his mom fell into her usual routine of crying and hand-wringing.

Everything was back to usual. Like his dad hadn't threatened to kill him in the kitchen.

They didn't even notice Kyle as he stormed past them, flung open the door, and hopped on his bike. Alongside the gravel drive, he sped through the grass, trying to outrun the fighting he'd left behind.

His parents weren't the only thing he wanted to distance himself from.

The new-found friends in the cellar might not be as "friendly" as he'd first thought them. During all the craziness, they'd wanted Kyle to kill his father. A shocking thought, one he couldn't even imagine. It scared the hell outta him.

How could he have been so blind? Sure, the creatures were harmless; cute, even, not that he'd ever say that out loud.

But where had those images come from? What did they mean?

He'd never lost control of his own anger like that before. Once he'd had a playground blowout where he had thrown down with a buddy. Over dumb stuff he couldn't even remember. But by school day's end, no real damage was done, and they were back to being friends again.

This was different.

Kyle stood up on the pedals, brought the bike up to hair-whipping speed. On the lonely country road, he flew down a hill. Reckless, dangerously fast. He didn't care. Nothing mattered. Tears stung his eyes. The wind caught them, unrolled them back across his cheeks.

Come back, Kyle…

The voice hit him hard, right between the eyes with the impact of a baseball. He panicked, the bike getting away from him. The handlebars wobbled. The rest of the bike followed.

He dropped his feet to the ground trying to stave off a wreck. His feet caught, bounced, dragged, and sent him into the ditch. He flew off the bike, rode the natural tumble down the slight decline. Couldn't have planned it better if he'd actually possessed some mad moves.

Dazed, he sat up. Next to him lay the bike, the wheels still spinning. Other than a scraped knee—nothing new there—he'd got off easy.

Except, of course, for his pride. In the field beside him, he heard laughter. From out of the woods, two boys foot-raced toward him.

The first kid, the shorter and clearly younger one, reached him in no time. He knocked back his mop of hair with a head jerk. He wore a cool Daft Punk t-shirt, so maybe there was a little hope for this town after all.

"Dude, you okay?" Concern hardly colored his tone, as he asked the question around laughter. "I mean, you really wiped out."

Kyle stood, brushed himself off. "Yeah, no problem. Happens all the time."

"Whatever. I'm Jonah." Jonah turned, waited for the larger kid, hefty and tall, to join them. He'd slowed down, now walking toward them. With apple-red cheeks, blue eyes, and curly blond hair, he looked to Kyle like a Swedish foreign exchange student. "This is Dag."

Dag jerked his chin. "What up?"

"I am now, I guess," said Kyle. "I'm Kyle. Man, I'm kinda glad to see you guys. I was beginning to think I was the only kid around here." Kyle didn't like calling himself a kid but didn't quite feel right proclaiming himself an adult either.

"Nah, there's some others. But we're spread out. Kinda sucks," said Dag, finally reclaiming his breath.

"Yeah. Gotta take your fun where you can find it." Jonah

nodded back toward the woods. "Wanna hang? Got some cig-arettes."

Kyle didn't want to smoke, had no desire to—even though he knew he'd have to try it eventually, one of those secret rules to enter adulthood—but he didn't want to throw away a chance at new buds either. He shrugged, noncommittal. "Yeah, I've smoked before, not for me. But I don't mind if you guys do. It's cool."

"Cool, cool," said Jonah. "Let's bounce. You can leave your bike there. Ain't no one gonna bother it."

Used to the Kansas City crime rate, Kyle hesitated, then realized there was no one around. Jonah led them through the knee-high field of weeds, puffing on a cigarette. His breath-ing sounded bad, worse with the smoke pulling in and out. "You live around here?"

"Yeah. Just moved," said Kyle.

"No shit? You gonna go to Piedmont?" asked Dag.

"I guess. Wherever seventh grade is."

Dag nodded. "That'd be Piedmont. Shitty town can't even afford a shitty junior high. We're stuck there 'til eighth grade. Shit."

Already, Kyle felt better. At least he'd know two kids once school started in the fall. As long as he didn't piss them off or something.

Jonah pulled back a low-hanging branch and ushered them into a small clearing. Two rocks had been maneuvered in, Jonah and Dag's thrones no doubt. Between them sat a small pile of distinguished butts.

A human chimney, Jonah wasted no time lighting a ciga-rette from his existing one. "Sure you don't want one, dude?"

"No, that's okay. Thanks anyway."

Jonah and Dag sat on the two rocks. The newcomer, Kyle sat in the dirt at their feet. Hopefully, he'd work his way up to rock status one of these days.

"So, where you live anyway?" Jonah leaned forward, the lead interrogator.

"Oh, um, on Oak Lane. That old piece-of-crap house, the one made of stone and wood that's pretty much falling apart."

Jonah lowered his smoke, stared at his partner.

Finally, Dag cleared his throat, said, "Shit, man, you mean the old Winstead place?"

Kyle shrugged. "I dunno. My parents never tell me any-thing. But it's about, I guess, a mile that way and—"

"Dude! No one ever tell you about that goddamn place?" Jonah tittered.

"No. What's there to know? It sucks."

"Dude, it more than sucks. It's friggin' haunted. Shit, man, can't believe no one tol' you about that shitty place."

Frustrated, Kyle thought they'd never get around to telling their tale. But a deep rock of dread settled in his gut, one that seemed pretty reasonable considering what he'd left back in the house. "Well, I know there's some weird crap going on. But what else should I know?"

Jonah and Dag shared another look. Jonah passed his butt over to Dag, the better to prepare for the telling of the story. "I only know what I hear, man. But it's a lot. That ol' house has been abandoned for, like, forever. The last family that lived there all died. Some say the mother went crazy, stabbed her husband, their twins—"

"Triplets," interjected Dag.

"Whatever, dude! She killed everyone in the house. But nobody knew about it for a long time, right? It's not like every-one knocks on your door around here. Finally, someone, some church lady or something, came to see if they were all right. She found the husband dead in the front room. That was all it took for her to go get the sheriff. When they got back, the sheriff found all the other bodies. And they found the crazy lady in the basement. You know what the crazy bitch was doin'?"

"No."

"She was tryin' to burn the house down. Sittin' on the dirt floor trying to light it up. They say she went through thousands of matches, man. Everybody knows you can't burn dirt." Jonah rocked back, laughing.

"Crazy shit." Dag coughed around his words.

"Man," said Kyle, "that'd pretty much explain why my parents got the place so cheap."

"No one wants to live there, dude! And now they say the Winstead family haunts the place."

Dag had been playing with his phone. Frankly, it surprised Kyle he even got service out in the boonies. Kyle's phone had been one of the first things to go once they moved.

"Here, check this shit out." Dag handed Kyle his phone.

Local Woman Slays Family, screamed the headline. Below that: *Dolores Winstead committed for life in Osawatomie mental facility*. The story rang true to Jonah's colorful recounting but carried no additional news, especially no mention of what could've possibly caused the woman to snap.

Dag took back his phone. "So, shit, dude, good news and bad news. The good news? You live in a haunted house. That's wicked cool. The bad news? It sucks for you, dude. Crazy shit." He shook his head as if saying: *glad I'm not you*. "Just bat-shit crazy."

"Yeah, it's crazy," said Kyle.

Yep, crazy pretty much described it. But Kyle also knew it as truth. And that the woman hadn't been nearly as crazy as Jonah and Dag or the rest of the town seemed to think she was.

By the time Kyle bicycled back home, the fight had gone out of his parents, but they still had plenty of anger left for him. Like a baby, they'd sent him up to bed without his dinner. Good. It gave Kyle more time to plan. Besides…after what had happened, he didn't feel right sitting around eating potatoes with his dad like nothing had happened.

But it had. And it was up to Kyle to save his family.

The creatures had been quiet since he'd arrived home. Which didn't feel right. He knew their reach was long, freaked him out they'd hit him up so far away. But he still felt their presence, felt them poking around the corners of his mind, feeling him out, prodding him with their crazy wishes. Planning.

Simply put, he couldn't wait for something to happen. He had to take the fight to them first.

In bed, he waited in the dark, awake, past midnight. Until his parents' not-so-shushed arguing had stopped. And then some. He hopped into his jeans, put on his sneakers, wore the same t-shirt he'd been wearing for days: his battle armor.

He slipped out of his bedroom, tip-toed past his parents' room, and down the stairs. First, he stopped by the breezeway. Gently, he eased open the door, which usually screeched like a stirred-up cat. In the breezeway, he found his weapon of choice. He picked up the plastic gasoline container, gave it a few good sloshes, feeling its reassuring weight.

The voices kicked in once he entered the kitchen. False, friendly, sing-songy voices…

What are you doing, Kyle?

We're your friends.

Not the adults who always want to hurt you.

The ones who must be stopped…

Kyle fought them. Tried to throw up mental blocks. Reminded himself he loved his parents, as screwed up as they were. Then his will weakened.

He worried about those days and nights he couldn't remember in the cellar. What the creatures had said to him, *done* to him. Had they programmed him to kill his parents? Taught him to hate? Gave him real adult feelings before he wanted them?

It pissed him off he couldn't remember.

He opened the cellar door. Quietly, but sternly, he whispered, "Shut up." And descended into the beasts' dungeon.

He hit the light, flicked on the flashlight. And the voices hammered him hard.

We're your friends.

Your parents hate you.

Your father despises you…

Wants to kill you…

Stop, Kyle. Listen…feel…

Kyle took a deep breath, as if that would expunge the heinous voices. His head pounded like a full-on construction site. He flung back the curtain. In his absence, the creatures had grown yet again. Maybe feeding on hatred. They wove together, hypnotic in their swirling, snakey bodies. Reaching forward, teasing, drawing back. Their peculiar music gelled into an angelic choir, all together, all beautiful. United as one. A peaceful, tranquil feeling…

Part of him wanted to continue, a part that seemed to be falling away from him. But he couldn't. He set down the gas can. Got on his knees, entranced by his friends performing their seductive dance. Then he curled up next to them, watched their bodies, their shadows jump in the meager light. So soothing… Eyes so heavy…

That's good, Kyle.
Don't fight us.
Just do as we tell you.
Destroy the older ones.

Kyle basked in golden memories, his mind a wide-screen of childhood events. But one image burned stronger than the others, practically burned a hole in his mind: *his parents.*

His parents who sometimes sucked and made him move and leave his friends behind to punish him for being eleven and…

The parents he *loved.*

With a small cry, Kyle jumped to his feet. "Shut up, shut up, shut up! I'm not gonna listen!" Scattershot, he moved the flashlight around the cellar searching for his gas can. Shadows played hide-and-seek. Creatures zipped up the walls like bats skittering away in a cave. But he found the container, something physical he could grasp.

What are you doing, Kyle?
Stop.
Listen to us.
We're your friends.

"Just…shut *up.*" The can weighed heavy in Kyle's hand. He gave it a good shake. Liquid sloshed up, seeped out a hole at the top. The pungent aroma of gasoline swept all of the falsely pleasant smells away. Using a heave-ho motion, he dumped the gas onto the stalks. "Here's your damn dinner."

No.
Don't do this.
You're killing us.
Killing us….
Killing….

From elsewhere in the house, a long and loud shriek penetrated his heart.

Mom.

The hellish stalks wilted, then sprang back up like a car dealer's air dancers, renewed with hope. But he couldn't deal with them now.

He dropped the can. Gas spilled, trickled a muddy path across the dirt. He ran, bounded up the stairs two at a time. Didn't stop. Hurdled up the next stairwell to the bedrooms.

His mother screamed again. Hellish, something he'd never heard her do before. Ice picks stabbed his heart, the damned voices screamed in his head, a wild, confused jumble. He tried the bedroom door. Locked.

"No, God, Robert, don't do—"

"Hold on, Mom!" Kyle put his shoulder into it. He bounced back with a grunt. His shoulder throbbed. He tried again. The house was old, the construction weak, the door gave, just a little crack. Still not good enough. He remembered the flashlight in his hand, brought it down on the knob. Did it again, this time in conjunction with another shoulder bash.

The door gave. Kyle flew in with it, nearly tumbled to the floor. Almost did it again when he saw the horrible sight before him.

His dad humming. Smiling sleepily. Casually sawing through his mother's ankle with a steak knife.

Screee, skritch, screeettt...

Blood darkened the sheet below her ankle, the bedspread heaped onto the floor.

"Dad! Stop it!"

Screee, skritch, screeettt...

His dad either didn't hear him or didn't care. Just kept about his work with the calm behavior he'd shown while destroying his salad.

Arms out, Kyle raced across the room. No idea of what he'd do. Until he did it.

He lassoed his father's neck. Using the momentum of the leap, Kyle ran into it and pulled him off the bed. They landed on the bedspread, Kyle on top, his hands still around his father's neck.

"Son?" His father's eyes cleared. He looked at Kyle, furrowed his brow. "What're you doing?"

Kyle didn't let up. He didn't—*couldn't*—trust his father. Not any longer. Not while those damned monsters had him.

Tears welled in both of their eyes. Kyle tightened his grip. His father's face turned red, then an angry purple. Kyle watched as his father's eyes dried up, cloudy, no one home. Rage replaced confusion. *Love?* He gripped Kyle's hands, ripped them away. Shoved Kyle over like he weighed no more than a baby.

Kyle rolled, sat up. His father retrieved his knife. Began humming again, the same melody the creatures had forced into Kyle's head. He brought the knife back over his wife's foot.

Kyle knew what he had to do. Knew where the weapon was even though he wasn't supposed to. But curious kids explore. He clambered up, whipped open the closet door. Dragged out the step stool, tip-toed onto it. His fingers explored the top shelf. An avalanche of boxes toppled over. And the gun spilled out of one.

With shaking hands, sobbing, he thumbed off the safety, aimed it at his dad's back.

"Dad?" Too soft, weak, a toddler's voice. "Dad! Stop! Don't make me kill you! But I will!"

He ignored Kyle.

Scree…scritt…scrik…

Tears flooded Kyle's voice, choked his words. "*Dad!* They got you! Don't listen to them! I don't wanna do this…but I have to! *Please…*"

Pointless. Too far gone. He wouldn't stop until his wife was six-feet-under gone. Kyle aimed. Closed his eyes. Bit his lip. And pulled the trigger on his childhood.

Krak!

The reverb slammed Kyle sideways, back into the closet door. He dropped, crying.

When he dared to open his eyes, he saw his father sprawled over his mother. One final hug. Blood spread across the back of his t-shirt, close to his shoulder. Kyle tucked the gun into his jeans, crawled over to his parents. Climbed up with the aid of the nightstand. He managed to roll his father off and to the floor. His mother's chest rose, lowered.

Still alive.

More tears bubbled over, something Kyle thought he'd put behind him. He was wrong. Serious wrong. He imagined he might never dry up.

He shook his mother's shoulder. "Mom? Mom? Don't leave me… Please, God, don't take them both…"

Her eyes fluttered open. She grabbed Kyle, pulled him to her. Hugged him so tight, too tight. Kiddy tight. And he didn't give a damn. He hugged her back.

"Mom," he said, "I gotta call 911. You're bleeding. Bad."

"Your father…" Her eyes filled with fear. "Where—"

"I took care of him. Don't worry." He glanced over the side of the bed, saw his father's unmoving corpse. And he hoped his mother wouldn't see him until later.

Quickly, Kyle bundled the bedspread around his mother's ankle. He tied it as tight as he could, a crappy tourniquet, something he halfway learned back in cub scouts. In a shaky, uncontrollable sob, he phoned 9-1-1. He cut the story short, just pleaded for the ambulance to hurry.

Due to shock, pain, maybe blood loss—Kyle couldn't afford to think about it, couldn't expend any more emotion—his mother lay calmly, hands folded. But awake. She stared at the ceiling, unblinking. Unlike her.

"Mom, I've got to do something." Kyle kissed his mother's cheek, squeezed her hand. "I'll be right back. Then we're leaving." After a quick check of her ankle—he couldn't tell for sure through the bedspread's thickness, but the bleeding appeared to have at least slowed—he stumbled out of the room.

"Kyle? Kyle?" From the room, his mother kept calling him, a broken record.

But he had one goal in mind, eyes set on the finish line. Kill the beasts before they killed again.

Half-lucid from his ordeal, from the craziness of it all, he didn't even remember walking to the cellar.

The voices had quieted, nothing more than whispers. Non-melodic, last-chance murmurs of life. Most of the stalks had crinkled up into old, black banana peels. Their corpses had stretched toward one another, possibly seeking brotherly comfort. The tallest of the bunch still stood tall, though it shook, vibrated, its mouth open. Screaming in a horrific whisper, its hatred so strong Kyle could almost touch it.

Kyle tossed another round of gas. He favored the eyeball stalk with an extra dose. The internal voices dissipated to a hiss. The stalks shriveled and collapsed on themselves. Their dried husks curled up into small kernels.

Finally, the voices stopped.

Except for another scream upstairs. Terrified he hadn't killed his father, Kyle raced up the stairs.

The door flew open. His father held his favored weapon: the bloody steak knife.

"What're you doin' to my friends, you little *bastard*?" The knife swung over Kyle's head, chunked into the stone wall. Kyle turned, nearly tripped. He gripped the rails, then throttled down the steps.

His dad roared, yanked the knife from the wall. Faster than Kyle'd ever seen him move, he zipped down the stairs.

"What'd you *do* to them? Goddamn you!" Kyle all but forgotten, his father ran for the dead creatures. He fell to his knees, screaming over the death site. "I'm gonna kill you for this, you little shit! You *hear* me? Gonna make you pay with your damn *soul*! They were the only things I ever cared about, the only things that understood me, my pain!"

Rattled, Kyle couldn't get a solid grip on the gun. With a tug, he freed it from his waist-line. It slipped from his hands, fell to the dirt.

Back on his feet again, his father came at him.

Kyle bent to snatch the gun.

The ground trembled. The walls shook. Plaster, dirt, debris fell from the rafters, snowed down. A pipe loosened, dropped, spat out a murky, dark liquid.

From within the earth, something groaned. The house shuddered as if alive.

Both Kyle and his father froze.

Kyle figured it for a fact. An earthquake—the Big One—ready to gobble them up, bring them back to the earth.

Beneath, something approached. The entire cellar trembled, wavering into double, triple vision.

The rumbling sound grew, a monstrous freight train bearing down on them.

Kyle covered his ears, thought the horrible noise couldn't get worse. It blossomed from a moan, pitched into a shriek. Agony, it felt like to Kyle, something he'd recently experienced.

The ground exploded. Earth erupted. From the six-foot diameter hole, a giant stalk, the mother of all stalks, shot out, quicker than Kyle's eyes could follow. Pink, wet, segmented, the body rose, kept rising, thumped into the top of the cellar. The ceiling cracked. More debris, including flooring from above, crashed down.

Kyle's dad screamed.

So did Kyle.

The beast's network of eye-covered stalks wagged around, then landed on Kyle's father. The beast's maw opened wide. Hundreds of crooked, dagger-like teeth clamped down on him, nothing but his boots showing, wiggling from the monster's jaw. Just as suddenly, the creature sucked back down into the hole. Its moaning retreated like traffic in the night.

The house stopped shaking. Kyle didn't. On unsteady legs, he stood. Retrieved the gas can. Warily, he stepped up to the hole, peeked over it to make sure the creature—the mother beast?—wasn't lurking, ready to gobble up Kyle, a father-son buffet. It probably didn't matter, not really. The beast had moved so fast, it would be impossible to outrun it.

He poured the rest of the gas down the hole, dropped the canister after it. Then launched the rest of the gun's bullets into the hole until he heard a reassuring *floomph* sound. Flames rose, nearly singed his hair and the tip of his nose.

Kyle listened. Nothing. Just the plinks and tinks of rafters shifting beneath the house's weight, telling stories of the past. One last touch, Kyle hefted up the bookshelf and buried the hideous garden beneath it.

"Earth to earth, dust to dust, hell to hell…something like that," said Kyle.

He wiped his dirty hands on his jeans, then raced up the stairs.

In the kitchen, he met his mother. Pale, out of it, lower jaw shaking. She held onto the door jam, the bedspread unraveled and trailing behind her like an unspooling mummy.

Outside, sirens wailed.

Kyle meant to be strong, he did. Strength is what it meant to be the man of the house. Instead, he collapsed into his mother's waiting arms. And wouldn't let go. Together, they stumbled toward the front door.

And beneath them, Kyle imagined—*oh, God, please let it be my imagination*—he heard something shrieking louder than the wail of the ambulance.

The Dental Dam Breaks

Oral hygienists are the chattiest people on earth, so thought Henry. Particularly when they jam tools and prod fingers in your mouth, rendering it impossible to reply to their incessant questions. Of course, finding a new dentist is like trying on a comfy pair of socks—when they fit, it's awesome; when they don't, blisters may develop.

"So, what do you do, Henry?"

The tube sucked at his mouth like a miniature vacuum cleaner. With a slurping sound, the tip of his tongue swept up, blocking the air flow.

"I mean, like, for work."

"Ah a ahhpha ahtiss."

"That's cool, that's cool."

Henry doubted the mohawked hygienist truly thought his graphic artist position was cool. No way could she have possibly understood him. Then again, she'd probably been schooled in dental translation skills. Either way, her blatant apathy made it clear she'd rather be anywhere but here.

Behind Henry, a timid voice peeped up. "Hello, hello, I'm Doctor Barrows." A hairy-knuckled hand appeared in front of

Henry. As Henry shook the hand, he couldn't help but worry about all that hand hair. He twisted, tried to see the dentist, but the awkward chair—a contortionist's dream chaise—held him captive. After all, if their relationship was intimate enough to allow this man to poke around inside his mouth, Henry at least wanted to *see* his partner.

The tube gulped down his remaining saliva. Henry managed, "Ha, Docta, I Herry."

"Nice to meet you, Henry." Dr. Barrows sounded less than gung-ho, no rat-tat-tat patter other dentists knocked off like teeth plaque. Rather, Barrows struck Henry as tentative, quiet. Maybe not a bad thing, really. At least Henry wouldn't be forced to talk. "I see you're in for…" Paper rattled. "…root canal surgery."

Henry's eyes snapped up like spring-coiled shades. "*Wha?* No! Cahity! *Cahity!*" Henry spat the tube out. It landed limply on his baby-sized bib, hissing like an angry snake. "*Cavity.*" He sat up, jacked a thumb toward his mouth, ensuring there'd be no question as to why he was in the dentist's chair. No, not a chair. *Torture rack.* But he damn sure wanted to make sure it was the *right* torture.

"Hmm. Guess Rita got confused over the x-rays." Assuming "Rita" was the raccoon-mascaraed hygienist, she'd apparently fled the scene of the near crime. Otherwise, Henry imagined, she'd be apologizing, trying to save her job. Good for her, not so good for Henry. For some reason, he felt more comfortable with a witness. "Ah. Here we are. Yup. A cavity."

Relief settled Henry back into the rack. He squirmed, attempted to make the chair hump nestle comfortably against his back.

Dr. Barrows sighed. Paper ripped. Seconds crawled. The dentist cleared his throat, whispered something inaudible. Then, he said, "Okay, Henry, here we go."

Henry still hadn't seen Dr. Barrows, but he sure as hell saw the huge needle waving in front of his eyes, a mutant hornet stinger. He clamped his eyes shut. Rubber-covered fingers kneaded his gums. Something hit the offending cavity. Electric pain struck. His stomach pot-bellied up, while his feet scrabbled at the bottom of the chair. Then the hypodermic dropped anchor.

"I'll give this a few minutes to work, then come back and check on you. You may need nitrous oxide. You're kind of a big guy. Ever had nitrous before?"

Already, a not unpleasant, slight tingling sensation crawled up his face. His lips turned elastically lazy, refused to mold words properly. "Yeth."

"Good, good."

Dr. Barrows's footsteps receded, dress shoes clacking across the linoleum. The soft rubber of tennis shoes swept in. Rita's face loomed large in front of Henry. Her eyes widened, her apathy gone but replaced by something far worse: *fear.* "Oh my God, Doctor Barrows is *crazy*," she whispered. "Don't let him know I said anything. Just *be* careful."

"Wai…*wha*? Wai a *mimmute!*"

Too late. Henry's mohawked angel of mercy whisked away on rubber-soled flats, his pleas unheard, unanswered.

What the hell's going on here?

Better to suffer through a sore tooth rather than go under the drill of possibly crazy Dr. Barrows. Henry pulled at the bib. Attempted to sit up. Suddenly, hairy knuckles exerted pressure onto his chest.

"Whoa, now, settle down, Henry." Barrows chuckled as he pushed Henry back into the chair. "It's not uncommon for people to panic before surgery."

Surgery? I'm just getting a filling!

"Nuh. Ah feelin' bettah."

A plastic shell clamped down over Henry's mouth and nose.

"Yep. Seen it before. Jitters. You just relax now. The nitrous will send you off to sleepy-land."

A hissing sound seeped out of the mask, bubbled into his ears.

Crazy. Hairy knuckles. Gonna drill my mouth.

Henry smelled nothing. He thought he tasted something slightly sweet, maybe not. While his body relaxed, his mind gyrated, wanting to rabbit in multiple directions. But his body persevered, coasting along on good-time waves.

Dr. Barrows's sigh echoed in Henry's head, far away as if from the far end of a tunnel. A blurry face floated in front of him. A fringe of lumberjack-orange hair surrounded it. Twin green specks of light bounced off Barrows's glasses. And Henry *still* couldn't make out the dentist's features.

"You know something, Henry? I feel like I can trust you." Barrows's voice sounded tired, yet lilting, soothing. *Sooo soothing.*

"Did you know dentists, as a profession, hold the highest rate of suicide?" continued Barrows. "It's true. I used to wonder why that was. Not any longer. 'Cause I know why." His voice dropped even lower, softer. "Guess it first happened—what?— two years ago. That's when I first heard the voices."

Voices? What's he yammering about? Where am I?

"I was finger-deep—finger-deep, sorta a dental joke—inside a patient's mouth. Then I heard singing. High-pitched voices, complete gobbledygook. But definitely singing. A chorus, a hellish chorus. Coming from the patient's mouth. Thought I was going crazy. I wrote it off, went home, and tied one on. But it kept happening. With more and more patients. And the worst part, Henry, the worst part…you know what the worst part was?"

Barrows paused again, clearly waiting for an answer. He was in for a long wait. Henry couldn't say anything even if he wanted to.

"Well, I'll tell you. When I took the drill into my patients' mouths…just doing my job…the voices screamed. Itty-bitty shrieks. Painful, *agonized* shouts. Like how a lobster screams when it's dropped into a boiling pot. Or…or rabbits. I…I was killing unseen, living beings…communities, perhaps…*worlds*. As Oppenheimer said, 'I have become death, the destroyer of worlds.' I couldn't take it, Henry. I tried to talk to my wife, my friends…they abandoned me, thought I was crazy. Yet…and yet, here I am. Still drilling, still operating, still… *killing*. What I'm killing, I don't know…not sure what…"

Barrows's voice traveled down a long hallway and dissipated like fine smoke. Then: silence. *Nothing.*

Henry woke with a jolt, drenched in sweat. Something banged inside his skull, his brain under construction. He struggled into a sitting position, checked out his surroundings.

The dentist. That's right. Cavity. But…what happened?

He had a vague recollection, a half-remembered dream that felt ready to completely immerse itself into oblivion. Something about…*Dr. Barrows?*

When he stood, he nearly toppled back into the chair. *No thanks, not today.* He felt his cheek. Chipmunked out to grotesque proportions, sore, but not too bad. Apparently, Dr. Barrows had completed the dental surgery while he was out cold.

With the back of his hand, he wiped drool from his chin. Then he stumbled into the reception area.

"Hi. Um, I guess I need to make a follow-up appointment with Doctor Barrows."

The receptionist stared at him, her face crinkling like cellophane. "I'm sorry, sir…you said 'Barrows'?"

"Uh-huh." Henry didn't particularly believe Barrows was an exceptional dentist, not by a mile. But, hey, Henry couldn't recall any pain, and that had to count for something.

The receptionist continued to stare at him, ol' stone-face. "We have no Doctor Barrows here, sir. Maybe you mean Doctor Stillson or— "

"No. I'm sure it's Doctor Barrows."

She craned her head around, bird-like, as if hunting for worms. Abruptly, she stood. "Um...wait right here, sir. I'll be back." She scuttled off.

After ten minutes, Henry had had enough. He tossed down his business card and hurried for the exit.

Weird. In fact, the whole day seemed weird.

Not that he remembered much.

As he rode down in the elevator, Henry dug through muddied recollections. Then he noticed the annoying Muzak.

Only problem was, the song spilled from his mouth, not from the elevator. And most assuredly not in his voice. Henry couldn't carry a tune, his warbling known to scare off cats. But this—*this*—sounded far worse. A sped-up record, a chorus amped up on helium.

Singing a toothpaste jingle.

UNDERDWELLERS

Darby sat at the back of the diner, eyes on the front door. Every time someone entered, the bell jingled and goosed her heart. She waited, desperately anxious to get the search for her brother underway. She'd been waiting too damn long as it is.

Kelton, the only brother she had, the big brother who looked out for Darby even when she didn't want him to. Try stopping him, a true force of highly caffeinated nature.

She only wished Kelton had been there to kick-start her ass into gear earlier. Kind of hard to do, though, since he'd vanished.

Six months ago, straight out of college, Kelton had landed a cushy, jealousy-inducing job at one of Kansas City's larger architecture firms. Sure, she was happy for her brother, but no one was more amped than Kelton. Golden boy made even more golden (if that metallurgic standard could be surpassed and Darby's parents certainly thought so).

Which made Kelton's sudden disappearance even stranger. His friends hadn't heard from him, his weekly calls home had stopped. Even more disturbing, Kelton's internet presence had dried up, blew away like so much cyber-dust. These days no one just stops, not cold turkey. Especially when you're Kelton, king of the party boys. Constantly, he posted pictures of his debauchery-filled nights whenever the feeling suited him. And it suited him often, wearing it with a brilliantly white smile and a model's self-confidence.

"More coffee, hon?" Clearly sick of Darby's coffee-only stake-out, the waitress folded her arms. The coffeepot dangled from a well-honed finger, tipped at a precarious angle. But, hey, life as a college student meant priorities: coffee first, food later. When Darby could afford it.

"Please." Darby inched her cup forward.

Kelton hadn't shown up for work for three months. When Darby spoke to Kelton's boss, he made it quite clear Kelton's future with Dignam and Boyce was questionable. Whenever Kelton resurfaced, though, he'd probably charm his way back into the company's good graces. If he *did* resurface, that is. Just like internet activities, people don't walk away from career-making jobs. They just don't; it was unheard of.

Her brother had always had a rock-solid head on his shoulders. Whenever he wasn't partying, of course. But he always remained sharp, sharp as wolf's teeth. Straight A's all through school and college. No surprise Dignam and Boyce had snatched him up. A huge surprise Kelton turned his back on it all.

Darby raised her cup. The bell jangled. Coffee spilled onto her hand. She shook her hand, clenched her teeth to avoid shrieking a litany of curse words.

Instead, she repeated the silent mantra her mother used whenever she stubbed a toe or banged into something: *dirty words, dirty words, dirty words...*

Naturally, Darby's parents were absolutely frantic over their missing favored child. That was the way they rolled, big drama being their favorite hobby. If drama lagged in the Smithfield household, they'd find a way to create some. Mountains out of molehills. Waiting for the sky to fall. Just as long as the drama didn't involve Darby. That special niche of drama tended to get swept under the rug.

But for once, her parents' drama seemed warranted.

At first, Darby thought Kelton had just embarked on one of his spur-of-the-moment, harebrained adventures: a booze cruise, an impromptu road trip to Mexico, something ludicrous and grandiose. Maybe even shacked up with a sugar momma somewhere. But Kelton's parties never lasted three months. It scared the hell out of Darby.

She should've searched for Kelton earlier. She wanted to, she truly did. After all, he'd comforted her, encouraged her, loved her when her parents had inexplicably shut that emotional door on Darby. He'd protected her, stood up to the internet bullies. He was always there for her. Especially after "The Incident."

Guilt coursed through her, rode her spine like ants on parade. She should've come to Kansas City earlier, no excuses, but she'd just entered the third semester of her final year at the University of Kansas, art her major. Something Kelton had encouraged ("You can do it, Darbs!"), something her parents had poo-pooed ("It's just a passing phase. Switch to business."). Surely, Kelton of all people—*especially* Kelton—would understand the importance of school and getting good grades.

Wouldn't he?

She sipped from her cup. Her hand shook. Coffee lapped up the side, settled. Caffeine stimulated her already fried nerves. As she lowered the cup to the saucer, it clacked several times before she landed it.

What had finally triggered Darby into action, what had kept her up nights, was the call she'd received fourteen days ago.

Asleep in her dorm room, a bird chirped. As she climbed

into consciousness, the bird sound regulated into her phone's tone. She hopped out of bed, banged a knee into the desk (*Dirty words! Dirty words!*), grabbed her jeans that had been hastily flung over the chair. She dug into the pocket, hoped she'd reach the caller before they hung up. It could be news of Kelton.

She looked at the number, didn't recognize it.

"Hello?" She cleared her throat. "Hello?" She despised the nervous strain in her voice, recognized it as loathsomely familiar. The same voice she'd developed during high school, especially after The Incident. Scared, uncertain, and above all, weak. She conjured iron into her voice and repeated herself. "Hello?"

No one answered. In the background, a low, insistent sound droned, almost but not quite electronic. An eerie sound.

"Kelton?" Although silent, the caller's presence was strong even over the phone. A jolt of pain cramped her gut, pierced her brain. Intensity, nearly supernatural in power, charged through the telephone. Like siblings do, she absolutely knew it was Kelton. "Talk to me, Kelton! Are you okay? *Say* something, any—"

"Dar…by?" Barely coherent, undeniably her brother. "Darby?" He whispered as if hurt. Or frightened. And if anything could scare her fearless older bro, it absolutely terrified her.

"Kelton, oh my God! Where've you been? Are you alright? Talk to me! You—"

"Help…me…sis…" He sounded hollow, a shell void of hope. "They've…got me…"

"Who? My God, what're you… Kelton, where are you?"

Wet, sluicing noises—*shhhh, swshhhh, sllsssss*—rose. So did Kelton's urgency.

"*Please*…help! You've *gotta*—"

Radio silence. Nothing.

Darby collapsed on her bed. Her arms shook, then the tremors moved to her knees and legs. On the other side of the room, Darby's roommate stirred.

Darby breathed in, out, harder, faster, desperately trying to control it. The wheezing followed, inevitable as death.

"Darby!" Kim raced around the center desk, whipped open Darby's top drawer, plucked out the inhaler, and crammed it into Darby's mouth with the nervous energy of a soldier plugging a grenade into a bunker's tiny window. "Breathe!"

Darby did. She inhaled the medicine, felt it work immediately. Her heart rate settled. She took another whiff. Braced her arms solidly against the bed. Her breathing slowed. Kim stood over her, hands over her mouth and nose, terrified.

Exactly how Darby felt.

"I'm okay, Kim. Thanks."

"What happened? Who was on the phone?"

"My brother."

"Kelton?" Kim sat on the bed next to her. "Is he okay?"

"No." Darby didn't know Kelton's condition. She just knew he was definitely far from okay.

That's when she decided. Grades be damned. She packed up her stuff and left for Kansas City in the morning.

Ting-a-ling!

God, she hated that damn diner bell! She wanted to yank it down, heave it into the street, but her already put-upon waitress would toss her out right after it. She couldn't afford a replacement bell, anyway, not on a college student's budget.

Already, she had to bite the bullet and hit up her parents to finance her search-and-recovery mission. Something she detested doing. Their relationship had been strained for a while anyway. That wasn't quite accurate; more like her parents had just been going through the motions with her because of societal expectations of how parents should act. It made her skin crawl asking them for anything.

Still, her brother came first. She had to foot the private detective's bill somehow.

The cops had been no help whatsoever. Clearly bored with the mundanities of looking for a missing person, they rote recited how many people went missing in Kansas City a year. Told Darby not to get her hopes up, most of the missing are never found, blah, blah, blah. Then Sgt. Stick-Up-His-Ass tossed the meager folder summing up Kelton Smithfield's life on top of a heap of forgotten souls in his out basket, then returned to his coffee in a jiffy, as if that took precedence. Turned his back toward Darby. Case closed! Or more like out of sight, out of mind.

On her way out the precinct door, Darby stopped and yelled, "So sorry my missing brother doesn't interest you, dickhead!"

After that, she hurried down the stairs and dashed to her car. The possibility of arrest worried her. Just a bit. But by the time she wheeled her car out of the parking lot, she broke out a smile—a dumb, ear-to-ear, buffoonish, open-mouthed smile. An honest smile. She hadn't had many of those lately. She laughed, hollow but hard-bought. Never in her life had she thought herself capable of such an act of rebellion. But she'd done it.

The way Kelton had taught her. He would've been proud.

If she ever got the chance to tell him.

It became apparent she couldn't find Kelton alone. Kansas City overwhelmed her, a big, sprawling place; bigger than Lawrence where she went to school; much bigger than the hick town of Karlton where she'd grown up. Where her maturity had been forced on her before her time.

Two weeks ago, she'd met Ed Vicenzo at a nondescript and unassuming—very much like the detective—coffee shop. When she'd arrived, Vicenzo was waiting for her. He stood, smiled, offered a firm handshake.

His appearance shocked her. He resembled his website photo accurately: balding, paunchy, short, and sweaty. Immediately she liked him for his warts and all self-acceptance.

"Pleasure to meet you, Darby. Coffee?"

"If you're buying, I'm injecting."

With a snort, he scraped his chair back, stood to catch the waitress's attention, and spun a stubby finger in the air: *the usual*. Then he sat back down. "Best damn coffee in K.C."

"How can you tell? There's, like, thousands of coffee shops."

"Okay, fine. Best cup I've tried. Or, hell, best one I can remember. Tell me 'bout your brother." He folded his hands on the table. Friendly Ed morphed into serious Ed. Serious lines rippled across his forehead.

She told him.

He sat back, massaged his cheeks with a gummy sound. Then he spoke through his hand like someone trying to cover bad breath. "Wow. This *is* strange. I mean, your brother isn't really the kinda guy who vanishes." Quickly, he added, "Hey, not that I'm trying to worry you, you understand."

"I've already heard the uselessness of looking for lost people act from KCMO's finest."

"Yeah, they're peaches, right?"

"Overripe and sour. But you've had luck finding missing people. You're supposed to be good."

"Well, Darby, tell you the truth, you kinda hit the nail on the head. A lot of it is luck. A little smarts. Mostly, the right connections. Connections I've got in barrels." Serious Ed turned dire. He leaned forward. "Some of what the cops told you is true. A lotta guys go missing, and they're never seen again. And the fact your brother was successful, had everything going for him…" His next thought faded away.

Darby finished it for him. "You think he's dead."

Ed's eyes went south, his chin nodded north and south.

"He's not. I talked to him a couple days ago." She told him about the call.

Ed gave his cheeks another solid workout. "Okay. Five hundred dollar retainer plus expenses. And by expenses, I mean if anything gets dangerous, you'll have to pay more."

"Fine and done. How dangerous do you expect it to get?"

"You never know. Maybe I've watched too much TV. But it's always wise to expect the worst. And I'd advise you to do the same."

"Expect the worst, hold out for the best."

"Or somethin' like that. Alright, let's start with Kelton's buddies…"

The next forty minutes were a solid question-and-answer session. His thorough nature encouraged her. Yet when she hadn't heard from him in nearly a week, panic set in. Constantly—for lack of anything better to do—she reread Vicenzo's reviews, reassuring herself she hadn't been rooked. Small town girl in the big city and all.

After another week of sweating it out in her lousy hotel room, Vicenzo finally called. Said he had a good lead. But he needed to tell her in person.

And this time when the infernal bell above the door clanged like a cathedral bell, it finally signaled the entrance of Ed Vicenzo. A blind black man followed him.

She stood, waved her hands in a silly, exaggerated—but couldn't be helped—fashion. "Over here, Ed! Over here!" Embarrassed, she sat down, ashamed she'd overcompensated for the blind man's benefit. Whatever the hell was he doing there?

"Hi, Darby. This is Vince. Vincent Durand."

Durand switched his cane from one hand to the other, stuck out his right hand. He aced the targeted area first try, fingertips pointed toward Darby's chest. She shook his hand. He held it for a beat, squeezed harder. At first, she'd pegged him as a weak old man. His face displayed a life hard lived, his gray whiskers weathered by many seasons. But his grip held solid, strong as a man half his age. "Nice to meet you, Darby. Call me Vinnie. Everybody else does." His voice had a nice, deep fluidity, a soothing tone, one that could fix a hostage crisis just by the timbre.

"Fine. Vinnie." She sat, puzzled. If the blind guy had an idea about her brother's whereabouts, why the necessity for his appearance? Ed could've easily relayed the information to Darby.

"Coffee here's okay, Darby," said Ed. "Can't touch *Bean Seeing You*, of course."

"Of course." Before the two men settled into the chairs opposite her, she hit up Ed with the million dollar question. "Where's Kelton?"

Ed patted the air in a condescending manner. A move she hated and had experienced too often from so-called authority figures. "Hold on. I'll get to that. The news may be good. Maybe not so good. Just don't get your expectations up. There might be a complication that—"

"For God's sake, just get to it. I'm a big girl."

Vinnie listened to the interchange with a hint of amusement. He drew his lips tight together. The corners of his mouth upturned, wrinkles swam around them. Even though he wore dark glasses, he appeared to be focused unwaveringly on Darby. Kinda creepy.

"Okay, yeah. I heard from one of my sources. Reliable guy. Your brother was seen about a month ago with the Underdwellers." He raised his eyebrows, waited for his revelation to sink in.

"The Underdwellers. What? A band?"

"No, not exactly. Well, sort of. I mean, not of the musical

variety." Vinnie chuckled, shook his head. "They live underground."

"Underground." Darby's hopes sank. Maybe she'd aligned herself with a charlatan—or a lunatic—after all. "Explain."

Ed's gaze darted about the diner. He lowered his voice to a near whisper. "Just like it sounds. The Underdwellers—and you'd better never let them hear you call them that—live underground. Beneath Kansas City."

"Uh-huh, right. And a nuclear explosion transformed them into mutant monsters that—"

"*Darby*." Vinnie thumped his cane onto the floor like a judge's gavel. "I suggest you hear the man out. Believe me…the Underdwellers are nothing to make light of."

"What? Are you one of them?"

Darby practically heard—*felt*—Vinnie's eyes narrow. "Girl, just 'cause I'm blind, you think I'm homeless? That what you think? Let me tell you something…" He jabbed a finger inches from her nose. "…I have a nice home up on 39th street, cost a pretty penny, too. I've got a decent job, teaching at the UMKC. Sociology. I have—"

"I'm sorry, Vinnie. Peace, okay? It won't happen again." Chastised, she tossed up *I give* hands. Anxiety didn't give her a right-to-be-rude card. Not that she'd admit it, but Vinnie was right: she had made the homeless presumption. More than willing to derail the train of awkwardness, she turned to Ed. "So these Underdwellers…they're homeless people? Can't really see Kelton hooking up with them." She almost added "No offense, Vinnie," but realized she'd be back where she started.

"Darby, he may not have had a choice. Yeah, some of the Underdwellers are homeless. I guess you'd say they all are now. But they're not the lounge-about-alleyway drunks everybody associates the homeless with. The Underdwellers are the forgotten, the embittered. Souls who were thrown away by people up top. And they're *angry*. The majority are savages, absolutely out of control. They don't make up top appearances often, but when they do, pray you're not on the streets. Violent crimes, murders, sometimes for food, mostly for the hell of it. I mean, they don't need cash anymore. Have no use for it. Nothing in our society matters to them. And rumor has it they're cannibals."

"More than rumor," sniffed Vinnie.

Ed stopped, shot a nervous look at Vinnie. With both men so strong in their conviction, clearly frightened, Darby knew they weren't crazy. And it froze her to her inner core.

"And you're saying Kelton joined these…Underdwellers?"

"Not necessarily. Sometimes they take people. For what, who knows? Some say they eat their captives, others say they use them as sex slaves…"

Darby cringed. The thought of her brother being sexually abused forced her eyes to moisten. But she held her tears in check. Only little girls cry.

"…some say they just physically beat them, break them emotionally, physically, and mentally to the point where they become one of them. A beast." Ed took one of Darby's hands in his. She flinched, yanked her hand away.

"They took Kelton?"

"That's what a source of mine says. Happened about three months ago. Which fits into the timeline of things."

"Your source… Did he say if they hurt Kelton?"

"When my source saw the Underdwellers, he hid. And watched. A guy fitting your brother's description sounds like he was their latest…acquisition. Apparently, he put up quite a fight, too."

Definitely her brother. Darby closed her eyes, sought out her quiet place, the place Dr. Sherlasky had told her to visit in times of stress. She couldn't find it; closed, shuttered, the

"Gone Out of Business" shingle up.

"Darby? Darby, you all right?"

Ed's voice sounded tiny. Her hopes felt even tinier.

Dear God, please let Kelton be okay, don't let him have been abused...

She couldn't bear that, anything but that. Suddenly, she felt very weak, fragile around the edges. Probably how Lot's wife felt when she glanced back at Sodom and turned to salt. When the Bible meant a damn in Darby's life.

"Darby?"

Darby swam back, anchored into resolve. The way Kelton had always been, solid; the way he had always wanted her to be.

"Okay, let's go then."

"Um, come again?" said Ed.

"I assume you're going underground to find Kelton. I'm going with you."

The two men chuckled, a sexist good ol' time. She swore if one of them dared pat her hand, she'd stab a fork into his offending fingers.

"Hold up a minute," said Ed. "You're not going anywhere. We decided—"

"'We'? What's this 'we' crap, Ed? I'm going down there with or without your help. And why in hell's an old, blind black man deciding my brother's fate and not me?"

Another thump of the cane. "Now, hold on there, Darby. You're gettin' dangerously close to the racist's edge. Yeah, I may be all of those things, but they hardly have anything to do with my abilities or—"

"Abilities? You can't see, for God's sake!"

With a heavy sigh, Vinnie turned toward Ed, then back to Darby. "Challenge accepted, girl. And since, for whatever reason, you threw down the race card, let's start there. You're a blonde-haired, blue-eyed, white protestant…24 years…no, 23 years old. But something bad happened to you in the past, something that changed you. You're bitter, more than someone your age has any right to be. Raised in Kansas, small town I'm guessing from your accent. You're lonely. You have friends, none very close, more like casual acquaintances. You don't wear perfume but smell like cocoa butter. Let's see…I could give your weight and bra size, but I've found women don't care for that too much."

Darby sat back, stunned. He'd hit everything on the nail, banged it good. She wanted to write it off as a cheap parlor trick. Or maybe Ed had filled him in. But she hadn't told Ed about her past. Her own personal shit-storm that didn't even make it into the local newspaper.

Vinnie grinned, waited for an acknowledgment. A friendly, warm grin.

Darby let out a laugh. Not because anything struck her as funny. Just a way to diffuse the tension, hers more than theirs. "Yeah, let's keep quiet about the weight. Vinnie… God, I'm sorry." He offered a gentlemanly nod. "I'll watch my presumptions. And no more racist, ageist, anythingist—"

"I'm used to it, Darby. And don't go making promises you can't keep. Old dog, new tricks and all that. I know you don't believe you're racist. No one does. But we all are, some more than others, even me. Can't be helped. Instinctual, like a dog. Imprinted on our collective consciousness."

"You truly believe that?"

"I truly do. But enough ethics lessons."

"Yeah, Vinnie's pretty amazing, isn't he?" said Ed. "One of my more-valued assets. Everyone always underestimates him. He knows the underground. Knows the tunnels, the things to watch out for. More importantly, he knows a few of the key players down there."

"But...how do you know them?"

"Years back, I wrote a thesis about their fascinating society. Got to know a few of the leaders. Now, I don't know if they're still living or still in charge, for that matter. But they'd kill you on sight if you tried to go down there without me."

"Um, and again, you're not going," said Ed. "I can't allow—"

"Try and stop me."

"Dammit, Darby, I don't even want to go. But Vinnie talked me into it. He—"

"I'll double your pay. Triple it."

Ed looked down at his hands, clearly weighing the offer. "I can't accept your money. It'd be taking advantage of your grief. Mom raised me better than that. And you'd probably be facilitating your own death. No way."

"There's no way I'm not going. Point me in the right direction."

"Jesus Christ." Ed looked upward as if pleading for Jesus's help. "Not even the cops will go down there, Darby! Hell, they don't even want to acknowledge the Underdwellers' existence. You're *not* going. I *won't* do it."

"I'll find a way. I always do."

"You listen to me, and you listen *good*, Darby." Suddenly Vinnie sounded like everyone's stern grandfather. "The underground isn't any place for a young girl. You'll—"

"Oh, wait! Hold on! *Now* who's being sexist and ageist?"

Vinnie turned toward Ed and shrugged. "Touché. But there's another reason I'm valuable down there. Something you don't have, Darby. You've got to rely on other senses than sight. Down there everyone's like me. Even playing field. Senses other than sight are the only things that'll keep you alive. I highly doubt—no presumptions—your senses are that honed."

"I can take care of myself." She opened her jacket, flashed the .38 Special revolver she'd liberated from her father's safe.

Ed conceded and sat back with folded arms. Smart man.

Vinnie laughed. "I do believe she can, indeed." Even smarter man.

On a quiet downtown street, Ed parked his car. From the back seat, he gathered his backpack and rummaged through the contents. Vinnie sat shotgun, pulling his lower lip.

Darby wanted to get the show on the road, save her brother, end it with a "happily ever after." Terror coursed through her like blood, pumping in and out of her heart. She whiffed her inhaler and pocketed it, hoping the men wouldn't notice.

"Asthmatic?" asked Vinnie. "I smelled the drugs when I met you. Just thought it was one of those things better left unmentioned."

"Darby, for God's sake," said Ed, "that's just one more reason why you shouldn't go down there. Asthmatic and walking through that…that crap is just—"

"I'm going." Standing firm, taking no prisoners. *Booyah!* "How're we getting there?"

"You'll see." First out of the car, Vinnie stretched. He brought nothing with him, just his rumpled self and quiet confidence. Darby assumed he didn't need a weapon. His hyperhoned senses probably packed more firepower than she or Ed had. Clearly, she was ill-prepared for this impromptu trip, but she wouldn't postpone it, absolutely not. If she did, her common sense would catch up to her, keep her safely ensconced at home. Crazy or not, she fully intended on going down.

Ed strapped on a backpack and quickly set off with Vinnie.

Darby hustled to catch up, half-suspecting they meant to ditch her. At Eighth and Washington, they entered a small, uninhabited tunnel, one apparently forgotten by most commuters once new freeways became all the rage. The cement foundations had begun to crumble. Even the graffiti looked forlorn and aged, tipped with psychedelia, hieroglyphics from the past: *Make Love, Not War; Peace; Keep on Truckin'*. A thin sidewalk edged one side, probably built more for utility workers than pedestrians. Chunks of it canted up like shark fins in a dark, gray ocean. Traffic swished by overhead, then receded into the night.

Half-way into the tunnel, Ed stopped. An old metal door sat in the cement. Based on the rust, it hadn't been used in years. Ed knelt in front of a corroded keyhole and dug into his backpack.

"Shouldn't take much to get it open. This door's the fastest, safest access for us. Hold the flashlight, Darby." The flashlight weighed a ton, an industrial job, but Darby held the beam steady. Ed slipped two items—both looking like nail files, only thinner—into the hole and jimmied them around. Something clicked. He stood, whipped out another tool, this one similar to Kelton's T-Square. Ed slid it into the slot next to the door, then yanked. With a groaning crunch, the door opened.

"Okay, Darby, last chance," said Ed.

"It's Kelton's last chance, too."

"Fair enough." Ed reached into his seemingly endless bag of tricks, pulled out a hard hat, complete with safety lamp. He strapped it on, looked ridiculous—but Darby couldn't help but feel a tinge of jealousy—and flipped on the light. "Let's go. Darby, keep the flashlight. Hold it out to your side as far as you can."

While Darby pondered that cryptic instruction, Ed slipped in through a foot-long opening. Darby set to follow, but Vinnie grabbed her shoulder. "Hold up a sec."

"Why?"

"You'll see."

Impatiently, she waited. Seconds stretched into agonizing minutes. In actuality, probably not, but to Darby, it felt like valuable time slipping away. "Can I go now?" As soon as she'd said it, she thought she sounded like an impatient little girl longing to cure her boredom.

"Go," said Vinnie.

Darby squirreled through the opening. She realized why Vinnie had her wait. The door led to a small room, four by four at most, nothing but a closet. Her flashlight landed on an old ladder sticking up against the grade of the tunnel's curved wall. It vanished into the floor, a tight fit. She wondered how Ed had managed it as big as he is. But she heard his heavy feet clanging down the ladder.

"Into the rabbit hole, girl," said Vinnie, his face framed in the door's opening.

Although bolted to the wall, the ladder wobbled at her touch, unstable. Darby took a deep breath, caught the ladder between her hand and flashlight and started her descent. The air had that odd smell of dirt: filthy, yet fresh at the same time. As her head lowered to floor level, she bid a silent farewell to the last of the light. She slipped into darkness, thankful for the heavy flashlight. The heft of it would make a decent weapon, too, should the need arise, and she truly hoped it wouldn't.

If it happens, I'm ready. Bring it.

False courage buoyed her. Then insecurity and fear pulled her under.

Okay, maybe don't bring it. Just bring my brother.

The ladder went on forever. Seemed to, anyway. The flashlight slowed her progress. Above her, she heard Vinnie enter the closet. The door slammed with a rumbling *dumph*. To Darby, it sounded like a coffin closing for the final time.

Ed landed safely, his head light beaming up at her. Never one for heights, Darby kept her eyes on the moss-encrusted brick wall in front of her. Finally, her feet splashed down into mud. Squelchy and sticky, but nothing had ever felt so blessedly beautiful. In no time, Vinnie shimmied down, comfortable as a sewer rat in his surroundings.

Darby studied the tunnel they'd entered. Brick walls, layered with a thick, dark substance Darby couldn't identify—nor did she want to—formed an arch above them. Fallen cables lay half-buried at her feet. Old wooden supports on the ceiling had long rotted away into splinters. Honestly, she thought it not nearly as bad as the men had described and said so.

"Girl, we're not underground yet! This is just the passageway." Again, the two men shared a chuckle, and Darby was damn sick of it.

Vinnie commanded the lead. Ed, more than willing to relinquish it, fell back next to Darby. "This used to be a trolley tunnel. Nearly a hundred and twenty-seven years old, by my estimation. Took folks from downtown to the Bottoms and then some. But with the advent of cars, folks didn't need it anymore. Just sealed it up and forgot about it."

"Where's it go?"

"Into the city."

The city. What the hell?

Ed stopped, turned to Darby. "You doing okay?"

"I'm *fine,* dammit!" Ice chilled her voice. She knew what Ed was doing: trying to big brother her. But she already had a big brother. She intended to keep Kelton that way. And she sure as hell didn't need to be coddled like a little baby bird every step of the way. "Sorry. Didn't mean to snap. I'm fine. Really. And I'll keep being fine. Can *you* be fine?"

"Best I can do is try, Darby. Still don't like it. It's dangerous as shit down here."

Darby had never considered "shit" dangerous, but Ed's constant warnings did nothing to allay her fears. Hard enough to control her fear without added drama.

"Always keep one hand free," continued Ed.

"Mm-hmm, sound advice." Vinnie had scurried so far ahead of them, Darby couldn't see him. But his deeply resonant voice of authority echoed everywhere, God speaking from on high.

"Why?" She'd already considered carrying her gun in her free hand.

"You need one hand free at all times. It could save your life. You'll need it to help guide you. So choose wisely: the gun or the flashlight. Make that decision count. And if you pull the gun, don't be afraid to use it. Because these…things down here won't hesitate to kill you. Just don't think of them as people. They aren't. Not anymore."

"I'll be ready." Darby's brave alter-ego talked a big game, but she didn't know if she could shoot anyone, Underdweller or otherwise. Hadn't considered it, not really. But if it meant saving her brother's life, hell yes, she'd rise to the occasion.

Muddy water soaked her shoes and socks. Large clogs of mud clung to her feet and weighed her down as if gravity had doubled below ground.

Ahead, a small light bobbed and danced like a firefly. Ed saw it, too. In a militaristic manner, he held up his hand to stop. From a distance, a man's voice grew louder. Singing.

"Buffalo gals won't you come out tonight, come out tonight…"

"Smoke! Hey, Smoke!" called out Vinnie. Darby heard Vinnie's stride pick up, rapid splashes practically skimming the water.

Ed lowered his hand, nodded at Darby: *It's okay.*

When they reached the source of the light, Darby saw Vinnie sitting cross-legged next to a grizzled, old hobo on a ramshackle elevated platform. Darby caught herself, realized the homeless assumption she'd just made. Then again, the man was obviously homeless. *Duh.* Sometimes a hobo is just a hobo, assumptions be damned.

The two men were involved in a quiet conversation, occasionally broken by companionable laughter, just two old friends catching up. Darby assumed the rickety wooden platform they sat on had been an old trolley station loading area. The faded sign behind the men confirmed her suspicions. *Down*, something, something, *Trolley*, smudge, fade to nothing.

In front of the seated men, a small fire burned beneath a coffee can, probably not the safest place to cook, but Darby imagined the hobo knew that or simply didn't care.

Ed started up the steps, each footfall grinding like teeth beneath his weight. Darby didn't want to chance the possible death-trap, but better than staying below by herself.

Yeah, some badass you are.

Oh, shut up!

"Smoke, these are my friends, Ed and Darby," said Vinnie.

"Pleased ta meet ya." He doffed his shredded knit cap, coughed out a hearty laugh that seemed inappropriate for a social greeting. "*Ar, yar, yar!*"

"Smoke and I go way back," said Vinnie.

"Way back," Smoke confirmed. "*Ar, arf, yar!*"

"I was just tellin' him 'bout your brother, Darby. Ed, you got that photo on you?"

"Sure do." Ed took a step forward. The platform shook like a minor earthquake. Darby felt the reverberations from her stomach into her bladder. She gripped the railing until it settled. From his pocket, Ed plucked out Kelton's photo.

Smoke grabbed it. The photo wagged in his gloved hand as he studied it, one eye shut. "Can't be sure, but… Yeah, I think

I 'member this boy. Some time ago. The U.D.'s dragged him kickin' and screamin' through these parts. Carried him right on down the line."

"Was he hurt?" asked Darby.

Smoke stared at her, mouth gaping open, before unleashing his hell-hound of a laugh again: "*Arf, ar, arrrr!*" Once he got that out of his system, he said, "Hard to say, girlie. The way he was carryin' on, though, I'd put money on it that he was just fine."

Hope. Much needed hope.

Vinnie nodded, clapped Smoke on the shoulder. "We got a job to do. If I can, I'll stop by on the way back, sit a spell."

"I'd like that, Vinnie."

"Me, too."

Vinnie stood, turned sideways, and gracefully glided between Darby and Ed. He climbed down the stairs, no need for the handrail. Ed followed.

Darby said, "Thank you, Smoke."

"Don't mention it, girlie. You jes' be careful down the ways. *Arf, yar, yarrrrr!*"

Mesmerized, Darby watched the old man prepare his meal. He manipulated two sticks—not very sanitary by the looks of them—to fish out the coffee can's contents. He pulled his still-smoking bounty directly into his lap.

Darby couldn't help herself. She flashed her light onto his dinner. The creature he had cooked belonged to a species Darby had never seen. Black, singed fur covered its tailless body. A pale white tongue lolled out of its mouth, pointed teeth ringing it. And on the side of its head, nestled next to one another like darkly colored marbles, sat three open eyes.

Darby gasped, stumbled back. Her flashlight rose and alit on Smoke.

"Get that goddamn thing outta my *face,*" he growled.

"Come on, Darby" yelled Vinnie. "Sorry, Smoke, it won't happen again."

"See that it don't!"

Vinnie huffed, "Let's go, let's go."

Darby ran down the stairwell fast, her hand riding the rail. She wished she'd have brought gloves. A splinter sliced into her palm. The railing snapped crisply behind her like popcorn.

Vinnie stormed off. Darby and Ed broke into a near jog to catch up.

"I'm sorry, Vinnie. I didn't mean—"

"That might be a fine excuse in school, but you're in a different world now, girl! From now on you only speak when we tell you to and only do what we tell you to!"

"Alright." Again, her weak side shoved its way forward. If she could fistfight that sniveling part of her, she would. Teach her a thing or two. "Sorry."

"She didn't mean anything by it, Vinnie. Take it easy on her," said Ed.

They walked in silence for a while, allowing Vinnie time to cool off.

When Darby felt the air clear, all hostility holstered, she said, "Smoke didn't seem so bad, really. I mean, for an Underdweller."

Vinnie laughed, stopped. Darby bumped into his back. "Smoke's no Underdweller. He's just one of life's casualties. Yet he's still managed to hold onto some dignity and humanity. Even under such conditions. And he knows the rules. He pays no attention to the Underdwellers, and they ignore him. It's the city folks they got a bone to pick with. Believe me, you'll *know* when you meet an Underdweller."

She let Vinnie race ahead again. Quietly, she said, "Ed, that guy…Smoke. I saw what he was eating. It didn't look like any animal I've ever seen. And I think—pretty sure—it had three eyes."

Ed hung his head, looked at his feet. "Different rules apply down here, Darby. You eat what you can, anything to survive. Different creatures are on the plate, too. I try not to think about it too much."

"But, where did—"

"Darby, I *said*, 'I try not to think about it too much.'" He broke away to join Vinnie.

End of discussion.

They trudged at least two miles through the endless tunnel; there was no respite from the crumbling walls and muddy floor covering. Ahead—*finally*—the tunnel ended, just ran smack into a dirty gray and red brick wall. To the right stood another unsound wooden platform.

"End of the line." Vinnie turned toward Darby, aimed a sharp barb her way. "No backin' out after this. If you're scared, turn tail."

"You're kidding, right?" Darby had something to prove. Not only to herself, but to Vinnie in all his condescending glory. "Want me to lead?"

"Heh. That ain't gonna happen. Up we go." Vinnie tackled the wooden steps with gusto, side-stepping the weak spots as if he had a GPS implanted into his brain. Darby did her best to mimic his path. No doubt a scurrying rat with one misplaced step could take down the stairs. They reached the top. Worried about Ed's extra weight, Darby pinpointed the safe spots with her flashlight. She needn't have bothered. Ed moved fleet-footed with the grace overweight men inexplicably carried.

Ed tugged on another rusted metal door set into the shadows. This time he didn't need his breaking-and-entering tools. The door opened easily. "You want point, Vinnie, or do I take it?"

"You're the boss, doesn't matter to me. But as soon as we run into the U.D.'s, it's probably best if I'm the first person they see."

"No argument here." Ed gave a little bow and swayed his hand. "Lead on."

Darby caboosed the trio, not her favorite position. A cool breeze caressed the back of her neck, soft as a ghostly whisper. Goosebumps hatched on her arms, the fine, minuscule hairs standing at attention. She looked behind her, saw nothing. Just in time, she swiveled back around. One foot wavered in open space. Her hands rotated wildly, her body perched on an uneven foot. Ed reached out, snagged her arm and pulled her to him.

"Darby, you have to be careful, dammit! Listen to things around you, echoes, everything! *Feel* the difference between enclosures and open spaces!" Ed flashed his helmet light downward. She'd nearly tumbled down a steep set of cement stairs.

Vinnie's head bobbed into the circle of light. "We tried telling her, didn't we?"

"I know, yeah, I know," groused Darby.

Ed grabbed her shoulders and gave her a little shake. "Look, I know you're worried about your brother, but you've gotta get your head straight down here. Nothing can occupy your thoughts but survival. Believe me, it's the only thing the U.D.'s think about."

Darby froze, stiffened at his touch. "I will…just *please*… let go."

"Sorry, sorry." Ed backed away. He hung his head, shamefaced, as if he'd punched her in a fit of rage. Honestly, the end result felt the same on Darby's end. "Tell you what, how 'bout I follow you?"

Darby nodded, tried to affirm verbally. She cleared her throat, banished her weak inner self, and said, "Alright, I'm ready."

She pointed the flashlight down, eyes locked on her feet. Deep and squat, the stairs appeared to be made for men with longer legs than hers. As a safety precaution, she did a one-two plant on each step before proceeding to the next. She touched the wall, planned to trail her fingers along it. Quickly she retracted her hand. Thick, mucous-like sludge covered her fingertips, a blood-moon color. Repulsed, she risked the descent with only her legs to guide her. If her slow going bothered Ed, he didn't let on. Several times, she risked a look beyond her feet, couldn't see or hear Vinnie. Couldn't see or hear anything for that matter. A crazy thought poked her mind: *What if I get vertigo and tumble down the steps? What if I go out of my mind and fling myself down?*

The downward plunge lasted for a good half-hour at least, a descent into the middle of the earth. Or maybe the bowels of Hell itself. Her ears plugged, then just as suddenly popped open.

Who built these stairs? And why?

The humid, suffocating air lifted. Icy fingers encased her in a cocoon of cold. An active breeze blew by her, lifting her hair. A welcome sign they were still tenuously linked to the world above—the real world. Perhaps it indicated movement around them.

The stairway took a sudden turn. Her feet stubbed onto solid ground. Carefully, she inched her toes out beyond the range of her flashlight onto the ground to ensure no more surprise steps lay in waiting. Down here, mud had dried to dust, sprinkled over what looked like a brick-inlaid road.

I don't think we're in Kansas anymore, Toto.

When she moved the light up and around, she nearly dropped it.

A city. Decomposing, dilapidated buildings lined both sides of the narrow road. A ghost of a once-thriving downtown area, now dead. No civilization, no life, like everyone had been suddenly blasted into dust. She thought cars belonged down here, wondered what had happened to them, then realized how stupid that thought was. Surely the inhabitants had been given time to evacuate before the city…well, before it ceased to exist.

Pitch black, a black so solid it manifested into its own physical entity. Darby grabbed her flashlight tight, held it to her chest, her saving beacon. She imagined how horrific it would be down here without it.

Glass in the buildings' windows had long ago given way to rot or vandalism, the frames long gone. Most buildings still stood—at least partially. Brick or cement foundations propped up their skeletal remains. Remnants of fallen—or foraged—building construction cluttered the building fronts. Darby looked up, half-expecting to see stars spread in the black night skyline. She saw only shadows, some deeper than others. Even in total lunar eclipses, a ring of hope always shone.

Vinnie joined them. "Take a good gander, girl. Get it out of your system. It's something, isn't it?"

Darby wondered if Vinnie had actually ever seen it. But it truly *was* something. At once awe-inspiring and terrifying. "What is this? How come I've never heard of it?"

"No one knows," Vinnie whispered. "Some say years ago—longer than anyone still living could verify—city planners just started adding more stories to buildings, paved over the old ones. Others say it's part of the Underground Railroad, the refugee's own hidden city. Nowadays, people either don't know it exists, plum forgot about it, or don't want to think about it."

"But…where are the Underdwellers?"

"Quiet! *Don't* use that term down here. They're here. Just a matter of time."

Terrors—similar to the night terrors Darby frequently had—set her body trembling. Shadows darted to her left, her right, melted into larger ones. Unseen water droplets plipped and plopped and magnified into gunshot cracks. For a second (she didn't dare do it longer), she closed her eyes, tried to feel what Vinnie felt. Something—a minute sound, possibly an auditory phantom—hissed. Very far away. A whispered conversation. Or feet carefully negotiating swampy ground.

Like the sound she'd heard when Kelton had called her.

She opened her eyes and immediately dug her hand into her pocket until she felt the smooth, plastic comfort of her inhaler. She took a whiff, more of a precaution, a nerve-settler, than treating an attack.

"Okay, Darby?" asked Ed.

She nodded. "Yeah."

"Let's go," said Vinnie. "Imagine we'll be gettin' visitors soon. Let me do the talking. And do *not* draw your guns unless I say so."

The dreaded "matter of time" seemed to wind into hours. At every far-off click or clack, Darby's mind jumped, and her body followed. But nothing happened. Just ruins settling, she supposed. She thought she'd prepared for this, but her mind being a fickle lord and master proved her wrong.

They walked down the middle of the street like sole survivors of the apocalypse, the darkly ashen sky above them blotting out everything else in the universe. Darby heard a noise to her right, immediately identified the small but disturbing sound.

Oh, God, I know that sound!

Someone licking their lips. In predatory, hungry anticipation. She flashed the light to the right, shone it into the building's first-floor window. A speck of white swam by, then blinked out of existence in the otherwise black hole. Another *smack*. Darby backed up a step, matched stride with Ed. Safety in numbers.

The road curved, not a sharp turn, and led them up the hill. When they reached the top, Vinnie stopped.

"They're here. Stay calm."

Shit!

Calm was out of the question, not now, not in this alien landscape. Darby spun as if out of control, her light blazing a dizzying circle.

"Stop *moving*," hissed Vinnie. "They'll see it as a sign of aggression."

Darby stopped. Scooted a bit closer to Ed. This time she welcomed her surrogate big brother. Her shoulders rounded, she shrank, one step away from wrapping herself into a worthless crying ball of fear.

"It'll be okay," whispered Ed. But she could tell he didn't believe it either. Hard to read a whisper, but his voice had definitely wavered.

Then silence. They waited. For what, Darby could only imagine. No, she didn't need to *imagine*. She'd lived through the worst possible scenario before.

"Hello?" Vinnie's voice startled Darby, cutting through the silence like a motorboat on calm waters. "We mean no harm. I'm looking for Tulip. Tell him Vinnie would like to talk to him."

More maddening silence. Broken only by that far-off, sanity-challenging, constant, torturous drip-drip-dripping of water.

Whispers broke around them. A nest of hissing snakes, growing in number. A sudden shriek forced Darby's heart up against her ribcage.

"*Aieeeeeee!*"

"Raise your hands," ordered Vinnie.

Darby's first instinct was to go for her gun. Instead, she raised her hands but held onto the flashlight so she could see their visitors. She wished she hadn't.

Pale figures rushed from open doorways, filthy and scarcely clad. A ludicrous image of a clown car popped into Darby's mind, one clown after another impossibly piling out. Full throttle and bare-footed, the Underdwellers hurtled toward them, hopping over debris, splashing through mud. Darby pulled into herself, tried to find her quiet place, tried to bestow her full trust in Vinnie. She failed.

Long, wild hair draped over the savages' faces, impossible to distinguish male from female. A few carried torches. Some brandished weapons: rusted hatchets and wooden stakes. Shrieks rose, gathered into one monstrous howl.

And they kept coming. Coming to rape, then kill Darby. Running at her, insanity glowing in their eyes. Saliva streaked from open and toothless mouths.

"I'm a friend of Tulip's! Tell them Vinnie—"

A mud-covered hand slapped Vinnie. Darby didn't give a damn about his instructions now. She wouldn't just stand there and wait for death.

She jammed her hand into her coat pocket, felt the butt of the revolver. Behind her, strong arms locked around her, pinned her arms to her side. The beast hoisted her up, held her against his chest. A male crouched in front of her. His tongue lapped out, explored a full circle of his lips. He thrust his hips forward. His penis wagged up and down. Shrill laughter penetrated her mind, her soul.

Not again, dear God, this can't happen to me again…

Torches lit up the dark city. The Underdwellers led Vinnie away, the top of his head visible over the circle of his captors. Ed struggled with another group, took a blow to the head from the blunt end of a stake. A metal pipe bashed his legs, took him to the ground.

Slavering, laughing, drooling, grotesquely erect males closed in around Darby. One dove in, pressed a solid steel finger into her belly's flesh.

Darby screamed, louder than the chaos around her. She kicked her feet, hit one beast in the shin. Another grabbed her legs, lifted them.

"*Nooo!*"

They carried her down the street. Darby rocked, tried to free her hand, grab the gun. She'd take out as many of the bastards she could, every last one of them. But arms secured her, hands caressed her, fingers pinched her. Tongues lashed at her.

I can't go through this! Not again!

Where no one would ever find her. Or know that she died. Deep, deep underground.

Her brain shut out the lights. A simple, little, vulnerable twig snapped in her mind.

Not again! Not…

"The Incident" occurred during the last, dreamy, near-summer month of Darby's Peyton High junior year. Everything had been going well. Her grades had stabilized into a solid and safe—but not too strenuous—"B" level. She'd enjoyed a couple dates with Chad Donovan, a sort of hot, kind of smart, yet not too arrogant football player. She could count on a small squadron of decent friends. Her parents weren't too much of a drag as long as she ignored them. They certainly had no problem ignoring her, all of their accolades reserved for Kelton.

Even when she'd been diagnosed with asthma, they'd rolled their eyes, wondered how much it would put them out, basically viewed her as a pain-in-the-ass.

Whatever. Parents didn't matter to teenagers, not in high school.

Over the last year, she'd blossomed from a gawky, tall, and awkward junior high school girl into a pretty woman of normal height. Or rather everyone else finally caught up to her height. She thanked the Fates she'd filled out in all the other right places, too. Naturally, she didn't see herself as pretty; that old lack of confidence proved a tough opponent to conquer. Every time she looked into a mirror, she saw flaws: the asymmetry of her face, how her teeth showed too much when she smiled, that damn mole on her chin she couldn't talk her folks into having removed. "It's your beauty mark," they had said. Whereas she saw it as a glaring, billboard-sized Mark of Cain. But if the new attention she'd garnered from boys gauged her spring awakening, then awaken she did, an ugly duckling into a swan.

Chad had been nothing but a gentleman on their dates. At the end of their second outing, they'd necked in his car a little bit. He didn't even go to second base, although her nether regions kind of wished he'd gone further. Not that she'd experienced anything beyond kissing before (self-pleasure hardly counted), having lived a rather chaste life. And, really, she didn't even know if she'd let Chad go there. But it warmed her with a nice day- and night dream. Always realistic, Darby didn't suffer any silly illusions she'd end up marrying Chad. On the contrary, she'd already set her mind on studying art at college, wouldn't let any pesky boy get in the way of her more important dream. Then again, maybe someday, if Chad lobbed the "L" word her way, she might just change her mind. Silly in a fluttery school-girl way, natch, but these days her entire world seemed fresh and new.

One night in early April, a car laid on the horn in front of her house. Chad's car. Before her dad could throw a bitch-fit, she zipped outside. Bent down to Chad's open window. Two of his buddies,—one riding shotgun, the other in back—had clearly been drinking. Dead beer soldiers lay at their feet, a loaded case next to Ron in the back.

"What's up, Darbs?" She loved the way Chad called her "Darbs." It always chilled her in a good way. Like a fine wine, she imagined.

"Not much." She swayed, testing her flirting skills.

"Hop in. Let's party!" The other boys roared in drunken agree-ment.

"I don't know…it's a school night and—"

"Ah, live a little, Darbs."

Of course, he had her at "Darbs." And the dimples, the ones she dreamily swam in. And, truth be told, she *hadn't* lived much, let alone a little. Her brother, Kelton, always lived like a rock star and Dad never crushed his fun. Why not her time? With friggin' football players, no less!

One last look behind her. No lights on the lower level. No peering eyes behind curtains. The coast appeared clear. "Alright, boys, let's go!" She couldn't believe she said it, couldn't believe she'd decided to leap on a spontaneous whim. Sponta-neity and she were strangers. Hell, she even had her future for the next five years mapped out. But this felt good, liberating.

"Chris, get the hell in the back seat. Make room for Darbs."

Chris obeyed, and Darby took his place. Even more daring, Darby scooted close to Chad. Encouraged by her newly born rebellious side, she grabbed his hair, pulled him toward her. She kissed the hell out of him, her tongue darting, teasing, ex-ploring. The boys in back approved, caterwauling like they were watching a football game instead of participating for once.

When she let Chad up for air, she said, "Beer me!"

Ron did. And kept them coming. She'd never been much for booze, wondered what the big deal was. Thought she could handle it. Four beers in and she was ready to quit.

"No, no, Darbs, we're just gettin' started," said Chad. "Chris, how 'bout makin' her one of your special cocktails." Laughs all around.

"I dunno. I probably better get back."

"Don't be that way, Darbs. Let's par-tay!"

From the backseat, Chris handed her a glass of nearly clear liquid.

"What is it?"

"Drink it and find out." Chad smiled at her, flashed his gorgeous teeth. "Come on! We do it all the time."

"Thass right," echoed one of the boys, "alla time!"

"I don't know…"

"*Chug, chug, chug…*"

"Fine. Last drink. Then I go home."

"Whatever you say."

Other than snickers, they remained silent as she took her first sip. It tasted terrible, burned deep in her chest. A very bitter taste, one she'd never experienced before, stayed with her. "That's horrible!"

"Come on, finish it! Chug, chug, chug!"

She did. She didn't want to be talked about the next day, called a wuss.

She woke up on her front stoop, sore, aching. Vaginally bleeding. Her clothes torn. Her makeup streaked. Her eyes dry and blurry. Still drunk. She heaved into the bushes. Wiped her mouth. Tried to clear the fog from her brain. Couldn't remember a damn thing after she drank that awful alcohol.

She touched the tender area beneath her skirt. Grimaced at the pain, pulled away thick drops of blood. Her bra and panties were missing. All but one button on her blouse had vanished. The only thing that remained whole were her boots, and even they were speckled with blood.

She threw up again. She sobbed in silence, mourned her lost virginity. Mourned how it'd been stolen, not given. Mourned how someone she'd trusted had abused and raped her. Mourned her devastating and complete loss of dignity.

Quietly, she opened the door and tip-toed in. Her father sat on the sofa, waiting for her.

"Where in the hell have you—" He stopped, mouth and eyes wide. "*What* did you *do*? Go to bed! We'll talk about this in the *morning*!"

That's all he said. Didn't ask how she was. If she was okay. If something had happened to her. Just assumed she'd been slutting it up. And, honestly, that was fine with her. She didn't want to talk to him about it. She didn't want to talk to anyone about it. She knew how she would become a pariah at school.

Turned out it didn't matter that she'd kept her mouth shut. After staying at home that first day of school ("cramps!"), the next day students buzzed about her, whispered about her as she passed. She supplied them squalid entertainment born of her misery. Soon, the social media blitz came, and it demolished her. The haters called her everything from "slut" to "whore" to "porn queen" and worse. Said she'd begged for it.

She'd avoided her rapists as best as she could. They weren't in any of her classes, but as Peyton was a small school, she couldn't help but see them. Chris and Ron smirked knowingly at her. Even more painful, Chad ignored her, just carried on, star running back, head up, eyes forward with a friendly grin on his ugly, ugly face.

Rumors of a video started around that time. About the same time, she fell into a deep depression. She couldn't stop crying. Seriously considered suicide. She quit going to school.

Her mother forced her to see a shrink, which just made matters worse. And she never told her shrink what had happened. Just kept quiet. Pretty much how her father treated her. All she got from him was a roomful of silence and eyes full of disappointment.

Then Kelton showed up. He'd blown off his college finals to come back for her. Her savior.

She couldn't tell him what happened. Couldn't stand the pain, the embarrassment, the life-changing humiliation. Couldn't even look him in the eye. Day by day, he stayed with her, talked her through the awful summer months. Coached her back to life. Darby knew it drove him crazy, but he never asked questions, although she suspected he intuited the truth. But he remained there as her friend. Her protector.

When she felt half-human again, she caved, told him the story. With one caveat: he couldn't tell anyone.

For days, they argued. Eventually, the well ran dry and they talked about other things, anything other than The Incident. Life began to look not so dreary. The clouds she'd been living under opened up, just a peep, but a tiny ray of sunlight broke through, nonetheless: *Kelton.*

And she finally decided to go forward with what happened to her before it happened to someone else.

The Incident (that's what her parents called it as if afraid to mention the "rape" word) turned into a three-ring circus. A circus not many people supported.

The rapists denied any culpability. Claimed no video existed. Said Darby came on to them and only one of them, Ron (taking one for the team), had mutually consensual sex with her. The bastards' parents had deep pockets, deep enough to buy and import lawyers from New York. They swayed the jury into believing Darby concocted The Incident. Likewise, the Sheriff denied Darby's claims (big high school football supporter), and the local news (true-blooded football fans) smarmily tsk-tsked their way through the meager coverage of the events.

Ron ended up with a slap-on-the-wrist probation, while the other two skated free.

Kelton spent the summer with Darby. The only one who did. Her friends abandoned her. Her parents took off emotionally, not physically (and God, she wished they had). She suspected her parents didn't believe her either. But Kelton was there. He taught her how to shoot a gun, too, very cathartic. And, by the end of that strange summer, she'd hugged her brother, something she thought she'd never do again with anyone.

Sometimes, late at night, she'd wake up in a sweat. Half-remembered nightmares—but all too real—would come back to her in red and violently fragmented images: her clothes torn from her struggling body; sweaty, beefy bodies pinning her to the car seat; a smack to the face, a punch to the gut; leering faces; giddy laughter; and the pain of being internally broken, internally violated, emotionally destroyed time and time again…

Darby didn't stay out for long. As the savages carried her into one of the decrepit buildings, the jostling jolted her awake. Surfing an adrenaline surge, she struggled. She pulled at their iron grips, trying to reach her hidden gun. If she had to, she'd reserve the last bullet for herself. Under no circumstances would she let them violate her. Never again.

"Let me *go*, you fuckers!"

They carted her through a large, empty room. Torches were mounted on the walls. The flooring had rotted, newer planks laid out for a walkway. In the corner lay a pile of debris, chunks of cement, slats of moldy wood, discarded office equipment. A door, surprisingly still intact, opened. They entered a smaller room equipped with a functional desk and several folding chairs. Vinnie and Ed occupied two of the chairs. An old man, fully clothed, sat behind the desk. Long gray hair rode his shoulders.

Savages filled the back part of the room, jockeying for better positions. Darby's captor thrust her down into the last folding chair.

"Darby, meet Tulip," said Vinnie. "Tulip, this is Darby."

Darby's new world order made no sense. Out of breath and nearly out of her mind, the puzzle pieces stubbornly refused to fit. She sought calmness, took solace in Ed and Vinnie's apparent relaxed states.

Tulip didn't look like a Tulip, and he certainly didn't carry the flower's disposition. He growled at Darby. "What do you want? Why are you in our city?"

If Vinnie and Tulip were old friends, they had a strange way of showing it. Vinnie said, "We mean no offense. No harm. In the spirit of friendship, I'd like to ask you a favor."

"I owe you nothing. You come into my city and ask for a favor. What's in it for me? My people?" Behind Darby, growls and yips rose. Restless natives tonight. Slowly, Darby moved her hand to her jacket. Pretended to scratch while she inched her fingers closer to the gun. Ed caught her eye, gave a subtle shake of the head.

"I'll be in your debt, Tulip," said Vinnie. "I know your people need food. I can bring enough canned goods to last your people a week. I'll leave 'em in the tunnel so I don't bother you again. Sound good?"

Tulip remained still. He rested his arms on the desktop, folded his hands corporate style. Not at all what Darby had expected. "Depends," he said. "What do you want in return?"

With a tranquil coolness Darby couldn't imagine given the circumstances, Vinnie pulled out Kelton's photo. "This boy. We'd like him back. It's the girl's brother."

Tulip glanced at the photo without touching it. He looked at Darby, back at Vinnie. "We had him. Not anymore."

Darby scooted up in her seat. "*What*? Where'd—"

"That's a pity, Tulip." Vinnie's voice rose until Darby took the hint. "What happened to him?"

"We couldn't use him. We need able bodies. He wouldn't commit. No matter what we did to him."

Darby cringed. She wanted to grab Tulip and shake an answer out of him. She shuddered out a breath and sat on her hands.

"I see. So…where is he now?"

"We had no choice. We had to offer him to the Below Gods. A sacrifice."

Even the natives silenced at the mention of the "Below Gods."

Darby's stomach swirled. Bile rushed up in her throat. She clamped her hands down hard on her seat. Blinked away horrid images of Kelton's torture and death. *Mind over matter, mind over matter…*

For once clearly stymied, Vinnie asked, "What are the Below Gods? I've never heard of them."

"They haven't always been here. Or maybe they have and are just now making themselves known. They're…beings you don't want to anger. I don't understand them. I don't *want* to know about them. They had come at night, ripped our people apart in their sleep. There were teeth marks on the bodies. Most of the flesh, most of their organs, gone. The Gods ate them. Angry, vicious, pissed-off Gods. They wanted food, so we gave 'em food. We leave above-grounders as sacrifices for them. As long as we keep doin' that, they leave us alone."

Oh...my God, no...

"Tulip, surely you don't believe they're really Gods or—"

"Watch what you say. I don't care if we were friends a long time ago. You don't say anything about our lives, our beliefs. Thought you understood that."

Vinnie nodded solemnly. "I do. My apologies. I didn't mean to offend." He moved his cane to the side of his chair, crossed his legs. Pulled his lip. *Strategizing.* "Can you take us to the Below Gods?"

"You wanna be sacrificed?"

Vinnie considered it. "No. But if you take us to them, I'll still honor our deal. Food next week. As long as you guarantee us safe passage back through your city."

"Won't need passage when you're dead. I see your mind's made up. Foolish." Tulip shrugged. "We won't take you to the Below Gods. We've never been all the way down there. But we'll show you where we leave our sacrifices."

"That's all I'm askin'. Thank you, Tulip. The food will be here next week."

"Doubt it. Not when you're dead."

Slowly, Vinnie stood. Held out his hand. Tulip looked at it, sneered. "That's above-ground custom. Offensive."

"Sorry." Vinnie jerked his hand back.

"Go. Stem, Boulder!" barked Tulip. "Take these fools to their deaths."

Slowly, Darby stood, cautious to not move too fast, the way to confront a snarling dog. Ed did the same. The Underdweller contingent in the back of the room parted. Two males stepped forward, naked as God—whatever God they believed in—made them. Silently, they left the building. Vinnie jerked his head. Ed quickly followed with Darby close behind.

They returned to the brick road—a distant reminder of

humanity—and followed it down a slope. Underdwellers had gathered on both sides of the road to watch the interlopers trudge by. Hisses, growls, and phlegm were flung. Darby waited for the first instance of violence, the kicker that would incite a riot. She patted her comforting gun. Tried not to look any of them in the eye. Just heard them moving, always moving, shifting with pent-up hatred.

Eyes straight ahead…

Down they walked. The crowd of onlookers had dispersed. Darby guessed they walked another half a mile. Then the two escorts deviated from the road, slipped into a mud-filled alley between two buildings. Behind the city, at the cavern's wall, they stopped before a small, roughhewn opening. Their torches still lit, they waited for Darby and company to catch up. One of them rocked impatiently on his bare heels. The other kneeled to peer into the dark hole. Both appeared nervous. The standing Underdweller jerked a finger toward the opening, but said nothing.

"Thank you," said Vinnie.

The escorts took off at a trot, then broke into a hair-flying sprint.

"In we go," said Vinnie. "I'm done on point. I don't know this place, never even heard of it before. It's outta my comfort zone."

Hesitantly, Ed squatted, waddled through the entrance. Darby didn't have to duck far. Once she reached the other side, a blast of hot air hit her like a furnace. She roamed the flashlight's beam above her. Tall enough to stand straight, cutting it close for Vinnie.

But the tunnel dead-ended at 200 feet, no other way in or out.

"There's nothing here." Ed sighed, sounding both relieved and frustrated.

"Yes, there is." Darby spotlighted the small crevice near the floor. At one and a half foot wide, Ed would have a hard time squeezing through.

Ed threw up his arms, his helmet's light bouncing everywhere. "Darby, I think it's time to finally give up."

"What? No way! No way in hell!" As if summoned, a bat swooshed over her. In another time, in a different place, the bat would've terrified Darby. Now it merely supplied background noise.

"Ed's right, girl. This is a fool's errand. Rushin' to our deaths."

"Can't believe you guys are wussing out. Especially after all the bullshit you gave me! See ya on the other side!" Darby dropped into the dirt on all fours, ready to foolishly do or die to prove her point.

"Hold on, stop!" Vinnie stepped up and planted a boot in front of her. Two more inches and he would've cracked her nose. "Darby, we don't know *what's* on the other side. I've never been down there before."

"I haven't either. Didn't even know it existed," said Ed.

"Exactly," continued Vinnie. "I'm as useless as a blind man down there. At least I know the Underdweller's city! And now, all this talk about Below Gods—"

"Tell me you don't believe that shit," said Darby. "Vinnie, I thought you had more common sense than that!"

"Girl, there's common sense, there's no sense, and there's the sense to stay alive. Hell no, I don't believe in any 'Gods,' but I believe there's something down there! The Dwellers don't make shit up. And, frankly, I don't want to know what it is."

"I'm scared, Darby, I don't mind telling you that," said Ed.

"Makes two of us. Takes an idiot to not be afraid." Vinnie tipped his chin down, no longer the voice of casual machismo.

"I'm so damn scared, I'm practically pissing my pants," screamed Darby. "But I'm still going." The men said nothing.

She gawped at them, waited, hoped for a reprieve. She didn't want to do it, but she played her final card. "Kelton saved my life! Literally!"

She wouldn't elaborate, couldn't anyway, but it had to be said. What drove her. What the true stakes were. Let them munch on that for a while.

Ed cracked his knuckles, said, "Well, hell, I never leave a job unfinished."

"Thanks, Ed." Darby's voice cracked, and she nearly threw her arms around Ed's waist, buried her face in his chest.

Vinnie sighed. "Guess it's better to go out trying to do something good. Maybe get some bonus points above." He laughed, dry as a sidewalk in August.

Ed maneuvered onto his knees, aimed the headlamp into the hole. "Yep." He reached into his backpack, brought out a smaller bag. "Always be prepared." Darby recognized some of the equipment from her brother's excursions: mountain climbing tools.

Ed chocked a thick piton into the wall next to the opening with a hammer. Gave it a couple of tugs. Next, he attached a carabiner with a heavy-duty strap and draped it over the opening. He moved fast, with assurance, then threaded a nylon rope through a descender. Darby recognized the eight-figure knot he used, although she never could master it herself despite Kelton's patient lessons. The harness Ed strapped his girth into looked like an S&M jock-strap.

Darby grinned. "Ed, have I told you how glad I am I brought you?"

Laughter filled the small cavern, then just as abruptly stopped. Reality claimed them.

"You ever been climbing, Darby?" Ed continued unrolling the rope.

"I've been on rock walls. My brother taught me how to use

the equipment."

"Good. Vinnie?"

"Can't say as I have. But I'm up for the challenge."

"I'll go first, hammer some pitons in along the way. I can't see how deep it goes. There's no telling. I'm hoping not too far down. But Darby, if we run out of rope, that's the end of the line. Literally."

"I understand." She gave it lip service, had no intention of following through. If the rope ran out, she'd scurry down to the end, take her chances, take a giant leap of faith.

"Vinnie, you go next. Since Darby's had a little experience, she'll follow. I'll spot below with a guide rope."

After more rushed instructions, Ed said, "Wish me luck," then crawled into the crevice. The cave bit into his sides, a granite mouth eating his fleshy succulence. Then he vanished.

Darby listened. Tried to hone her auditory skills. She heard a sleek *zzzz*, the sound of the descender gliding down the nylon. An occasional *tumph*: Ed's feet landing on the wall. Then a grunt as he kicked off again. Metal hit metal. She heard—more than felt—her throat wrestle down a gulp. Vinnie's cane tapped out an increasingly chaotic beat. She smelled his fear.

"I'm down!" Ed's voice echoed up toward them. Darby stuck her head in the hole. "It's not too bad," Ed continued. "Not that far. You're probably better off walking down the wall using the rope to guide you. Hand over hand. Take it slowly."

Vinnie exhaled a sigh of relief. Darby pulled the rope, Ed fed it from below. She hooked Vinnie into the harness, double-checked his connections. "Be careful."

"Girl, there's *nothing* careful about this." He sounded put out, a little pissed off. All for show, of course, to mask his fear. Darby realized he wasn't superhuman, more like her than she initially thought.

She watched his descent, her flashlight on him strictly for

her own benefit. Getting the lay of the land. Once grounded, he clapped dust from his hands. "Nothing to it," he called out.

Darby tested the strength of the initial spike again, would've knocked on wood if there'd been any. Stepped into the harness, pulled it tighter than necessary, tugged the connections. Although it left her feeling vulnerable, she secured the flashlight into her coat pocket. Then she entered the darkness.

She zipped down the first part of the wall with ease. Too easy and much too fast. Her torso dipped down over her legs. Feet over her head, she locked her legs straight out, strained on tip-toes to grab purchase with the wall. Carefully, she yanked on the rope. No give, no pull, tight as a guitar string. Precariously she hung, locked into that awkward position. Blood rushed to her head. "Um, I think I'm stuck."

"Dammit. Give the rope a sharp tug," Ed yelled. "Then fast as you can, kick off the wall."

She breathed in deeply. An alarming whistle emanated from her chest.

Not now, please, not now!

Afraid to let either hand off her life-line, she couldn't dig for her inhaler. Her back strained, thigh muscles screamed. She tugged hard. Pain jabbed her shoulder, but she kicked with all her lower strength. She flew back into dark emptiness, a nauseating feeling. Her body wobbled, a battle for head over feet dominance. She bent her legs at the knees, attempted to add bottom weight. But if she over-calculated, she'd smack her head into the wall when momentum snatched her back. Just in time, gravity righted her. Barely got her feet up, knees to her chest. With a teeth-jarring crack, her feet slapped the wall. The rope released an inanimate sigh of relief.

Wzzzz…

The rope unspooled fast, dropping her freefall. She tried swinging back against the wall to slow her descent, couldn't control her trajectory. She had to plant her feet before the inevitable snap-back jerk of the rope yanked her into a face full of rock. Panic claimed her.

Something buzzed by her ear, swooped back for another pass. The buzzing grew into a beastly growl unlike anything she'd heard before. A foul odor tripped her gag reflex. The unseen creature's wings fluttered, mechanical in sound and repetition. A warm breeze generated by its wings brushed her hair, warmed her face. She wanted to swat it, no matter its size, but wouldn't let go of the rope.

She arched her back, kicked her legs against the wall. Thrust one hand out wildly, blindly, found a protruding rock and grabbed it. Hugged the wall. The rope jerked up, carried Darby half a foot. Then settled as Darby dangled in the air. She took a wheezy breath, gave the taut rope a gentle tug. The rope loosened. She continued down.

Ed's lamp lit at her back. "Thatta girl."

With no way to judge how far to go, her butt splashed down into the mud, her feet still on the wall. She took advantage and rested there a minute. No one dared laugh, not this time.

She unhooked herself, framed a very false smile. "Ready?"

They walked down a gradual slope in the cave, the only way to go. No other entrances connected, no other way out.

Vinnie stopped. "Listen. You hear that?"

Darby didn't, not at first. But once she closed her eyes, stashed everything else away, she heard it. "Water. Running water."

"Yep. Maybe not such a good thing for our travels."

They followed the sound toward the source. The rush of water grew, an incessant and powerful flow. Darby expected to smell stagnant water, not the slightly skunk-like odor that filled the cave. The farther they walked, the stronger the smell permeated.

"Smells like…natural gas," said Ed.

"Not any kinda gas I ever smelled," said Vinnie. "But I imagine that's the closest way to describe it."

The trail ended at a volatile pond. The water roared. To Darby, it sounded like a mass of voices stirred to anger. Water swirled and bubbled, raced in circles toward the center vortex as if boiling. Small waves licked the muddy beach they stood on. Darby swore the water breathed and hated.

Darby found the origin of the commotion: on the right side of the cavern, a mini-waterfall of sorts. The cascading water carried the color of a deep, dirty crimson. The color of life's essence: blood.

The pond extended for three hundred feet or so. On the other side, where the water calmed, the path continued onto welcome dry ground.

"Can you tell how deep it is, Ed?" Vinnie stuck the tip of his cane at the edge, fished around in a few other spots.

"Not by looking."

"Damn waterfall's throwing off my depth perception," said Vinnie. "Guess we're going swimming. Probably safer to walk it if we can."

Oh, hell yes, Darby planned to walk the bottom. Not that swimming frightened her. Dirty water, sure, hepatitis, damn straight. But not swimming. Under no circumstances would she ruin her flashlight, gun, or inhaler, though.

Side by side, Ed and Vinnie drifted in. Darby stayed close behind them, but not too close. Taller than her, the men would provide an accurate measure of sudden, unexpected drops. They tread slowly. Sludge moved beneath Darby's feet, shifted, slid into her shoes. The bottom took a downward slope. Water crept up to her knees. Regardless of what she'd been told about keeping one hand free, she held her necessities above her head: the flashlight in one hand, the gun and inhaler in the other.

Vinnie and Ed strode with ease, Ed's belly riding the water like an inner tube. He held his backpack out and above the water. For all the good it did Vinnie, his cane went down, then came up with gunk—not quite mud—stuck to the bottom. He shook it off, rinsed, repeat.

Next to them, the waterfall thundered. Backsplash drenched them. Darby turned away, using her back as a shield to protect her survival tools. She took a deep breath and held it. No telling what toxins were in the water.

Behind her, she heard, then felt a splash. Not one of the waterfall's incessant gushes, rather a solid, deep *ker-thunk*. Something rubbed against her ankle.

Don't think about it, don't worry about it, don't wonder about it, it's gone now…

Half-way through the pond, Darby resorted to standing on tiptoes. She held her head back. Water lapped her chin, threatened to enter her mouth. Her hair floated atop and behind like a wedding dress train. Her arms strained from carrying her items, grew heavier. The ice-cold water chilled her, stabbed her arms. Her fingers wavered, loosened. She forced them to close, open, close until they woke up, until they hurt.

They passed the waterfall. The opposite beach beckoned. Able to lower to flat feet, Darby expelled her breath. The water slapped her shoulders.

Thank God.

Over the din of the waterfall, she heard another hollow *thunk* behind her. A mini-wave washed over her shoulders. She just wanted out of the pond, felt like fighting the water and running. Above all, she didn't want to look.

She turned around. Nothing. Rings expanded and skimmed the water. Just a fish, that's all, the kind she'd never eat.

Her legs warmed. Pressure pushed at her belly.

A creature broke the water. It rose, kept rising, insanely

rising. Pale, sickly moist folds of flesh ringed the large, writhing worm. It swayed high above Darby as if manipulated by invisible ropes. Brown, cancerous spots spattered its belly. It turned, twisted, swirled. It lowered its head to face Darby. But it wasn't a head. Just a baseball-sized knob. Lumps shifted beneath the skin.

Darby choked on a scream, managed a squeal.

"What's wrong?" Ed whirled. "Jesus *Christ!*"

The knob flowered open. A gaping maw exposed hundreds of sharp teeth. Two undulating lumps snapped open. Frog-like eyes—yet somehow human—glared at her. The monster shrieked. So did Darby.

"*No, no, no…*"

Darby manipulated her finger onto the revolver's trigger and took aim.

Ed grabbed her wrist. "No! The gas! You'll blow us all to Hell!"

The monster snaked in, trumpeted like an elephant, darted back out. Ed swung his backpack at it, not even coming close.

Without deliberation, Darby shifted her gun to the flashlight hand. Held her inhaler at arm's length. The creature jagged in. Its mouth widened. A black tongue unfurled. Eyes broke out on the tongue like swollen taste buds. Darby hit the inhaler. The creature shrank back. She did it again. The monster's mouth snapped shut into a compact fist. It dove back into its habitat. An explosion of water followed.

"*Run!*"

Darby trudged, forcing her legs against the powerful water. The water receded to her waist. She pushed.

Move, dammit, move!

The creature banged into her calf. She jolted, nearly pitched over. From the shore, Ed and Vinnie shouted delirious nonsense. Behind her, water whooshed, then splattered down in rivulets.

The creature broke the water again. A wave smacked her back, subsided. She turned, whiffed the monster with her inhaler. It dodged the mist, then reared its body back like a cobra. Ready to strike.

Darby's knees broke the surface. She picked them up, high-stepped to the shore. Didn't stop until she raced fifty feet from the waterline.

She bent over, hands on knees. Out of breath, dizzy, her chest tightened. She hoped to hell she still had medicine in her inhaler. Hyperventilation nearly seized her.

What if the goddamn thing can walk on land?

The water settled. Ripples atop the surface skated toward the waterfall. Almost a signature farewell: *See you next time.*

Darby shivered. "Oh, my *God!* What *was* that?" Between loud wheezes, she hit her inhaler hard.

"You okay, Darby?" Ed's complexion had turned chalky.

"Will be in a minute." She inhaled deeply, sucked on the life-giving piece of plastic like it was manna from Heaven. Her breathing settled. "But...what in hell was that thing?"

"Told you before I don't think about things down here too much," said Ed. "I like to sleep too much. What you knew above? Doesn't apply a lick down here."

Vinnie grunted in acknowledgment.

She understood. In fact, tonight she understood a great deal more than she had her entire twenty years of life.

"Swear to God, though, never seen anyone win a fight with an inhaler." Ed shook his head, stuck somewhere between incredulity and amusement.

"I'd say you got lucky. We all did," added Vinnie. "But... brave move, girl. Damn brave."

Finally, she'd been indoctrinated into the "boy's club." She couldn't hide her grin, no matter how she battled her cheek muscles. Proudly, she marched on ahead of the men.

They walked on. No more surprise lakes, no more monsters. Just disturbing sounds, unearthly ones: buzzes, tortured shrieks, contented sighs, ecstatic moans. The sounds of Hell as Darby had imagined them as a child.

The path led them down, always inexorably down.

"You hear that?" Darby grabbed Vinnie's arm.

Torn from reality, Darby thought she'd imagined it at first. She needed corroboration. Needed to know even though they were treading through an unfathomable world, sanity still tethered her.

She heard it again: chanting. Not organized tribal chants, nothing like that and far from musical in nature. Instead, she heard a cacophonic riot, each voice different, each one beating its own drum. Voices that may have been human once but certainly weren't now. Grunts, squeals, moans, screams.

The Below Gods.

Closing in on their final destination. Maybe in more ways than one. A shudder ran down her back.

"You ready?" asked Vinnie. He looked decidedly not ready. With his head tilted down, Darby thought he was praying.

"Let's do it," said Ed.

Connected at the hip, they descended. Blacks became blacker. Inhuman screams rose to glass-shattering heights, amplified by the cave's acoustics.

Ed stopped, dug through his backpack for one last trick. He pulled out buggy looking goggles and strapped them on. "Night vision. Guess I shoulda led with this, huh? Darby, if I'd known you were coming, I'd've brought another pair."

"It's okay, Ed." She spoke loudly into his ear and patted his arm. "I'm just glad you're here."

The corners of his mouth turned up, just a hair, but his eyes cast downward. Saddest smile Darby had ever seen, as if he had abandoned all hope. Perhaps she was stupid not to do the same.

Sound overwhelmed them, bounced off the cave walls above and beyond. A rush of hot air tightened Darby's face. She swallowed, tasted something foul and stagnant.

The trail ascended slightly. Then stopped, the path half-blocked by a large boulder. Clearly, the source of the sonic bedlam lay beyond the boulder in a lower cavern. They stood at the lip of Hell.

Screams blistered Darby's ears. Voices climbed beyond any man-made scale, sustained at an unreachable length. All of them somehow different.

Vinnie raised his voice to be heard. "Dowse the light."

Darby covered the flashlight with her hand, pointed it toward the ground. She edged around the boulder. Ed hovered next to her, his chin practically resting on top of her head.

The muted flashlight provided more than enough light to see, and that was too much. Darby's internal world exploded at sights that would break anyone's mind. The cave's claustrophobic walls no longer pressed in. Her mind accepted all, rejected everything as the truth.

Darby shrank back. Her legs refused to work. They gave out. Stunned, on her knees, she couldn't move.

"My... I..." That's all Ed said, and he'd said it all. He stumbled back. Fell on all fours and vomited.

"What is it?" asked Vinnie. "Tell me...*what*?"

Ed pulled off his goggles, handed them to Darby. "I don't want 'em anymore. I can't unsee..."

Darby's hands shook. Her heart raced. Her breath skyrocketed. She sucked on the inhaler, gave it an extra squirt. Did something she hadn't in a long time. Prayed, this time with commitment. She waited to reclaim her breath. Strapped on the goggles. Looked at Ed and Vinnie through the weirdly disorienting green night vision. Fortified her weak legs, stood, and looked around the boulder again.

Below, in a vast cavern, deformed beasts prowled. White in color or maybe the unnatural green of the night vision. Their bodies were hairless. Flaps of skin appeared soldered over their eyes, melted into their skin. Noses existed as dangling skin flaps. Where ears should've been, orifices drilled into their skulls. Dark-rimmed, lamprey-like mouths were filled with tiny razor teeth.

They fought one another. Constant, vicious, to-the-death battles. A group beat one creature to the ground with fists and claws, then tore him to shreds. The victim's remains instigated another fight. The victor jumped onto the body, dug his claws into the fallen creature's abdomen, and ate his innards.

The most identifiably human in form appeared long of jaw, short of upper skull. These creatures appeared to rule the roost, the others giving them wide berth. Others sported tails, prehensile snakes that moved of their own accord. Some had long, curved horns, some had holes poked into their thinly sheathed skulls.

They clambered over one another. Bounded off walls. One beast impaled itself upon a stalagmite. Its body didn't go to waste as the others swiftly devoured the remains.

All beasts were bare of genitalia. No gender difference, at least as far as Darby could see.

So…how in the hell can there be so many of them?

Then Darby saw the cage against the wall. Below her and to the right. Constructed of bones, tied together with God knows what, hardly stable in appearance. The cage's prisoners looked even less stable.

She pointed toward Ed's binoculars. He handed them over. Doubling them with the night vision gave her vertigo at first, then she recovered. If her mind hadn't snapped yet, it never would.

She ran her finger across the small wheel, focused the binoculars. Closed in on the cage's inhabitants. *Humans.* A handful. Some barely able to stand. All of them hovering at the back of the cage as far away from the monsters as possible. A man sat huddled in the corner, distant from the others. Lean but muscular arms wrapped around knees drawn to his face. The long hair—curly locks, clearly blond or so she wished it to be—belonged to her brother. She knew it. Absolutely.

"I'm going down there," Darby whispered.

"No, you're not." Ed wouldn't look at her. He stared at his hands as if he expected them to do something surprising. "It's suicide."

"Kelton's down there. Locked up. I came to get him. I'm not leaving without him."

"It's impossible."

"I don't think it is. They're animals. They're blind, running into everything in their path. They're mindless, too, eating each other, whatever. Just gotta be careful, stay out of their way."

"If they're so mindless, how'd they lock up your brother?"

Darby thought about it. Couldn't come up with a good answer. "I dunno. But…I think they live on some sort of animal instinct. They have what looks like noses and ears of a sort. So they might be able to smell and hear. But that's it. They won't see me."

"Puts me on equal grounds," said Vinnie. "But it does sound like you're egging on death. You got a plan?"

For once, Darby didn't want to think that far ahead. If she planned it, it would give her more time to chicken out. She had made up her mind. And she wouldn't pressure these two brave men—her friends—to go with her. They'd already done so much.

"It's cool, guys. You don't have to go. I get it. It's not your brother. But…I've got to try." She felt the tears coming on. Fought them like a warrior. She drowned a sob with a cleansing swallow. "I've got to do it for Kelton."

Slowly, tiredly, Vinnie stood. His knees cracked. "It's a good day to die."

"Sorry, Darby, I'm still not goin' down there," said Ed. "Way above my pay grade. Give me the flashlight. You keep the goggles. I'll lay down fire from here if you need it."

"Appreciate it, Ed."

"Wait! Got one more thing for you." Like a magician, a knife appeared in Ed's hand. A magnificent killing knife with a blade that gleamed green beneath her night vision.

"And you kept this secret 'til now?" said Darby.

"Some secrets are best kept to the cuff. God—or whatever's out there—go with you."

"You, too." Darby took the blade, weighed its heft. Then handed it to Vinnie. "Ready, Vinnie?"

"No. Let's go."

Around the boulder, Darby discovered a ledge about two feet in width set off the wall. In gradual increments, not too steep, it led down into the cavern. She tapped Vinnie's shoulder. He leaned down, and she whispered into his ear about the ledge.

Before Darby could object, Vinnie set off on the narrow trail, nimble-footed as ever. Instead of using his cane, he trailed fingertips along the wall. Darby hurried, followed closely behind, her gun up and ready.

As they descended, the cacophony rose to deafening heights. Most of the creatures remained embroiled in the massive free-for-all at the center of the cavern, far from the prisoners.

Except for the two guards by the cage. Even without genitalia, they dry-humped the make-shift bars, hunger possibly driving their base instincts.

Vinnie and Darby set foot onto level ground. From the battlefield's commotion, the world shook below Darby's feet.

Again, she tapped the blind man's shoulder. "There're two by the cage. I can't use the gun. They'll hear it. You'll have to use the knife." She left the order unfinished. She wasn't used to delegating. Especially sending people to kill.

"Just lead me over there," he whispered. "Then I can sniff and snuff 'em out."

"Grab my belt loop."

He did. Awkwardly, they shuffled toward the cage. So far, so good, no attention from the beasts by the cage.

Closer. Their feet scuffed across the dirt floor, inch by inch. Vinnie's breath whiffed down on top of Darby's head with each exhalation.

The two guard beasts pulled at the bars, rattled them. Then one leaped on top of the cage.

A female captive froze. She gripped the bars, looked at Darby through squinted eyes. And squealed.

Dammit.

Darby stopped dead, held her breath.

On the edge of the battlefield nearest Darby, a beast stalked away from the fighting. Sniffed the air. And manipulated a horrific approximation of a frown, its mouth dragged down into tight folds.

Darby moved ahead toward the cage, faster. "Six feet in front of you," she whispered to Vinnie.

With its four limbs wrapped around the cage's binding bones, the beast on top of the cage turned toward Darby, head at an unnatural angle. On long, ape-like arms, it lowered itself to the ground. It smelled the unmoving, stagnant air. Tilted its head as if dialing in radar.

It shrieked, penetrating as a bullet between the eyes.

Vinnie took off at a clip, shoving Darby aside. He followed the beast's scream, the knife above his head. With perfect aim, he arced it down into the beast. But the creature's chest deflected the blade. Vinnie bounded back, surprise on his face. His cane splashed into the mud. Vinnie dropped into a crouch, knife in both hands. The creature loped toward him. Vinnie shot up and rammed the blade into the creature's throat. The creature staggered, then toppled. Vinnie jammed a foot onto the fallen beast's chest, yanked out his weapon.

Darby raced over, swept up Vinnie's cane. The other cage creature stumbled their way, sniffing blood in the air, claws out. Confused, it tottered through several false starts, unable to find a direct path toward the fallen meat of its partner.

Darby grabbed Vinnie, pulled him near the wall. "The other one's going toward the creature you killed," she whispered.

"How far's the body from the prisoners?"

"Close."

"Then I'll move the dead thing farther away."

"No! Vinnie, wait!" Helplessly, Darby watched Vinnie shuffle toward the dead creature. He swept the cane in front of him, then pushed it through the dirt to pick up speed.

Vinnie's cane tapped into the monster's torso. Cane under his arm, he grabbed the dead creature's legs and dragged it. The other beast stumbled ever closer in a drunken, zig-zagged pattern.

Frantically, Darby waved her arms, momentarily forgetting Vinnie's disability. Vinnie dropped the beast dangerously close to the outskirts of the battlefield and tapped his way back.

The wandering creature stopped, held its malformed head up, inhaled deeply. Then changed course, headed directly toward Vinnie. Shambling on all fours.

Vinnie must've sensed him coming closer. He stopped, thrust his cane out in a circle clearing the immediate circumference. The monster stopped three feet in front of him, just out of cane's reach. A blind stare-down. The monster released an ear-shredding cry. Cue enough for Vinnie. He stepped around it, hustled into a jog, his cane flapping wildly.

Darby broke from cover, ran toward him. "Over here," she croaked, just loud enough. With keen hearing, Vinnie corrected his path and ran toward her.

A female prisoner crammed her face between the bars of the cage. "Hey…" Her voice cracked like an old phonograph. "Over here. Hey…" So far she couldn't muster a scream, but Darby knew damn well it was her intent. Darby had to choose between shutting her up or getting Vinnie to safety. Easy choice. Vinnie narrowed the gap, almost there. He'd make it, she knew it. He always did.

She raced for the cage. She grasped the bars, jiggled them to rouse the inert prisoners' attention. Dirt—or some other substance— crumbled off the top. "Listen to me! All of you! The only way you'll get out of here is if you keep quiet!"

More of them stirred, all in varied states of malnourished stupor. They clambered toward her, desperately reaching, bony fingers outstretched.

"Shhh. Keep it—"

"Oh, my God! We're *saved*!"

One single, simple proclamation—one Darby couldn't fault the woman for, truth be told—and their covert operation blew away like ash.

At the tip of the battlefield, several beasts stopped fighting. Chins tipped into the air, one after the other. A sound of locusts rose as more creatures smelled the rancid air.

"Christ." Darby rushed around to the cage door.

A hand dropped onto her shoulder. Her heart banged. She whirled, gun up. Vinnie brandished the knife, flipped it in his hand, offered the handle to Darby. "Take it, girl."

Darby cut through the strange vines holding the door closed. Liquid, thick and sticky, oozed from the vines. One of the vines scuttled away, a living entity. Several more followed.

She jabbed at the remaining moving strands.

A male prisoner pulled on the door, pleading, "Hurry, please, God, hurry!"

Quickly, Darby looked behind her. On all fours, two creatures galloped her way. Picking up blistering speed.

The door loosened. She thwacked it back. "Fast and quiet as you can, run up the ledge. Hurry."

She forgot they couldn't see in the pitch dark. But they moved like they could. Like underground animals, they'd probably grown accustomed to their dark prison. The first freed captive found the ledge, then another behind him. They linked together like train cars and moved fast as one, too.

Several bodies in the back of the cage lay in a clump, dead. Next to her brother. Sitting, quiet, frighteningly lifeless.

Her heart thumped. Her hand wavered over his shoulder. His unmoving shoulder.

Don't let him be dead. Dear God, after all this, let him be okay. Please, anything but—

"We gotta move, Darby!" Vinnie's voice sounded shaky, for once firmly aboard the panic wagon.

Darby shook her brother's shoulder. As if in a drugged haze, he looked up. Emaciated, bony, weak. But undeniably, beautifully Kelton.

"Kelton, it's me, Darby!"

"Darby? Can't...be..."

"Get on your feet. We gotta go. Now!"

She slapped him. Felt it in her stinging hand, deep in her hurting heart. Tough love. Kelton attempted to get to his feet, made it to his knees, then toppled over. Darby grabbed his underarms. She couldn't believe how light he felt. But his legs showed cords of muscle, lean and mean. Even with meager—if any—food, he'd practiced some sort of exercise regimen.

Vinnie thwacked his cane against the bone bars. "Move,

Darby!"

Beneath the oncoming stampede, the ground trembled.

"Move your ass, Kelton!" With power she didn't know she had, Darby yanked her brother to his feet.

He moved like an old man, arthritic and doubled over at the waist. They didn't have time for it. "*Now*, goddamn you!" She slapped him again, this time harder.

He straightened, rubbed his cheek. Looked at her with sad, glassy eyes. Darby grabbed his wrist, wrenched him behind her. "Come on!" She tapped Vinnie's shoulder as she passed him. And ran like hell, Vinnie hot on her tail.

Harsh reality smacked Kelton out of his stupor when he saw the approaching horde. He stumbled, righted himself, wagged his arms like a newborn learning to walk. In seconds, he drew upon his reservoir of stamina and kept up with Darby.

Behind them, several rushing beasts dropped onto the fallen monster, the one Vinnie had taken out. A God-sent delay. New fights broke out. Flesh ripped, entrails flew through the air as they fought over the carcass.

But a couple of beasts bypassed the meal, the smell of fresh, living meat apparently more appealing. They came running, slavering like hyenas with their tongues lolling out.

Darby hit the ledge first, Kelton next. Vinnie lagged behind. A monster galloped toward them, heaved a claw onto the ledge. It snared Vinnie's ankle. Vinnie grunted, fell on all fours, the monster's claw still wrapped around his ankle. Then he slipped over the edge.

Krak, krak!

At the top of the ledge, Ed stood beside the boulder, his pistol smoking.

With one hand braced against the rock wall, Darby leaned over the ledge. On the cavern floor, Vinnie shoved the beast that Ed had shot off him. Clearly disoriented, he sat up, shook his head.

"Get up, Vinnie, get up!" yelled Darby. She edged Kelton around her. "Just hug the wall, Kelton. Follow it to the top. I'll be up in a second."

"I can't—"

"Just shut up and go!"

Darby left no time for a rebuttal. She raced back down the ledge. On the ground, she helped Vinnie to his feet. When he landed his left foot, he cringed. He buckled and nearly took them both over. More beasts approached, coming at them at a frenzied speed. Darby stood over her friend, torn, unsure. Terrified.

"Go, girl. Save your brother."

"I'm not leav—"

"My ankle's broken. I'll never make it. I'll buy you time. Just tell my family. Hell, tell the world."

Roars flared. Feet—hooves—trampled the dirt. A good dozen of them coming on strong.

"But I can help you!" She bent, impotently tugged beneath his underarms. He didn't—wouldn't—help.

"Nope. No, you can't." Vinnie grinned. "Complete your mission. Without me."

"Please, Vinnie! I can get you up there! I know I can!" Again she tried lifting him. He shut her down, dead weight.

His arms flopped to the ground. "Dammit, girl, no sense in everyone dying. Now go!"

She understood the sense in Vinnie's argument. Didn't like it. But she didn't have a choice. She took out her gun, handed it to him. "Take out as many as you can."

"Girl after my own heart."

Quickly, she dropped, kissed his cheek. Didn't even think about it. And she ran.

She scaled the ledge in no time. Ahead of her, Kelton struggled. She put a hand in the small of his back, gently pushed him into the cave.

Vinnie shouted, full of color and curses. Five shots rang out. Then a final, lonely *bang*.

"Christ, was that Vinnie?" Antsy, Ed bounced from one foot to the other. New life possessed him. The others ran ahead, some sobbing, others screeching like sirens.

"We'll talk about him later, Ed. Ready?"

"Always."

Hand in hand, they ripped down the path, Kelton the bridge connecting them. With Ed's added strength, they swung Kelton, dropped him, picked him up again, acting as Kelton's crutches. Light as a feather, Kelton practically flew. Darby's shoulders and arms strained. In a good way. But, Christ, they still had a long way to go yet.

Barely jogging, they bypassed most of the other survivors. A few had slowed to a walk.

"Hurry up, they're coming!" Darby called out to each prisoner on passing, the best she could manage.

Ahead lay the lake. The one she dreaded nearly as much as the hideous creatures following them. But she'd beaten the lake monster before. After all, she had her conquering inhaler.

Some of the faster refugees had already splashed into the pond, almost giddy at the feel of the water.

"Wait, stop!" Her voice barely wheezed past her tortured lungs.

Behind them, the beasts had entered the passageway. Their hateful, relentless screams boomed through the cave, rendering it impossible to tell how far back they were.

But several shrieks rose above the others, more defined, more present. Above Darby.

Two beasts dropped from the ceiling. One landed on top of Ed. He tumbled. With a hand around the monster's throat,

Ed used his weight and managed to wrestle the creature beneath him. He beat its forehead with the butt of his gun until gore flew. It stopped writhing, winding down with a deflating-tire hiss.

"Go, Darby," Ed shouted.

No other option. Survival mode.

Run! All I've been doing, all I can do, can't do anything for Ed, for Christ's sake, run!

Without preamble, the lake monster reared. It clamped its mouth onto the first swimmer's shoulder. He shrieked. His back arched as if he'd touched a live wire. The monster wrapped its serpentine body around the man's torso and whipped it in the air like a rag doll. Predator and prey vanished beneath the rolling water.

Darby looked back. Ed was up on one knee, gun poised in a shooting stance. One of the monsters drew up to him. Unbelievably, Ed didn't fire. The beast flew into him. Their bodies collided with a loud, wet thump.

"Shoot it, Ed," Darby yelled. "Kill it!"

Instead of the easy option, Ed continued to beat it with his gun, his fists. The monster caved. Ed wobbled to his feet. Green and red liquid soaked his shirt. "Just go, Darby." He said it nonchalantly, adding a casual hand wave as if he were dismissing an annoying house guest. Even from twenty feet away, his wounds didn't look good. If nothing else, Darby knew Ed was a realist.

Darby had a more immediate fish to fry. The pond creature would blast out of the water again, count on it. The waterfall was impassable. The opposite side, though, could be shallower, a quicker route.

"Everyone, follow me!" Toward the left, she darted to the water's edge, light on her feet until she reached the wall. Kelton followed, as did the rest. Darby had guessed right. Rocks tore at her shoes, but the water didn't rise above six inches. They made rabbit time. She reached the shore first, Kelton next, then the other survivors safely dry-docked.

Across the lake, a throng of beasts thundered into the cave. Ed ran into the lake, stopped once the water reached his stomach. Stone-faced, he turned, waited for the oncoming horde, gun up.

"Ed?" Darby's tremulous voice sailed across the water.

Ed didn't look back. Just spoke in an iron voice. "I'm gonna end this. The only way I know how, Darby. But you'd better run. Run like hell. I'll wait as long as I can."

She knew what he planned to do. It made solid military sense. Sad sense. The reason he hadn't fired the gun earlier.

"Thanks, Ed…for everything." Darby wanted to say more, but couldn't. Wouldn't. She had a responsibility to get everyone else to safety. "Hurry! Run fast as you can or die!"

She led the group. Several times Kelton lagged behind. She went back, retrieved him. Like a steady racehorse, Darby always pulled ahead of the pack.

They rounded the curve in the tunnel, extra protection. Up hill all the way, she pushed herself, demanded everyone do the same. Her knees strained. Her legs weighed heavier than lead.

Far behind them, bullets fired, steady and methodical. And kept going. Obviously an automatic.

They ran. Ed's gunfire synched up to their plodding, tired footfalls. The creatures howled, voices pitched even higher in death. And Ed wouldn't quit. He'd keep firing, keep living, until he detonated the natural gas. After all, he'd said he never left a job unfinished.

The world exploded.

Darby woke to dazzling light and a sterile white environment. Her first thought: *Great. After storming the dark below, I'm now in freakishly bright Heaven.*

Then pain brought her back to mortality. The bed was overly complicated, wires crisscrossing, doo-dads and what-nots running into and out of her aching body.

A hospital.

And all around her: *beep, beep, beep.* Worse than the ringing in her ears.

First things first: Kelton. She wrenched the oxygen mask away and coughed. When she reached for a cup next to her bed, her leg caught worse than a charley horse. She pulled back the blanket to reveal a cast. So much for deciding to ditch the hospital.

What happened after Ed had blown Hell to…well, Hell?

She pressed the call button.

A nurse pattered in. Hands folded beneath her chin, doe eyes round and sad, she sported a very doting and matronly look. Fragile to the point of porcelain, the nurse looked like she needed a hug worse than Darby did. "You're awake, honey."

"Yeah…" Darby croaked, singing old-time blues. "Kelton?"

"Your brother? He's fine. Or will be. He's malnourished, dehydrated, weak. But he'll get better."

"Where…is he?"

"Down the hall."

Broken leg or not, Darby shoved the intricate web of tubes and hoses out of her way and slipped her good leg next to the guardrail.

"Nurse Figurine" raced to her side. "No, no, honey! You need to stay put. You've been through quite an ordeal. You have a broken leg, a rib, and who knows what else." Her hands flapped beside her as if drying her nails. "You need to stay in bed until doctor's orders say otherwise."

"I don't give a…damn about…" Literally, her words dried up. She pointed at the elusive paper cup just out of reach.

An "aha" moment struck Nurse Figurine as her wide eyes grew even moonier. She grabbed the cup of ice chips, held it to Darby's mouth.

"Slowly. There we go, that's a good girl. Take it easy, nice and slow. *Good* girl." The nurse stroked Darby's hair like she was a lap cat. Either Darby had entered a new circle of Hell, one she hadn't yet visited, or she'd mistakenly ended up in the children's ward.

Didn't matter. Kelton was okay. She had to see him.

"Thanks." She pushed the nurse's fidgeting hands away. "I'm…gonna see my brother."

"I don't think that's such a good idea, honey. You—"

"Don't care." Darby rattled the bed guard to no effect. Her energy drained; she tried moving it, but it proved too formidable. A weak and final hand smack to the metal finally nudged the nurse into action.

"Oh, my! I can see you're not going to take no for an answer. Stay right there, okay?" She presented radiant eyes and a sunset of a smile. "I'll call Doctor Nevins and explain. Okay? I promise, honey…"

Darby had fought the denizens of Hell to see her brother. A Heavenly nurse wouldn't stop her.

When Nurse Figurine rolled Darby into Kelton's room, nothing had prepared her for his appearance. He resembled a skeletal version of the muscular, vital brother she'd grown up with. His once-thick blond hair strung down the side of his face in strands so wispy she thought early male pattern baldness had set in. His eyes were sunk, deep and dark, into his emaciated skull. Smoky circles around his eyes provided his only color. Pale as bone and slight as wet tissue, it seemed a miracle he could sit up.

She couldn't help herself, couldn't stop the tears. Now was the time to unleash them, especially after holding them in for so long. She wept over how Kelton looked, over what they'd been through, over the deaths of her new friends, and finally, over the fact her brother was alive. Kelton started crying, too, something Darby couldn't stand, which just loosened her waterworks more.

Quietly, Nurse Figurine closed the door behind her as she left.

Kelton raised a stick-like hand. He grimaced. Darby rolled her wheelchair toward him, gently grabbed his hand. Their entwined hands dropped to the mattress, his hand cold and unable to sustain a grip.

"You're alive," said Darby. Enough was enough. She forced cement into her veins and wiped the last of the tears from her eyes.

"Thanks to you," he said.

"We had help. From my late, great, new brothers. What happened anyway? I don't remember—"

"The explosion knocked you out. A chunk of stone clobbered you. Scared the hell outta me, but…I'd pretty much grown a rhino skin by then." A weak smile. "Couple times you came to. You were delirious. But able to tell us where the rope and harness were. We would've never found it. Had a helluva time hoisting you up, though."

"Yeah, I'll bet. I don't remember any of that. I don't even remember walking—"

"You didn't. A couple of the newer prisoners were stronger than me. They weren't strong enough to carry you, but…between a couple of 'em taking turns, they kinda dragged you to safety."

"Huh. Glad I don't remember it."

"Doctor Nevins told me memory loss is sort of a defense mechanism. Protection, I guess, against…crazy…things…" Kelton lost it like she'd never seen before. Her tough, star athlete, life-of-the-party, big brother cried like a baby, unable to stop, nearly hysterical. Words poured out, garbled beyond comprehensibility. She cradled his head, stroked his hair much like the nurse had done to her earlier, but not too hard, too afraid he'd break.

"I didn't tell them…anything…," he continued through the tears. "Who would believe us? Told them…I didn't remember…" After a while, Kelton stopped crying. Darby knew he could continue, probably needed to continue, crying. Hell, he'd earned it. But dehydration put an end to it.

Darby asked, "How long have I been out?"

He tried lifting his arms again in a "who knows?" gesture, gave up. His hands smacked limply back to the bed. "Darby… I don't know. I've sorta lost all sense of time since…since… you know." He turned his head, looked out the window.

"How many made it out?"

"Two died in the explosion. The rest are somewhere in

the hospital."

"Have you seen them?"

"No." He fixed her with an icy cold glare. "And I don't really want to. The less I think about that…nightmare, the better off I'll be."

Darby nodded. She understood. Probably not the healthiest way to handle the situation, but God knows she'd adopted that method after The Incident. She'd quit talking to everyone at school, friend and foe alike. In many ways, Kelton's experience paralleled her own trauma. And her heart broke over it. Particularly over the thought that he, too, may have been sexually violated. Maybe with time—as he'd been so patient with her—he'd open up to her. But not now. Because she knew. She *understood*.

"I take it you got past the, um…human Underdwellers okay?"

"Never saw anyone. Not one of those bastards who first took me."

"Huh." She supposed the Underdwellers had honored Vinnie's agreement. Wondered if she should take up his end of the canned goods deal. Then the thought of going back down there sent a chill careening down her back.

"Weird thing is we about gave up," said Kelton. "The trek seemed endless. But some homeless guy found us, went and called the cops, ambulances, whatever."

"Smoke? Dirty, poor teeth, laughs a lot?"

Kelton managed a smile. "Think you about described half the homeless population. But, yeah, I think that's what he called himself."

"Thank God he helped us."

"God had nothing to do with what went on down there, Darby. God's not real. But…other things are." A hard, metallic sheen strengthened his eyes. Lines formed on his face, those of an old man. He lowered his voice, not that it had been loud to begin with. Almost a whisper. "What…what *were* those things?"

She wished she had an answer. But, like Ed, she'd rather not dwell on it. Therein lay the path to insanity. Darby shook her head, muttered, "Just that. Things."

"You think we got 'em all? When Ed blew them up? Every last one?"

No. Hell, no! A thousand times no! You can't kill something that's already dead! Right now, the inhuman monsters are tearing and rending flesh, wolfing it down, clawing, yowling, screaming…right below our feet!

But that's not what Darby told her brother. "There's nothing to worry about any longer, Kelton. Not while we have each other."

Outside the window, night had fallen. Beneath streetlamps, shadows moved, shadows that had no physical origin. Something loped across the street, something big and dark and featureless. She heard a shriek carry on the wind, followed by other caws of blood-boiling anger. Other disfigured mutants joined the lone figure, growing into one large entity comprised of sharp teeth and slick, pale, featureless skin.

Darby rolled closer to the window. With her back turned to her brother, she closed her eyes, then dared another look.

A strolling couple entered the circle of light cast by a streetlamp, a blessedly human couple.

"What's wrong?" asked Kelton.

"Nothing." Regardless, she drew the shade shut, hardly the impenetrable barrier she wished they had. She put on her game face, smiled big for her brother.

Again, she took his hand in hers. "Kelton…I'm sorry."

"For what?"

"I'm sorry I didn't come sooner. When you went missing. I…"

"Shh. It's okay, sis." His grip felt physically weak but powered ten-fold by heart. "You came. You saved me. *Us.* I owe you everything. You're my hero."

"You're mine. Always will be, big brother. Love you."

Even though it hurt like hell—for both of them—Darby managed to position her head on his shoulder. She let the tears fall again.

ABOUT THE AUTHOR

Stuart R. West is a lifelong resident of Kansas, which he considers both a curse and a blessing. It's a curse because…well, it's Kansas. But it's great because… well, it's Kansas. Lots of cool, strange and creepy things happen in the Midwest, and Stuart takes advantage of them in his work. Call it "Kansas Noir." Stuart writes thrillers tinged with horror and horror tinged with thrillers, both for adult and young adult audiences. He writes at the crossroads of horror and sneaky humor. *Twisted Tales from Tornado Alley* is Stuart's first short story collection and third book with Grinning Skull Press, and Stuart feels funny talking about himself this way. Stuart spent twenty-five years in the corporate sector and now writes full time. He's married to a professor of pharmacy (who greatly appreciates the fact he cooks dinner for her every night) and has a twenty-two-year-old daughter who's still deciding what to do with her life. But that's okay. It took him twenty-five years to figure that out.

Stuart's blog can be found at http://stuartrwest.blogspot.com/. Drop in on him at Facebook at: https://www.facebook.com/stuartrwestwriter

If you liked the stories you've just read, consider checking out Stuart R. West's novels: *Dread & Breakfast* and *Ghosts of Gannaway*, both currently available and can be ordered from your local bookseller.

"Heart-stopping horror infused with page turning suspense."
--Russell James, author of Dark Inspiration and Q Island
DREAD AND BREAKFAST
Stuart R. West

Chapter One

"*Why* are you *doing* this?" The chains binding her wrists drew taut as she lurched forward. Her chin cracked down onto cement, triggering her bladder. Urine warmed her legs. Dignity didn't matter, not anymore. Nothing made sense. As she dragged her locked hands toward her, she pushed up on her knees. Pleading, her last hope. "*Please* don't do this, oh God, please don't hurt me. Just … tell me *why*."

Two figures stepped in front of the floodlight. Joined at the hip, hands entwined like lovers on a stroll.

A dry voice, crisper than crackers, said, "Why? Because it's date night."

The hatchet swung down, delivering date night's goodnight kiss.

❆ ❆ ❆

Snow swirled in the wind, dropping like feathers. Rebecca knew a storm had been forecast, hardly good driving weather. But she wasn't about to let up. Not 'til she put Hollington far behind her and then some. Dangerous? Absolutely. But navigating through a snowstorm sure as hell felt a lot safer than what she'd left behind.

The wipers beat the windshield, struggling to clear it. Snow piled on the hood. Rebecca brushed a hand through the condensation and hunkered down to peer out the narrow opening. She cursed herself for not getting the Chevy's defrost fixed; it never had worked worth a damn. Of course, she also didn't think she'd be fleeing for her life during what one weatherman had gleefully called "the Storm of the Century." Maybe she should've thought this out better. Should've, would've, could've; the old game she'd been playing a lot lately.

She glanced at Kyra, sound asleep. The seatbelt looked tight, confining her daughter's small frame. Kyra's stuffed dog rode with her, the safety belt covering its mouth, its eyes: say nothing, see nothing. The way Rebecca had lived the past ten years of her life.

But enough.

Rebecca had thought—if not accepted, exactly—she understood Brad's violent streak. It didn't happen often, but when he hit her, it hurt. Not so much physically; she'd developed a surprising tolerance to the pain. Emotionally, though, it pummeled her worse than fists. Yet she accepted it, justified it as the norm. After all, her daddy treated her mother the same way. And, as Brad often told her, his job weighed heavily on him, the stress too much. "Being a police detective is a load-and-a-half for any good man," he'd said before punctuating his insight with a blow to her cheek. Now Rebecca thought it nothing more than a load of shit.

Was Brad a good man? At one time she'd thought so. But when he hit their daughter last night, her perception, her entire world, changed.

Enough.

Kyra had sought safety in Rebecca's arms, crying, asking why Daddy hated her. The breaking point. And Rebecca hated herself for not having made the decision long ago. She knew then, absolutely knew, she and Kyra would leave in the morning. After Brad went to work.

Right now, he probably just arrived home and found her note. Then flew into a rage. Fine. Let him find a new punching bag.

As Rebecca tapped the brakes, the car swerved, the back tire edging toward the ditch. Finally, the car shuddered to a stop, Rebecca's heart threatening to stop as well. With white knuckles over the steering wheel, she blew out a deep breath, staring into the storm. Nothing but endless snow, drifting into dunes along the road. Fear fueled her; not just fear of the storm, but fear of the future, the unknown. Starting over at the age of 32, no college degree, no practical work experience. All very scary. But she still had her life. And Kyra's. This time she'd make it count.

Last night, after Brad had struck Kyra, things turned even worse. She knew Brad wouldn't let her leave, so she suffered in silence one last time. She'd consoled Kyra the best she could, even though she'd lied through her teeth. Hanging a pretty picture on abuse isn't easy. After Kyra had settled down, Rebecca dragged herself up to the bedroom, dreading what she knew awaited her. Five minutes later, Brad was pawing at her, acting like he hadn't hit their daughter. As if his abuse had turned him on. Business as usual, Rebecca a sex object purely for Brad's pleasure.

It felt like rape, torture of body and mind.

Enough.

Once the tears started, she couldn't stop them. Ten years' worth of bottled-up sorrow finally spilled. She covered her mouth with an arm, muffling her sobs. A small whimper birthed in her chest, a sad, little thing that matured into a growl.

That bastard. That miserable bastard. And I took it.

"Mommy?" Kyra yawned, staring at her. "Why're you crying?"

"Shh, honey, it's okay. Mommy's just tired, that's all. Everything's fine." Rebecca wiped away the tears and erased all thoughts of Brad. Time to pull it together. Kyra counted on her.

"Where are we?" Kyra leaned forward, wiping a viewing space through the windshield.

"I think … the sign said Hilston, Missouri." A place she'd never been, nor ever heard of before. Not that that was uncommon. Brad never took her out of Hollington, Kansas. Her entire life she'd been trapped in a lousy Kansas City suburb, her prison.

"Is this where we're going?"

"No, honey. We're going to stay with Aunt Jill and her family for a while. Like we discussed."

"And Daddy's not coming?"

"No, he's not."

Kyra said nothing, reacted indifferently. But a barely audible sigh escaped from her, one possibly of relief. Of course, Kyra loved her dad, warts and all. Yet she wasn't blind. She'd seen Brad at his worst. But he'd never hit Kyra before. It'd been foolish thinking he never would either. Brad was a ticking time bomb more often than not. Hell, she may as well have triggered the bomb herself. She should never have kept Kyra in that situation. Not for six years. *Shoulda', woulda', coulda'.*

"Mommy, I'm sorry I knocked over Daddy's beer. It was an accident. I'll never do it again." She blinked at Rebecca, sincerity sparkling in her eyes.

"I know, honey. Accidents happen." Slowly, Rebecca backed the car up and straightened it out; she noticed the snow was already covering her tracks. Nice and steady, twenty miles per hour. Maddening, like her life, steadily going nowhere. But not any longer.

"That's why Daddy hit me, isn't it?"

Again, Rebecca felt an emotional punch to the stomach. She couldn't have Kyra accepting Brad's abuse as just punishment. Not the way Rebecca had. "Kyra, Daddy's sick. He doesn't—"

"Is he dying?"

I wish. "No, honey, he's not sick like that. He…he has something wrong in his head. Something that makes him do bad things. Like hitting you. He can't help it. It has nothing to do with his feelings for you. He loves you. But he should never have hit you. And I don't want you blaming yourself. You understand?" Rebecca watched Kyra carefully, ensuring the message took.

Kyra nodded. "Daddy's sick." A simple reiteration, but delivered with firm resolve. Relief coursed through Rebecca, a realization that Kyra would survive to live a healthy life. She marveled at her daughter's resilience, the kind children uncannily possess.

Rebecca reached over and dropped her hand over her daughters'. "Love you."

"Love you…*Mommy, look out!*"

She had only taken her hand off the steering wheel for a few seconds. Not that it really mattered. The car took on a life of its own, angrily determined for the ditch. Rebecca tromped on the brakes. The car fishtailed, the back end sliding. In a panic, Rebecca cranked the steering wheel, forgetting to steer opposite in the snow. Kyra screamed. A complete 180 tossed Rebecca's stomach, then they twisted into a second loop. Closer, closer to the edge of the road. Snow sprayed from the drift they plowed through. The front of the Chevy lowered into the ditch, the back two tires banging down. Trees rushed up. Rebecca flung an arm over Kyra's chest, an impotent shield. Metal roared as they smashed into the tree. Rebecca flew against the steering wheel, sharp pain jagging into her chest. Glass tinkled, something hissed.

She held onto the wheel for another few seconds, uncertain their wild ride had ended. Smoke drifted up from beneath the sprung hood.

"Kyra, you okay?"

Kyra clutched her stuffed dog to her chest, eyes wide. She nodded, not reassuring enough for Rebecca.

"*Say* something, Kyra. You okay?"

"I think so. Gotta potty."

The damage to the Chevy appeared extensive. The front end resembled an accordion, a web-like vein crossed the windshield. A heavy tree limb lay over the hood. No signal on her cell phone. And the snow kept falling, God's frozen tears.

Rebecca wanted to cry. But she didn't. Instead, she laughed. Just a little at first, then it swelled, nearing hysteria. Nothing else seemed appropriate. Kyra joined her, a nervous titter.

Welcome to the first day of my new life.

Harold really shouldn't have done it, pretty much a no-brainer. Betraying the Kansas City mob is hardly the smartest career move. But money can be a strong motivator. Over the last several years, Harold had managed (or "mismanaged" might be more apt) Vincent Domenick's books and financial affairs, skimming a few tips off the top for his hard work. It's not like Domenick would miss a few bucks; the man had more money than several countries combined. Besides, the money had blood all over it, supposedly the net gains from Domenick's trucking company. But Harold knew better, knew where the cash really came from. Not exactly stealing from charity.

Things had heated up, though. Fast. Men wearing dull suits and flashing shiny badges had taken a sudden interest in Mr. Domenick's affairs, poring over his financial records and asking Harold uncomfortable questions. They had instructed Harold to keep Mr. Domenick blissfully unaware. No problem, he could live with that. But what really sealed Harold's bold career move was when one of the feds flat out stated that ignorance of Domenick's crimes wasn't a valid legal defense. He said it with a shit-eating smirk, as if he enjoyed watching Harold squirm. Harold received the message loud and clear: once Domenick goes down, Harold would be dragged to prison along with him. No thanks.

After Domenick's goon dropped off the monthly briefcase of cash that morning, it practically beckoned to Harold, screaming like a wild lover, "Take me, Harold, take me!" He would've been a fool to turn a deaf ear on such wanton lust. The time felt right to get out of town, his start-up funds handed to him in an easy-to-take briefcase, perfect for the man on the go. He'd always wanted to visit the Caribbean, never thought he'd live there. Life is sweet.

By now, Dominick had probably realized his money had vanished. Then again, maybe not. The man never did have an eye for numbers. Still, jumping on the first available plane seemed risky, too easily traced. And Harold swore he had spotted several suits following him over the last week. Pretty damn lousy at their jobs if an accountant could sniff out the feds. On the other hand, it could've been his imagination. Seven hundred thousand dollars' worth of hot can make a guy paranoid. But he hadn't seen anyone on his tail over the last couple of hours. Hell, in this weather, even the feds must've called in for a snow day.

He had a plan. As far as winging it goes, a pretty decent plan—catch a flight out from Los Angeles. Dominick's reach didn't extend to the west coast. But first Harold had to get there. And the damn snow didn't make it easy.

Married to his work, as they say, he had no real good-byes to make. He could always call his ex-wife from the Caribbean, rub it in her nose a little. She'd always wanted to go there. A smile crossed his lips as he planned what he'd say to her: *Eat it, Barb.*

But now he needed sleep. Absconding with mob money wears a man out. He couldn't get very far in the storm anyway. The sign he'd just passed had read, "Welcome to Hilston, Missouri. A lovely place to antique."

Of course, the sentiment made him gag. Pretty twee using "antique" as a verb, not to mention bragging about it. And he really hated "antiquing." Barb had forced him to join her on some of her expeditions, wasting numerous hours in musty shops full of crap the owners tried to pass off as collectibles. But Hilston was the closest place to stop. Surely he could stomach it for one night.

He followed a sign pointing toward the downtown district. Downtown amounted to basically one block lined with antique shops. At a stoplight, he stepped out onto the empty street. Snow buried his shoes. Squinting from the blizzard, he looked beyond the one-storied shops, searching for a tall building along the skyline. Nothing. Crummy little town didn't even have a single hotel. But he knew there'd be a bed and breakfast, possibly several, a mainstay for those foolish people who just can't get enough "antiquing" done in one day.

Several blocks over, on a hilly street so narrow only one car could safely drive down it at a time, he spotted his destination. His tires lost traction, plunging him into sickening helplessness. At the bottom of the hill, the car slowed, then popped up on a curb, delivering him in front of the "Dandy Drop Inn." Even the name nearly made him wretch. Everything in this damned town wanted to be "cute." "Cute" was about as relevant to him as nipples on men. But the inn promised a bed, and what the hell, breakfast to boot.

❋ ❋ ❋

"Got his location, boss."

"You gonna give it to me or have I gotta guess?" Winston's patience had run thin. Not only did he despise driving in the snow, but talking on the phone while driving was something he rarely did. Just not safe; kinda stupid, really. But tonight it couldn't be helped. He wanted to get the job done, get out of the storm, get back to Julie and the kids. Tonight, multitasking trumped safety.

"Sorry. You're never gonna believe it …" The kid paused, still forcing Winston to play "Twenty Questions." Yep, patience had about run its course. Still, in Winston's line of work, patience is a virtue.

"For Christ's sake, just tell me, Lenny."

"Yeah, uh, sorry, boss. The accountant's holed up at a bed and breakfast. In some shithole called…let's see…Hilston, Missouri. Want the address?"

"No, I'll just read your mind. Yes, *give* me the damn address." He really shouldn't snap at Lenny; the kid had proven himself time and again with his crazy computer and hacking skills. If he wanted to find anything or anybody, Lenny was his go-to guy. When you're in the "security consulting" business, assets like him are invaluable. Sometimes he wondered how people in his line of work made do before the advent of computers. Didn't matter. Lenny'd sussed out the missing accountant's location in no time at all. The accountant may be a whiz with numbers, but apparently didn't know jack about technology. The fool didn't realize his cell phone could be triangulated. Gotta love progress.

"Okay, got it." Winston pulled over, then entered the address into his G.P.S. Quickly, he switched the "creepy man's" voice his kids delighted in to a British woman's voice. On a night like this, Mr. Creepy made a lousy traveling companion. "Thanks, Lenny. We'll talk soon."

Hilston, Missouri. *Crap.* Another forty miles or so. Since he'd only been able to travel about fifteen miles over the past hour, he still had a good three-hour trip ahead of him. Long night. Better call home.

"Hey, Julie, it's me."

She laughed as she always did when he identified himself. Old habits and all. "I know, Win, we have Caller I.D."

"Yeah, yeah, right. Hey, the storm's not letting up, and I'm still trying to get home. I'd better find a spot to hole up for the night. It's coming down like…I dunno, blankets. It's bad."

"Blankets, huh? Lame metaphor, hon."

"Hey, a poet, I ain't."

"Just be careful, 'kay? Promise?"

"Promise. Love you, honey. Kiss the kids good night for me."

"Will do. Love you back."

Spending nights away was a necessary evil in the security field. Lousy beds, paper-thin walls, diner food that could start a grease fire in your belly. But, mostly, Winston hated being away from his family. He lived for his wife and two daughters, pretty much the reason he extended his field of expertise in the security industry.

Of course, he'd been hesitant at first. Ever since childhood, he'd never had a stomach for violence, always preferring to talk his way out of a bad situation if possible. But Mr. Dominick had planted the idea in his head. Just a small seedling at first, but it blossomed, watered by Dominick's pushing. And, frankly, when Winston looked at the resources he had available—the entirety of his company, "Ashford Security Solutions" (unfortunate acronym and all)—pushing "Security Consultant" to the next level seemed like a natural step. Via Lenny, he could access anyone's personal accounts and files; false identities and papers were a snap to acquire; and, of course, his business led him to people who had no qualms about securing untraceable weapons for him. Sure, his company was profitable, but just not quite enough. When he considered his house mortgage and his daughters' costly private school tuition, well, pulling the first trigger wasn't so bad after all. Just as long as he never made it personal.

Family came first, though, one hundred percent. Several years ago, when he had first started taking on out-of-town assignments, Julie had grown aloof, her frustration evident in her uncommon silence. Once—and only once—she'd straight out asked him, "Are you having an affair?" Her lower lip had trembled, obviously dreading—yet anticipating—his answer.

He swept her up in his arms with an amazed chuckle. "No, Julie, I swear to you I'm not. I never would and never will." Within his hug, he felt her physically lighten, her tense shoulders relaxing.

"I know, Winston. I'm just being silly. Forget I said anything."

And they both had. She never questioned him again. He told her about the more mundane details of his workload, the majority of it. But he never mentioned anything about his extra duties for Domenick. If she suspected, she never let on. Sure, guilt gnawed at him from time to time for withholding the complete truth, but he didn't outright lie. He reasoned it was for her benefit. What she didn't know wouldn't hurt her.

He glanced at the glove box where he stored his gun on

road trips. The .22 LR handgun was small enough to conceal, yet packed a punch like a charging rhino. It hadn't let him down once.

Yet he dreaded using it. Sometimes completing duties for Domenick left a sour taste in his mouth. Especially when the assignments pleaded for their lives. Usually why he liked to take them out without any personal contact. Never put a story to the face. It helped him sleep at night.

How this job was shaping up worried him. He couldn't very well sleep in his car, not in this storm. And there didn't appear to be a motel in Hilston, not according to his phone. Against his better judgment, he'd probably have to stay at the bed and breakfast until the storm blew over. Then he'd make his move.

As his car crunched over the snow-packed highway, he flipped the visor down, kissed his fingers, and tapped the photo of his family. *This one's for you.* Then he drove on into Hilston.

❄ ❄ ❄

From an early age, Heather Peterson knew she was different. She just couldn't quite put a finger on how. Her schoolmates had shunned her, running in exclusive packs, which suited Heather just fine. She had other interests; not the typical sort either, the ones the silly girls thrived on. Growing up on a farm enabled her to pursue her new-found hobby. But she'd longed to share her passion with somebody, something that seemed out of the realm of possibility.

Until God, in His kind and gracious manner, led her to Tommy. Or rather, led Tommy to her. Miracle of all miracles, Tommy had strolled up to her at her first Young Christians meeting, drawn to her inner light, and boldly stuck his hand out. Handsome, and with more confidence than a movie star, Tommy Goodenow regaled her with tales of his accomplishments. Heather had listened with rapt attention, drowning in his blue eyes, and swimming in his deep, soothing voice. Smitten like a silly schoolgirl—which, she supposed, she was—Heather knew Tommy was the man for her. Knew it as sure as she knew God had gifted Tommy to her. Once the meeting had ended, Tommy asked her out. Her hopes soared, then crashed back down to earth. What if he found her strange like the other students did? What if he found her impossible to love, the way her parents had?

But she should have had faith in God. Things worked out better than she dared hope.

Holding her ring up next to the car window, a street lamp caught a glint of diamond. Her smile stretched, grew even wider when she looked at her new husband behind the steering wheel.

Mrs. Tommy Goodenow. Heather Goodenow. She couldn't believe she was now a married woman. Something she had only dreamed of before.

Tommy must've sensed her thoughts, the way he innately knew so many things about her. He swept his brown hair out of his eyes and flashed his killer smile, incredibly toothy and white. "Penny for your thoughts, Missus Goodenow?"

"Why, Mister Goodenow, a girl has to keep some secrets." Truly a miracle how he brought out her playfulness, a daring flirtiness. Still, she didn't want to tell him what really bothered her, something that caused butterflies to swarm in her stomach. While her newlywed status thrilled her, to be frank, the inevitable consummation terrified her. Momma'd never been much help in such matters, never taking the time to explain things. Heather'd pieced things together as well as she could from stories overheard in the high school locker room.

She thought she knew what to expect. But did she truly? Was it possible to be petrified and exhilarated at the same time? Something burned in her lower regions, a warmth that spread throughout her body and spiked in her brain. Her mind toyed with her, teetering on the verge of unlocking the secrets of the human body. All led there by God, of course. She turned toward the window, hiding, but not out of shame, never shame. Rather, she didn't want Tommy to see her surely pale complexion. Fear of consummating their love. *Sex.* There she said it; well, not out loud, but she put a label to the act. And it didn't sound dirty at all, not really.

Tommy's hand crawled on top of hers. "We'll be there soon, babe." Always so darn self-assured, Tommy had enough confidence for both of them, and then some.

"Both hands back on the wheel," she chided. "With this crazy storm, you'll need all your attention on the road." She swept back a lock of her blond hair and tucked it behind an ear. "You'll have all the time in the world later to attend to me." Had she just said that? She couldn't believe her audacity. Tommy had that effect on her.

She'd told Tommy she was a "V." Honestly, she'd never even had a boyfriend until him. Sure, she kissed a few frogs, stupid boys hopping around on the playground. But never one like Tommy. And he'd handled the news of her virginity like a true Christian gentleman. He didn't laugh, as she suspected he might. He didn't ridicule. Instead, he'd seized her hand within his, held it to his heart, and said, "Then we're meant to be together. I've been saving myself for marriage."

Which totally blew Heather away. How in Heaven could a boy this gorgeous have gone untouched? She pretty much assumed Tommy had indulged in "lighter" petting, making out, who knew what. Part of being a boy. But she never asked, he never volunteered. Some things are better left unknown.

God had smiled down upon them both that fateful day. And they had agreed to help others see the light as well. Spreading the wealth of God.

As they approached a traffic light, Tommy tapped the brakes. The car slid a few feet into the intersection before crunching to a halt.

"My goodness." Heather fanned herself with a hand. Mostly to calm herself from the slight scare, maybe to cool herself down for more intimate reasons. "Be careful, babe." Funny how comfortable she'd become calling her new husband "babe." Before, she would've thought it juvenile, vulgar even. Now it sounded daring, liberating.

"Always with you, babe. I'd never put you at risk." Again he patted her hand. This time she allowed it since they were stopped. "We're almost there." Another knowing grin. "G.P.S. says just a few more blocks."

Anticipation crawled inside her, an uncomfortable scratching at her private parts. Only several blocks separated them from their marital bed. How far they'd come along God's path, all building to this moment. "Can't wait," she said quietly.

After months of chaste dating, she had expressed her innermost feelings to Tommy, told him of her unusual passion. Bravely, she'd demonstrated her hobby, leaving any judgment in God's hands. At first, he'd watched slack-jawed, an uncommon look for him. Nothing ever seemed to faze him. When she finished, she stood up, looking at him in silence. Waiting. Finally, his grin fell back into place. He strutted forward, the cock in the henhouse, and kissed her. Then, dropping to his knees, he picked up where she left off. Finished the job and followed it with another kiss, full-on, sensual, exciting. *Forbidden.*

She closed her eyes, basking in the blissful memory, and silently prayed: *Thank you, God, for leading us to one another.*

Tommy jarred her out of her reverie, concern tightening his handsome features. "Okay, babe?"

She nodded. "Never been better. Just … praying. I'm thankful for us and wanted to let God know."

"Amen," he said.

The wedding had been a small, slap-dash affair. With no friends to speak of, Heather's side of the church had been fairly barren, occupied by a few relatives she didn't really know. Tommy, on the other hand, had invited a raucous group of male friends who laughed and hooted throughout the ceremony. Since Tommy had graduated a year before her, she didn't really know them either. To be honest, based on their childish actions, she didn't think she wanted to get to know them. The louder they carried on, the redder Reverend Paxton burned. Not nearly as bad as her father, though. He sat in the front row, red as dawn, ears on fire from a head full of hate. He had been dead set against the wedding, actually believing it to have been a "shot gun" affair. *Hardly.*

After the glorious event, they stopped by home to say goodbye to her parents. Her father had grown even more sullen, falling into a whiskey fit. And he hadn't even blessed them with a wedding gift.

But that was okay, though; turn the other cheek as the Good Book says. Heather and Tommy had left her parents with the ultimate gift, the true Christian thing to do.

Heather smiled at the memory, warm in the afterglow.

Close-set, quaint houses and trees lined the street. Heather's heart knocked, practically jumping up the hill ahead of them. Ready for the final mystery to be unwrapped. She swallowed, an audible dry click.

The car hurtled down the hill, Tommy grinning behind the wheel, letting gravity take over. At the bottom of the hill, he pumped the brakes, *thunk, thunk, thunk, hiss.* The car slalomed to a stop, deep tire grooves in the snow-laid street behind them. Wind rattled the chains on a sign reading, "Dandy Drop Inn."

"We're here, babe." Tommy leaned over and kissed Heather. His tongue darted into her mouth, a hand gently caressing her breast. His reward for having conquered the snow storm.

"Tommy!" Heather pushed him back, not too much. She couldn't resist a smile, giving away her true desire. "Not in public!"

Tommy looked around, seriously puzzled and nearly comical. "This ain't exactly public. No one out on a night like this but us."

"I'm no slut, Tommy Goodenow, to be pawed on the street. You just wait."

"Reckon I can, at that. Reckon I will. Lookin' forward to it."

"Me, too." She tossed her arms around his neck and gave him a quick peck. Just a tease, enough to titillate, not enough to ignite his male hormones again.

"Okay. Ready?"

Not really. "I suppose. As long as you're gentle," she whispered.

"Always, babe. Always."

They stepped out into the snow. Heather cinched her coat beneath her chin against a sudden, brutal gust. Snow blew into her face, biting cold. "*Oh.* Don't forget the knives."

"Right, babe." Tommy pulled open the car door, reaching into the back seat. He gripped the knife sleeve, waving it as validation. "Can't forget God's work."

The wind seized and conquered his words, everything except for "God." But she intuited what he'd said. With her gloved hand coiled around the crook of Tommy's arm, he escorted her down the sidewalk to their honeymoon abode.

Stuart R. West

Author of *Dread and Breakfast*

GHOSTS OF CANNAWAY

Chapter One

1929…

Something looked off about Karl, no doubt about it. Tommy Donnelly saw it in Karl's eyes the minute they got in line. Not the usual red-eyed glassiness that accompanies miners' fondness for moonshine, either. Karl's gaze flicked back and forth, unfocused and yellow, like a desert lizard's eyes.

Tommy didn't know Karl well. Just by reputation and his daddy's mining tales. An old-time roof-trimmer, Karl's responsibilities included clearing loose rocks, making the mines safe for the other men. Apparently, he'd been in the mines since before the turn of the century. But on this gray Kansas morning, Karl stayed to himself, mumbling. He stared into the dirt like he was prospecting for gold. Hardly in keeping with what Tommy'd heard about this legendary miner.

Truth to tell, though, as it was Tommy's first day in the mines, Karl's odd behavior just set him more on edge.

Big Ed took it all in stride, of course, as he did everything. He chuckled deep within his formidable belly. "Kid, first-day jitters? Stay by my side and you'll be fine."

"Thanks, Ed. Guess I'm just gettin' my feet underneath me."

"That so?"

"That's so." Tommy forced a weak smile. It didn't make him feel much better, but the fact Big Ed had taken him under his wing gave him a small cushion of comfort. Tommy's daddy would've wanted it that way. It bothered him no end that Big Ed didn't think Karl's behavior seemed peculiar. But maybe that's the way Karl always acted.

The line of denim-clad, ruddy-faced men snaked across the grounds. The closer Tommy came to the pull derrick, the more his stomach flip-flopped. Watching the men disappear into the earth in a large bucket increased his anxiety.

Big Ed picked at his teeth with a dirty fingernail. "*Pfft, pfft, pfft!*" Big Ed launched his excavated oral debris onto the ground.

"Tommy, you're gonna start as a dummy. I talked to the ground boss, told him I want you. You'll carry my drill bits. You do good, show you're a man who ain't afraid to work, you'll move up to mucker in no time."

Karl lifted an eyebrow, appraising Tommy as if seeing him for the first time. "They're down there. Told me what I gotta do." He stared at Tommy, waiting for a response.

Big Ed ignored him. Tommy followed Ed's lead.

"All greenhorns gotta start somewhere, kid." Ed raised his voice to be heard over Karl's muttering.

"They come to me, no matter the time, day or night, they talk to me, tell me what I gotta do…"

They were next. Tommy hoped Karl would go down in the bucket in a different grouping. No such luck. Luck wasn't on his side today. Never a good thing for miners.

Jim Reaper, a particularly taciturn man who lived up to his name, was hoister man today. The empty bucket clanged down in the shaft as Jim cranked the hoist handle. Every time the bucket banged into the shaft's wooden walls, Tommy's heart jumped right along with it.

Big Ed let out a long sigh and climbed the platform. The boards creaked beneath his weight with every step. He grabbed the cable and swung a leg up and over the bucket's rim. "Come on, kid." He jerked his chin toward Tommy.

Tommy stepped up onto the platform. Karl followed behind him. *Closely.* So close Tommy felt Karl's breath on the back of his neck. Ed reached out a helping hand, and Tommy hopped in. Karl gripped the bucket's rim and gave it a spin.

"Come on, Karl," said Ed. "Quit horsin' around. Time to get into the mines."

Karl's lips pulled back, showcasing his yellow-toothed smile. He looked around at his surroundings, lost, a man awakened from a dream. It rattled Tommy, but at least Karl had stopped babbling.

Didn't take long, though, for Karl to shrug off sanity and resume his ongoing private conversation. He turned, asked a question of someone not there, laughed at an unheard response. Finally, he hopped into the bucket, his long legs neatly clearing the rim.

The bucket rocked back and forth over the shaft's collar. The bail holding the cable hook above them groaned. The gaping opening sat at about 12 feet wide by 12 feet across. The darkness reminded Tommy of the hole in the ground they put his daddy in when he passed. Miners work underground, die underground, get put back there again when all's said and done.

"All right," said Jim. It was more a declaration than a question, but Big Ed nodded anyway. Tommy grabbed the cable, a tenuous lifeline at best.

Karl stared at Tommy, his eyes dull. Rather, he looked right through him. "They won't let me rest, gotta do what they say…"

"God damn, Karl!" said Ed. "You liquored up or the devil on fire inside your belly?"

Karl didn't answer. He just gave a lopsided, lazy man's grin.

The square of skylight shrank as they lowered into the ground. A few torches lit up the shaft wall's cribbing of strategically placed 2" x 6' timbers.

The light played across Karl's face, shadows obscuring his eyes. Ed hummed a mostly melody-free ditty, something Tommy didn't recognize. When Karl fell silent again, Tommy couldn't help but steal glances at him. His stillness unsettled Tommy more than the constant mumbling.

Karl's arms shot up. He lurched toward Tommy. The bucket rocked, bashed into the walls. Tommy stumbled, his back against the bucket's rim.

"Karl!" Ed roared. "Jesus Christ!"

Karl shot Ed a puzzled look, then reached a trembling hand toward Tommy. He stroked Tommy's shoulder like petting a mining mule. "It ain't time yet," Karl said. "Not yet, they tol' me…"

"Sorry, kid," said Ed. He glared at Karl. "He ain't usually like this."

Echoes rose above and sank below as the bucket landed on a wooden platform four hundred feet below ground. Water bubbled and churned below the wood planks. Tommy couldn't distinguish the sump-pump from the pulse pounding in his ears.

Tommy hopped out of the bucket first. He didn't want to spend any more time with Karl than he had to. Ed must've had the same thought. He hefted himself out with surprising speed for a man his size. Karl dawdled behind as Tommy and Ed walked down the drift.

Ed clapped a hand on Tommy's back. "Time to light 'em up." He struck a long wooden match and held it to the lamp on Tommy's helmet. "Gotta be careful with fire down here, kid." The welcome light illuminated the dark drift. The match hissed out in a puddle at Ed's feet. "You're lucky, boy. Wasn't too long ago we made do with cloth helmets. Didn't protect us worth nothin'. Damn Gannaway was one of the last mine owners in the tri-state area to give us hard helmets."

Their boots squelched through the water. Using the steel rails as guides, they walked toward the light. After three hundred feet or so, the drift opened into a large stope, already mined and hollowed out for the most part. Artificial orange lantern light painted the cavern's walls. Carefully chiseled pillars of unmined rock braced the cavern roof for support. Nothing looked particularly steady. Boisterous voices greeted them.

"Big Ed! Who's the dummy with you?"

"Is he outta his momma's diapers yet?"

"Ground Boss," said Ed, to a sweaty, short, round man, "this is Tommy, my new dummy. Matthew's boy."

The man's eyes brightened. "Matthew was a good man and a better miner. If you're half the miner he was, son, you'll do just fine down here. Call me Ground Boss. Or sir."

"Yes, sir."

Against the wall, a man stood on a tall ladder, twenty-five feet above the cavern floor. Two miners pulled attached guide ropes taut. The ladder man stabbed a ten-foot-long spear into the rock above him. "Look out below!" he yelled. *Clump.* Loose rocks rained down from the ceiling.

"They tell me what to do…" Karl brushed past them, drowning out the Ground Boss's instructions. Karl walked toward the men steering the roof trimmer on the ladder, purpose in his stride.

A mule brayed once, then again.

Water around Tommy's feet bubbled. Invisible raindrops pelleted down, circular ripples spreading outward. The ground trembled. A hush fell over the miners. Big Ed looked puzzled. Worse, he looked *worried.*

The ground shook again. A roar ripped through the cavern walls. Not a horn exactly. Something deeper, more resonant. An inhuman moan, far away and all around them at the same time. A one-note, unending blast from the bowels of the earth.

Tommy felt the vibrations in his legs first. Then it traveled up into his chest, rattling his ribcage.

"Cave in!"

Panic. Water splashed, churned by fleeing feet. Miners dashed by Tommy, running toward the bucket.

Big Ed held his own, solemnly shook his head. "Nope. This ain't no cave-in. Nothin' like one I never heard."

Screams erupted by the ladder.

"What in *God's* name?"

A pickaxe dangled in Karl's hand, a skull-faced grin on his face. A man lay crumpled at his feet. The other rope-holder lunged at Karl. Karl sidestepped and the man went head first into the wall. With the grace of a dancer, Karl swung around and brought the pickaxe down onto the man's head.

A man on the ladder scrambled down. Karl kicked at the bottom rungs. The man flailed his arms about as if trying to sprout wings. The ladder slowly teetered, then crashed onto an outcropping of rock. The miner's eyes popped clean out of his head. His teeth shattered, spreading small white gems out on the rocks.

"God *damn!*" said Big Ed.

Karl propped a boot onto the dead man and yanked out the pickaxe. He licked the tip. Lovingly, almost. He opened his mouth, his smile crimson. Karl snatched the spear from off the ground. Then he raced straight for Tommy.

Tommy froze, standing still as miners rushed past him. The bellowing sound churned his innards, filled his bladder.

Without breaking stride, Karl ran the spear through another man's stomach. The tip poked out the man's back. He gave it a twist and withdrew the weapon as smoothly as a knife slicing through butter. Intestines slithered to the ground, smooth as a snake over a rock.

A bear of a miner tossed his arms around Karl's neck. Karl thrust the pickaxe into the man's neck repeatedly, missing his own face by inches. He studied the pickaxe, then dropped it.

"Good God in heaven!" the Ground Boss moaned.

"Come on! We gotta get outta here!" Ed yanked Tommy's arm. *"Tommy!"*

Karl dug through his newest victim's burlap bag and pulled out a handful of cylindrical-shaped objects.

Dynamite.

The hellish moaning loosened rock from the ceiling. Small pebbles at first, then a thunderstorm of larger debris. Groundwater danced, shimmied, and rippled.

Karl struck a match, held it to the wick of a dynamite stick. *Fssst.* He dropped the dead match, grabbed for another.

Something struck Tommy's cheek, pulling him out of his horrified stupor. Big Ed had his hand pulled back, preparing for another slap.

"Oh…lord," said Tommy, tears stinging his eyes.

"Let's *go*, goddammit!" Ed clamped down on Tommy's arm, nearly pulling him off his feet.

Karl chased after them, cradling the dynamite to his chest while he swung his spear.

They stormed down the drift. Tommy stumbled, his shoulder catching against the wall. The Ground Boss struggled to keep up, his panting loud in the drift. Tommy risked a glimpse back. Karl stood at the drift's entryway. Singing in an eerie, high-pitched tone.

A gospel song.

"If you could see inside insteaddd, you'd see a brand new mannn..."

The bucket had vanished. There was no way out.

From somewhere far away, a mule whinnied, mocking them.

Hysterical shouts echoed down the shaft. The bucket crashed in front of them. The bottom flipped out like an open can of beans. Its broken cable swished back and forth above it like a horse's tail swatting flies.

"Jesus God!"

"...'cause the old man is deaddd..."

Karl walked slowly down the drift, three sticks of dynamite tucked under his arm. He scrabbled at a matchbox. He struck a match against the rock wall. It snapped in half.

"Go!" Tommy pointed at the swinging cable. "Our only chance! God, it's our only chance! *Go! Now!"*

The Ground Boss grabbed hold of the cable, his knees and ankles entwining around the line. He scurried up inch by inch.

"You would see a brand new man..."

"Ed! Go!"

Ed shook his head. "You go, boy. Your daddy'd never forgive me if I left you down here."

"But I'll be *faster!"*

"More the reason for you to go, kid! *Dammit* all to hell, now *get!"*

As soon as the Ground Boss cleared the top, Tommy jumped onto the cable. Hand over hand, he scrambled up quickly. Faces peered down the hole. The skidoo bell warning clanged.

And over it all, Tommy heard Karl's death dirge.

"… 'Cause the old man is deaddd!"

Tommy looked down. Ed steadied the cable with one hand, his other held out, warding off Karl.

Karl's singing dried up. The loud thrumming noise diminished. Silence. Except for the scritch-scratching of a match head.

Halfway up the shaft, Tommy spotted a niche carved out of the rock. A hole for the workers who laid down the cribbing along the shaft walls.

Tommy knew Ed couldn't make it to the top. Not before Karl lit his dynamite. Tommy swung toward the niche. His arm and leg took hold, and he crawled in.

Tommy heard Ed talking quietly to Karl.

"Ed! Come on! *Move* it!"

Ed squinted toward Karl before hopping onto the cable. With a grunt, he inched his way up. His weight tugged at the cable Tommy held, burning his hands.

Karl shoved the ruined bucket off the platform. He crawled on top and sat down. By all appearances, he didn't have a care in the world. He chuckled and scratched a match.

Ed struggled hard. For every five feet he climbed, he had to pause to catch his breath.

"Just get to me, Ed!" Tommy leaned out of the niche, extending his hand toward Ed, straining so hard his muscles shook. Willing Ed to keep going.

Ed climbed and clawed, gasping for air.

A tiny spark of light flashed at the bottom of the shaft. Karl stared into the match's flame. Then he wedged a stick of dynamite into his mouth. The fuse caught, sparkled, brightened, then continued on its trail to destruction.

"Oh sweet Lord, Ed, hurry! Hurry!"

Ed surged forward, using every bit of energy he had.

Karl lit the other two sticks of dynamite. Then he lay

down like Jesus on the cross, arms outstretched, the lit dynamite in his hands.

Tommy's fingers swept the tip of Ed's outreached hand. *Missed.* Ed jumped up an inch and grasped Tommy's hand. Tommy pulled, throwing himself back. His backside scraped along the rock toward the shaft, Ed's weight dragging him out. He anchored his feet against the niche's edges, slowing himself. But not enough.

"Ed! Climb! You gotta climb more! I can't pull you in!"

Ed clawed a foothold into the niche and rolled in on top of Tommy.

The first explosion ripped through the shaft, followed by two more. Wood-reinforced walls shook. Rock crumbled. Fire roared up the shaft, bathing them in blistering heat. A cloud of black smoke roiled up and out into the open air above. Tommy and Ed clung to one another like early morning lovers.

The flood of falling rocks dwindled, became a rare pebble. The dead quiet after the chaos should have been comforting. Instead, it seemed an additional threat, devouring Tommy with false hope.

The smoke cleared, and Ed and Tommy separated. Tommy had soiled his pants. Ed wouldn't hold it against him, though. Or say anything about it. Ever. He'd done the same thing.

Chapter Two

1969...

The music stuttered, stopped, sped up. Then it faded out.

"Damn it." Dennis pulled the van onto the shoulder of US69.

He reached down and tugged at the eight-track cartridge. Wrinkled tape trailed from the player like ribbon on a gift.

The one concession Dennis had asked Meyers for was an eight-track player installed in the research van. He knew Kansas radio would be hellish. Especially out in the boonies. Nothing but country music and preachers ranting about saving souls from damnation.

It didn't matter much, not really. Just moving on and doing something different renewed him with a vigor he hadn't experienced in a very long time. Getting away from Los Angeles, at least if for a while.

Meyers had seemed reluctant to send Dennis to Gannaway, Kansas. He'd never given a reason. But he saw it in Meyer's distrusting look. A look filled with pity and doubt. Obviously, Meyers didn't feel Dennis was emotionally up to the task.

But Dennis needed the job. Anything to take his mind off what had happened six months ago.

A flash of movement caught Dennis's eye. An American Indian man stood just off the highway, knee-deep in dried bushes and weeds. He looked as startled as Dennis, but recovered with ease and tipped his fedora. Dennis nodded a greeting. The man dropped a potato bag and spread his hands in a "what the hell" manner. Then he pointed across the two-lane highway.

A modest home sat on the other side of the highway, nothing memorable. But the yard burst with a carnival of color. A white-painted garden jockey statue guarded the graveled driveway. Psychedelically colored birdbaths decorated the yard, a pop-art fever dream. Metallic pipes and rods clung to one another, pitched somewhere between sculptures and warnings. A giant peace sign covered the garage door. Above it hung a basketball hoop, wind chimes replacing the net.

The man pointed inside the van, and his lips moved. Appearing frustrated, he cranked his hand around like an organ grinder. Dennis scooted across the bench seat and rolled down the window.

The Indian leaned over the sill and Dennis extended his hand. The man surprised Dennis by foregoing the traditional handshake and offering his thumb instead of his hand. Their thumbs entwined in a soul handshake.

"Peace, brother." He gestured toward the ruined cartridge Dennis held onto. "Can I have that?"

"Sure. You know it's no good anymore, right?"

"Can see that."

Dennis shrugged and handed over the tape. The man cradled the draping tape as tenderly as a gardener would an uprooted plant. He eyed the tape's label. "Good band."

"Yeah, real rock and roll."

The man's smile burned warm and brilliant, his teeth dazzlingly white against his sun-drenched skin. "Come back some time and see what I do with it."

"I might just do that. Peace."

Dennis looked back in his rearview mirror as he ambled on down the highway. The Indian flashed the two-fingered peace sign. Dennis stuck his hand out the window and re-turned the gesture.

He thought he might enjoy the people of Kansas.

Judging by the desolate surroundings, Dennis knew he didn't have much farther to go. The trees lining the highway were barren. Permanently bowed, the dead ushers pointed the way to Gannaway. Tornado devastation had splintered and weathered the roadside signs, but they were still legible. Competing chicken restaurants battled for the traveler's taste buds and cash. Chicken Rosie's, Chicken Greta's, and the under-achiever of the bunch, Lazy Harry's OK Chicken. The board demanding passersby to *Cherish God's Gift* seemed miraculously untouched, probably not too much comfort to Gannaway's past residents now.

Hawks nested on sagging power lines, heads craning, watching Dennis's progress. The only sign of life he'd seen for a while.

Dennis nearly missed the faded "Welcome To Gannaway—A Perfect Piece Of Heaven" sign. He parked the van in a lot filled with abandoned tires and hopped out. He took in a deep breath as he walked by the remains of a building, now nothing more than a crumbling stone foundation. A sour tang of metal filled his mouth, so overwhelming he could taste it.

Next to the destroyed building rested a small, fence-enclosed graveyard. A defunct electric tower loomed high above the gravestones, a guardian of the dead.

Across the highway, he spotted the Gannaway Mining Museum, or at least its remains. The wrap-around porch slanted like a storm-tossed boat deck, rising and falling by nature's whim. Several of the wood pillars holding the roof over the porch had toppled. The few survivors looked ready to join them.

Dennis's walking tour brought him to the main strip, four stores in a row. What used to be stores, anyway. A bathrobe hung behind a *Closed* sign on the Gannaway General Store's door, the owner's final word on the topic, no doubt. Boxes and a flattened shelving unit spread across the floor. Earl's Machine Shop crumbled to pieces next door, the front window, door, and back wall all blasted out. Graffiti decorated the walls, forgotten artwork for a dead town. The next two establishments were in even worse shape. Impossible to tell what they once were. One block over, the Old Minetown Pharmacy appeared open against all odds, a soda sign lit up in the front window.

Across the two-lane road stood a water tower, ballyhooing the high school's football team: "Gannaway—Home of the Lions Since 1918." Below it, a statue of a lion sat, one paw perched up. Rusted and discolored, it stood proudly amid the devastation like the king of the jungle it once was.

Towering over it all were the chat piles. Man-made anthills hollowed out from below the surface, the earth's unwanted refuge stacked skyhigh. They dotted the horizon. For over forty square miles they covered the landscape, some of them perhaps 300 feet in height.

Alongside them, the remains of mining equipment rusted away, relics from a different era.

Before he left Gannaway's city limits, Dennis saw the only other open business in town. Durwood Funeral Home. *Telling*.

How could one of the once most thriving mining towns in the country come to this? Once it was proclaimed "A Perfect Piece of Heaven." Now Gannaway felt more like hell on earth.

A knock on the door jolted Dennis awake from his nightmare, the same nightmare that had plagued him for six months. He owed his unexpected visitor his gratitude.

He slipped on his glasses, flipped on the lamp, and checked his watch. Nine-thirty. Early for him to have fallen asleep, too late for a visitor.

"Who is it?"

"County Commissioner."

Dennis opened the door. An overweight man in a sheriff's uniform grimaced at him, toeing at the gravel. The holstered gun at his side weighed down his pants. He constantly hitched them up by the belt loops.

"Um, hi." Dennis rubbed the sleep from his eyes and stuck out his hand. "Sorry, you caught me sleeping."

"You sleep in your clothes?"

"Don't usually. Just wiped out." Dennis stepped back and waved him in. "I'm Dennis Lipstein. What can I do for you?"

The Sheriff waddled in, studying the small motel room's interior. He pulled out the desk chair and fell into it with an exhausted sigh. "I'm Eddie Stokes. County Commissioner and Kwashau, Kansas sheriff. I reckon you can also consider me sheriff of Gannaway, too."

"That's a lotta titles for one man." Dennis sat on the bed.

"I'm a lotta man." Stokes laughed at his own joke, although Dennis thought he just stated the obvious. "Lipstein, huh? You a Jew-boy?"

Dennis blinked, unsure if he'd heard the man right. "Excuse me?"

"Son, I don't stutter. I asked if you was a Jew-boy?" The chair creaked beneath Stokes as he leaned forward.

"Yes, I am. Not currently practicing. Are you an ignorant bigot?" The instant the words tumbled out of his mouth, he wished he hadn't said them. But Dennis didn't tolerate bigotry easily. Not after growing up with it most of his life.

"Did I hear you right, son?" Stokes patted his chest, then his holster.

"Like you, Sheriff, I don't stutter."

Stokes gave a one-note chuckle. "I reckon not. You got a smart mouth on you, son."

"Sheriff, I'm sorry. I apologize. I shouldn't have said that. You just caught me off-guard. I wasn't expecting—"

"Well, now, you've done gone and gotten on my bad side,

Mr. Lipstein."

"Dr. Lipstein."

"Come again?"

"I'm an environmental scientist. Dr. Lipstein."

"Well, hell, now, Mr. Lipstein, if this is your'n way of getting back on my good side, you're sure not very good at it."

Obviously, Sheriff Stokes carried around more than a few chips on his shoulder. But Dennis didn't want to begin his stint in Gannaway with the local law harassing him. "Okay, let's start over." Dennis crossed the room, hand outstretched. "Peace?"

"You a hippie, too, Mr. Lipstein?" Stokes leaned back, relishing his intimidation.

"No, I'm not a hippie."

"Smoke a li'l grass, maybe?" Holding two fingers to his lips, Stokes made a sucking sound.

"No, I *don't* smoke marijuana."

"With that long hair and that scraggly beard—"

"What can I do for you, Sheriff?"

Stokes's face turned redder than a twelve-hour sunburn. "Well, believe it or not, it's what I'm supposed to do for you."

"I don't follow."

"Mr. Gannaway told me you was coming. Some high muckety-muck from the United States Corps of Engineers."

"That's right. Wouldn't consider myself a high muckety-muck, though."

"From the looks of things, I wouldn't either." Stokes passed a huge hand through the air. "But Mr. Gannaway told me to give you assistance. *Supervised* assistance. Now, I gotta tell ya', folks around these parts don't cotton much to strangers nosin' about their business. Just what is it you're hopin' to achieve, son?"

"We, ah, don't really know yet. That's what I hope my research will—"

"And you're a scientist? Back in my school days, I learned science is based on hard facts."

Dennis toyed with the idea of asking him what his education entailed, then common sense prevailed. "Finding the facts is my research."

"And what facts are you lookin' for?"

They could go around and around all night. Dennis cut to the chase. "Gannaway used to be one of the richest mining towns in the tri-state area, if not the wealthiest. The zinc and lead mining industry boomed, particularly in the '20s and '30s."

Stokes seemed disinterested, nodded nonetheless.

"It's a fact the mines under Gannaway have been depleted. Or nearly so. Mr. Gannaway shut down his last mine in 1968 due to lack of minerals. And now the overseas countries have grabbed a large portion of the market."

"Damn commies." Stokes scowled. "Still doesn't tell me what you're doing here."

"There've been reports the water's contaminated in Gannaway. Acid mine water from the minerals. Air contaminants are also a concern. There's—"

Stokes jumped to his feet, faster than Dennis thought possible. He yanked his pants up again. "Son, you *still* ain't told me what you're doing here."

"I'm testing the water and the air. Preliminary investigations. Find out—"

"What's the bottom line?" Stokes wandered off toward Dennis's open suitcase on the floor. He leaned over, one foot off the floor, and peered inside.

"We're going to determine what to do with Gannaway. Make recommendations. Maybe turn it into a wetland."

"You know there's still folks livin' in Gannaway. You gonna take their homes from them because of some scientific nonsense?"

"We'll do what we need to do." Dennis crossed the room and closed his suitcase. "We're trying to save these people's lives. Seems to me there's been plenty of lives lost already in Gannaway."

Stokes prodded a finger into Dennis's chest. "And I'm tellin' you, son, you'd best watch what you look into. It ain't your concern. You may not like what you find." He poked Dennis again before he dropped his rounded shoulders. His face sweetened with a baby's smile. "But I'm here to help you." He tucked a piece of paper into Dennis's shirt pocket. "My number. Mr. Gannaway says I should help you. But don't you go off on your own, now, hear me?"

"I hear you."

"Think I can find my way out." Stokes left the door open behind him. Dennis slammed the door and pulled back the curtain. Stokes sat in his Sheriff's car, speaking into a walkie-talkie. He replaced the walkie-talkie with a flashlight and swept the beam across Dennis's window. Dennis jumped back.

He had to reconsider his earlier assessment. Maybe Kansas was going to be a huge bummer.